STEALING KISSES
in the SNOW

D0974405

**Also available from
Jo McNally
and HQN Books**

Slow Dancing at Sunrise

JO McNALLY

STEALING KISSES
in the SNOW

HQN™

HQN™

ISBN-13: 978-1-335-04148-7

Recycling programs
for this product may
not exist in your area.

Stealing Kisses in the Snow

Copyright © 2019 by Jo McNally

www.HQNBooks.com

Printed in U.S.A.

Family is love. This book is dedicated
to my three stepchildren and their spouses,
who welcomed me into their family twentysome years ago
and graced us with seven amazing grandchildren.

Acknowledgments

It was easy to get myself in the mood for writing my first-ever holiday romance because I'm married to a guy who loves Christmas just as much as I do. His Santa collection fills our house every December, and he's tolerant of my rather obsessive approach to decorating the tree. He knows now to just walk away and leave me to it, because I know where every ornament "belongs" and that anything he does will just be redone. By me. I love him for trying to help, but I love him even more for knowing when to walk away. A true partner. His support (and cooking!) makes it possible for me to write, and I am deeply grateful for his love (and foot rubs...).

A special thank-you to my funny wine-drinking friends who helped inspire the feisty Rendezvous Falls Book Club. Thanks to my globe-trotting mom and her sister, who redefine "old age" for anyone who can keep up with them—you helped me envision eighty-year-old Iris and her strength. To my brother and sister-in-law, who are pretty good globe-trotters themselves, and sometimes let us join them on an adventure. Thanks as always to my agent, Veronica Park of Fuse Literary. And thank you to my dear readers—you uplift me every single day with your support, reviews and the fun conversations we have on social media.

CHAPTER ONE

PIPER MONTGOMERY WAS plunging the toilet in Room Twelve of the Taggart Inn when her four-year-old daughter announced she wanted to dress up as Deadpool for Halloween.

It wasn't even ten o'clock on a Wednesday morning, and this was already turning into one of *those* days. Piper was pretty sure she already knew the answer to her next question, but she asked anyway.

"Lily, where did you even *hear* of Deadpool?"

Lily brushed her white-blond curls from her face with a big smile. "Ethan told me! He said Deadpool was a superhero and he wears red and red's my favorite color, so it's perfect!"

Piper sat back on her heels on the marble bathroom floor. Mr. and Mrs. Carlisle would be finished with breakfast soon, and they'd expect their bathroom to be fully functional when they got back. But Lily's grandmother would have some expectations, too. She could just imagine the look of horror on Susan Montgomery's face if her granddaughter dressed up as a foul-mouthed superhero. It would be just one more thing Piper had failed at since Tom's death.

"But Gigi already bought you that pretty butterfly costume, remember?"

Lily's face scrunched. "Ethan says butterflies are stupid. He says…"

"Yeah, Ethan says a lot of things." Her grip tightened on the wooden plunger handle, crinkling her rubber gloves. She had no doubt this whole Deadpool idea was her thirteen-year-old son's payback because she'd suggested he might be too old for trick-or-treating this year. Or it could be payback for her working two jobs up until a week ago. Or for moving them into a house he claimed to hate. Or it could just be payback for the fact that Piper was *here* and his father was dead.

She missed the sweet little boy who used to cling to her legs and declare his love for her so loudly that strangers would laugh. It was hard to reconcile that child with the sullen teen Ethan had grown into, but he'd been through a lot in a few short years. They all had. She sighed in the direction of the clogged toilet. "I think Ethan was teasing you, honey. He knows you're too young to be Deadpool. It's not appropriate."

"Oh! I know what approp-rat means!" Lily loved big words. "It means what people expect, right? So people wouldn't expect me to be Deadpool and they wouldn't like it?"

Piper could think of one person who definitely wouldn't like it. "That's right, honey. So let's talk later and we'll come up with something for you to wear that will make everyone happy." Except Ethan, of course, but making her son happy seemed a lost cause these days.

She put her frustration into her plunging efforts, and was relieved when the toilet drained with a whoosh. Lily clapped her hands and started dancing. Victory dances for toilets that flushed. *Livin' the dream.* Piper wiped down the bathroom, then shooed her daughter out to the hall.

Plumbing wasn't normally her responsibility at the inn. She usually handled cooking breakfast and doing some cleaning for the owner, Iris Taggart. But Iris broke her hip a week ago, leaving Piper, the only employee, as the temporary Woman In Charge. Since Iris was eighty, "temporary" could last a while. As long as Piper was in charge, she was not paying a plumber a hundred bucks for a job she could handle on her own.

She'd just peeled off her rubber gloves and tucked them, and the plunger, into the hallway closet when Mr. Carlisle came up the stairs. Just in time—she doubted the guests she'd served salted caramel pancakes to forty minutes earlier would want to see their cook with a toilet plunger in her hand. She gave him a bright smile as she grabbed Lily to stop her from twirling and singing about toilets.

"Your room is all set, Mr. Carlisle. So sorry for any inconvenience. If you'd like, I can box up some of those cookies your wife liked so you'll have a snack while you tour the wineries today."

"That was fast. Then again, you probably have a plumber on call with a place this ancient." He looked around the hallway, with its bold floral wallpaper, and wrinkled his nose. She understood the sentiment. She'd been campaigning for a few months now to get Iris to update the decor, but the old woman wasn't a fan of change. Mr. Carlisle shook his head as he put his key in the door. "No offense, but coming to Rendezvous Falls was my *wife's* idea of a good time, not mine. But

I've heard there's a distillery around here, so I'm hoping that'll be worth the drive from Philly."

"Eagle Rock Distillery? Oh, you'll love it. Ben Wilson has done a great job up there, and the views this time of year are spectacular. You'll drive right by one of my favorite wineries on the way up there—Falls Legend Winery on Lakeview Road." She moved past him toward the main staircase. "That way you'll *both* have a good time today."

Lily nodded solemnly, precocious as ever. "Yes, the views at Ben's are spectac-alar this time of year."

Mr. Carlisle chuckled, leaning down to the little girl's level. "So you've spent a lot of time at the whiskey distillery, have you?"

Lily's blue eyes shone. She loved being talked to like an adult. The girl was in way too much of a hurry to grow up.

"Oh, yes! Gigi and Grandpa take me there. Mr. Ben has a donkey named Rocky, and I feed him carrots. Mr. Ben was my daddy's best friend, but my daddy's dead, so Mr. Ben says he's *my* best friend now."

The words sent their usual slice of sorrow through Piper's heart. After four years, it was still hard to accept that Tom was gone. She had to give Mr. Carlisle credit. He hid his shock well, his smile barely faltering as Lily info-dumped all over him. Piper added *talk to Ben* to her to-do list. Ben Wilson was a great guy. Her in-laws adored him, and she'd already suspected Susan had decided he was the "anointed one" to take over Tom's role as husband and father. But, like so many other things, that wasn't Susan's—or Ben's—decision to make.

"Come on, Peanut. Momma has work to do." She

tugged Lily toward the stairs. "Enjoy your day, Mr. Carlisle!"

Once downstairs, Piper started clearing the dining room. There were only three rooms occupied last night, but the weekend ahead was fully booked. Not only was it the peak of leaf-peeping season, it was also Harvest-Fest weekend in Rendezvous Falls. The festival would take place downtown, just a few blocks from the Taggart Inn. Iris usually had the porches decorated and set up for folks to enjoy tea and spice cookies to showcase the inn. But it was already Wednesday and Piper had no idea how she would get the decorating done in time, much less the food.

She'd check her to-do list and figure out a way. Maybe if she baked cookies at home at night and froze them? Maybe she could decorate the inn at night, too, if Ethan could be convinced to watch Lily. But if she *decorated* at night, she couldn't *bake* at night. Her shoulders sagged in defeat. She was so damn tired, and she didn't see any rest in sight. Between the kids, the house, two jobs, and now Iris's accident, Piper was nearly groaning from the weight of her responsibilities.

"Look, Momma! I'm an Iroquois princess!" Lily grabbed a garland of brown-and-gold silk leaves from the bannister of the massive mahogany staircase in the lobby and wrapped it around her head like a crown. Piper had been reading a children's book aloud to Lily before bed about the rich Native American history in the Finger Lakes region of Upstate New York, and the many legends handed down through centuries.

"Very pretty, Lily. Just be careful not to pull those garlands down by accident, okay?" At least Piper had

managed to get autumn decorations up *inside* the inn—
mostly pumpkins, gourds and silk leaves. Iris had been
hauling out the boxes of decorations—without asking
for help—when she took the fall that led to her broken
hip. Thank god Piper had been cleaning a room on the
second floor and heard the awful thud and Iris's cry of
pain from upstairs. Another half hour and Piper would
have been gone. Iris could have been lying up there for
hours before anyone found her.

"Momma, I'm going to go feed Mr. Whiskers, okay?
Because I'm respons-bull for him." Lily had been
thrilled when Iris pronounced her the cat's caretaker
while she was recovering.

"Just be sure not to let him out of Iris's apartment,
and lock the door when you leave." Lily started to skip
away as Piper called out one more order. "And no playing in the guest areas!"

The Victorian mansion, built in the late 1800s, had
three floors plus a full attic and a scary, horror movie-
style basement. The first floor held common areas
for guests to enjoy, a large dining room, the kitchen,
a few guest rooms, and Iris's living quarters in the
back. Piper had bought the house next door that January. She'd started helping Iris part-time, eager for any
job she could find once her pretty pink house turned
into a money pit. The elderly woman gradually added
more duties to Piper's list, and she was glad for the
extra hours. Even better, Iris didn't mind her bringing
Lily with her. Piper didn't have live-in babysitters these
days, unless you counted Ethan. But he was barely a
reliable babysitter in the afternoons, much less in the
early mornings. Lily bounced out of bed every day rar-

ing to go, but Ethan was more of a don't-talk-to-me-until-noon sort of kid.

Iris insisted she didn't mind the endlessly active girl being around while Piper worked, as long as she didn't disturb the guests. Of course, Lily *did* that on a fairly regular basis, but most of the time the guests seemed charmed by her. She was so much like her father, with her ability to make people like putty in her hands. Tom had been so genuinely kind and friendly that everyone just…relaxed around him. And smiled. Piper used to smile all the time too, when her husband was alive.

She loaded breakfast dishes into the commercial dishwasher. The kitchen was the one area in the inn where Iris didn't mind a modern look. There was stainless steel everywhere, including the oversized appliances. It was overkill for making breakfasts, but Iris had once served dinners at the inn. That had become too much for her to manage, but she still talked about reopening the restaurant somehow.

"Momma!" Lily's shriek as she ran into the kitchen startled Piper so much she almost dropped the platter she was holding. She should be used to her own child by now, but tell that to the heart that just tried leaping out of her chest.

"Lily! *Please* don't scream like that. There are guests…"

"But Momma, I saw a *giant*! He was walking right down the hall—a real live giant!"

Piper probably had Ethan to thank for *this*, too. He constantly told Lily the inn was haunted by monsters. Luckily, her fearless little daughter loved that idea, so his plan to scare her failed. But Piper was going to have yet another talk with him. Seriously? *Giants* now?

"Lily, it's not nice to tell stories." She talked over her daughter's objection. "I know, your brother loves tall tales, but we should always tell the truth, okay? Did you take care of Mr. Whiskers? Did you lock Iris's door?"

"Yes, but Momma, that's when I saw him! A big hairy giant dressed in black!"

Piper slid the door open on the dishwasher and rolled the steaming tray out onto the counter. She glanced at her watch. Damn, she was supposed to stop at the insurance office this morning to pick up her final check. They'd been more than understanding when she'd had to give her notice for the part-time job in order to help Iris. Arguing with her daughter would just slow her down. *Choose your battles.*

"Okay, Lily. If you see that giant again, bring him to me so I can tell him to stop hanging around here. It's bad for business."

Lily giggled and dashed out of the kitchen before Piper could tell her they were leaving soon. She put away the rest of the dishes and tossed the dishrag into the bin to be washed. She was mopping up the last corner of the floor when she heard the kitchen door open again. Good—Lily hadn't wandered far.

"I'm glad you're back, sweetie. I'm almost done, so—"

"Momma! I found the giant! Isn't he hoomongus?"

Piper turned and froze, clutching the mop handle tightly. Lily was standing in the doorway, holding hands with a stranger. Well over six feet tall, with straggly, wet hair hanging to his shoulders and a scruffy beard, the man was clothed entirely in black leather, including leather chaps on his long legs. He had the deepest-set eyes Piper had ever seen, shadowed under heavy, dark brows. With his size and overall menacing appearance, it was no wonder Lily thought he was a giant.

And he was holding her daughter's tiny hand.

Piper bristled, her exhaustion gone in a flash. She'd gladly battle *actual* monsters to save her children, and big or not (and he *was* big), this was just a man. A man who was about to regret touching her little girl. She brandished the mop handle in front of her like a sword as she went toward him. "You let her go right this minute! And get out of here! I'm calling the police…" She fumbled to get her phone out of her back pocket while still aiming the mop at him. Her voice was fast approaching a scream. "You get the hell away from my daughter!"

LOGAN TAGGART HAD been thrown out of plenty of places in his lifetime, but never by a pretty little ponytailed momma wearing a ruffled yellow apron. He managed to squelch his smile, knowing it would be a mistake to laugh.

The golden-haired munchkin clutching his fingers right now was clearly the woman's daughter, and he probably looked like an ax murderer. He gently freed himself from the child and stepped back, raising both hands and modulating his voice carefully.

"Ma'am, I'm sorry. The little girl said she wanted me to go to the kitchen, and I was heading here anyway…"

The woman seemed flummoxed. Her chest rose and fell rapidly, her blue eyes wild as she stepped closer. She raised the mop higher with one hand, then dropped her phone on the counter with the other so she could snatch her daughter's hand, tugging her to safety behind her. She waved the mop again, as if that would really protect her if he posed a threat. He was a foot taller and a good seventy pounds heavier than she was. The biggest danger to him was in her other hand—the cell phone she'd picked up again.

"Please don't call the police," Logan said, trying to sound as reasonable as possible. "It'll upset the customers and I haven't done anything wrong."

The woman hesitated, glancing back at her daughter. Momma Bear had saved her cub. She swallowed a couple times, then gestured to the door with the mop. Her voice still shook, but the volume lowered.

"You need to go."

"I'm sorry I startled you. I've had a long-ass…" He glanced at the kid and grimaced. "It's been a long trip, and I got caught in a rainstorm just south of here. I haven't eaten since yesterday's dinner…"

Her eyes softened a fraction, even as she held the mop out firmly. She nodded toward the door. "The Methodist church three blocks over has a food pantry, and the Catholic church does soup and bread every Wednesday for whoever stops in. Father Joe might be able to help you find a place to sleep. But you can't stay here."

Logan couldn't stop his bark of laughter, even though it made her jump. She thought he was *homeless*? He couldn't decide if he was offended or impressed. Clearly scared out of her wits, she was still kind enough to offer him a chance at hot food and a bed. Yeah, definitely impressed. It was no surprise she worked for his grandmother, who was also a tough-as-nails woman who cared about others far more than she ever let on. Her eyes started to narrow again, so he tried to clarify that he wasn't some random vagrant.

"Actually, I *can* stay here."

She lifted the cell phone. Not good. His words tumbled out. "I'm Logan Taggart. This is my grandmother's place. I know I look like Sasquatch right now, but I'm honestly just here to help my grandmother." There was certainly no other reason he'd ever come to Rendezvous Falls with all its froufrou festivals and Gran's kitschy old inn that should have been sold ten years ago.

The woman froze. "You're *Logan*? But Iris said…" She looked him up and down. "Iris said you worked on an oil rig somewhere." Her chin rose defiantly. "And she didn't tell me you were coming."

Right now he *wished* he was on a rig somewhere. He'd be more comfortable in a screaming hurricane than standing here in Rendezvous Falls, defending his presence to this woman raking over him with her suspicious blue eyes. He bit back a tired sigh.

"She didn't *know* I was coming. She told my sister and me not to come, but we knew she'd need help, and I was the loser…I mean…the lucky one who had time to come to Rendezvous Falls." The truth was, he'd lost the bet with Nikki a week ago, and had no choice but to uproot his life, stuff it into a duffel bag, and ride his Harley from Alabama to New York. He rolled his bum shoulder and tried not to groan. "I assume you work for Gran. Nice to meet you, Mrs…?" He held out his hand and waited. The woman was attractive in a fresh-scrubbed, wholesome way that had never been his style. But there was something about her ferocity when she first saw him that was…interesting. She stared at his hand before her shoulders dropped a fraction and she let out a long breath, lowering the mop at last. She reached out to take his hand, but she clearly wasn't happy about it.

"Piper Montgomery. I work for Iris part-time, and a little more than that now that she's laid up. I'm sorry, Mr. Taggart… I…"

"Your reaction was one hundred percent understandable. And please, don't ever call me 'Mr. Taggart' again. It's just Logan. And *I* should be the one apologizing for frightening you and your daughter…"

The girl jumped out from behind her mom. They were so much alike—long blond hair, big baby-blue eyes and porcelain skin. The girl flashed him a toothy grin.

"*I* wasn't scared! I knew you were a real giant, and Momma didn't believe me. But now she does! My name's Lily, and I'm gonna call you Logan the Giant, 'kay?"

Oil rigs were no place for kids, so he didn't have much experience talking to them. And he was still wary of Lily's mom, who'd just released his hand to hold Lily back. Either she didn't believe he was Iris Taggart's grandson, or that fact didn't automatically make him "safe" in her book. She shook her head at the little girl.

"You will call him Mr. Taggart…" She glanced up at him. "Or maybe Mr. Logan?"

He nodded. "As cool as Logan the Giant sounds to my ego, Mr. Logan is probably the better choice. It's nice to meet you, Lily." He extended his hand to her, and she grabbed his fingers and shook them up and down with a great deal of enthusiasm, making him grin.

"Hi, Mr. Logan! Are you staying at the inn? Miss Iris lives in the back. I can give you the key. But you'll have to watch Mr. Whiskers if you stay there, because he likes to escape. Or are you going to take a room? Or you could stay with us! We live right next door and there's a bedroom in the attic that my brother wants but I bet he'd let you have it..."

Piper held up her hand to stop the seemingly endless flow of words. "Mr. Logan is *not* staying with us. You can't just invite strangers into our home, Lily. Why don't you go to the library and find a book to read while Mr. Logan and I have a chat?"

Uh-oh. Logan's gut tightened. Whenever a woman said they wanted to have "a chat" in that tone of voice, it was rarely a friendly conversation. He'd been on the receiving end of more than one through the years. Piper may not think he was homeless anymore, but she wasn't giving off a "welcome to the Taggart Inn" vibe, either. She picked up her phone, shaking her head at his look of concern.

"I'm not calling the cops on you. Yet. But I do have to make a call." She tapped on the screen and turned away from him.

"Chantese? It's Piper. Look, I know I said I'd pick up my check this morning, but it's probably going to be after lunch. I have a little situation... Yeah, everything's fine... No, no need for Hal to stop by..." She glanced over her shoulder at him. "Unless he wants to meet Iris's prodigal grandson..."

Logan grimaced. Great. That's just how he wanted the locals to think of him. She noted his expression and for the first time, he saw a glint of amusement in the eyes that had been icy until now. She'd said that just to goad him. He had to admit, he liked her sass.

"Yeah, you heard right… Well, he's…scruffy…" She laughed at something Chantese must have said. Her laugh was light and soft, and he couldn't help thinking that it fit her somehow. "He seems fine, I guess. I just have to get him settled. Then I'll drop Lily off at St. Vincent's for preschool and come to the office, okay?"

He seems fine… I guess? So he hadn't exactly won her over with his charm yet. She turned back to face him after the call ended. Her voice was brisk now, all business.

"Okay. Let's figure out some logistics. How long are you staying? And where?"

Logan scrubbed the back of his neck. Probably would have been nice if he'd thought that far ahead before he got here.

CHAPTER TWO

HER QUESTIONS WEREN'T that complicated, but she seemed to have stumped him. Piper gestured for Logan the Giant—it really was an appropriate title—to have a seat on one of the stools near the pastry counter, but he didn't move right away. For the first time since he'd arrived, she looked past the wetness and leather and tried to take in the man. There were deep lines under his golden-brown eyes. Weathered grooves around his mouth. The guy was exhausted. Against her better judgment, her heart softened.

I haven't eaten since yesterday's dinner...

"Let me scramble up some eggs for you, okay?"

He nodded, shrugging off his jacket and wincing as if he was in pain. Then he unzipped his chaps, removing them and folding them neatly on top of his jacket on the floor by his feet. Losing the leather made him a little more approachable, even though she could see dark tattoos peeking out under one sleeve. She wasn't against tats—Tom had several. But on this guy, the swirling blue-and-black ink served as another reminder that she didn't know anything about him. He didn't at all match Iris's stories of her grandson and the oil job that kept him away from Rendezvous Falls. Piper cracked two—she glanced at the size of the man—*four* eggs into a bowl and splashed a little water in before whisking them.

He lowered himself onto the stool with a low groan and swept his wet hair back over his shoulder.

"Are you hurt?" she asked, holding the whisk still above the bowl.

"No. I was just thinking what Gran's reaction would be if she saw me show up at her precious inn looking like this." As rough as his body was, his voice was the opposite—deep and smooth. "She probably would have worked me over with the business end of that mop and chopped off my hair herself with a dull kitchen knife. Thank you for your self-restraint."

Piper poured the eggs in a hot skillet and smiled in spite of herself. "If I had any doubts whether you were really Iris's grandson, they're gone. Because that's *exactly* what she would have done."

"*Do* you have doubts? I can show you my ID."

She hesitated, half wanting to take him up on the offer. But it would be crazy-rude to demand his ID when she was already cooking him breakfast. And why would he lie about being related to Iris? There was nothing to gain from that other than an opinionated old woman who would indeed beat him with a mop if she thought he deserved it. Piper shook her head.

"That won't be necessary."

She buttered some toast, then placed Logan's breakfast in front of him. His wallet sat there on the counter, opened to his driver's license. She looked at him, realizing this was the closest they'd been so far. And whoa—close up was a really good look on him. His eyes were brown, with sharp flecks of gold in them, as if lit from behind. And they seemed gentle. That knocked her back a bit. Just like his low, steady voice, his eyes didn't match the overall visual he projected.

He was all hair, beard and leather to look at, and he smelled of rain and sweat. But his eyes were deep with some emotion she couldn't quite define. Whatever it was made something flutter in the general vicinity of her heart. She blinked, looking at his license again.

"I said I didn't need…"

His mouth slid into a crooked grin. "Your words said one thing, but your hesitation told me something different. Go ahead. Look at it."

She swallowed her guilty conscience and picked up the wallet. Logan Anderson Taggart. Mobile, Alabama. His hair was either shorter or pulled back in the photo, showing a striking, clean-shaven face full of angles and shadows. Next to her, the grungier version of Logan scooped a huge pile of eggs into his mouth and groaned.

"Oh, man. So good. Thanks." He talked as he chewed, gesturing toward the wallet with his fork. "Satisfied?"

That wasn't exactly the word she'd use. Yes, he'd established he was Logan Taggart. But between the kids, the inn, juggling jobs, the house, and her in-laws…she rested her hand on her chest, willing her heart to slow down. The last thing she needed was this guy adding more complications to her jam-packed life.

"Why are you here?" She closed her eyes tight. Damn it, she hadn't meant to just blurt that out. His heavy brows rose in surprise. He *was* her employer's family, after all. She struggled to regroup. "I mean…are you just checking on Iris, then gone? What are your plans?

You have a plan, right?" Once she knew his intentions, she'd be able to slot him into her schedule.

He grinned as he ate, unperturbed by her machine-gun interrogation. He wiped his mouth with the back of his hand and leaned away from the counter, appraising her until her face started to heat. The man was a fascinating contradiction. Rough, but with gentle eyes. Tough, but polite—although not exactly well-mannered, since he didn't use a napkin. Intimidating in appearance, yet laughter seemed to hover just below his words.

"Piper—can I call you Piper?—I've spent the past six days packing up my life and riding twelve hundred miles on a motorcycle. I never once worried about any of those things."

Her mouth fell open. "You drove here without a plan? And what do you mean by packing up your life?"

Good grief. Who did that? And how long was he planning to stay? A shudder of fear went through her. Was he going to try to take over Iris's business? Iris mentioned once that her grandchildren wanted her to sell the place. Was he here to force that to happen? Was she about to lose her job?

"Whatever I can pack in a duffel bag is what I refer to as my life." He noted her thunderstruck expression. "But I do have more stuff in a couple storage lockers somewhere. The only 'plan' I have when I travel is the destination. Once I get that far, plans generally figure themselves out."

She still hadn't closed her mouth. Her brain was leaving skid marks trying to catch up with what he'd just said. *Plans figure themselves out?* Logan's eyes lit with laughter. At her. Was he just playing with her? She had a teenage son. She knew how to deal with someone trying to yank her chain. She straightened and finally got her mouth to work.

"So, you just hopped on a motorcycle…in *October*…and drove north to Rendezvous Falls to 'help' your grandmother…" She made air quotes. "And you have no idea… What do you think you're going to help her with?"

He moved easily to his feet, towering over her. Granted, many people were taller than her five-foot-five, but he was a *lot* taller. He took his plate to the sink and washed it himself. Okay. That was a nice surprise. He set the dish in the drying rack and turned back to face her, crossing his arms on his chest.

"It's not complicated. My grandmother owns a business, and she can't run it from a hospital bed. I'm here to do that. As far as where I'm staying, Gran's doctor told us Gran was going straight to a rehab center for a month or two, so I'll sleep in her apartment. She still has the spare room, right?"

Piper grabbed the counter to steady herself. Logan the Giant was not only going to *live* here, he also thought he was going to *run* the place? A nervous laugh bubbled up. For one thing, that was *her* job, and she couldn't afford to lose it. For another…he couldn't be serious.

"*You're* going to run the Taggart Inn?"

He shrugged. "Well, my name *is* Taggart. And I once ran an oil rig in the middle of the North Sea during a blizzard when the rig manager dropped dead on us, so I think I can handle a bed-and-breakfast in East Podunk."

"We're west of Podunk, actually." She couldn't help

herself. It was one of the factoids tourists got a kick out of, but this guy wasn't a tourist.

"What?"

She sighed. She'd started this, so she may as well finish. "Podunk is a real place, and it's right here in the Finger Lakes. Little tiny place with just a handful of houses. But it's east of here, so we can't be *East* Podunk."

"O-kay." Logan shook his head. "I guess that's something a B and B manager should know?"

"It's something *this* manager knows." She sounded pissy, but this...this *giant* was not going to take her job. Her title had never been formally designated as manager, but that's the job she was doing now. And Iris said her grandson hadn't been here in *years*. What was he up to?

"Ah...*that's* what this is all about," he said. "Nikki and I never thought Gran would allow someone else to run the place unless she was forced to." He definitely seemed familiar with Iris and her love of control. "She's never hung on to an employee for more than a few weeks before she decided they didn't meet her standards."

Piper had heard about Iris's reputation for rarely hiring help and never keeping them. For some reason, she'd apparently managed the impossible and remained employed. "Well... I'm not *officially* the manager, but I've been working here since January, and after Iris fell last week, I've been running things."

Which was why she'd had to leave the other job. Thankfully Iris had given her a nice raise this week to compensate her for the extra hours she was working, and promised to keep it in place until Iris got back to work, which could be a while. The woman was eighty, after all. Piper was leaving the kids with her in-laws too much as it was, and it wouldn't be long before Susan and Roger would start giving her more heat about her parenting skills. They still hadn't forgiven her for buying a house and moving out on her own, taking *their* grandchildren with her.

Logan rubbed the back of his neck. "So let me get this straight. You're not actually the manager? You just took over when my grandmother wasn't in any position to prevent it? That's a little opportunistic, isn't it?"

Piper eyed the mop, now safely in the corner. Taking it upside this guy's head was feeling like a really good idea right about now. She raised her chin and stared straight up into his eyes, doing her best to ignore that odd little hint of a flutter that rippled through her chest. *Shut up, flutter.*

"I was just thinking the same about you." His right brow arched, but she didn't slow a beat. "You show up out of nowhere, without telling anyone you're coming, and announce that you're taking over a successful business while your elderly grandmother is incapacitated? It's not a good look, Logan. From what little I've heard of you, it seems you haven't visited Iris for a few years now." She warmed up to her anger, putting her hands on her hips. "Your grandmother may be injured, but her *mind* is as sharp as ever. She knows I'm running things here, and she knows I'm the only one who can. How dare you insinuate I'm pulling a hostile takeover of the place. If anyone's actions are suspect, they're *yours*. The locals won't appreciate it, either. They adore Iris Taggart."

That might be overstating a bit, but the people in Rendezvous Falls definitely *respected* Iris. She'd been instrumental in the town's rebirth decades ago, and had sat on nearly every community and charity board within twenty miles. She could be abrasive as hell, but she was smart and ambitious, even at eighty.

Logan shook his head, a low laugh rumbling from his chest. "So, what—you're threatening me with the town-folk now? As if I care what the 'locals' think of me?"

"Momma?" Lily was in the doorway, clutching a book almost as big as she was. "Do you think Miss Iris would let me take this home to read? It's a dictionary!"

Piper was happy for the interruption *and* for a chance to get out of this kitchen and away from a smirking Logan Taggart so she could gather her thoughts. She headed for the door, grabbing her purse off a shelf and slinging it over her shoulder.

"Why don't you leave it here, but put it on the table by the window so you can read it while I'm cooking tomorrow morning?" She glanced back at Logan, who hadn't moved from his position, leaning against the sink with his arms folded. "Unless Logan the Giant is planning on making breakfast?"

His amused smile deepened. "I've fed hungry teams of roughnecks. I think I could handle breakfast for a few guests." He must have seen the panic on her face, because he raised his hands in innocence. "But I'll leave the kitchen duties to you, Mrs. Montgomery. I'm going to clean up. Then I'll visit my grandmother and hear directly from *her* how she wants the business to be run."

If he thought he was going to scare her with that comment, he'd failed. She was sure Iris had her back. At least...*fairly* sure. But she'd have to be more careful about throwing out challenges to him—he'd almost called her bluff on cooking breakfast. She gave him a tight smile, trying to show she hadn't been ruffled by his veiled threat.

"I'll let you into Iris's apartment..."

"No need. I have a key, unless the locks have been changed in the past..." He hesitated, and for the first time she saw his cool confidence slip. He cleared his throat. "In the past three or four years?"

"The locks haven't changed that I know of. Enjoy your visit, Logan, and be sure to say 'hi' to Iris for me." She'd be damned if she'd let him think she was intimidated just because he was going to see his grandmother. And her employer. "Let me know what she says about that hair of yours."

LOGAN FORGOT HOW frilly Gran's apartment was until he walked through the door. She'd always embraced not only her own obscurely royal British bloodline, but also the era of the Victorian mansion she lived in. So there were porcelain teapots and Wedgwood figurines everywhere, and furniture with narrow curving legs that never looked strong enough to support him.

Just inside the door was a narrow console topped with a fancy porcelain bowl filled with keys, pens, buttons and random spools of thread. Beyond that was the living area and kitchen, with two bedrooms off to the left. There used to be three, but Gran had remodeled years ago, so now her own suite was supersized, leaving one smaller guest room, which he'd be using.

He carried his duffel into the guest room and dropped it on the floor. He'd unpack later. Right now? He needed a long, hot shower. He'd been more than ready to leave Mobile, even if Rendezvous Falls and all its homespun charm, located in the winery-laden Finger Lakes area of upstate New York, was far from his dream destination. He'd already been off the rig for two weeks on disability, and boredom had him pacing the floors. At least these were new floors to pace.

An orange tabby cat glared at him from the doorway. Mr. Whiskers had been following him from the time he arrived. Seemed like everyone in this place was looking at him with suspicion. He started to pull his rugby shirt over his head and let out a hiss of pain. It might be easier to cut the damn shirt off with scissors. He blew out a few sharp breaths and tried again, keeping his left shoulder as low as he could. The doc said it might take surgery to make the rotator cuff right, but Logan wanted to save that for the last resort. He'd had a cortisone shot, but spending four days on the bike had pretty much nixed any effects from that. By the time he'd pulled into the Taggart this morning, his shoulder was screaming.

The hot water hit his back and he let out another loud groan, but of pleasure this time. Damn, that felt good. He stood there for a few minutes, hands on the back of the shower, letting the warmth soak in. When he finally stepped out and dried off, he felt a lot more human than he had when he'd arrived. He looked in the mirror and chuckled. Yeah, Gran was going to hate his hair. But she'd have to deal with it for today. He pulled it back into a tight knot so it would at least look neater than what Piper saw earlier. Man, the expression on her face!

She wasn't young—probably just a couple years behind his forty years. She had some fire in her, too. Not only when she was in Momma Bear mode, but after that, too, when she thought Logan was there to take her job away. Then she'd turned around and recommended places for him to go when she thought he was a vagrant, and she'd cooked *breakfast* for him. Whoever she was married to was a lucky guy. If she was married.

She hadn't corrected him when he called her Mrs. Montgomery, but she wasn't wearing a ring, either. She had at least two kids, though—Lily mentioned a brother. He knew nothing about kids, other than they came with the baggage of whoever fathered them being around forever. The few moms he'd dated always seemed distracted, and were constantly trying to push their kids on him. No, thank you. His own father hadn't known how to raise kids, so how was Logan supposed to? Besides, he never stayed put long enough.

He dug some clean, dry clothes out of his duffel, making sure to choose a button-front shirt instead of a pullover, just to give his shoulder a break. That damn rookie roustabout hadn't been paying attention last month, and would have been knocked right off the platform and into the Gulf if Logan hadn't grabbed the rigging and manhandled it into place. But he'd been doing shit like that for too many years, and his body was starting to suggest he'd had enough. He looked around the bedroom and shook his head.

This was as far from living on an oil rig as he could

get, with the lace-topped canopy bed and delicate settee by the bay window. Outside, his black Harley-Davidson sat in the parking lot. Beyond the lot was what made Rendezvous Falls such a successful tourist trap—the famous Victorian houses in all their wild color combinations. They called them the Painted Ladies of Rendezvous Falls, and the town was filled with them, each one fancier and more colorful than the last.

Perfect example? The house across the parking lot. It was *pink*. Not just a little pink—all shades of pink. Everywhere. There were sharply peaked dormers over the windows on the second floor, with elaborate gingerbread trim that looked like the lace on his bed. Beneath each window was a framed rectangle of dark pink with a lighter pink wooden heart in the center. Between the dormers were smaller round windows bumping out of what must have been the attic. Even the garage behind the house was pink on pink on pink. *Yikes*. Who would want to live in a cotton candy house? A little girl's enthusiastic words came back to him.

We live right next door and there's a bedroom in the attic that my brother wants but I bet he'd let you have it...

Could he picture the blonde, blue-eyed mother and daughter living in a house that looked like a birthday cake? Uh, yeah, actually. Lily had been wearing a pink top, and she was as girly as a little girl could get, with her curls and infectious giggle. And Piper, with no makeup and wearing jeans, had the same rosy pink cheeks as her daughter. Her smile, even if it had been fleeting this morning, was as sweet as the fancy house next door. But still…a *pink* house? If she *was* married, the guy wasn't just lucky. He was a saint.

Speaking of sainthood, it was time for him to go see Gran. The nearest hospital equipped for hip surgery was in Geneva, fourteen miles north. He hated the thought of putting on his leathers again, but there was definitely a sharp chill in the air. He hoped Gran still had her barge of a car in the garage, because he was going to run out of motorcycle weather pretty quickly if he stayed here any length of time. The clouds had cleared, though, and it was a nice ride up Route 14. The trees were bright gold and yellow, with the occasional shot of red from a giant maple. The colors made Seneca Lake look even more blue than usual at the base of the long valley, with vineyards on many of the slopes above and below him. He passed half a dozen wineries—the other thing that made this area famous.

It wasn't hard to find Gran's room when he got to the ortho unit at the hospital. He could hear her complaining about the food as soon as he stepped off the elevator. Christ, the woman never changed. He grudgingly smiled to himself. It was both a blessing and curse that Gran was such a fireball. That feistiness was what kept her going, even if it drove the people around her crazy. Her voice rose.

"Young lady, this so-called soup tastes like dishwater! My god, I understand it being low-sodium, but there are other spices besides salt that are perfectly healthy. You have that cook come up here and I'll teach…" She looked to the doorway where he stood and her gray eyes went wide. "Logan! I…well, I never expected… Come here, you big brute!"

The poor aide getting the soup lecture scampered out of the way, and out of the room, when Logan headed for Gran. He crouched to hug her, afraid to sit on the bed and disturb her hip.

"Hi, Gran. You didn't really think we'd leave you all alone, did you?"

Her hug was fierce, but he felt a little tremble in there too, as if she was fighting tears. Sure enough, she sniffled a couple of times before regrouping and pulling away. Other than his father's funeral, he'd never seen her shed a tear. But her eyes were clear and sharp. Whatever it was had passed, probably by her sheer force of will.

"I don't need anyone's help, but damn, boy, I'm glad to see you!" She gestured to a nearby chair when she finally released him. "How long are you staying? Have you been to the Taggart?"

He nodded. "Just long enough to shower and change. And grab a quick breakfast from your new cook."

The old woman smiled. "Piper was still there? Good. That girl's a hell of a lot more than a cook. She's been a godsend over the past year, and especially now."

Despite him and his sister trying to convince her for *years* to hire help, his grandmother had always been the one to do everything at the inn. Mainly because her standards were so high she couldn't tolerate anyone else's attempts at doing her job. This wasn't the time to bring it up, but eventually he and Gran would have to have "the talk" again. The one about selling the Taggart Inn.

He studied her. Hospital beds never made anyone look good, but Gran looked small and…worried. She'd somehow managed to be fully made-up, with her hair styled neatly, if a little more fluffy than usual. She was wearing a bright yellow jacket of some kind. But he could see the strain of pain in her eyes, and an overall tiredness he'd never seen in her before.

They'd had their disagreements through the years, but he'd somehow figured Gran would just live... forever. She was too stubborn not to. But now? Now he could see she was mortal after all. The realization left him shaken. His voice softened.

"Tell me how you are, Gran."

"Isn't it obvious?" she scoffed. "I'm stuck here in a hospital bed with a cast-iron hip that hurts like hell. They're moving me to the rehab place tomorrow, and then the real fun starts with the physical therapy. Of course, they've already had me up and walking, the sadist bastards."

He laughed. This was the headstrong woman he remembered. "At least they haven't dampened your spirits, Gran. I know you don't want to hear this, but you're going to have to be patient. It's a long process."

"Bah! Patience is for wimps. I have an inn to run, and I can't do it from here. We're headed into our busiest season. I didn't even get the fall decorations up!"

He thought of the silk leaves and pumpkins he'd seen all around the lobby. "Somebody decorated. The place looks like a pumpkin spice latte blew up inside of it."

Gran smiled and patted his hand. "That must have been Piper. Did you meet her? She's a godsend."

Logan frowned, a shaft of worry hitting his chest. Gran was repeating herself. He kept his tone level so he didn't upset her. "Yes, I met her. She cooked me break-fast."

"Oh, right. You told me that." She scowled. "Damn drugs. I've been fuzzy all week and I hate it." She took a hard look at him, reaching up to turn his chin to the side and examine his hair. "Lord, Logan, speaking of drugs—you look like you're *dealing* them. I can't imagine what Piper thought. She's such a good girl." Gran wagged her finger in his face. "And you stay away from her!"

"Why?" Not that he was interested in Piper—wasn't she married?—but he felt the sting of Gran's disapproval. Because Piper was a "good girl," that meant she was off-limits to him, which made him...what? A bad boy? Back to the same old argument with Gran, about his so-called "wasted life." She was still talking at him.

"She has enough going on in her life without dealing with a rolling stone like you. She's a sweet woman with a heart of gold." Gran made Piper sound like some sugar-frosted saint. He thought of the way Piper had come at him with her blue eyes blazing, threatening him with a mop. Gran's voice turned affectionate. "And the guests love her."

"What exactly does she do there?" Piper had seemed genuinely upset when he'd inferred she was taking advantage of Gran, but he had to be sure.

Gran waved her hand. "Everything, really. She started helping in the kitchen. She's a whizbang cook. Then she picked up doing the cleaning on the days she didn't work at the insurance office. Piper buying the pink sister next door was the best thing that could have happened to me."

"Pink sister?" Well, that answered that question. Piper, Lily and family *did* live in the pink confection across the parking lot.

"Don't you remember? The three smaller houses on the street are called the Three Sisters. One's pink, one's blue, and one's green. Other than the color schemes, though, they're almost identical."

Logan had no reason to remember that. His visits to his grandmother were pretty irregular as a kid. Usually his dad packed him and Nikki off to Gran's when there was some kind of trouble with one of Dad's big ideas. Being sent to Gran's meant his father was about to uproot them again. Or was afraid of going to jail—which he somehow always managed to avoid. Logan never paid attention to the stories she told about Rendezvous Falls and its houses.

Rendezvous Falls had always been as foreign to Nikki and him as landing on the moon. People were so…happy here, with all of its "charm" and the way people knew each other and helped each other. They were all so invested…so *rooted*…in the community. It was like some 1950s sitcom—the kind that got mocked on *SNL*. Frankly, the place had always scared the crap out of him.

Gran sagged back against her pillow. Maybe he should leave her to rest. But she wasn't finished.

"Anyway, Piper started working more hours for me, and learned how to do pretty much everything at the Taggart, other than handling the books." Made sense Gran wouldn't give up the money managing part of things, not even to Saint Piper. "She was part-time, but now…" Iris gestured to her hip under the bedsheets.

"Now I'm paying her full-time to run the place, at least for the time being." That explained why Piper had been so afraid to lose her job. Gran fixed him with a hard look. "Unless you've finally come to your senses and decided to take over the family business?"

The dig was no surprise. Gran had tried her best to con Nikki into taking over, but that had blown up years ago. Now she was turning her sights on *him*? Yeah...no.

"Gran, it was never a family business. The inn has always been *yours*. And we agreed that when it got to be too much, you'd let the place go."

Her chin quivered. "I did no such thing!"

"Gran, you did. Maybe you were just placating us, but you said it. We don't need to talk about it today, but we do need to talk about it. In the meantime, I'm here to take care of things while you recuperate. But once you're back in fighting shape, I've got a rig in South America with my name on it. This is only temporary."

His grandmother stared at him. The woman still had the power to make him feel like a misbehaving twelve-year-old. He waited her out, having inherited his stubborn streak from her. One of the machines she was hooked up to beeped gently every few seconds, and he could hear nurses giggling at the desk outside her room. He didn't take his eyes off hers, but she nearly broke his resolve by the time she spoke again. Even aged and temporarily infirm, she was tough as nails.

"Everything in your entire life is temporary, Logan. I'll need you here until at least Christmas." She kept talking over his objection. "That's only a couple of months, and South America can wait. It won't kill you. But you are *not* working at my inn looking like *that*."

He looked down at his slightly rumpled cotton shirt and jeans. "What? Perfect Piper was wearing jeans."

Back came that pointing finger of hers, perilously close to his nose, reminding him that when he was a boy, she hadn't been afraid to pinch that nose to get his attention. She wouldn't do that now, would she? He leaned back, just in case.

"First, don't get sarcastic about Piper Montgomery. Second, I was talking about all that hair. Good lord, boy, when's the last time you held a razor in your hand? I can't have you scaring the guests, even if it is almost Halloween. You get over to Slim's on Main Street tomorrow and get all that…" she gestured in the general area of his entire head "…under control! Lose the beard, and bring that awful hair up above your collar." She glanced at his arm, where a shadow of tats showed below his shirt cuff. "And keep that nonsense covered up. We don't want people think we're owned by the Hells Angels."

The woman loved to be in charge. Of everyone and everything. It was a waste of his energy to resent it—it's just who she was. And for all their disagreements through the years about his lifestyle and that damn inn, he loved her as much *because* of her feistiness as in spite of it. Logan stood, stooping to kiss his grandmother's forehead. "Got it. Slim's tomorrow. Only for you, Gran. But stop saying 'we' as if that place isn't one hundred percent Iris Taggart."

She rolled her eyes. "It was never meant to be one hundred percent mine. It was supposed to be your father's, but he wanted to chase bigger dreams. I was hoping you or your sister might see the light, but that never happened, either. You're both just like him."

"Hey, he was *your* son."

Gran chuckled. "Good point. But that wanderlust you all have didn't come from me. I put the time and the work in to build something *permanent*, and never once thought about leaving." She gave him a sharp look. "You might want to give it a try sometime."

She just couldn't give it a rest. Her insistence on the virtues of "staying put" had led to some of their biggest arguments in the past, including the one three years ago. The last time he'd come to Rendezvous Falls. It was easier to ignore her thinly veiled hints on the phone, where her gray eyes couldn't bore into him. But now, when she was at her weakest, something resonated inside him at her mention of permanence.

"Whatever you say, Gran." There was no anger in his voice. He turned to go, but she called his name as he got to the door.

"You just do what Piper tells you to do, and everything will be fine."

Logan nodded and left, but he couldn't help thinking that following Piper's orders for the next two months was probably not going to make him feel "fine" at all.

CHAPTER THREE

"FOR GOODNESS' SAKE, Iris, hold still before I end up burning you with this curling iron!"

Iris Taggart stopped moving, but not before giving her friend the stink eye first. "You burn me with that thing and *you'll* be the one in the hospital bed. Hurry up!"

Cecile Harris was fussing over Iris's hair with that damn hot stick, trying to keep it out of sight from the nurses. The hospital staff probably wouldn't appreciate a red-hot beauty appliance being used next to oxygen tubes and cotton sheets.

Still fluffing Iris's hair, Cecile set the curling iron down and handed her a mirror. Iris swatted her friend's hand away before she ended up looking like an ancient Dolly Parton. Hair this big wasn't even close to being her style, but it would have to do. Being eighty was bad enough. Being eighty against pasty white hospital sheets was a no-go for Iris. She refused to let people see her like that, so she'd strong-armed her book club friends to come in here every morning to "fix her up."

This was Cecile's morning, and Cecile liked to fluff Iris's bob and use lots of pastel makeup. Tomorrow would be Helen Russo's day, which meant Iris would have hardly any makeup at all. And then Vickie Pendergast would come in on Saturday and have her ready for a fashion runway by the time she was done. Iris didn't like the inconsistency, but what could she do? The hospital was a good drive from Rendezvous Falls, and the ladies were driving here first thing in the morning to help her. As a *favor*. So she couldn't complain. She just *couldn't*. She looked in the mirror and bit back a sigh. Good lord—powder-blue eyeshadow, *sparkly* eyelashes and bright pink lipstick. She looked like a ventriloquist's dummy. All she needed was a feather boa. But she summoned up her brightest smile.

"It's lovely, dear. Thank you for doing this."

Cecile waved off the thanks and sat down with a cup of coffee. "Oh, please, I *like* doing it! It gets me up and going in the morning, and this hospital has the best coffee shop I've ever seen." She took a sip, being careful that none drizzled on her sunny yellow sweater. "I may keep driving up here after you leave just for the coffee!"

Iris was a tea drinker, in deference to her mother's rumored royal British lineage. But she nodded absently in agreement. Ten days in, and she still hadn't come to terms with being trapped in this damn bed. Her friends were wonderful, but the thought of smiling her way through weeks of recovery made her feel exhausted. And sad. Cecile leaned forward, brushing her out-of-the-box-blond hair back as she lowered her voice, as if asking for nuclear codes.

"So tell me all about your grandson. It's been years, hasn't it? Is he really going to run the Taggart? Do you think he'll stay?"

Iris pulled her pink chenille bed jacket tighter around her shoulders. The color was Cecile's favorite, not hers, but the jacket kept her from exposing her paper-thin hospital gown to every Tom, Dick and Harry who walked by. A lady needed to maintain her dignity, after all.

"I don't know if he knows *how* to stay anywhere…" Lord knew that boy was allergic to settling down, just like his father. "But he agreed to stay through Christmas."

Iris figured if either of her grandchildren were going to show up, it would be Nicole. Nicole's last visit to Rendezvous Falls had ended with the usual argument about selling the inn, though.

She smoothed the bed covers, plucking at a loose thread on the blanket. Logan agreed with his sister about selling the inn. *His* last visit had ended in an argument too, after he told Iris she should retire. *Retire.* Screw that. She ran her hand along the blanket again. Give up the inn? She may as well just lie here and die. And she wasn't ready to do that quite yet.

It had been a shock—and a relief—to see Logan walk into her room yesterday, declaring he was here to take care of things.

"What's he going to do? Piper Montgomery is running the inn, right?" Cecile asked, startling Iris out of her thoughts.

"She's doing the cooking and cleaning and checking people in, but she has two kids. I don't know if she can juggle it all." A chill of panic went through her. The inn was her life. What if Piper couldn't—or didn't want to—do it? What was she going to do? She'd never really prepared for the possibility of losing it all.

A male voice interrupted from the doorway. "Is this a private party or can anyone join?"

"Rick! Come on in!" Cecile bounced up and gave Rick Thomas a big hug. He was currently the only male member of their little book club, which Iris herself had founded years ago. She didn't make as many meetings these days as she used to, but the friendships were as strong as ever. Rick pulled up a chair next to Cecile, giving Iris's hand a quick squeeze as he sat.

"You look very…colorful…this morning, my dear." He was careful to conceal his wink from Cecile.

"Doesn't she?" Cecile exclaimed. "I think pink really suits her coloring."

"But maybe not her personality?"

Iris huffed out a laugh. "Screw you, Rick. What brings you out this early in the morning? And all dressed up, too. Did someone die?"

He glanced down. "You think I'd wear a sport jacket and chinos to a funeral? What kind of drugs do they have you on in this place? I'm doing a guest lecture in Buffalo, and I thought I'd stop on the way by. How are you feeling?"

In constant pain. Helpless. Old. Frightened. Angry as hell.

"I'm fine, Rick." Iris smiled as she lied. "I should be out of here and into the rehab facility in a couple days, and then I'll work on getting back into fighting shape. Maybe I'll even run in the marathon next spring."

Her friends laughed right along with her, but Iris felt the sting of tears behind her eyes. She was in this mess because she'd tripped over a rug. A *rug*. There were dozens of them in the Taggart, and she'd been walking on them for half a century. But she was tugging on a box of harvest decorations that morning and somehow found herself tangled up on the rug in the hallway. She'd gone down like a redwood. As soon as she hit the floor she knew she'd broken something. Thank god Piper had been there. They ended up replacing her right hip with some fancy titanium thing. Her friend Helen said they'd have to call her the bionic woman now. Iris didn't want to be bionic. She wanted to be the way she'd always been. But, as her mother used to say, *if wishes were horses, beggars would ride.*

Cecile was filling Rick in on Logan's arrival, and Rick started to laugh.

"A hot single guy who's been working on oil rigs all over the world? Does this mean the matchmakers will be back at it again?"

Cecile's eyes went wide. "Oh, I hadn't thought of that! Iris, what do you think? Should we find a nice young lady for your grandson? We have a meeting coming up…"

Iris shook her head sharply. "For one thing, Logan's not the 'nice young lady' type. He's long-haired and tattooed and rides a motorcycle. As much as I'd like to see him settle down, I don't think a sweet thing will ever keep his interest."

Rick nodded. "A bad boy, eh? Just my type. But I'm assuming he doesn't swing my way?"

Iris rolled her eyes. "Not only is he hetero, he's at least twenty years younger than you, you creeper."

"I wasn't offering myself as an option." Rick was tall and lanky, and he stretched his legs out in front of him with a half laugh, half sigh. "I don't have the energy for trouble like that anymore. But surely there are some…" he formed air quotes with his fingers "…'bad girls' out there for Logan."

Cecile sat up straight. "Oh! Connie Denton's daughter rides a motorcycle, and she's built like a brick shi… well, you know what I mean. And Lena is friends with that tattoo artist with the blue hair. I'm sure we can find someone who'd catch his attention."

Logan would never go for it. Then again, he wouldn't really have to know…

"We'd have to do it in stealth mode. He's a stubborn one."

"*Your* grandson? Stubborn? Go figure!" Rick laughed, ignoring the hand gesture she gave him. "We'll talk about it at the meeting and let you know if we come up with any promising prospects."

Cecile swatted Rick's arm. "You hated the idea of us playing matchmakers for Helen's niece!"

Rick shrugged. "But then I found a professor for her, remember? It was a mismatch, but we can learn from our mistakes. And don't forget, now Whitney's engaged to be married."

Iris scoffed. "She's engaged to a man who was right there all along, and you guys never even considered him for her."

"True," Cecile nodded. "But when Luke and Whitney hit a rough patch, *we're* the ones who got them back together, so I count that as a win. Hey, what about Piper Montgomery?"

Iris recoiled at the thought. She adored her grandson, but he was so much like his father. He never stayed. Not in one place. Not with one person. The only thing Logan would be interested in with a sweet single mom like Piper would be a one-night stand, and Iris couldn't let that happen. She dismissed the suggestion with a shake of her head.

"Did you not hear me say he wasn't into sweet things? Piper's a go-to-church-on-Sunday kind of woman, and she has two kids and meddling in-laws. I love my grandson, but I know his type, and she ain't it." She started to laugh. "But I doubt we have to worry about it. Piper wouldn't want a rough-around-the-edges drifter like Logan anywhere near her kids." That truth made Iris feel better. Piper had enough going on in her life without tangling with Logan.

"ETHAN, I SWEAR to God, if you don't get out of that bed, I will dump a pitcher of ice water over your head. I've got to get back to work!" Piper was in the midst of her weekday morning ritual. She'd bundle up Lily and take her to the inn while she got breakfast started. Then they'd dash back to the house, where she'd get Lily dressed and Ethan off to school. Easily the worst part of her day.

Lord knew she'd never planned on being a single mom. Tom was supposed to be here. Helping her. Laughing with her about Ethan being a typical teenager. But Tom, the man who'd been her whole world, was gone. And she was doing the best she could to hold everything together. Including herself.

She gave it one last try, resorting to her mad-mom screech. "ETHAN!"

She let out a squeak of surprise when she heard her mother-in-law's voice behind her.

"Really, dear, is *screaming* at the boy the best solution?" Susan Montgomery stood in the side-door foyer, dressed in designer wool from head to toe. The beige color matched her mother-in-law's perfectly coiffed hair and catlike eyes. She tugged off her leather gloves. "You shouldn't take your personal frustrations out on Ethan."

"Gigi!" Lily came barreling down the hall and into her grandmother's arms. Susan had been emphatic from the start that the children were never to call her Grandma because it "aged" her.

"Hi, Princess!" Susan knew Piper didn't like that nickname for Lily. Little girls could be so much more than princesses. Maybe she should let her daughter dress up as Deadpool for Halloween after all, just to make her point. Susan straightened, speaking to Lily, but looking at Piper. Just in case Piper missed her not-so-subtle message. "Sounds like Mommy is having a bad day. Maybe you should come stay with Gigi and Poppa this weekend?"

Piper's teeth ground together so tightly she was surprised Susan couldn't hear it. They'd discussed this. The woman knew better than to extend an invitation to the children without consulting her first. Before Lily could answer, Piper reclaimed her time, her voice in Suzy Sunshine mode for Lily's sake. But her level gaze made her feelings clear to her mother-in-law. A woman she'd once treasured as a second mom. Their relationship was just one more thing Tom's death had left in tatters.

"Aw, thanks for asking, Gigi, but Lily is going to help me decorate the inn today. And I'm taking the kids to HarvestFest this weekend. Maybe you and Poppa can meet us there?" She didn't want the Montgomerys out of her children's lives. But *she* was the parent.

Lily's head bobbed up and down, sending her curls flying. "And before the festival, you can come see the decorations at the inn! It's going to be so pretty!" Lily looked up at Piper with a bright smile that reminded her sharply of Tom. "And spooky, too! We even have a giant!"

"Okay, Lily," Piper took her daughter's hand. She didn't need to be discussing Logan the Giant with Susan. Hopefully he'd be gone by the weekend, once he saw that she could handle everything just fine while Iris recovered. "Why don't you go make sure your brother is up and getting dressed for school?" Lily galloped up the painted wooden stairs. It was a mystery how thirty-five pounds of little girl could sound like ten elephants.

Susan twisted her gloves in her hands. "I'm a little surprised you're letting an impressionable child like Lily work on 'spooky' decorations. Is that really a good influence?"

Piper bit her tongue. Literally. She bit it hard, just to keep her from reacting in anger. The Montgomerys meant well. She *knew* that. She and the kids had moved in with Susan and Roger three months before Lily was born. Which was ten months before Tom died in Afghanistan. Piper had been in too much shock at first to see how she'd gradually relinquished her parenting duties to them. Now that she was taking charge of her life again, Susan and Roger—especially Susan—were having a hard time letting go. It might have been easier if Piper had moved closer to her dad and his new bride in Texas, and cut the ties more cleanly. But she didn't want to do that to the children or to the Montgomerys. Tom, even in death, would bind them all together for the rest of their lives, so they were going to have to figure it out.

"Lily will be fine," she finally answered. "The decorations are all kid-friendly." If she ever finished putting them up.

"But she's talking about a giant!"

"Oh, she's just being silly." *Quick! Subject change!* "What brings you by so early?"

Susan used to watch Lily on the mornings Piper worked at Peterson Insurance, since Hal Peterson wasn't as open to the idea of children at work as Iris was. Susan had complained about Piper working two jobs, but now that she was working one and didn't need a sitter as often, Susan was even more unhappy.

"I've got an early dentist appointment in Watkins Glen, and I noticed your lights on when I drove by."

It made sense for Susan and Roger to have keys to her house. That didn't mean Piper was okay with them just walking in unannounced. She glanced at her watch. She needed to cook breakfast for guests at the inn, so that discussion would have to wait for another day. She was turning to yell up to Ethan again when she heard the resentful thud of her son's sneakers on the stairs. Maybe it was her imagination, but he managed to make every action seem like a condemnation of her parenting skills. Sure enough, when he got to the foyer, he just kept on walking into the kitchen without uttering a word. He even gave the gift of jerking away from her when she reached out to tame that mop of light brown hair. Just a few short years ago, he'd soaked up her hugs like candy.

"Ethan, ignoring *me* is one thing, but at least say good morning to your grandmother."

Ethan's monotone voice rolled lazily out from the kitchen."Morning, Gigi." Then he started to whine. Loudly. "Mo-m! Do we really not have any milk? Come *on!*"

Piper blew out a long breath. "You know how much I love it when you create two syllables out of a three-letter word, son. Try moving something. It's in there." She looked at her watch again. Room Five had requested breakfast at seven thirty. She gave Susan a cheery smile as she ushered her to the door. "Thanks for stopping by, but we have a busy morning. We'll see you at the festival, okay?"

Fortunately Mr. and Mrs. Chappell in Room Five were running a few minutes late. By the time they helped themselves to coffee and juice from the sideboard and sat down, Piper was serving them turkey-stuffed French toast with cranberry-orange compote. She barely had time to run outside before the eight o'clock seating to make sure Ethan got on the bus. She waved and called out a goodbye, but he ignored her. *Shocker.*

She tried not to take it personally. All boys got varying degrees of "attitude" when they hit puberty. The family therapist told her that the surge of testosterone turned many of them into little bundles of random anger, even if they had an intact family unit to support them. And Ethan's family unit was definitely not intact. Tom was gone, and Ethan was angry about it. Hell, Piper was angry, too. She got it. She also got that she was the nearest, easiest target for her son's rage and loss. But understanding that in her *head* and understanding it in her *heart* were two different things.

At least she had eight or ten years before Lily hit puberty and turned on her. For now, the Happiest Girl in the World was sitting by the window in the corner of the Taggart kitchen, drawing sunny pictures of their pink house just across the parking lot, while Piper finished cleaning up. All the guests had been fed. Her son caught the bus. Her daughter was happy. Today was sliding into the "win" column.

"Are you done serving breakfast?"

Piper spun around at the booming male voice. Lily jumped up and ran to Logan Taggart in the doorway, wrapping her arms around his legs. "Logan! I'm drawing pictures of our house—come see!"

Logan froze, staring down at Lily with wide eyes. He raised his hands and his mouth opened, but no sound was coming out. He looked…terrified. Lily was putting on a full-court press of cuteness, resting her chin on his leg and staring up, up, up at his face.

Piper wondered at her daughter's instant fascination with the man. Lily was always friendly, but she acted as if Logan was a familiar family member instead of a complete stranger. A stranger who was looking down at Lily like she was a cobra about to strike.

He finally found his voice, his eyes darting from Lily to Piper and back. "Good morning, Lily. Uh… I don't know if your mom wants you to…uh…"

He wasn't afraid of *Lily*. He was afraid of *Piper*, after she'd threatened to beat him with a mop yesterday for being near her daughter. She wiped her hands on a towel and walked toward him.

"Lily, Mr. Logan is here looking for breakfast. Again." She arched a brow at him, and the corner of his mouth lifted in recognition of her sarcasm. "Why don't you go draw something special for him?" Lily skipped to the kitchen table, and Piper turned to fire up the front burner on the stove, placing the flat griddle over it. "It's a little late for breakfast, but I have a couple more servings of stuffed French toast assembled in the fridge. I always make extras of those in case someone's super hungry. Give me a few minutes to grill it up."

He shook his head. "You're busy. Point me in the right direction and I'll cook it myself."

She blinked at him in confusion. "You'll...what?"

He lifted one of those heavy, dark brows. "I told you I can cook, especially on a griddle. Have *you* eaten, by the way? Want me to cook one for you?"

A man who cooked. And who offered to cook for *her*. That was something different. For all of Tom's qualities, his cooking skills had never gone past flipping burgers on the grill. Logan bent over in front of the refrigerator to pull out the platter of uncooked sandwiches, displaying a very fine... Piper looked away quickly, shocked at where her mind just went. She had no business admiring any man's ass. She wasn't blind, of course, but noticing and *admiring* were two very different things.

He glanced at her over his shoulder and cocked his head.

"Piper? Breakfast?"

"Oh...um..." She ran her hand over her hair, pulling her ponytail tight. "I couldn't eat a whole sandwich..."

He straightened. "Good. One isn't enough for me,

so I'll eat one and a half. These look great, by the way. After breakfast, let's talk about my training program."

She took a sharp breath. "Excuse me?"

"Gran's orders." He gave her a crooked grin before turning to the stove. "You're stuck with me until Christmas. She said you know more about running this place than anyone else, so I'm your apprentice. Gran and I will handle the bookkeeping while you and I do the day-to-day stuff." He tossed an alarmingly large slab of butter onto the griddle. The first thing she'd have to teach him was moderation before he single-handedly clogged someone's arteries.

Lily looked up from her drawing, eyes wide in alarm. "No, Momma, you can't train him today! We're decorating for the festival! You *promised*!"

Piper looked from her daughter to the imposing figure cooking breakfast. His long hair was pulled back into a "man bun," and it highlighted the sharp angles of his face. He was dressed in well-worn jeans and a dark rugby shirt, with thick-soled work boots. How could Iris think Logan was suited for working as the face of the Taggart Inn? Until *Christmas*? As if Piper didn't have enough to worry about this Christmas, with her house falling down around her head and a promise she had to keep.

"Well, I guess Mr. Logan's first lesson will be how to decorate the front porch, won't it?"

Lily laughed. "He's so big, I bet he can hang the garlands without a ladder, Momma! Mr. Logan, we have a bunch of flowers to put on the steps—I'll show you where they go. And pretty orange tablecloths. And a *scarecrow*! Miss Iris told me where he goes, so I can help with that, too!"

The griddle sizzled. Logan looked at Lily, then over to Piper. "My grandmother didn't tell me I'd have *two* bosses in this place, but I already know better than to argue with either one of you." He aimed the spatula at Lily and waggled it playfully. "Especially you. If today is decorating day, then we'll decorate."

Piper watched him cooking breakfast. He seemed comfortable at the stove and unconcerned about the prospect of having a woman and a little girl bossing him around. Judging from his smile, Lily's instant connection with Logan was mutual. There was something about his…steadiness…that made him very appealing. She turned to wipe the counter. Not to *Piper*, of course. Appealing in a *general* way. To a woman who might be in the market. But *she* wasn't.

Piper was lonely. Had been for a while now. But the last thing she needed was a man in her hectic life. If she did, though…she glanced over her shoulder at Logan.

Nah. He'd never be her type.

CHAPTER FOUR

LOGAN WAS USED to taking orders. He understood the importance of structure and hierarchy, particularly in a setting where one mistake could cost someone their life, or the lives of everyone on the oil rig. He'd had bosses he'd liked, and bosses he'd strongly disliked, and a healthy number of didn't-care-much-either-way bosses in between. And he'd *been* a boss of sorts lately, as chief mechanical engineer. He knew those pumps, drills, and engines inside and out, and he was confident in the decisions he made.

So it was disconcerting, to say the least, to find himself holding an armful of fake fall leaves and a plastic pumpkin...with no clue what to do with them. His bosses all afternoon were two very opinionated blondes.

"Mr. Logan, you're not very good at decorating, are you?"

Lily Montgomery's calm assessment was right on the mark. He looked down at the tiny yellow-haired girl with her mother's bright blue eyes. She smiled up at him as if she'd just pronounced him God's gift to decorating rather than the exact opposite. The kid was more than just cute. She was smart and funny. She went at everything she did with conviction. He liked her, and he couldn't remember the last time he'd said that about anyone's kid. He had nothing *against* children—he'd just never related to them quite the way he did with this little one.

She pointed at the white metal tables scattered around the porch, with their fancy metal chairs to match. "Tomorrow there'll be a plastic pumpkin on every table, but you have to tie them down or the wind will blow them away." She held up a chubby fistful of twist ties. "Momma uses these. And the leaves go up on the ceiling."

On the ceiling? Logan looked up. Ah...there were hooks just inside the gingerbread trim, spaced at about the same distance as the small rings on the garlands in his arms. Leave it to Gran to have a system for everything at the inn, including the decorations.

Piper had left them alone a few peaceful minutes ago to run inside to answer the phone. Why peaceful? Because the woman never stopped bossing. Where to get the boxes from. What order to carry the boxes out in. Where to put each one before unpacking it. How to unpack it. He thought his grandmother was organized, but Piper took it to a whole new level. She was emphatic that all the decorations had to be up today because customers were arriving for the weekend festival.

And for now, at the Taggart Inn—regardless of his last name—Piper was the boss. Gran said so.

"Are you just going to stand there or what?"

He looked down at his diminutive assistant. Lily's hands rested on her hips, her head tipped to the side. This damn kid was cute as hell.

He gave her an exaggerated wink and spoke in a

conspiratorial whisper. "I'm afraid to move until your mother gets back. I'm afraid I'll get in trouble."

Lily pursed her lips, then nodded very seriously. "You might. She's very fussy. Momma says she's... pah...pahticler. She likes things done right. My brother says she's a control freak, but he doesn't say that to Momma's face, just to me and Gigi."

There was a lot to digest in that little speech. And none of it was any of his business. Lily pointed at the garlands in his arms.

"I know how to hang those. They're just the same as the grape ones Miss Iris decorated with for the wine festival last month." She pointed up. "You put the rings over those hooks all around the porch. Miss Iris used a ladder. I don't think you'll get in trouble with Momma if you do that."

Ignoring the horrifying image of his grandmother climbing ladders, Logan bent over to look Lily in the eyes. "Will you help me?"

Her mouth dropped open. "Really? How?"

"I can't quite reach by myself. But if I hold you up there, I bet you could hook up the pretty leaves, couldn't you?"

Lily's face lit up. "Yes!" Her head bobbed up and down, sending her curls bouncing. "Oh, yes, please, hold me up, Mr. Logan!"

By the time Piper came back to the porch, Logan and Lily had nearly finished hanging the fall garlands on the front and side porches. It was a bright, sunny October day, the kind that liked to trick people in the northeast into thinking maybe winter wouldn't come after all. The little girl's laughter had attracted a small crowd on the nearby sidewalk, watching their progress, waving and smiling.

"Decorating *and* providing entertainment. Nice multitasking, Logan."

Still holding Lily high, he looked over his shoulder to where Piper stood, arms folded on her chest. The pose was stern, but her smile wasn't. As bossy as she'd been all day, that bright smile made up for it.

"Momma! We're decorating! And I'm *flying*!"

Lily put the last loop over the last hook, and Logan couldn't resist zooming her around in the air like a plane before setting her down. Yeah, his shoulder was aching a bit, but she wasn't heavy enough to make it any worse than it already was. Before he could straighten up, the little girl wrapped her arms around his neck fiercely, holding him in place.

"Thank you, Giant Logan!" Lily planted a wet kiss on his cheek. She giggled and ran to her mother, who looked as surprised as Logan by her daughter's sneak attack.

"Lily, why don't you go wash your hands after handling that garland?" Piper said, staring at Logan the whole time. *Uh-oh.* As soon as the door closed behind Lily, he raised his hands in innocence.

"I'm sorry for putting her to work like that, but she seemed to be having fun, and I promise there was no danger I'd ever drop her." The kid barely weighed thirty pounds. "In my defense, you *did* leave us together out here, and you were gone a long time, and…" He dropped his hands. "Actually, you *were* gone a long time. How did you know we weren't hanging things backwards and making a mess?"

Humor sparkled in her eyes. "This house has these amazing innovations called…" she gestured toward the inn "…windows. Lily seemed to be having a ball out here, and…" She looked at his biceps. Her look seemed to linger longer than necessary. Interesting. He had a brief juvenile urge to flex those biceps for her. She met his gaze again. "I never worried that you'd drop her. I cleaned up the lobby while you were keeping her busy. Or vice versa… I wasn't sure who was in charge."

Logan shook his head, still wondering about that lingering look she'd just given him. Maybe she wasn't quite as saintly as Gran thought? Nah—he had to be reading her wrong. His woman-reading skills were getting rusty. With a start, he realized she was still waiting for his answer.

"Lily was definitely the one in charge, believe me."

"I don't doubt it." She finally broke eye contact, and her cheeks showed a blush of pink. She looked around the porch. "We need to get these boxes back in the attic. These decorations will stay up through most of November, with a few additions for the Ghostwalk tours." She paused, her brows furrowed in thought. Then they shot upward. "The *cornstalks*! That's what we're missing. I'll call the nursery and see if they can deliver some. We need those before the weekend."

She pulled out her phone and started tapping on it before she was done talking. She'd been doing that all day. Piper was clearly a multitasking whiz, and she had some sort of organizing app on her phone where she stored all the random tasks that popped up. Logan looked around the porch, which was already groaning with decorations.

"Why do we *need* cornstalks?"

Piper looked up. "You're asking why we need corn-stalks for *HarvestFest*? That's the quintessential fall decoration, and Iris always has them tied to the porch posts. Trust me, we need them."

Logan rubbed the back of his neck. "The inn is already fully booked this weekend. Are you saying someone might cancel if they get here and don't see dead corn on the porch?"

Her eyes narrowed again, but not in concentration this time. She was annoyed. With him. It was a look he was beginning to recognize, even after just a few days. Narrowed eyes. Steely gaze. Rigid chin, slightly raised. A voice he suspected she reserved for small children. And men who annoyed her.

"You're saying we have their money already, so who cares about their experience while they're here?"

It sounded bad when she said it *that* way. "No, I understand this is a customer-driven business. I'm just having a hard time wrapping my head around cornstalks or no cornstalks making or breaking a customer's visit."

"For one thing, they're *guests*, not customers." She slid the phone back in her pocket. "A gas station has customers. We have *guests* who trust us to provide a certain atmosphere for their stay. And every little detail contributes to that atmosphere..."

Her voice trailed off as a yellow school bus stopped at the pink house across the parking lot. A tall, skinny boy with a mop of sandy-brown hair hanging over his eyes came off the bus, head down, scuffing his feet as if he was walking to his doom. Logan felt like he was watching a film of himself at that age—gangly, with-drawn, mad at the world.

Piper went to the porch rail, her lecture to Logan forgotten. She called out to the boy.

"Ethan!"

The kid stopped, lifting his head slowly and staring wordlessly at Piper. She was undeterred by his care-fully blank expression.

"I have to work for another couple hours. Come get your sister, okay?"

Ethan's head dropped back until he was staring straight up at the sky. His despair was palpable. "Mo-m, no! I was gonna go to Josh's..."

"You're not going anywhere because you're *grounded*, remember? Drop your books and come get Lily. Now." Logan bit the inside of his lip to keep from laughing at the sharp change in Piper's voice, which had gone from friendly callout to hardened steel. The sweet little mom wasn't going to take any shit from her son.

"Man, this is bull..." The boy whipped his backpack toward the pink porch and headed their way. Interest-ing family dynamic—hyperorganized prim and proper mom, sweetheart of a little girl, and...*this* kid. A walk-ing bundle of sullen resentment.

Piper's voice grew heavy with warning. "Ethan, you come off your grounding tomorrow. Don't push your luck."

The boy's muttered "Whatever..." made Piper's shoulders go tight. She took a deep breath and slowly released it. Logan could almost hear her counting to ten in her mind. She turned to him, her smile brittle but determined.

"Excuse me while I go have a conversation with my *precious* firstborn." She marched down the stairs and met Ethan halfway across the parking lot. Logan couldn't hear her low words, but he could tell from the boy's rolled eyes and thin, angry mouth that she wasn't making much headway.

Lily bounced out onto the porch and over to Logan's side. She followed his gaze to Piper and Ethan, then shook her head.

"That boy will never learn. He's pushing Momma to test her, and he's always gonna lose."

Logan chuckled. Lily spoke with a wisdom far beyond her years, clearly repeating an overheard adult conversation. "Really? Is that what your daddy says?"

She didn't look up, her voice level and matter-of-fact. "My daddy's dead. Miss Iris is the one who said Ethan would always lose against Momma."

His mouth opened, then closed again. What was he supposed to say? Lily was four. And her father—Piper's husband?—was dead. Lily didn't seem traumatized, but what did he know about little girls with dead daddies? He finally blurted the only thing he could think to say.

"I'm…I'm sorry about your daddy."

Lily looked up at him with an eerie calm. "He was a soldier. He met me once but I don't remember. Momma says I was a little baby. Then he went somewhere to be a hero and got dead." She looked back to her mother and brother. "Momma says it's just us now. Her, Ethan and me. That's why she bought us a house—to make us a family. But Ethan doesn't like it."

Logan was stunned to silence. He'd been imagining

Piper going home at night to play happy housewife with some lucky guy. Picket fences and all that. He looked at the pink house. Sure enough, there was a picket fence surrounding the backyard. A little crooked and with peeling paint, but it was there. She was a single mom, working long hours to support two kids on her own. No wonder she was hyperorganized—that was her survival mechanism. Logan already liked Piper's spunk, but now he had a new respect for the load she was carrying.

"Al*right*!" Ethan surrendered dramatically. "Geez, okay. I'll watch her, but I'm not cooking."

"Seriously?" Piper's voice was tinged with humor now. "Are you referring to popping the occasional frozen pizza in the oven? You're off the hook for 'cooking.' I'll make sweet-and-sour chicken when I get home. Your favorite." She reached up to ruffle his hair. He pulled away, but not until she'd gotten one affectionate pass at him.

Ethan looked up to the porch. His hair was darker than Lily's, and his eyes were brown or hazel instead of blue. He lifted his chin at his sister.

"Come on, brat."

"Bye, Giant Logan!" Lily galloped down the stairs and ran to her big brother. "Ethan! You won't believe what I did today! Mr. Logan held me up up *up* in the air and I hung the decorations myself! Are we going home now?"

Ethan flashed his mother a dark look, but surprised Logan by rubbing his knuckles affectionately in Lily's hair. Not unlike what his mom had just done to him. "Guess so. Come on." He turned to go and saw Logan's motorcycle parked next to the inn. He halted abruptly in a classic double take. He glanced up at Logan. "Yours?"

Logan nodded in reply. Ethan studied the bike again, tipped his head, then shrugged. The universal language of teenage boys trying hard to appear unimpressed.

He decided to poke the kid a little. "You ride?"

Ethan's eyes went wide for a minute, until he realized what he was doing and looked away while regaining his composure and shaking his head in the negative.

"You want to?"

He'd almost teased a smile out of Ethan, but Piper broke the moment with a firm rebuttal.

"I don't care if he *wants* to or not, he won't be riding any bike that doesn't operate under pedal power." She shot Logan a puzzled look. No, that was annoyance in her eyes. Again. "But thanks so very much for offering."

He gave an exaggerated shrug, not unlike Ethan's. "I just asked the guy a couple of questions."

Her eyes narrowed at him in warning. *He's always gonna lose...* Yeah, he was starting to see more of that solid steel spine Piper Montgomery had.

"Well," she said, "whatever you were doing, you can stop. He's not a 'guy.' He's thirteen and he's not riding a motorcycle or getting interested in riding a motorcycle or answering questions about motorcycles."

Ethan interrupted. "In five years I'll be old enough to do..."

Piper rounded on her son, shaking a finger in his face. "Yes, I know. You'll be able to do whatever you want. But let's face it, you'll be lucky to *survive* five years at this rate. Take your sister home, Ethan."

Ethan opened his mouth, took one look at his mother's

face, then snapped it shut again. *Smart man.* He took his sister's hand and stalked to the house, muttering something Logan couldn't hear. Whatever it was made Piper clench her hands into tight fists before she turned and walked to the porch. She headed for the door before stopping in front of it, still staring straight ahead. Logan waited, figuring he was about to get a lecture.

"I'm sorry for my son's behavior." Her voice was low and tired. She frowned and glanced back toward her house. "Ethan is going through…something. Everything. I don't know."

"Lily told me about her father." Her back stiffened, but Logan wanted her to know that she didn't have to tiptoe around the issue with him. "I'm sorry. That's a lot for anyone, much less a boy going through puberty."

Piper chewed her lip, then shook her head with a sad smile, turning and leaning her back against the door. "I don't know how to get her to stop telling everyone that."

His stomach dropped. "It's not true?"

"Oh, it's true. It's just not something a four-year-old needs to announce to everyone she meets." Piper thunked her head against the door a few times, her eyes closed tight. "She's my little people pleaser. When the therapist told her it was good to talk about losing her father, Lily took it to mean she *should* talk about it. All the time. To everyone."

Logan tried to picture Lily sitting on some shrink's couch. "She has a therapist?"

"We have a family therapist. Lily and Ethan both see her. And me, of course." She straightened, her eyes snapping open and her cheeks going pink. "And that was *way* too much information. I'm sorry—I guess I know where Lily gets her oversharing from." She laughed nervously at his silence and waved her hand to dismiss the topic. "Okay, if you'll get these boxes off the porch and upstairs, I'll decorate the tables in the morning."

"You know, I *can* do more for you than carry boxes, Piper."

PIPER'S FACE FELT like it was on fire. First the guy flexes some eye-popping inked-up biceps at her, then he witnesses her family drama. She shouldn't be daydreaming about this guy and his backside or his arms or… anything. Maybe it was a good thing she'd blurted out all that information. *Yes, my entire family is in therapy.* None of this would have happened if her husband—the love of her life—was still alive. But he wasn't, so here she was, dealing with it. Poorly.

Instead of staring at her in disdain, Logan was looking all sympathetic, offering to do more. She could think of a few things she'd like him to do… *Nope.* Bad idea. He tipped his head to the side and raised a brow, waiting patiently for her answer. Oh. Oh *hell*. He was offering to do more for the *inn*. Of course.

"Um…yeah. I'm sure you can." She pulled herself together, going over the to-do list that was on a constant loop in her head. "But right now, the boxes need to be gone. We have guests arriving tonight, and I don't want them driving up to all this clutter." She gave him a pointed look. "Even if we *do* already have their money." He rolled his eyes—the grown-up version of her son's favorite expression.

She ignored it and pulled out her phone to check the reminder app always open on her screen. "We need to make sure they get checked in and find out what time they want breakfast, and I need to get the egg-and-sausage casseroles prepared for the morning. I already set the dining room for breakfast. I'll come back after the kids are settled tonight to pick up the final breakfast schedule and make sure there aren't any issues."

A soft breeze rustled the flame-red leaves on the giant maple in front of the inn, and a few of them gave up the fight and fluttered to the lawn below. She added *rake the leaves* to her list of issues to deal with. Issues like overflowing toilets or someone who couldn't figure out the thermostats. This place was almost as unpredictable as her unexpectedly needy old house across the lot. And somewhere along the way, she'd have to put up the still-missing cornstalks, find time to clean the rooms tomorrow, plan Sunday's breakfast, set the dining room again, serve cookies on the porch according to Iris's tradition, and get her children to HarvestFest so her mother-in-law wouldn't be breathing down her neck with disapproval. A familiar weariness weighed on her shoulders.

"You don't have to do all that alone, although I probably can't help with the mother-in-law issue." Logan was looking at her in amusement, and perhaps a bit of concern. She clapped her hand over her mouth in horror. Had she blurted that long list out loud? What was it about this guy that gave her verbal diarrhea? His mouth curved up into a crooked smile. "But if you'll let me help with some of the other stuff, you'll have time to get to the festival. How do you usually check people in after you've gone home?" He turned away to stack the boxes.

"I put a sign on the door and the desk with my cell

number, and ask them to call or text. Then I run over and get them settled in." It wasn't a perfect system, though it had worked well when Iris had an occasional night out and asked Piper to cover. But now Piper was basically on call all the time. Once in a while her friend Chantese covered the inn when one of the kids had something going on and Piper couldn't be in two places at once.

"Okay. You're not doing that anymore." Logan's voice was firm. "When you go home at night, you should be off the clock. I'm living right here, so I think I can handle handing out room keys."

As much as she appreciated his offer, now it was *her* turn to roll her eyes as she tossed a smaller box his way to stuff into a larger one. "There's a little more to it than handing them a key, Logan. If that was all, I'd just leave the keys in envelopes for everyone. You have to verify the reservation, including any special requests and dietary restrictions, run their credit card, sign them up for breakfast, and make sure they get the information booklet on Rendezvous Falls. Then you take them to their room and show them how everything operates, so we don't have third floor bathtubs overflowing into the rooms below because someone didn't tuck the shower curtain in properly."

That had been a particularly bad day four months ago, and it cost Iris a small fortune to repair the damage and refund the stay for the people in the flooded rooms.

Logan straightened, looking at her in disbelief. "Who stays here? Five-year-olds?"

"Shhh!" Piper looked around in a panic, then dropped her voice to a low hiss. "Rule number one—don't ever say anything about guests if there's the slightest chance you could be overheard. Which basically means, never on this property. Even if you're not talking about them specifically, no one wants to think their host is mocking them or complaining about their business."

He considered her words for a second, then nodded. "Fair enough. Sorry. But…" His voice dropped and he stepped closer. He smelled like…man. Oh, yeah. Definitely that spicy, man-sweat scent that she hadn't been close to in a long time. It took her a second to catch up with what he was almost whispering. "…how to use a shower curtain? Really?"

She was rattled by his scent. His presence, looming over her like that. His raspy whisper. His deep-set brown eyes, sparkling with warm humor. She blinked away and tried to remember how to pull some much-needed air into her lungs. What the hell was wrong with her? She sidestepped away to regain her equilibrium, fussing with a couple of chairs.

"Yes, really. Assume nothing. This house is over a hundred years old. Most of our guests don't have experience using a claw-foot tub as a shower, which can be tricky. They may not even have shower curtains at home. I mean, everyone has glass doors these days, right?" Was she babbling? Why was she talking about showers, where people were normally naked? And why was she wondering how Logan would look naked? *Deep breath.* "Repairs are expensive. Unhappy guests are even *more* expensive. When I tell you something has to be done a certain way…"

"Okay, okay." Logan raised his hand. "I get it. Keep

the customer happy... I mean, the *guest*." His smile faded. "Have there been a lot of repairs?"

"I've only been working with Iris since January, but yeah, it's an issue. Last winter the ice backed up on the roof because the gutters were clogged, and water got in through the shingles. And the boiler is always a challenge. I had to go down there last week and flip switches and turn valves and kick it a few times until it finally decided to start."

Logan turned to her, looking pained. "You *kicked* it? Did you even know what switches you were flipping? Or what the valves were...?"

"I'm not a mechanical engineer or anything, but I had to do the same thing a few times last winter. Iris showed me. She said she's been keeping the old thing going that way for years." She shrugged. "It worked."

"Well, I *am* a mechanical engineer, and I'd really like it if you didn't assault any more machinery." Logan grabbed all the boxes and waited for her to open the door for him. "I'll take a look at the boiler."

"Oh, good. A *man* to the rescue." She sounded petulant, but there'd been more than a touch of condescension in his voice.

Logan looked over his shoulder as he propped open the door to the inn, his arms full of boxes. "Really? Weren't you just using my manhood out here all afternoon? If you'd rather carry these boxes yourself..."

"I'm just saying..." What *was* she saying? Tom used to tease her when she pushed back at him for trying to take over, saying she was having a superhero moment. But Tom was gone, and it was a damn good thing she'd learned to stand on her own. She followed Logan inside and gestured for him to head up the stairs. "I'm just saying that your grandmother has been running this place without a man for a very long time. So don't come sweeping in here and think you're 'saving' us from our foolish ways. Iris has done just fine, and so have I since she got hurt."

She couldn't see his face, but his voice was resigned. "Fine. But I'm here through Christmas, and I have skills that might come in handy."

"And what happens after Christmas?"

He stopped on the landing, looking over his shoulder. His mouth was straight and...grim. "I guess we'll have to wait and see. My grandmother's getting a little too old...hell, she's been too old for years...to run this place. And I'm sure as hell not doing it. But until a decision is made, I want to help. Let's get rid of these boxes. Then you can show me how to check guests in."

She hesitated, then nodded, watching as he headed up the massive spiral staircase. Biceps bulging. Tight buns. Tapered thighs. The man was just as fine from behind as he was from the front. She shuddered. Sure, *hot* was every woman's type, but this guy, with his tattoos and long hair and scruffy beard and motorcycle and general air of...steady calm. That might be what agitated her more than anything else. He was so unruffled about everything. Even about forcing his grandmother to sell the inn, while knowing this place was what Iris lived for. Nothing seemed to be a problem in his eyes, other than hearing that they beat on the furnace.

But he sure was pretty to look at.

CHAPTER FIVE

"GRAN, HOW OLD *is* that boiler of yours, anyway?"

Logan stretched his legs out in front of him. His grandmother had moved to the rehab center yesterday, and her room was a little more spacious. The long shelf near the window was lined with floral bouquets and cards.

Gran shifted in her bed, trying to hide a sharp wince of pain. He remembered when a former coworker had a hip replacement a few years back. Vince said the pain was so deep it was like finding out you had a cosmic black hole in your body that had no end. But Vince was golfing a few months later, so there was hope. Of course, Vince was a healthy, active sixty-two at the time, and Gran was eighty. She gave him a sideways glance and straightened the fluffy blue sweater she was wearing over her hospital gown. He squinted—did she have *glitter* on her eyelashes?

"Why? Is the heat acting up again?"

"*Again?* Maybe it's time to replace it."

She laughed and shook her head. "Don't be stupid. Piper and I know how to keep it going. A good thunk on the side with a big wrench usually does the trick. I thought I told you to get a haircut?"

He put his hand up to the long ponytail and grimaced. "Sorry, Gran. Piper had me working Thursday and Friday, and yesterday Slim's was closed for HarvestFest. What kind of barber shop closes on a Saturday?"

"The kind where the owner is president of the Rotary and is in charge of running their barbecued chicken tent at the festival. Get that cut this week, before you scare guests away."

"I signed five custom...guests...in over the weekend, and no one ran out the door screaming. But yes, I'll go this week. Give me a break—I'll get there."

At six-foot-four, he tended to intimidate anyway, but standing in the fancy lobby where the mahogany check-in desk was located, right across from the ornate staircase framed by stained-glass windows, he felt a little like the monster in some dark Victorian movie.

"You're registering guests, huh? How do you like Piper's system?"

"I thought it was *your* system?"

Gran chuckled. "Oh, please. When Piper saw me using the old roller style of credit card receipt maker with the carbon paper copies, she just about flipped." Gran leaned forward a little and dropped her voice like a conspirator. "But those carbon copies worked just fine for years." She sat back again, pushing her white hair behind her ear. "When Piper showed me that we could put that little cube thing on the electric tablet and get paid just like that...well, I signed right up."

"*You* use the tablet?" Gran despised change. It was one of the things they'd argued about on his last visit. He'd pushed her to update the place to make it easier to sell. That conversation hadn't gone well. He knew he'd stepped in it again when Gran's eyes went cold.

"It's *my* inn, Logan. Of course I use it. I'm not afraid of technology. Haven't you seen the Facebook page for the Taggart Inn?" Her chin rose proudly. "We're on Insta, too. I'm old, but I'm not a dinosaur."

"Sorry, Gran. I forget you've always been a renaissance woman, ahead of your time. Too bad Dad couldn't have inherited some of that talent." He knew his father could be a sore spot for Gran. She just shook her head.

"Your father had *talent* up the wazoo. And enthusiasm. What he was missing was common sense." She plucked at the blanket with her fingers. "He wanted bigger and better and richer and faster. Always chasing some scheme that never panned out, as you well know."

Yeah, he knew. Logan and Nikki had been dragged all over the country as kids, moving every year or two as Dad followed one new sure thing after another. Every move was "the last move" according to Dad. They'd stopped believing him by the time Logan was ten. He and his sister learned early not to bother making friends or getting attached to a particular place, because everything was temporary. They always left town, their friendships and memories lost in the dust of Dad's dreams.

Gran gave Logan a hard look. "His failures weren't because he didn't have talent. Brian was addicted to that damn horizon. Always looking. Always chasing. Never seeing what was right there in front of him." She sighed. "He knew the inn was waiting here, but he told me he'd be 'going backward' if he came home. I never did get that. How is destiny going backward?"

"Like you said, Gran. Dad never could settle down, not even here." Especially not here—Dad had a strong aversion to the Finger Lakes, and Rendezvous Falls in particular. He told Logan it was because growing up in the inn made him feel like he'd grown up in a museum. A place that never changed, and Dad was born craving change just as much as Gran hated it.

"And his apple didn't fall from the tree, did it?" She gave him a pointed look, and Logan squirmed in the chair.

"Hey, I'm not him. I have *one* job…pretty much, anyway. It just happens to be in multiple locations." He shrugged, hiding his own grimace of pain at the motion. "It's all I know, Gran. I grew up on the freaking road. But at least I have a steady paycheck, which is something Dad rarely experienced. And I've gotten to see the world with this job."

"Sure," she scoffed. "You've seen the world's *oceans*. But is the North Sea all that different from the Gulf of Mexico?"

Lately? Not so much. "It's colder, that's for damn sure. But I've seen more than water. And it's been amazing."

"It's *been* amazing? As in past tense?"

"Don't twist my words. I've always loved my job."

"Interesting. Another past-tense expression. You *have always*, not you *do*." Gran sat up, her eyes bright with interest. "What's going on, Logan?"

Damn his grandmother's spooky ability to read people like a freaking psychic. The truth was he *had* been growing more dissatisfied with his life, and it bothered him. He didn't know where the feeling was coming from or what it meant. But it was there, simmering under the surface.

"Nothing's going on. I can't wait to get to South America." Which would look just like every other place he'd been. He shook off the thought. Time to divert. "Hey, speaking of cold..." He leaned forward. "Do you still have that old Buick?"

"Watch how you use that word *old*, bucko." But she nodded. "Of course I still have it. What else would I drive?"

It was tough enough trying to discuss selling the inn. He dreaded the day someone had to take Gran's keys away. For now, she seemed in full control of her faculties.

"Do you mind if I use it while I'm here? It won't be long before it's too cold—and snowy—for the bike."

Gran nodded. "The keys are in the bowl on the console table." She wagged her finger at him. "Just be careful. There's hardly a scratch on her, and I expect her to be that way when I get home." Her face fell. "Whenever that might be."

There was a faint gray tinge to her skin. Her new round of physical therapy was wearing her out, and he'd stayed too long.

"I'll let you rest up, Gran. There's probably a mountain of laundry waiting for me at the inn." He and Piper had done several loads yesterday, even though some guests had opted to be environmentally conscious and not have the sheets and towels changed nightly. Piper explained she'd started offering the option to save both labor and money. And the environment, of course. But today was Sunday and everyone was checking out. He stood and gave his grandmother a peck on the cheek. "I'll stop by in a few days, but call if you need anything." He started to turn away, then stopped. "Hey, you never did answer my question before. How old is the boiler at the inn?"

"Hell if I know. It was there when I bought the place. Gets a little temperamental now and then, but it's been keeping that big place warm for a long time."

Yikes. Gran had owned the inn for forty years or more. If he and Nikki ever *did* convince her to sell, that was one thing that would have to be updated. "Mind if I take a look at it?"

She crossed her arms. "*Look*. Don't *break*. I don't believe in throwing things away just because they're old. And don't you go making decisions there without me. Piper's the boss until I get back."

"Are you sure?" he teased. "I'm thinking Lily might be the boss."

That raised a fond laugh from Gran. "Oh, that girl. I can't decide if she's going to save the whole damn world, or just take it over." Her brows gathered. "You and Piper getting along? I know sugar-and-spice moms aren't your thing."

No, they weren't, but having it thrown in his face again bothered him. Besides, Piper was more than a cliché. Watching her over the busy weekend made him think there was more spice there than sugar. She was smart and hardworking. She had a sharp sense of humor and a killer smile when she let her guard down. And those things—smarts, sass, laughter, ambition—were definitely his thing. But she was also a mom. Even if she was interested, and he had a hunch she was, she'd want more from a man than he could ever offer.

He thought about the sullen teenage boy. "Her son isn't quite as bubbly as his sister."

"Ethan?" Gran waved her hand. "He's all snarl and no bite. He loves to push Piper's buttons. I tried to tell her *all* boys hate their parents at some stage. Ethan wanted them to stay with his grandparents, where they'd been living. It was familiar. And he was being spoiled rotten there."

Logan shoved his hands in his pockets and frowned. "They were living with Piper's parents?"

"Oh, no. Her mom's gone, and her dad's remarried in Texas somewhere. Piper came to live with Tom's parents in Rendezvous Falls while he was deployed. Then he was…you know the story?"

He nodded, frowning at the thought of what she'd had to deal with. "I know he died, I assume in action. Lily said she was a baby, so three or four years ago?"

Gran stared out the window. "Tom only saw that sweet girl once, right after she was born."

"Why did Piper stay with his parents so long after he died?"

"Susan and Roger were a big help at first, stepping in when Piper was grieving, running the kids around and taking care of everything. But they haven't handled her decision to buy her own place well, even though they're lucky she decided to stay here in town. I think Susan figured *she'd* raise the kids, but Piper had other ideas. She's tougher than she looks." Logan didn't doubt that.

Gran settled back, her face falling. "I really hope she stays on. I *want* her to. If neither of my grandchildren are going to take over the family business, I *need* Piper around to keep it going."

"Or you could just se…" He tried to stop the words, but he was too late.

"I'm *not* selling the Taggart. And if you don't want it, then don't mess with it. Or Piper. Got it?"

He weighed her words for a moment, then nodded solemnly. He'd have to be more careful about bringing up the selling issue. At least for now. "Okay, Gran. Don't worry."

As he rode back to Rendezvous Falls, he rolled the conversation around in his head. *Sugar-and-spice single moms aren't your type. She's tougher than she looks. I need Piper to stay…*

Not one bit of it made the bossy blonde with the big blue eyes any less interesting to him.

"CHANTESE, THIS HAS BEEN great, but I have to get back to the inn. I know it's only Monday, but Ghostwalk is coming up this weekend and we are not ready. Thanks for inviting me, though." The to-do list was pushing its way to the front of Piper's mind, no matter how much she'd tried to relax on this lunch break with her best friend. Chantese had a son the same age as Lily, and the moms met when Malcolm and Lily started going to daycare at St. Vincent's Church.

Chantese raised her glass of iced tea in a mock toast, leaving a ring of moisture on the booth table. "It's always nice to have grown-up conversations without the rug rats…I mean…our adorable angels…pulling on our sleeves."

Piper snorted, then signaled to Evie Rosario behind

the counter that she wanted her check. Evie and her mom owned the Spot Diner.

Chantese leaned forward and winked, her lashes long against her dark skin. "So things are okay with Iris's grandson? I hear he's a hottie."

Piper groaned. "Please. As if I'd notice if he was a hottie or not." He was. "And things are fine. It's his family's business. I'm just an employee."

Piper was still getting used to having Logan around. Every time she turned, he was offering to help or giving her that crooked grin of his as he watched her work. He did that a lot—watching her. To be fair, that was her fault, since she almost always turned down his so-called assistance. He didn't take things as seriously as he needed to, and he tended to bump into the most expensive items in every room. He'd already broken a vase and nearly toppled Iris's favorite tea set. The guy meant well, but just watching him make his way around the rooms filled with precious antiques made her nervous. Or hot and bothered.

The first made sense. The second did not. It was so unexpected to feel this first flutter of attraction to any man since Tom's death. Why now? And why *Logan*? Tom had been her efficient, perfectly outfitted marine. Everything in place, even when he was off duty and playing with Ethan. She used to tease him about pressing creases into his jeans. He was a neatnik and proud of it. But Logan? Not so much. He *still* hadn't cut his hair or shaved that beard. He was more rumpled than pressed. He was basically the opposite of the man she'd loved. And yet it was *him* who made her skin twitch and heat up anytime he was near.

"Whoa, what's got you all red in the face?" Evie slapped the bill on the table, but Chantese reached over and grabbed it, laughing up at Evie.

"I asked her about Logan Taggart, and this…" Chantese gestured toward Piper's heated face "…happened. Don't you find that interesting?"

Evie, with her signature bright streak in her dark hair—it was hot pink this week—brought her hand under her chin and tapped it thoughtfully. "Yes, very interesting."

With that, Piper stood. "Why am I friends with you two again?"

"Because we love you and keep you sane?" Evie gave her a proud grin.

That was true. She'd leaned hard on them these past few years, including when she'd made the decision to buy her own place. And when that place ate up her savings. She arched her brow at Evie.

"Fine. But this ain't that. Don't go imagining cupids anywhere near me, okay? I have no time and no interest."

She left, bundling up against the wind and cold that had rolled in that week. She stopped at the hardware store for some plumber's tape. The kitchen sink at her house was leaking, and she was going to tackle the repair herself. She'd read a few online articles and figured she could handle it. After spending so much money on repairing the surprise foundation problems last winter, there wasn't much left in her emergency fund for plumbers.

But first she needed to get back to the inn. Susan was picking up Lily from day care today, and would keep her until dinnertime. Ghostwalk was an even bigger event than HarvestFest, and they'd have a full and lively inn come Friday. She had to plan the menus and check the pantry. She was also going to give the downstairs a good cleaning. She glanced at her watch. She'd have time to get through the library and parlor.

After gathering her supplies, she walked into the library and came to an abrupt halt. There was a man reading in the large wingback chair by the fireplace, which had a *fire* going in it. The sign on the mantel clearly stated guests needed permission before using any fireplace. She couldn't see his face, but his hair was short, dark and carefully groomed. He looked tall, and was wearing an ivory fisherman sweater. A log crackled and broke in the hearth, sending a spray of sparks up the chimney.

As of this morning, the only guests registered for tonight were four women in town for a voter registration symposium at the local college. Maybe this guy was waiting for them? But to have started a fire on his own... She cleared her throat loudly.

"May I help you, sir?" Her voice was firmly disapproving.

The man stood, and from the back his frame seemed oddly familiar. Tall. Broad-shouldered. Solid. He set his book down on the side table, then turned to face her. It was...Logan. But not Logan? His long hair was gone, cut into a style that made it look like he'd either just rolled out of bed and run his fingers through it, or paid a fortune to have it look like that. His once-scraggly beard was trimmed close to his face, accenting the strong line of his jaw even more than before. The look, combined with the cable sweater and dark, narrow jeans, made him look like one of those spice cologne commercials with the rugged fishermen. It was a really good look.

His presence filled the room. She set her basket of supplies on the side table and took him in. He was a rough-and-tumble oil rig worker, but right now, he looked like he belonged here in this paneled room full of leather-bound chairs and books. Damn it, she had no business feeling this way. She was a grown woman with two kids and a mortgage. Christmas was coming. She didn't have time to deal with ridiculous fantasies. But when she stared into his eyes...

His mouth slanted into a crooked grin. "I think I'm supposed to ask *you* that question."

Her mouth went dry. "Wh-what?"

"You asked if you could help. That's what I should be asking you, right?" He glanced at the fireplace. "Sorry about the fire. I visited my grandmother this morning and the ride back was pretty chilly on the bike." He chuckled at her expression. "Is it my new look that's left you speechless? Gran was on my case about the hair, so I finally caught up with the barber today." He ran his fingers through the dark, thick hair that barely brushed his ears. "Do you approve?"

Oh, yeah. She approved. Except...*no*. Sure, he'd been living in her head day and night, but she couldn't let herself get *serious* about a guy who'd looked like Aquaman. But *this* guy? This polished hunk reading a book by the fire, who could have stepped out of some men's fashion magazine? Something deep inside fluttered again, for *real* this time, and she took a physical step back.

"You look…different." She barely managed to avoid using the word *delicious*. "I'm sure Iris will approve." She glanced around the room, desperate for a distraction. Her eyes settled on the fire. "You opened the flue?"

"The room would be full of smoke if I hadn't." His smile faded. "You did tell me the downstairs fireplaces were in working order, right?"

"Yes, we had them all cleaned and inspected during the summer." Talking about the inn put her on more solid footing. "I wouldn't want a guest starting a fire in here, but I'm sure you know what you're doing."

He nodded. "I understand the general concept of lighting a fire."

Yes. Yes, he did indeed. After four years, she'd figured her libido was as dead and gone as Tom was. But… surprise! Her whole body was positively humming right now. And it was more than just Logan being eye candy. It was that calmness he always exuded that kept pulling at her. Maybe that was the answer to why him and why now. Her life was an out-of-control whirlwind and he possessed the steadiness she craved. Having a logical explanation would help her fight back the attraction. *Right?*

Her chin rose, and she reached for the basket of rags and furniture polish.

"I'm sorry if I interrupted your reading." She'd never imagined Logan Taggart as the curl-up-by-a-fire-with-a-book type. She could certainly do without the image now. "I'm just dusting. I'll start in the parlor."

"I'll help." He walked toward her and took the feather duster from the basket. "I can reach the high shelves, and I'm pretty sure you can't."

"Are you mocking my height?"

"I would never." The twinkle in his eyes said otherwise. "But why not work to our strengths as a team?"

She was glad to get her focus back on work. This weird energy between them was clearly one-sided, and she could ignore it now that she understood it. He was a guy stuck in Rendezvous Falls for a few months, and they were going to have to work together. As friends. She could do that. The way Logan swished the duster in and out around some of Iris's delicate antiques made Piper cringe, though. He toppled one tall pitcher, but caught it in midair before any damage was done. He looked back at her and conceded the wisdom of her more careful approach with a nod.

"I just finished gluing the handle back on the last vase I broke. I don't need to give myself any more repair projects. Slowing down now."

Piper started dusting the table next to the chair he'd been sitting in, mainly because she was curious to see what he'd been reading. Probably some motorcycle magazine or war story. But she wasn't even close. She picked up the leather-bound book and turned to Logan.

"*For Whom the Bell Tolls*? Seriously? Isn't Hemingway a little...I don't know...heavy?"

His voice was low and casual. Even the feather duster didn't do anything to reduce the raw maleness of him.

"It's the first thing I happened to pick up." That explained it. He'd grabbed it by accident. Then he continued. "I prefer *A Farewell to Arms*, but this one's worth a reread."

"You read Hemingway?" Now that she thought about

it, he looked Hemingway-esque today with the short hair and wool sweater. But still.

He lowered the duster and turned to face her with a wry grin. "Why, Piper Montgomery, are you shocked that a leatherneck like me appreciates Hemingway? After all, he writes about the common man."

"I didn't really picture you as the reading type, I guess. And if I did, I'd imagine a modern-day thriller. Why were you reading in here and not in Iris's place?"

He picked up a delicate piece of Wedgwood china and brushed the duster over it before setting it back on the shelf. "Don't tell Gran, but her apartment is a little…frilly…for me. I feel like a bull in a china shop. I'm always afraid her furniture is going to collapse when I sit on it." He glanced around at the library's hunting prints, dark paneling, and the deep red Oriental rug covering the hardwood floor. "This room is the closest thing to a man cave I could find."

"That makes sense." She thought about Iris's cluttered and very Victorian apartment. "I can't imagine you kicking back at Iris's any more than I can imagine you reading Hem…" She closed her eyes tightly. "I sound like such a snob, don't I? It's just…the motorcycle. The oil drilling and all the adventures at sea." She paused, then started laughing at herself. "I guess that sounds a lot like Hemingway, now that I think about it."

Logan rubbed his left shoulder absently, looking at the book in her hands. "There aren't a lot of entertainment options on a rig during the downtimes. Sometimes I'll join a poker game, but usually I relax in my bunk with a good book."

Piper tried to envision him lying in bed with a book

in his hand. But somehow her brain stopped at *in bed*. When her phone went off in her pocket, she jumped as if she'd been bitten. She'd fallen into the warmth of Logan's eyes again and lost all concept of where she was. He started laughing when he heard Ethan's ringtone—the theme from *Jaws*.

"It's my son. Trust me, it's fitting." She answered the call.

"Mom?" Ethan's voice was high and cracking. It was one of those rare times when he sounded like her little boy. Like he needed her instead of hating her. Her pulse jumped.

"Ethan? What's wrong? Where are you?"

"I'm at school. In Mr. Dillard's office. He wants you to come." He hesitated. "I got in a fight."

"A *fight*? With *who*?"

"Mom, just please come get me, okay? I got suspended."

"Suspended?" She was already headed for the door when she ended the call and turned to Logan. "I have to go… Ethan…" She looked at her cleaning basket sitting on the chair, but Logan picked it up and nodded his head toward the door.

"Go. I'll finish this. And Piper?" She'd started to turn away, but stopped. He smiled and held up the book. "He'll be okay. I was suspended more than once, and now I read Hemingway."

CHAPTER SIX

LOGAN FINISHED DUSTING and polishing in the library and took care of the parlor, too. He had to be even more careful in there, working around all the antiques Gran had collected through the years. He was used to precision work when it came to wiring or building complex machinery. But with a feather duster? Definitely out of his element. He stoked the fire again in the library and was just sitting down with his book when he heard the front door open. He didn't think they were expecting any check-ins that night. He headed toward the foyer.

"Mr. Logan!" Lily Montgomery let out a squeal and ran from the older woman standing with her, straight to Logan's legs, which she embraced. He winked down at her, and she tightened her grip and stood on his right foot as he took an exaggerated step, swinging her along for the ride. Yesterday he'd walked the length of the upstairs hall with her clinging to his leg like that. It was their thing. He had a *thing* with a four-year-old. Who'd have thought *that* would ever happen?

"Whatcha doin' here, kid?" he asked, returning her happy smile. He didn't know if all little girls were like Lily, but he suspected not. She had to be uniquely charming. Otherwise, people would be having twenty kids just to have little Lilys in their lives. She made people happy. She made *him* happy.

"Lily, get off that man's leg right now! What are you thinking?" The older woman, clad head-to-toe in chocolate brown, had dark gold hair and a sharp expression. Lily didn't react, still holding on tight as she answered.

"But Gigi, this is Logan the Giant! I told you about him. He's the one who let me fly when we put the leaves on the porch!" She looked up, resting her chin on his thigh. "Wow, you cut your hair! Where's Momma?"

He was reminded of his first morning here, when Piper brandished a mop at him to protect her little girl. *Gigi* was wearing the same "get away from that little girl" expression. He carefully removed Lily from his leg, speaking to the woman.

"You must be Lily's grandmother..." The woman recoiled a bit, but nodded. "I'm Logan Taggart. *My* grandmother owns the..."

"I know who Iris Taggart is." Okay then. Her expression was cool as she appraised him from head to toe. "I'm Susan Montgomery. Piper was supposed to be at the house waiting for Lily, but maybe she decided there was something more important than her daughter..."

His eyes narrowed. That was some heavy passive-aggressive shade she was throwing at her daughter-in-law. In front of Piper's daughter. Logan had grown up watching his father schmooze folks into investing in his schemes, so he'd learned a thing or two about dealing with people like this. He gave Mrs. Montgomery his best smile and most ingratiating tone.

"Nothing is more important to Piper than her children. She had a call to pick Ethan up from school." She'd been gone well over an hour now. He kept his smile firmly in place, wondering how serious Ethan's fight had been. "She'll be back any minute. Lily can stay with me if you're too busy to wait."

"Don't be ridiculous. I'm not leaving my granddaughter with a perfect stranger." She gestured toward Lily. "Come on, sweetheart. We'll wait over in your house for Momma and Ethan."

Lily skipped toward her grandmother, waving back at him. "Ethan's in big trouble again. Bye, Logan!"

"See ya, kid."

Mrs. Montgomery gave him one last long look before heading back outside. He watched through the window as they walked across the parking lot to the pink house. Piper's little blue car pulled into the driveway, and Lily ran to her mother. Ethan slammed out of the car and into the house without taking his eyes off the ground in front of him. Piper scooped Lily up, resting her on her hip as she talked to her mother-in-law. Judging from Piper's stiff posture and jerky shake of her head at something that was said, she wasn't happy. He'd known her less than two weeks, but he could tell her mood from a distance.

He'd been getting some weird signals from her. There were times when it felt like she was…interested. She didn't *flirt* exactly, but he was pretty sure he'd seen the occasional flash of heat in her eyes before she'd quickly tamp it down. He liked her. She was funny and smart and strong. He looked forward to their daily breakfast meetings after guests had been fed. She'd chatter on about her lists and plans. He liked the sound of her laugh. Ah, what the hell—he liked everything about her. Who wouldn't be attracted to a beautiful woman, right? But Gran made a good point. Piper wasn't his type. She wasn't one-night-stand material, and he was definitely a one-night-stand kind of guy. Anything other than that got a woman thinking he was going to stay, and they started expecting…more. He didn't do more. He did see-you-'round.

He went back to the library to gather up the supplies and put them away in the cupboard tucked under the staircase. The door squeaked, and he made a note to fix it. He looked around the lobby, with its slightly faded wallpaper and 1990s brass fixtures. The place needed a face-lift. It needed repairs. He closed the cupboard door. It needed to be sold.

He ran his hand along the wide banister and remembered sliding down it as a boy when Gran wasn't looking. The big old place might not be his style any more than Piper was, but it struck him that the Taggart Inn was the one constant in his life among dozens of different homes. This was the place that was always just… there. Waiting for him. But the Taggart was a commitment, and Logan wasn't ready for that. He probably never would be.

A gust of wind rattled the stained-glass windows behind the staircase. There was freezing rain in the forecast, so it was time for him to make sure Gran's old car was ready to go. His phone buzzed with a text. As he fished it out of his pocket, he saw Ethan come out of the pink house with a basketball in his hand. He hoped the kid wasn't in *too* much trouble. He sighed when he looked at the phone screen. There was a picture of a white beach, waves lapping at the sand beyond a stand of palm trees.

Sick of snow yet?

Ted Prescott was the guy who'd taught Logan how to do just about every job there was on an oil rig. Ted was ten years older, but they'd become as close as brothers through the years. Annoying, ball-busting brothers. Logan typed his response.

No snow. Just cold AF.

Ted responded.

How's Granny?

Logan snorted. God help the man who ever called her "Granny" to her face.

In rehab. Looks like I'm stuck here till Christmas.

Logan had grabbed his jacket and was headed outside before his phone pinged again.

How's the shoulder?

He frowned. Ted had been there when Logan made the foolhardy move on the rig, and he'd been there when Logan got the news from the doctor. Surgery might help.

Might not. Working the platform was no job for a guy with a bum arm. But it was the only life he'd known since he was twenty. He tapped out his reply.

Better every day.

Ted's answer came back quickly.

Liar

Time to change the subject.

You on the rig?

He watched as the dots floated on the screen, indicating Ted was typing more than a one-word answer. Oil rigs were the only life Ted had known, too.

Home. Lori's been on my ass to stay off the rig during hurricane season. Maybe longer. Says I'm getting too old for this shit.

Was Ted serious? Lori was a great woman and a good friend, with a ready laugh and a take-no-prisoners attitude toward protecting the ones she loved. She fretted over Logan almost as much as she did over Ted. She was always sending him care packages loaded with her home-baked goodies. It couldn't be easy having a husband who might be gone for weeks at a time, doing a dangerous job. But Lori had never complained. At least, not that Logan knew about. Before he could figure out how to respond, another bubble popped up.

She might be right. Gotta go—kid's got a game.

Logan checked the fireplace to make sure the fire was burning down safely before heading out to the garage. Ted didn't mention which of his two kids had a game. Probably Teddie, the oldest. *She might be right.* Damn. He slid the phone in his pocket and shook his head. *Nah.* Ted was a lifer.

The carriage house behind the inn had long ago been converted to a three-car garage. His Harley Low Rider was in the middle bay, safe from the weather. The mower and other lawn supplies filled the left bay. And a very large Buick filled the right. Gran had purchased the dark green two-door Riviera twenty-some years ago. It was the last year they made them, and Gran immediately declared it her favorite—and final—vehicle. The car was so long it barely fit in the garage. Then again, Gran didn't do much driving these days. She drove into the downtown section of Rendezvous Falls once in a while to shop or meet someone for lunch, and made the occasional trip to a doctor or dentist.

He turned the key and the Riviera started right up. He backed it out of the garage, wondering how he'd ever get used to driving this barge. Hopefully this cold spell would pass quickly, and he'd have more time to use the bike before he had to deal with driving this thing. Figuring he'd better check the oil, he shut it off and popped the hood. He was leaning over the engine when he sensed a presence behind him. Ethan stood a few feet away.

"Hey, kid."

"Hey." The single word was loaded equally with caution and curiosity.

He stayed under the hood, but gestured for Ethan to come closer. "Know anything about cars?" He found the oil at last, and pulled out the dipstick, wiping it clean with a rag.

"I like cars, but don't know how to fix 'em or anything."

"What kinda cars do you like?"

Ethan stared at the ground. "I dunno. Street racers, I guess."

Logan grinned. "Like in the movies?"

The teen made a grunting sound that Logan interpreted as a yes. Having conversation with Ethan was like pulling teeth. Had *he* been like this at that age? Yeah, he remembered Gran threatening to box his ears if he didn't start speaking up and making eye contact.

Logan put the stick back in, pulling it out again to check the oil level. Down a little, but not bad. He showed it to Ethan, pointing to where it should be and where it was.

"First step in fixing things is to learn how to keep them from breaking. Like with cars—keep all the fluids up to snuff and you'll get a lot more miles out of them."

Ethan watched every move Logan made. Transmission fluid was good. Wiper fluid good. Air filter was a little sketchy. He showed it to Ethan.

"I'll pick up a new filter and a quart of oil. If you want, you can put them in for me."

For just a moment, there was a glimmer of interest in Ethan's eyes. Then an edge hit his voice. Sullen? Defensive? Discouraged?

"I don't know how."

"I'll teach you. Want to join me on a test drive to see if I can handle this old boat?"

The corner of Ethan's mouth twitched. He was more interested than he wanted to let on. Just then, Piper's voice called the boy's name from next door. She must have been at the front door, because they couldn't see her. Ethan's shoulders dropped again.

"Go on," Logan said. "It'll be a couple days before I have the stuff I need. But I'll let you know, and you can help."

A carefully blank look went over Ethan's face. The I-don't-care-about-anything expression that protected teen boys from getting into a conversation that might leave them feeling awkward.

"Whatever." He started to turn away when Logan stopped him.

"Look, I know you had a shitty day." Ethan's eyes went wide in surprise. The kid was thirteen. He surely knew how to swear. "Don't act like you've never heard or said the word. Your mom's probably going to be on your butt for a while about fighting, but…by the time I was your age, my mom had been dead a long time. You're lucky to have her, okay?"

Half a dozen expressions flitted across Ethan's face before he settled on the familiar blank look. "My dad's dead."

Why had Logan brought the conversation to this point? Why was he even *having* a conversation with this kid? He cleared his throat and nodded. "I know. Mine is, too. I get it, man. I'm just saying…" What *was* he saying? "I'm just saying…you had something lousy happen to your family. But your *life* doesn't have to be lousy because of it. You get to decide. Got it?"

Ethan looked him straight in the eyes for a long minute. Logan had a feeling he was being sized up. The boy's expression softened fractionally, but his voice remained flat. "Yeah. Got it. Later."

And he was gone, saving Logan from rambling on any more than he already had. The kid had a professional counselor to talk to. He didn't need Logan preaching at him. But there was something about that chip on Ethan's shoulder that reminded Logan a lot of himself at that age.

He managed to park the Buick in the garage and get the door closed—no easy feat. His thoughts went back to his earlier text conversation. Was Ted seriously thinking of quitting the life? Ten years ago, he'd told Logan he'd probably die of old age on some godforsaken ocean, and they'd laughed in agreement.

Logan rubbed his aching shoulder. *You get to decide.* Maybe Ted had a point.

PIPER CRINGED WHEN the frying pan she'd tossed toward the sink hit the edge with a loud clang and then clattered to the bottom. She'd put a little more energy into that toss than she'd intended.

Ethan got into a *fight* at school. Well, more like a shoving match, but still. Her son was a grumpy bundle of hormones these days, but he'd never been one to lose control like that. And he'd certainly never gotten phys-

ical with anyone. He'd had to serve an in-school sus-
pension for one day, along with the other boy. It could
have been worse.

And then, of course, there was Susan. Piper scrubbed
the stove burner where the oatmeal had boiled over
that morning. Susan had been giving Piper the side-eye
and dropping thinly veiled insults ever since Piper and
Ethan came home to find her waiting there with Lily
the day of the fight. Susan was "worried" that Piper
was "working too much" and "leaving" the children on
their own. Just what Piper needed—more guilt. She'd
pointed out to Susan that Ethan pushed a kid. In school.
He wasn't hanging out in some dark alley at midnight
getting in knife fights.

She looked at Lily, sitting by the kitchen window
and flipping through *A Photographic History of the
Finger Lakes.* The girl had long ago stopped surprising
Piper with her curiosity and ability to absorb information like a sponge. So much like Tom, wanting to see
the world and learn everything he could. When Susan
heard about Lily's plans to be Deadpool for Halloween
next week, she'd been speechless. It was actually kind
of fun to watch, but it hadn't taken long for her to start
up with her unending sermon about how a mom should
be home with her children so she knew what they were
being exposed to.

Piper angrily told Susan that Lily wasn't being *exposed* to anything other than a loving home and a hardworking mother she could look up to. Because Piper
had this *under control* (she hoped). She hated fighting
with her former mother-in-law. The two women had
once been so close, Tom teased that if he and Piper

ever divorced, his parents would dump him and keep Piper. Susan used to be bright, happy and loving. She'd embraced Piper as the daughter she'd never had, and they'd gone on shopping trips together, finishing the day laughing over chardonnay like best friends.

But Tom's death changed all of that. Susan refused to even consider counseling for herself. She'd insisted Ethan and Lily would get her through the loss of her only child. But that was too much weight for the kids to carry. It wasn't fair to them, and was one of the issues that propelled Piper into moving out. The decision had come as a shock to the Montgomerys, and Susan still hadn't forgiven Piper for doing it. Piper didn't want to make an enemy of Susan. But she wasn't about to abdicate her role as her children's only parent. That thought just angered her more. She wasn't supposed to be doing this alone. Tom was supposed to be here. And damn it, she missed him just as much as Susan did.

She finished scrubbing the stove top and threw the metal scrub pad into the sink. Except she put so much force behind it that it bounced off the wall behind the sink and onto the floor.

"Shit!" She stomped over to pick it up. Lily looked up from her book, wide-eyed, her voice hushed and far older than her years in its censure.

"Momma! Ladies don't say that!"

"Who the hell…heck…told you that?"

"Gigi did. She says you swear too much."

Piper took a deep breath, walking over to kneel next to Lily's chair. This was one of those razor's edge parenting moments—how to make sure Lily didn't start walking around cussing like a sailor, and still make sure she understood that "ladies" could say whatever the hell they wanted.

"That *is* a bad word, honey. It's a grown-up bad word, meaning little girls should *never*..." she fixed her daughter with a serious look to make her point "...*never* say it. But grown-ups, in private, will say it sometimes when they're upset. And by 'grown-ups,' I mean men *and* women. If a man can say it, so can a woman. But it was wrong for me to say it in front of you. And it was wrong for me to say it here at the inn, where guests could have heard me. It would be unpro-fessional."

Lily's eyes lit up at the new word. "Un-profff-en-al?"

"Almost. Un-pro-*fess*-ion-al. That means doing something that's bad for business. It upsets people. And I care very much about the inn and our guests." She was caring for it more and more, now that she was spending so much time here. She looked out at the porch, deco-rated for Ghostwalk, and smiled to herself. She was proud of being able to keep the place going. Lily was staring at her expectantly. What was she saying again? "And because I care, I have to act professional. And that means no bad words." She frowned. "How did you and Gigi end up talking about curse words?"

"Ethan said that word in front of Gigi, and she told him not to say it in front of ladies and little girls." Piper sighed. Susan should have told Ethan not to say it at all. Lily turned back to her book. "I miss Gigi. Are you two fighting again?"

Piper felt a stab of guilt. She and Susan *had* been ar-guing a lot this year. "No, sweetie. She's just not baby-sitting you as much because I'm not at the insurance company anymore."

Lily flipped a few more pages of the book, studying the pictures intently. "I like my days with Gigi. She plays dolls with me and Poppa takes me to the lake to fish." Lily looked up. "They tell me stories about Daddy."

And now the guilt felt more like being skewered through and through. Susan and Roger were Tom's parents. They were good people who had lost their only child. And they truly loved Lily and Ethan. It wasn't fair to keep the kids away just because she disagreed with Susan on a few things. She pulled Lily into her arms.

"I'll see if you can visit them this weekend, okay? And tonight, I'll tell you a story about your daddy."

Lily grinned. "The one where he dropped your ring and the mermaid gave it back?"

"Yes. I'll tell the one about the ring and the mermaid." Tom's proposal had been picture-perfect—on a beach on the Outer Banks at sunset. He knelt on one knee at the edge of the water, then got so nervous when she said yes that he dropped the ring into the foam. For one horrifying moment, they thought it was lost for good. But the very next wave not only brought it back, but left it sitting right on Piper's foot. Tom jokingly said a mermaid saved their marriage. Lily's hand rested on Piper's cheek.

"You're smiling about Daddy, aren't you?"

Piper blinked away the sudden moisture gathering on her lashes. "Yes, sweetie. I'm smiling about your daddy."

Tom would never want this power struggle between

Piper and his mother. He'd also never want Piper to doubt her own parenting skills. He'd called her "Super Mom" when Ethan was little and she'd been left on her own during Tom's second deployment. She stood, rubbing her hand in Lily's hair with affection. "I'm going to call Gigi right now and see if she wants to have you spend the night. How's that?"

Susan didn't hesitate to come right over later when Piper called. But before Piper let her take Lily for the night, she needed to make a few things clear. They sat at Piper's kitchen table.

She loved her cozy kitchen, even if it was in a bit of disarray. Half the wallpaper had been scraped off. There were multiple layers of the stuff, the process was messy and exhausting, and there always seemed to be something else more important to do. The cupboards were original to the house, but they were a little tired. Some of the doors drooped on one side or the other. She'd removed most of the door and drawer pulls, and had new ones sitting on the counter to be put on. Someday.

The cupboard doors below the sink were missing entirely. Piper had removed them for easier access to the plumbing. Susan took in the white bucket under the sink and pressed her lips together in a firm, angry line.

"Christmas? You want to have Christmas in *this* house?" Piper didn't respond. She'd learned a few tricks from Susan over the past few years, including the one about not blinking first. Susan straightened, twisting her hands together and apart and back together again on the table. "Piper, dear, I hardly think you'll have this place ready in time for a big Christmas dinner."

She leaned forward. "Unless you're finally going to let Roger and me pay for some renovations here?"

"No!" If she let Susan and Roger sweep in to the rescue, this would never feel like *her* house. Piper took a breath. "I mean, thank you for the offer. But I've got this. The house will definitely be ready for Christmas. More than ready. It will be perfect. I promised the kids we'd put a big tree in the living room by the front windows…"

"Which still have no curtains…" Susan started. Piper ignored her.

"I'll have the new dining room light installed by then, so we can christen the room with a perfect holiday meal." The old light flickered and crackled so much that she'd had an electrician remove it, afraid it would burst into flames. He said the problem was in the cheap light, not the wiring. That had been a relief, considering the way the foundation ate up her reno budget.

The home inspector she'd paid for before closing on the house had somehow missed the fact that the century-old stone foundation had cracked and settled, knocking the house off-kilter and threatening its structural integrity. It wasn't until after she'd moved in with her children that she discovered the spider cracks in so many downstairs walls were signs her charming family home was falling apart. The repairs took all the money she'd set aside for remodeling, so she was just going to have to do it herself. Which she could totally do. After all, why else did online DIY videos exist?

"But Piper, it's Christmas. Tom's favorite…"

Tom's favorite time of year. Her tough marine husband had turned into an excited little boy every holiday season—decorating the house like a Griswold, buying trees that were always too big, going to every Christmas parade and celebration he could find. She used to tease him that the only reason he wanted children was to have an excuse to act like one at Christmas. Holidays at the elder Montgomerys' were formal and very…grown up. It was time she provided Tom's fun sense of adventure and happy Christmas memories for his children.

Susan's eyes went shiny with distress, and Piper felt a stab of pity. Tom's death had hurt them both. "Susan, with so many community events coming up, the inn will be busy, so I could really use your help with the kids on those festival weekends." She reached over and took Susan's hand. She wanted them to be a team again. "I won't be able to do it all without you."

That wasn't an exaggeration. The Rendezvous Falls Ghostwalk was coming up that weekend, quickly followed by the Holiday Craft Show, the Holiday Historic Homes Tour, and then the Celebrate a Victorian Holiday events every December weekend before Christmas. In between all of that, she had to get this house of hers ready for the perfect Christmas she'd vowed they'd have, come hell or high water. Piper felt tired just thinking about it all, but she brightened her smile when Susan nodded and squeezed Piper's fingers.

"Of course I'll help, dear. Roger and I miss the kids. But about Christmas…"

"I think Tom would want the kids to spend Christmas Day at their own home, don't you?" Susan's face fell, but she managed another nod as Piper continued. "*This* is their home now." Whether Ethan liked it or not. "It's our first Christmas here, and it needs to be special. So I'll be having Christmas dinner here and you are invited. You can host Thanksgiving, though, because that's right in the middle of the holiday madness and the inn will be open, so I won't have time to cook."

Susan blinked a few times, staring somewhere over Piper's shoulder, lost in thought. Finally she let out a soft breath of defeat, looking around the kitchen again. Her eyes stopped on the doorless cupboard under the sink.

"Fine. If you think you can pull it all together, then I won't stop you from trying. We can always change it to our house at the last minute if we need to."

Piper straightened in her chair. *Challenge accepted.* "We won't need to."

She had her kids and she had a house and she was... making it. But was *making it* going to be enough to last the rest of her life?

CHAPTER SEVEN

LOGAN SCRUBBED THE back of his neck, wondering how many meds Gran had taken that day.

"So…" he finally said. "Why am I meeting this woman again?"

She fixed him with her no-bullshit glare. "How about because I asked you to?"

"But Gran… I don't want another tattoo. And if I did, I already have a tat artist I trust in Mobile. Pretty sure I've paid off the mortgage on his house by now. Besides, I thought you *hated* my ink?"

She'd shocked the hell out of him that morning when she asked him to roll up his sleeves just a few minutes after he walked into her room. Any other time, she was barking at him to cover it all up. Today, she wanted him to meet a tattoo artist in Rendezvous Falls.

Gran gave a soft sigh. "Look, I've heard Kat Gifford is very good. She's active in the business owners' group and I…like her. Maybe she could do…" she waved her hand toward his arm "…something somewhere. If people see you there, and see the…uh…quality of your 'art,' then maybe…"

Logan squinted, trying to make sense of this conversation. "Gran, are you pimping me out to help some tattoo artist make money off *my* guy's work? No self-respecting artist would…"

"Oh, Kat doesn't know. I just thought…" She scowled and leaned forward, waving her hand at him. "You know what? Forget it. If you can't do your grandmother a simple favor, then just never mind." He sat back in the chair and stared at his grandmother in amazement as she continued her rant. "I don't need your help. I run my own damn business and I *founded* the damn Rendez-vous Falls Business Owners' Association. But I guess you think it's crazy for me to help a young female entrepreneur succeed in this town." She slapped her hand on the mattress. "If it's that much of a burden, forget it. I'm not gonna beg you."

Logan's father used to tell him that with Gran, you had to pick your battles. That there were times when she dug in, sometimes over the weirdest stuff, and once she did that—the fight was over. Until right this moment, Logan had never understood. But now? Staring into her steely gray eyes? Now he got it.

"Okay, Gran." He held up his hands in defeat. "You win. I'll call this Kat and go for a consultation. I'll try not to feel cheap and used."

Gran's mouth quirked into a smile. "I appreciate you sacrificing your obviously very high moral standards."

He chuckled as he stood. "So your spirits have returned, then?"

"Did you have any doubt they would?" She settled herself more comfortably against the pillows, then reached for her water glass. He moved to help her, but snatched his hand back when she glared at him. "How's the inn doing? Are we ready for Ghostwalk?"

The decorations had shifted slightly at the inn from just leaves and cornstalks to include jack-o'-lanterns and fake spider webs.

"Has she brought down all those old candelabras from the attic?" Gran shook her head. "Those are beautiful antiques, but for some reason people think they look spooky, so I only use them at Halloween."

"The inn is oozing with orange and brown and black. It's like living inside a piece of candy corn. If that's the look you were going for, she nailed it."

Piper had been bossing him around for days, and was eerily close to being even fussier about details than Gran was.

Gran's eyes sparkled. "I'm glad she was able to pull it off. Sometimes she likes to chase her own ideas."

"Perfect Piper?" He thought Gran considered Piper a saint in the flesh. "Are you saying she's human after all?"

Gran flipped her middle finger at him, making him laugh out loud. He liked this old woman just as much as he loved her. He'd only hurt *himself* by staying away so long. Whether or not she'd ever be able to run the inn again was a discussion they still needed to have, but not yet. He was glad she'd found Piper, especially with a busy season coming. Gran seemed to be thinking the same.

"Piper is wonderful. She works hard, and her moving in next door was a godsend, especially now. But she has lots of ideas for redecorating and adding different 'events' and stuff. I love her enthusiasm, but you know I'm not a big fan of change." She paused, tipping her head to the side as if considering her words carefully. Her expression softened. "Honestly, though, I don't know what I'd do without her. She's become really special to me. A single mom trying to make it—I was once where she is, and I guess we've bonded over that."

Logan thought about the busy little blonde and grinned. "I've thought more than once since I met her that you and Piper are two stubborn peas in a pod. I'm glad you hired her."

Gran nodded absently, then gave herself a little shake and looked up at him, all business again. "So you'll go see Kat? Today?"

"Today?" He thought for a moment. It was Wednesday, and things were quiet at the inn. He still didn't get Gran's insistence that he meet this woman, but it wouldn't kill him. He blew out a breath. What else was he going to do in Rendezvous Falls? "Sure, Gran. Today."

LOGAN STOOD OUTSIDE the Indigo Ink Tattoo Studio a few hours later and fought the urge to turn around and go back home. Maybe *all* the way home, back to Mobile. He was supposed to walk in there, peel off his shirt, and what? Let people think this Kat woman might have done the expensive ocean sleeve that took Andy months to create? No ethical artist would want that. He couldn't shake the feeling that Gran was up to something more than just being nice to some tattoo artist with a chair in a strip mall studio. But he'd already set up the appointment with Kat over the phone for a consult, so he may as well get it over with.

"Logan, right? I'm Kat. Come on back." She greeted him as soon as he walked in. She had short jet-black hair with bright blue highlights on the tips. She was tall and slender, with a swirl of flower tats on one arm that ran from her fingers up to vanish under her sleeveless top, only to peek out at her neckline. She smiled, her bright purple lips matching her long, sparkly fingernails. She was bold, that's for sure. The kind of woman he generally gravitated toward. But he was here on business.

She gestured toward the chair. The mirror was surrounded with tacked-up images of work he assumed she'd done. It was good stuff. He took his jacket off, and she gave a low whistle at the tattoos she could see below his rolled up sleeves. "Nice work. What brings you here? Oh, wait…you said you were a referral, right? Who can I thank?"

He settled into the chair. "Iris Taggart."

The shock on her face was photo-worthy.

"Seriously? Iris sent you to *me*?" She stared at him, then slowly smiled. "I definitely need to know how prim old Iris Taggart got into a discussion with a hunk like you over your ink." Despite her use of the word *hunk*, there was nothing flirtatious in her tone.

"I'm her grandson."

She didn't even bother to look embarrassed. Kat was a stunner with those dark eyes and high cheekbones, and she had a laugh as bold as her looks.

"That would explain it. I know her opinion on ink, though, so I'm still having a hard time imagining her suggesting you get *more*." She motioned toward his shirt. "Let me see the rest of it. Do you want me to pull the curtain?"

He shook his head and removed his shirt, tossing it on an empty stool nearby.

"Damn, Logan. That is freakin' amazing." She ran her fingers over his left shoulder and down his arm. The front of his shoulder was a blue-and-white sky, with birds flying under a blazing sun. The back of his shoulder was a stormy night scene, with the moon just visible behind angry clouds and bolts of lightning. Both scenes blended together on his upper arm. On his bicep was an oil rig surrounded by crashing, foaming waves. His forearm art was beneath the ocean's surface, with stingrays, sharks and dolphins swimming through the blue-green water. Kat's fingers traced every line, appraising the work and admiring the details Andy had achieved.

"Where'd you have this done?"

"A friend of mine has a studio in Alabama. Took almost a year to get it done right."

"All I can say is wow." Her eyes rose to meet his. "You work the rigs? I've got an uncle down there somewhere. Texas, I think. He said the ocean rigs are intense."

He shrugged. "They can be. But it's the only life I know."

"So why are you in…oh, that's right. I heard Iris took a fall. She okay?" He nodded. She looked at his other arm, free from ink except for a narrow band of Celtic knots around his forearm. "What are you looking for from me?"

Before he could answer, a guy walked up and put his hand on Kat's shoulder, smiling at Logan.

"Hi, I'm the owner, Chris. That's some nice work there." He nodded at Logan's arm.

Kat bristled, swatting the man's hand away.

"Take a hike, Chris. He's *my* client." From the tense set of Kat's jaw, Logan guessed this wasn't the first time the boss had tried to poach her customers. Or cop a feel.

Logan watched Chris walk away, dropping his voice so only Kat would hear. "That's your boss, huh?"

Kat's mouth twisted. "He's the only show in town right now. I just need save my pennies and build a clientele for another year or two. Then I'll open my own studio."

They chatted while he flipped through her binder of designs. She suggested a small sea serpent tat for his empty shoulder, and sketched out a quick image. They were discussing details when Kat's next appointment, a young woman with a flock of swallows inked on her arm and a swirl of bright green in her dark hair, arrived.

Logan stood to leave, and Kat set her sketch on the table. "I'm *still* trying to figure out why Iris sent you to see me when you didn't want a new tattoo." She held up her hand when he started to speak. "Come on, I had to *sell* you on that tat. You didn't come in here looking for one."

He pulled on his shirt. "I'm getting the tat because you're good at what you do, not because you *sold* me on it, Kat." That made her smile. "But I'll confess I don't know why Gran sent me. She hates my ink and usually barks at me to cover it up."

The young woman who'd just walked up interrupted. "Oh my god, are you Logan Taggart?"

He eyed her as he reached for his jacket. "I am."

"And your grandmother is Iris, right?" She looked between Logan and Kat and started to laugh. "And Iris suggested you two meet? Oh my god, they're at it again."

"Evie, what are you talking about?" Kat looked as confused as Logan felt, glancing back in his direction.

"Logan, this is my friend and client, Evie Rosario. She and her mom own the Spot Diner downtown."

Evie shook Logan's hand with a much-too-delighted grin. "Iris is part of the same book club Helen Russo is in, along with Vickie Pendergast, Lena Fox and a bunch of others."

Logan nodded. "I met a couple of them at the hospital last week. They've been helping Gran."

"Yeah, and I bet they think they're helping *you*, too." She looked at Kat. "How well do you know Iris?"

Kat rolled a gleaming metal tray of tools and ink closer to the chair as Evie sat down. "Barely. We've met a few times in business owners meetings. I know Lena Fox pretty well, though. We're in the art guild together…"

Evie snapped her fingers. "That's it! That's how they found out about you." She motioned to Logan's arm, now covered. "Nice work, by the way. What better match for a guy with ink than a tattoo artist?"

"What kind of match?" An idea was whispering to Logan from the back of his mind, but he couldn't let himself believe it.

Evie gestured between the two of them. "A *dating* match! It's their new hobby."

Logan's mouth dropped open in synchronization with Kat's. Gran had tried to play freakin' matchmaker. With *him*. What in the hell was she thinking? He turned to Kat.

"I am *so* sorry. I had no idea…" He couldn't remember when he'd felt more embarrassed. He knew he had to be blushing. "Gran has never done anything like this…"

"Oh, yes she has." Evie chuckled. "This summer the

same group played matchmaker for my friend Whitney Foster up at the winery. And they were terrible at it, so I can't believe they're trying again."

Kat frowned. "Wait, isn't Whitney Foster *engaged* now?"

"Yeah, but not to anyone *they* fixed her up with. That didn't stop them from taking credit for Whitney and Luke being together."

Logan scrubbed his hands down his face and groaned. Just what he needed—a bunch of geriatrics messing with his love life. "I'll put an end to this as soon as I see Gran. Kat, I'm…"

She waved her hand in dismissal. "No worries. You're a client, so there's no way I'd go there anyway."

"I get it. Hella awkward."

"Yup."

Logan stared hard at the wall, trying to figure out if his grandmother really was losing it. When he realized Kat was getting ready to start work on Evie's arm, he turned to go. "Um, look…if I come back for that ink…let's agree to never mention this conversation again. *Ever.*"

Evie snorted in laughter, but Kat held out her hand for a shake. "Deal."

Logan left the two women and headed to his car, bouncing between anger and confusion with every step. He was forty freaking years old. Why would Gran be trying to hook him up? Maybe he really *should* talk to her doctor, 'cause she was clearly losing it.

CHAPTER EIGHT

PIPER HAD A stare-down with the kitchen sink for an hour or so before tackling the repair. It would probably make more sense to replace the whole thing—faucet and all—but that wasn't going to happen before Christmas. The bucket under the sink was not part of the perfect Christmas ambiance she was determined to have. And she couldn't let this leak get any worse. Her tablet was propped on the counter. She'd watched the video at least a dozen times. Tom's small toolbox sat next to her on the floor, along with the bag of supplies from the hardware store.

"You sure you know what you're doing?" Ethan's voice behind her echoed her own thoughts.

She turned and gave him a bright smile.

"Of course I do! How hard can it be to take a pipe apart and put some magic tape on it to stop the leak? Then I'll just put it back together and we can finally get rid of this bucket and put the doors back on. Do you want to help?"

"Hell, no." He backed away.

"Excuse me?" She barely managed to avoid laughing at his response. She knew he knew how to swear, but as a mom she shouldn't encourage it.

"I mean…no, thanks, Mom. I think you got this."

He gave her a quick thumbs-up and vanished, probably off to play video games. He'd been on his best behavior since the incident at school. She wasn't sure if it was genuine contrition or a ploy to get off being grounded, but she was happy to bask in the joy of a relatively well-behaved son for a little while.

She turned back to the sink. She might not be able to fix all her son's issues tonight, but she could fix this sink. She scooched closer and picked up a wrench from the toolbox. First, shut off the water valve.

"Momma? Whatcha doin'?" Lily's voice, just inches from her ear, made Piper jump, smacking her head on the cupboard frame. Which, of course, made Lily laugh.

"I'm repairing our leaky sink, baby. All by myself, because women are smart and strong and capable, right?" She turned to see Lily nodding, her pigtails bouncing. "Aren't you supposed to be watching a movie in the living room?"

"Ethan said *he* needed that TV." Of course he did. He liked using the biggest screen possible when gaming.

Piper shook her head. "Go tell Ethan that I said *you* get the living room TV tonight. He'll have to suffer through using his computer for gaming. If he gives you any grief, send him to me." She gave Lily a quick kiss. "Now go on, because Momma's got to get busy."

Finally alone, with no other excuses not to get started, she turned the water valve off. It was too tight to move with her hands, so she used a wrench. It slipped off a few times, and she had to really put her weight into it. The valve looked ancient. There was an odd crackling sound when she turned it, but that was probably just some of the chipped chrome finish coming off. The position was awkward and she was glad she was petite, because she barely fit in there. As it was, she ended up lying on her back to work. She removed the cold water pipe, cleaned it, attached a new connector, and put everything back together, sealing the threads with the plumber's tape. Three wraps, just like the video said. She tightened the connection, her arms trembling from the effort of using the wrench over her head without smacking herself in the face with it. Now she just had to turn on the water to see if it worked.

She moved to her knees and reached in with the wrench to turn the knob. Boy, she'd really gotten it tight. She leaned on the wrench to try to get the valve moving, and… BAM! The lever snapped off and water started spraying with the force of a fire hose and the aim of a lawn sprinkler. It was soaking the inside of the cabinet and covering the floor. And Piper. She screamed, and heard the kids come running. Sputtering and blinking to protect herself from the water's force, she grabbed at the pipe, feeling the sharp edge of metal slice her palm. No time to worry about that now. Ethan was next to her, rapidly handing her random tools that weren't going to be any help. And he was yelling at her to stop the water—which *really* wasn't helping. It was late, but she needed help from someone who knew what they were doing.

"Lily! Call the inn!" If Logan could fix an oil rig, he could surely fix a kitchen sink.

LOGAN JUMPED WHEN Gran's landline phone rang on the table next to the sofa, sending Mr. Whiskers scampering. It was after ten, and the few midweek guests they had were all in for the night. Thinking it might be one of those annoying robocalls, he almost ignored it. But Gran had been adamant that this was basically her "Batphone" and must be answered; it was connected to the business line. The caller ID read Piper Montgomery. He shook his head with a smile. The woman never stopped fretting about the inn.

"Yes, Piper," he answered, sarcasm dripping from his voice, "I *did* pick up the Ghostwalk flyers for this weekend and yes, I remembered to lock the front…" The screams in the background stopped him cold. He was on his feet in an instant. *"Piper?"*

Lily answered him, nearly screaming herself. "Mr. Logan! Mr. Logan! Come quick! Mommy broke the kitchen and she's saying unproffenal things!"

"Lily, I'll be right there. Is the door unlocked?"

"I'll get it, Mr. Logan!" The line went dead.

He hung up the phone and headed out the side door without bothering to grab a jacket, running across the lot. What did "breaking the kitchen" mean? An accident with an appliance? A *fire*? He sprinted up the front steps just as Lily opened the door, wide-eyed and pale. Logan forced himself to slow down. There was no sense panicking the kid any more than she was.

"Hey, Lily! What's going on?" He could hear Piper cursing from somewhere in the back of the house, so he scooped Lily up and headed that way. Cursing was good. Cursing meant she wasn't unconscious. The front room was neat and tidy, just like Piper, and painted a soft, sunny yellow. The furniture was modern and functional, with clean, sturdy lines. Definitely more contemporary and less cluttered than Gran's. There was a family portrait over the sofa, with a handsome man in uniform holding a tiny baby and smiling at Piper and a young, gap-toothed Ethan. It was a stark reminder that this was another man's family.

The hallway was only partially painted—half yellow and half a faded blue. They passed the dining room, which had a gaping hole in the ceiling where a light should be. The house might look like a candy confection on the outside, but it seemed Piper had her hands full with the interior.

"See? Unproffenal words." Lily pointed toward the kitchen, where Piper was still swearing up a storm. She sounded more ticked off than in danger. He finally understood what Lily was trying to say.

"Unprofessional?" Lily nodded and Logan couldn't stop his chuckle as he heard a string of f-bombs ahead. "Yeah, those are very unprofessional words, and not for little girls to repeat."

He stepped into the kitchen, with some walls wallpapered and some not, and thought he'd wandered onto the set of a slapstick sitcom. Water was spraying everywhere from under the sink. The floors were wet and slippery. The lower half of Piper's jeans-clad body was visible near the sink, bare feet kicking against the soaked floor. Under the sink, she was shouting something he couldn't understand. Oh, wait...he knew *that* word. He just never imagined Piper did. Ethan was frozen in place, staring at the toolbox and sounding even younger than his years.

"What do I *do,* Mom? What do you want me to *do*?"

Logan set Lily on the counter, where she could watch from a safe perch. He waved his finger at her.

"Stay. Here."

She nodded, probably relieved not to be part of the chaos. Ethan looked on the verge of tears, and that was the last thing any of them wanted. Logan rested his hand on the boy's shoulder to settle him.

"Do you know if there's a main water shutoff valve for the house?"

Ethan threw his hands in the air, wild-eyed. "I don't know! How am I supposed to kno…"

"It's okay, bud. There may not even be one." In a house this old, who knew? Logan turned to Piper, still squirming under the waterfall in the lower cupboard. "Come on out, Piper. Let me look at it."

His heart tightened at the panic and embarrassment in her voice. "I *can't* come out! The valve handle broke and I can't get it back on and I'm trying to hold the pipe together but there's water every-damn-where!"

Logan smiled, peeling his shirt over his head and tossing it on the dry counter near Lily. He kept his voice low and steady as he knelt by Piper's legs. He'd learned that being a voice of calm helped keep others from freaking out. "Come on out, Piper. I can't fit in there with you in the way."

"I can't! Don't you see all this water? The kitchen's going to flood and if these cupboards get ruined I can't afford to replace them. Son of a *bitch*!"

She was rapidly leaving panic behind and heading straight for hysteria. She'd soon be hyperventilating *and* hypothermic. Logan glanced around, spotting the towels hanging on the oven door. He gestured and Ethan, glad to be doing *something*, grabbed them and tossed them his way. He had to slow down the spraying water before he headed to the basement, but he couldn't do it with Piper slapping at the valve with her bare hands. Was that *blood* running down her arm?

Muttering a few curse words of his own, he grabbed her calves and pulled her out from under the sink, ignoring her loud protests. Once she was out, he took hold of her wrists. He held up her hands in front of her face and gave them a gentle shake to get her attention. Her dark knit top was soaked with freezing water, and her hair was hanging in cold wet strands around her. Behind her, water was spurting and splashing everywhere, but he only cared about Piper. She finally looked at his face so he could be sure she was hearing him.

"You've cut yourself. You're wet. You're cold. And you're not helping. I've got this." She didn't respond, so he slid her across the wet floor to sit in the corner. He looked up at Ethan. "Hand me the duct tape and a plastic bag, then go get your mother some bath towels before she turns into an ice cube."

He pushed his shoulders into the narrow space, his face taking on a steady stream of water. Damn, it was cold. He had to lean his weight on his bum shoulder, and he groaned at the throb of pain. It couldn't be helped. He tied the two towels tightly around the gushing valve, then wrapped the plastic bag over them and covered the works with duct tape from top to bottom. The slapdash repair wasn't pretty and wouldn't last long. Water was leaking into a puddle at the base of the cupboard, but he'd contained the wide spray and slowed the water enough that he could leave it and go looking for another shutoff valve somewhere.

He twisted himself around and sat up on the kitchen

floor, looking to Piper. Ethan had dropped about five towels in her lap. She had one wrapped around her wet hair like a turban, and was sliding another over her shoulders. Her face was pale, blue eyes big as saucers. She looked up at her son, then over to Lily, who hadn't moved. And Piper started to laugh. He thought at first it might be hysteria, but her belly laugh was strong and genuine. Lily started giggling, then guffawing behind him. And even Ethan, usually so determined to be stoic, started to laugh—softly at first, as if he'd forgotten how to do it. Then he started to roar with laughter, his arms across his stomach.

Logan looked at the three of them, laughing in the face of their self-induced disaster, and grinned as he shook his head.

"In the words of my Alabama buddy, Ted…y'all are crazy."

That only made them laugh louder. He tried to hold it in, but his shoulders were shaking as he stood and reached his hand down to Piper to help her up. She wiped at her eyes, which deepened a shade or two when she looked at her son. The problem child walked over to his baby sister and set her on the floor, holding her hand so she couldn't get too close to the worst of the flooding in her stocking feet.

Their laughter tugged at something in his soul. He shrugged it off. They were a family. A package deal. A permanent package deal. That was a big *nope* with his lifestyle. And yet…their happiness in the midst of chaos touched his heart with an unexpected warmth. He turned back to Piper, wrapped in bath towels and beaming up at him. She had to be one of the most interesting women he'd ever met. He grabbed a towel for himself, then tried to get everyone refocused on the still-leaking kitchen sink.

"Do you have a flashlight?"

She reached into the toolbox and handed him one. The toolbox had the name Tom written on it in neat block letters with black marker. Another reminder. These children had had a father. A man Piper had loved. A man who'd never return. He swallowed hard, then looked over at Ethan. Logan might not be a perfect role model, but he could help Ethan learn a thing or two while he was around. After all, Logan had once been a sad, angry kid himself.

"Piper, do you know if there's a shutoff in the basement?"

Her face fell. "Sorry, I don't. Our basement isn't as scary as Iris's, but I still hate going down there. The lights don't work very well."

"Okay. I need to get down there before my quick fix has a blowout. If there isn't a shutoff, I'll have to turn it off at the street. Do you know where your meter is?" She nodded, and he noticed her clutching her hand. *Shit.* He'd forgotten she was hurt. "Let me see that."

"I think it's okay." She held it out and he looked for himself. It felt…weird…holding her hand like that. He cleared his throat more loudly than necessary, willing himself to get a grip and focus.

"Looks like a clean cut. I don't think you need stitches, but go bandage it up."

Her brow quirked upward. "Yes, sir."

He didn't respond. She was still giddy from adrenaline after the plumbing break, and now she was acting playful. But getting playful in return felt like a mistake. It would be crossing a line he didn't need to be crossing. He turned and grabbed his shirt.

"Ethan, come on down to the basement with me so you'll know what to do next time. That way you can help your mom." Logan looked at Piper, standing with Lily in her arms. She was grinning at him, laughter in her eyes and a towel around her head. Damn, she needed to laugh more often. It made her glow. Or maybe she always glowed and he hadn't seen it until tonight.

He turned to follow Ethan, and wondered if he'd ever be able to *unsee* Piper looking like that.

CHAPTER NINE

PIPER HAD BANDAGED her hand and was almost finished mopping the kitchen floor by the time she heard the guys coming back upstairs. Whoa. She just thought of her thirteen-year-old son as a *guy*. She wrung out the mop in the sink—at least the drains worked. She'd thrown the bath towels she didn't use for herself onto the bottom of the cupboard to soak up the water that seeped from the bulky-but-effective repair Logan did after physically dragging her out from under there. What a night. The puddle had stopped growing, so she figured the guys—damn, she did it again—had found the shutoff valve for the house.

Her son only had so many facial expressions these days. He generally favored his carefully crafted *whatever* expression. If he broke away from that, it was usually only a partial break. He'd sport half his *whatever* look and half of what he was really feeling. Sad and whatever. Angry and whatever. Amused and whatever. But when Ethan came back into the kitchen with Logan, he looked thoughtful and…grown-up. With barely a hint of his usual perpetually bored expression. Logan's hand was on Ethan's shoulder as he quizzed him.

"So, the water shutoff is where?"

"Toward the front of house, over in the corner."

"And you turn it?"

"Left-loose for on, right-tight for off."

"And the main electrical breaker is?"

"At the base of the stairs by the electrical box—the big red lever."

"And if a breaker fuse flips off?"

"Look for one that's flipped to red, and flip it back so the green shows."

"And if the sump pump stops running?"

"Check to see if the float is stuck on the side of the hole."

"But first…"

Ethan answered as if repeating the exact words he'd been taught, rolling his eyes. Nice to know she wasn't the only one who got that save-me-from-adults treatment. "Unplug it first because electricity and water don't mix."

Ethan hadn't had a lot of men around to show him these things. Roger was a loving grandfather, but he always joked that his handiest talent was writing checks to people who knew what they were doing. Tom used to love tinkering with things, but he never got the chance to pass that passion on to his son.

Logan laughed and clapped Ethan's back. "Exactly. Now you know where to start when your mom needs your help. You're the man of this house, so you should know how to keep it in working order."

Piper set down the mop and raised her hand to stop that kind of talk. "He doesn't have to be man of the house, because *this* house has a woman in charge." Ethan's eyes dimmed a little, and she hurried to correct herself. She'd been so quick to assert her place that she'd taken her son's away. "I mean…"

Logan cut her off and gestured around the kitchen. She couldn't stop thinking of all the colorful tattoos now hidden under that shirt. She'd seen glimpses of it before now, but had no idea that he had an entire ocean mural on one arm. She almost missed his question.

"Ethan, how many residents of this house are there?"

"Three."

"And how many are female?"

"Two."

"And male?"

"One."

"Thank you. The math alone makes you 'man of the house.'" He gave Piper a pointed look, and Ethan's elusive smile threatened to return, with an emotion she hardly ever saw these days. Pride. "Your mom is woman of the house, and…she's your mom. Which makes her the…managing partner. That means she's the boss. But you're still a partner here. And you have a responsibility to this family. Got it?"

Piper blinked back tears as her son straightened his shoulders and nodded. Tom would be so proud of him in this moment. When had Ethan turned into a young man? And why hadn't she been treating him like one instead of wishing he was still her little boy?

"And what about me?" Lily said. She rubbed her eyes, and Piper cringed when she looked at the clock. It was late. Hopefully all this excitement wouldn't give Lily more nightmares. She'd already had two that week. She gave her daughter a big smacking kiss on the cheek.

"You, my dear, are the superhero who called in reinforcements." She winked at Logan. "And tomorrow, you're going to be a *cranky* superhero if you don't get to bed." Piper started for the stairs, but stopped by Logan's side, looking up into his warm eyes and feeling a flutter of that unfamiliar sensation again. More than attraction and affection, although she felt those, too. No, this was definitely the heat of *desire* blossoming deep inside her. There was no sense in denying it. She'd known it once, and never thought she'd feel it again. But this man, soaking wet and bemused in her kitchen, had reawakened desire in her. It frightened her just as much as it thrilled her. She swallowed hard, but her heart was still too full for her to be articulate.

"Logan…this was…thank you…"

He nodded, then gave her a deep smile that nearly stopped her heart altogether.

"You're welcome. I'll replace the valve tomorrow morning, but until then, you have no running water in the house." He must have noticed the panic in her eyes. "Do you have bottled water? There are rooms open at the inn tonight if you'd rather camp out over there."

For some reason the thought of sleeping under the same roof as Logan Taggart, at least in her current frame of mind, felt dangerous. She shook her head.

"We have plenty of bottled water in the pantry for brushing our teeth and stuff. The kids have already bathed and showered. We'll all be asleep in no time, so we'll be fine. I can pay you…"

He stared at her, his face going blank. When he didn't want to be read, he was as good at closing himself off as her son was. "I'm sure you can. But you're not paying me, Piper." He reached out to pat Lily's head, which was resting sleepily on Piper's shoulder. There was some-thing about that—the way he treated her children with affection and respect—that made her warm inside all over again. It wasn't just the rugged good looks of this man fueling her desire. What was on the inside, at least what she'd seen so far, was even more appealing. His hand moved from Lily to rest lightly on Piper's arm. "And while I'm on the list of things you're not doing, you're also not cooking tomorrow morning. Sleep in."

That was a nice thought, but she hated not doing her job. "No, that won't be necessary. I'll…"

One heavy brow rose. "What's necessary is that you get some rest and take care of that hand. I've fed a rig full of hungry oil workers. I think I can handle the three doubles and two singles we have staying tonight." His face grew serious. "I mean it, Piper. As a Taggart, I am banning you from the Taggart Inn until at least ten o'clock. Once you get there, I'll come over here and get your kitchen straightened out. Deal?"

Her laughter bubbled up. "I'm sorry, was that sup-posed to sound like a negotiation and not a direct order?"

He chuckled. "I figured I had a better chance of you saying 'deal' than saying 'yes, sir' again."

"You figured right." Exhaustion crept over her. Her back was throbbing, her hand hurt, and Lily was far too heavy on her hip. "Fine. Deal. Ten o'clock." She turned to her son, who'd been watching the conversation with intense interest, particularly Logan's hand on her arm. For once, she couldn't read his mood at all. "Let's all get some sleep."

Logan started for the door, looking back at Ethan.

"You'll be in school when I do the plumbing repairs, but I still need to take care of Gran's car. Stop over later and maybe you can learn how to keep your mom's car running. After all, you'll be driving in a few years." As if Piper needed to be reminded. Ethan nodded, following Logan to the door.

"Can we work on your bike, too?"

Logan looked past Ethan to her. She gave a warning look, then a small nod. He understood her unspoken message. "Work on? Yes. Ride? No. Not until we show Mom she can trust the two of us. Lock up behind me, okay?"

Ethan nodded. The two males—she still couldn't quite bring herself to call Ethan a man—walked away. One she adored with all of her heart. And one who was beginning to occupy far too many of her thoughts.

"That breakfast was delicious, Mr. Taggart!" Mrs. Quinn from Room Eight smiled brightly. "Gotta love a man who can cook! Your wife is a lucky woman."

Logan nodded as he gathered the plates from the table. He gave an inward sigh at the large coffee stain on the tablecloth. Add that to his growing to-do list that morning.

"Thank you, Mrs. Quinn." He laid on the customer service charm, giving the old woman a wink. "There is no Mrs. Taggart, which is why I had to learn to cook."

The pewter-haired woman laughed, giving him a full-body sweep with her eyes that made him awkwardly uncomfortable. He was half afraid she was going to pinch his ass. "Young man, with your looks and your talent, women should be knocking the door down to marry you."

He muttered a quick thank-you and moved out of reach to clear the two empty tables nearby. Piper would have a fit if she knew he'd left dirty dishes sitting there after the guests left, but he'd had no choice. He'd been right in the middle of serving breakfast when he got the call that a bathtub was clogged on the third floor. This was his week to play plumber.

He'd dashed up to clear the drain, then back downstairs to wash up, don the apron again, and serve the next breakfast sitting, barely getting their Roustabout Scramble out in time. On the bright side, his meal was a hit with everyone. The few times he'd been recruited for kitchen duty on the rigs, he'd basically grabbed whatever he could find and thrown it into a skillet with a pile of eggs. A little ham. Some crumbled bacon. Sausage. Onions. Mushrooms. Peppers. Cheese. It was a filling meal, with enough protein to keep workers happy and satisfied until lunchtime. He figured the Roustabout Scramble would do the same for their guests.

"Excuse me?" Mr. Feldman from Room Ten raised his hand at the corner table, where he sat with his wife. "We're going wine-tasting today. Can you tell us if there are any wineries closed on Thursdays, so we don't waste our gas driving around?"

I have no fucking clue about wineries...

Logan smiled politely. "Let me get the wine trail booklet from the front desk…"

Feldman frowned. "We *have* the booklet. But it doesn't have the hours for every winery. That's why I'm asking."

Logan kept his smile in place and tried not to react to the guy's condescending tone while his brain spun, trying to figure out how to answer the question. His breath hitched when he felt a warm hand on the small of his back and heard a familiar female voice.

"Nearly all the major wineries are open Thursday through the weekends, Mr. Feldman." Piper was looking at the guests, not at Logan. Her hand stayed on his back, creating a buzz of energy under his skin as she continued. "Halcott Winery is only open Friday and Saturday. Windy Hill and Cardiff wineries are open on Saturdays only. And if you want a break from wine, I recommend trying Eagle Rock Distillery. It's not far past the Falls Legend Winery, and their whiskey has won several awards. They're doing small-batch vodkas and gin, too."

Mrs. Feldman looked at her husband. "See? I told you Piper would know the answer. She knows everything about this area."

The man across the table gave Logan a look. "I just assumed someone with the last name of Taggart would know the answer, too."

Logan stiffened, but Piper pressed her hand against him to silence him. It worked, since her touch made him forget what they were even talking about. The sensation left him feeling rattled. She was picket fences. He was open road. Yet the touch of her hand made him oddly breathless. He finally caught up with her laughing reply.

"Mr. Taggart's grandmother actually owns the inn. Logan is more of an…um…apprentice."

He let them all have a nice laugh at his expense. To quote Ethan…*whatever*. He and Piper turned away from the table together, and he saw the pointed look she gave the two—now *three* with Mrs. Quinn gone—tables piled with dirty dishes. She kept her voice low so the two remaining tables of diners wouldn't hear.

"Are you having a rough morning, Logan?"

He almost didn't respond, lost in the thought of how much he missed the feel of her touch on his back. "You could say that. I had to unclog a bathtub in the middle of cooking breakfast."

She grabbed a tray and started helping him clear the tables. "Room Ten?"

"How did you know?"

Piper gave him a level gaze. "You think I don't know which bathtubs, sinks and toilets like to act up around here?"

"Just like you know the hours of operation for every winery in a twenty-mile radius, right?"

Her mouth curved into a smile. "Maybe not twenty miles, but probably five or ten." They cleaned up the dining room and headed back to the kitchen together. Something had shifted between them since last night. She glanced up at him, apparently thinking the same. "Thanks again for last night, Logan. I can't imagine what I would have done without your help. You're my hero…"

Her words trailed off as she opened the kitchen door with her hip. Logan had a feeling his "hero" status was going to be very short-lived once she got a look.

"Um, yeah," he started. "I'm not real good at the clean-as-you-go method you use."

"I can see that." Shocked laughter floated just beneath her words. There were three dirty skillets on the stove. Several bowls piled in the sink. And whisks, spatulas, egg cartons and other stuff sitting around on the counters.

"In my defense," he started, "I *did* have to go upstairs to fix that bathtub in the middle of everything."

Piper set her tray down on one of the few empty spots on the counter, then slowly turned to face him. There was a lot less laughter in her voice now.

"I have had mornings—when the inn was *full*, Logan—and more than one room needed service. A backed-up toilet in one, an overflowing sink in the other, and a guest who thought she was having a *heart attack*." She looked around, her lips twitching. "The kitchen *never* looked even *close* to this level of chaos. Is this how your kitchens looked on the oil rigs?"

"Well…no. For one thing, I wasn't actually the cook. But there was a crew that cleaned up."

She picked up a towel and threw it at him. "Well, guess who's the *crew* today? Because this?" She gestured around. "This is all yours. I'll go do the rooms. And…good luck."

What Piper didn't realize was that Logan didn't mind hard work. He had the kitchen back in order—or something closely resembling it—in an hour. Then he was off to take care of her kitchen sink, using the key she'd left on the counter. Replacing the valve under the sink was awkward, but not really difficult. He worked with pipes and pumps for a living—this was just a little smaller working quarters than he was used to.

He was cleaning up when she walked in. She leaned over to inspect under the sink and grinned up at him over her shoulder.

"I'm glad to see you work more neatly than you cook."

He finished drying his hands and tossed the paper towels into the trash. "As your son would say...*whatever*. And you're welcome for breakfast. And the repair."

He was only teasing, but her cheeks colored. "I'm sorry—thank you for everything."

"Glad to do it, Piper." And he was. He was happy just to be around her. Even in this falling-apart house. He pointed his chin at the box full of hardware. "You want help putting those door pulls on? I've got time."

"Nah. That's one of the jobs I can actually do myself." She straightened and dug her hand through some of the pieces in the box. "Just takes a screwdriver."

"What are some of the jobs you *can't* do alone?"

There was a firm set to her chin at that question. She was so much like Gran—proud and stubborn. He thought about the dining room with no light and the half-painted walls. She had her hands full with this old place. He thought of her crawling under her kitchen sink the night before to tackle a repair on her own. He'd been thinking of Piper as cute and sassy. Or feisty. Spirited, maybe.

But she was more than that. She was *tough*.

CHAPTER TEN

PIPER TURNED AWAY, not wanting Logan to see panic in her eyes. She took two bottles of water out of the refrigerator, offering him one. Her voice was tired in her own ears. "Don't worry about it. One job at a time, right?"

Logan took the bottle, scrubbing the back of his neck before meeting her gaze. Then he glanced away again, as if uncertain. It wasn't a look she saw often from Logan. He shifted his weight on his feet, then sighed.

"This is probably none of my business, but I gotta ask. This place seems like…a lot. Were you trying to save money by buying a fixer-upper?"

She laughed so hard water almost shot out her nose. She grabbed a paper towel and wiped her face, still laughing as she covered her face with the towel. Mainly because she was afraid she was about to burst into tears. So much work to be done here, and so little time or skill to do it. Her chest went tight, and she sucked in a ragged breath before lowering her hands. Logan wasn't laughing. In fact, he looked concerned, as if he knew she was about to lose it. She gave him a bright smile. She totally had this.

"If that *was* my plan, it was a bad one. I knew the house needed cosmetic work, but I had enough money set aside to pay for it. What I didn't know was that the foundation was unstable." Which left her finances unstable. She told him how she'd used Tom's death benefit to buy the place, and how the home inspector totally missed the foundation issues, costing Piper a small fortune to repair. She flashed another smile. "The good news is this house will still be standing long after we're gone."

Again, he didn't laugh. He looked around the kitchen, and she knew he was seeing the work left to do. She stood up straight. This was *her* house, and she loved it. Or…she *would* love it, when she got the work done. Logan wasn't fooled by her bravado.

"Look," he said, "I've actually built houses. My dad was a contractor for a bit." He seemed lost in thought for a moment. "I'm saying I can help. Like getting the cupboard doors back on. Putting a light up in the dining room. And speaking of lights, those old fluorescents in your basement are straight out of a horror movie."

She laughed at that, taking his empty water bottle and tossing it. "I know, right? I'm always expecting to hear someone start up a chainsaw when they start flickering on and off. Thanks for offering, but… I'll get it all done. I watch a lot of how-to videos."

Logan cringed. "Please tell me you're not going to work with electricity based on what you learned on some video."

"Of course not." She was terrified of electricity. "Okay, maybe I'll let you help me with the dining room light. I need the downstairs done for Christmas, because I have big plans. But first you and I both have to get through Ghostwalk at the inn this weekend. It's a whole different crowd than HarvestFest."

She hadn't worked the inn for one yet, but she'd

lived in Rendezvous Falls long enough to know that Ghostwalk brought a younger, more…lively…crowd. Iris had already warned her to put some of the more fragile items away for the weekend, as guests tended to drink more and get careless. Iris said she'd caught guests tapping on walls, moving pictures, and trying to slide bookcases around to find secret passageways and perhaps a ghost lair inside the inn.

Logan leaned over and started gathering his tools together. "Is there a weekend when this town *doesn't* have a 'fest' of some kind?"

"Not this time of year. But even during the off-seasons, there's at least one festival every month. Half of them were your grandmother's idea." He grunted at that, and she bristled. "Rendezvous Falls is lucky to have Iris and her marketing smarts. Festivals bring people, and people bring business. A lot of our businesses rely on the holiday season to break into the black for the year. From now until New Year's, there's something every weekend."

"You've got big Christmas plans for the inn, huh?"

For a moment she was distracted by the way his shirt stretched tight over his broad shoulders. She hadn't had a chance to really look at that ocean tattoo running down his arm last night, and that felt like a damn shame right now. What had he just asked about? Oh, yeah. Christmas.

"The biggest." She blinked. "Oh, not for the inn. At home. I promised the kids that if we got our own house, we'd have a perfect family Christmas, and I'm gonna make it happen." She gave him a sideways glance, knowing he'd met Susan already. "And my in-laws are coming."

"Ah, I see. So you're not talking Santa's workshop

perfect. You're talking Martha-Stewart-level perfect."
He pulled on his jacket.

"Pretty much. It was Tom's favorite holiday, and I
want the kids to feel that connection with him."

Logan nodded, looking at the refrigerator door.
There, among all Lily's drawings and Ethan's school
schedule, was a photo of Tom, laughing as he swung
a five-year-old Ethan up in the air at the edge of the
ocean. Logan's voice lowered.

"Your husband?"

She nodded. The kitchen suddenly felt very small.
Logan was standing close now, and with that rugged…
Logan-ness…it felt like he was taking up all the air, as
well as her ability to think or speak.

He stared at the picture. "Ethan must miss his dad."

"We all do." It was true. Her friends used to tease
her that she'd hit the jackpot with Tom, and they weren't
wrong.

Logan turned to face her. "Of course you do. I didn't
mean you wouldn't. But boys and their fathers…" His
voice trailed off.

"I'm sorry," she said, reaching out to put her hand on
his arm. "I wasn't thinking. You lost *your* father, too."
She knew Iris's son was dead, but she didn't know any
of the details.

Logan stared down at her hand. "I was older than
Ethan—nineteen when Dad had the stroke. But it's tough."

"And your mom?"

"She died when I was eight."

He said it as if he was saying it might rain tomorrow. No emotion. No expression. The only sound in
the kitchen was the hum of the refrigerator, then that

stopped, too. Piper tightened her fingers on his arm, which felt like granite.

"Logan, how awful. I'm so sorry. I didn't realize…"

He pulled away with a shrug that seemed more calculated than sincere.

"That's life, right? Nothing's permanent."

Despite his flippant tone, she had a feeling there were far deeper emotions buried there beneath his laid-back persona. He'd been so nothing-bothers-me since his arrival. But the man read *Hemingway*. His still waters might run much deeper than she'd first thought.

LOGAN CHEWED THE inside of his cheek to keep from scowling, in case a guest caught his expression. Then again, this particular group of guests was getting on his last nerve and he didn't much care what they thought. HarvestFest weekend had been busy, but in a homespun, everyone's-buying-pumpkins sort of way. But Ghost-walk? Between the nerds here looking to find "real" ghosts and the people here just to party, the inn was busier and noisier than he'd ever seen it. They'd made it through Friday night without incident, but Saturday had a whole different vibe.

The group from Rochester was definitely here for a party weekend. Last night he'd had to gently usher them to their rooms after they started playing a loud game of poker—he was pretty sure they were thinking of trying *strip* poker—in the parlor. The four couples started their Saturday by hitting every winery they could find in the area—which was a lot. Then they came back to the inn and started sampling all the bottles they'd lugged in with them. Still not done, they filled the flasks they thought they were hiding so cleverly, and headed out to join the official Ghostwalk tour an hour ago.

Piper had explained yesterday how a number of historic homes opened their doors at nightfall and hosted actors who portrayed citizens of days gone by. Not only did the locals love it, but tourists came from all over, looking for a chance to see the inside of some of the famous Victorian houses. Logan didn't understand the desire to snoop inside someone else's home, but he had to hand it to Gran for thinking it up twenty years ago. Piper said it was a huge moneymaker, and sure enough, the inn was fully booked with a waiting list. Thank god this was the last night, though. It had been a long week, and he knew Piper was just as exhausted as he was.

The Rochester crew apparently thought this was the type of haunted house tour that would include fake blood and zombies. Add all that alcohol to the mix, and they ended up being so disruptive that they were asked to leave the tour. Which meant they were back at the inn, disgruntled and drunk, milling around the lobby arguing about what to do next. Logan glanced at his watch. Eight o'clock was a little early to send them all to bed, although the thought was tempting. Luckily, Piper showed up before he said anything. She stepped up onto the staircase and whispered that Iris's friend, Vickie, had called her about what happened and to warn her that some drunk guests were headed their way.

Devon White seemed to be the group's good-time ringleader. His girlfriend, Beth, was doing her best to rein him in, but here he was, singing the theme from *Ghostbusters* at the top of his lungs in the lobby. Logan was getting ready to play bouncer and tell them all to pack up and hit the road. But Piper, ever the business-minded one, pointed out in a low voice that none of them were in any condition to drive. Not to mention the inn would lose a lot of money if they left. Then she stepped up higher on the staircase and clapped her hands to get everyone's attention.

"I'm glad you all had fun tonight…" She smiled as a few of the guys hooted and hollered in agreement. "But you haven't heard *all* the ghost stories from Rendezvous Falls yet."

"Yeah, 'cuz they threw us out!" Devon shouted. Some of the other men clapped him on the back as if he'd just announced he was running for president. Piper's smile was like steel as she pushed on.

"Well, if they hadn't done that, you'd never have had the chance to hear *our* stories. Why don't you all follow me into the kitchen, and I'll tell you some of the tales of the Taggart Inn." Gran had never once mentioned the Taggart being haunted, but Piper was so sincere right now that even he believed her. As she came down the steps, she whispered instructions to him. "Grab every candle and candelabra you can get your hands on and bring them to the kitchen. We'll give them a show to take their minds off missing the tour."

It wasn't long before Piper had filled the kitchen with flickering candlelight. She turned off the overhead lights as she brewed a giant coffeemaker-full of a blend strong enough to melt spoons. Logan brought in extra chairs for the kitchen table so everyone could sit and sober up, while she told them dramatic stories of jilted brides and lonely children and cast-aside lovers who wandered the halls of the Taggart Inn. Her stories were so detailed, and her voice such a dramatic almost-whisper, that she soon had all of them enthralled, including Logan. Even obnoxious Devon seemed spellbound. Piper started baking chocolate chip cookies by candlelight as she talked, filling the kitchen with the cozy aroma.

Logan leaned against the back wall and watched in fascination. The stories, along with the coffee and the sugar jolt from the cookies, were lowering their guests' intoxication level. Eventually, other guests joined them as they returned from the real Ghostwalk. The candlelit kitchen was soon standing room only. Piper kept weaving ghost tales as she baked more cookies. If all those stories were true, it was a wonder anyone could walk down the halls of this place without bumping into an apparition.

It was after midnight by the time the last of the guests wandered up to their rooms, raving about what a wonderful evening it had been. Piper had kept them all in the palm of her hand for hours. But she'd started giving him darting glances of panic about an hour ago. He saw the exhaustion etched around her eyes.

He suggested everyone follow him to the parlor for a glass of brandy to fortify their courage for the night ahead. He got a laugh, even from the Rochester group, who were substantially more subdued and sober now. He knew Gran had tiny liqueur glasses in the cupboard, and he also knew where she hid the cognac. He limited everyone to one small glass, so no one would be getting drunk all over again. And they'd be out of Piper's hair so she could get the kitchen reorganized for the next morning. She mouthed a relieved *thank you* as he ushered everyone out.

Once everyone had gone up to bed, he gathered the empty glasses on a tray and made his way to the kitchen. The glasses rattled and clinked dangerously as he walked. Good thing he'd never tried to make it as a waiter. He turned and gently pushed the kitchen door open with his hip.

Piper hadn't bothered to turn on the lights. All but a few of the candles had been extinguished. She was sitting at the table, still wearing the gingham apron she'd donned earlier. Her arms were folded on the table. Her head rested on her arms, golden hair falling free around her shoulders. Her eyes were closed. She was sound asleep.

He stood there, propping the door with his hip, holding the tray of crystal, and took in the view. Logan had seen some pretty incredible sights in his travels. The northern lights flaming through the sky over the North Sea. Hurricane waves lashing at tanker ships in a rhythmic dance of survival and power. Slow-motion sunsets over the Gulf. A school of fifty dolphins making the water boil as they leaped and frolicked next to the boat on the way out to a rig in Malaysia.

But he knew, without a doubt, that he'd never seen anything as beautiful as Piper Montgomery sleeping at a candlelit kitchen table. Not just pretty to look at, but beautiful in a way that shook him to his core. It made no sense. He wasn't a settling-down kinda guy. He was a rolling stone, like his dad—although he liked to think he was less of a dreamer. But then again, maybe not. Because seeing Piper sleeping there, all pink and gold and soft and clever and strong... Well, the sight made him dream some dreams, for sure.

The crystal rattled on the tray again, reflecting the rattling of his foolish heart. He set the tray down, letting the door close quietly behind him. Gran was right.

Pretty little single moms were *not* his type. Especially ones who lived in pretty pink fairy-tale houses in a town full of other fairy-tale houses. This wasn't the place for him. Rendezvous Falls was picket fences and permanence. Logan wanted new sights and adventure. At least, he had until tonight. Tonight, he was thinking picket fences might not be so bad.

He walked over and knelt at Piper's side, resting his hand softly on her shoulder. She started and sat up, blinking in confusion.

"Did I fall asleep? What time is it?" She went to stand, but his hand was still on her, holding her there.

"Relax. You were only out a few minutes. Get your bearings before you stand up." He removed his hand and immediately regretted it. He wanted to be touching her. *No. Nope. Bad idea.* Her eyes were a little unfocused, as if she wasn't sure where she was or why. He grinned. "You were a hero tonight, Piper. Where did all those ghost stories come from? 'Cause if this place is really that haunted, I'm getting a hotel room somewhere."

Her pink lips slid into a soft smile. "When Ethan was younger, he *loved* ghost stories. He loved all kinds of stories, really. Wizards. Ghosts. Knights of old. I'd read to him every night, and sometimes he'd make up his own stories. I just I dipped into that well and pulled up whatever I could think of, and adjusted the stories to fit the inn."

Smart girl. Logan ruffled her hair with his hand. "Well, between the stories, the coffee and the cookies, you saved the night." She was staring at him wide-eyed, her lips parting. Then he realized…he'd just run his hand across her head, affectionately messing her hair. What a stupidly intimate thing to do. And damn if his hand wasn't still there, cupping the back of her head, fingers moving in her silky hair. He stood abruptly, stepping back and staring at his misbehaving hand. "I... I'm sorry. I guess we're both tired and loopy. That was... weird. I don't know why I did that..." Who was he kidding? He'd done it because he couldn't resist touching her. "It won't happen again..." Actually, if he had anything to do with it, it would. "Please don't be offended..." *Please tell me you liked it.*

Piper stood too, looking up at him with a bemused smile. "It's...um...okay. Like you said, we're both loopy tonight." As if proving her point, she swayed a little on her feet. And damn if he wasn't touching her again, reaching out to rest his hand on her hip. Her eyes flared wide, and darkened to almost cobalt in the candlelight. She ran the tip of her tongue across her lower lip, and Logan had to close his eyes to hold the heat in. This little spark between them was just that—a little spark that didn't mean anything. He was a man. She was a fascinating woman. There was candlelight. Of course they'd both feel a little kick of desire. That didn't mean they had to give in to it.

Piper seemed to come to the same realization, straightening abruptly and brushing past him. She slapped at the light switch on the wall like it was a fire alarm, setting the room ablaze with light, blinding them both for a moment. She bent over and blew out the candles on the table. "Sitting around in candlelight didn't help our loopiness."

Watching you put your lips together to blow out those candles isn't helping, either.

He looked away and took a deep breath. If she could pretend there wasn't an instant where they'd created a little spark of magic just then, so could he. *Single mom.*

Single mom. He frowned. That didn't raise the same alarm that it used to.

"You've had a long day, Piper. Go home and get some sleep." He looked across the parking lot to the pink house at the very edge of the streetlight's glow. "Is Ethan watching Lily?"

"No." She reached for her jacket. "I knew it would be a busy weekend, so I asked their grandparents to take them until Ghostwalk is over."

"So you're alone in the house? Hang on, I'll walk you over."

She tipped her head to the side. "I'm okay being alone in my own house, Logan." She grinned. "It's not haunted or anything." Her smile faded just a bit as she hesitated. Her eyes were dark and intense. "And…I think it might be best if you stayed here."

His heart jumped. She *had* felt it. Something *had* just happened between them. But what? And what should they do about it? Piper didn't seem to be having any problem with that decision. She shrugged on her jacket and headed out with a quick wave good-night. He stood on the porch and watched her until she reached her door. She looked over her shoulder, and he was pretty sure he saw a smile on her face when she caught him standing there. She went in, then flicked the light once to let him know she was safe and sound. If only he could say the same. Because he felt wildly out of his depth, and more than a little nervous about what had just happened. Nervous…and excited.

The hell if Piper Montgomery hadn't just rattled his damn cage like no one had before.

CHAPTER ELEVEN

PIPER GRIMACED WHEN Ethan appeared at the bottom of the stairs Halloween night in full zombie costume, complete with gruesome gashes and a missing hand. She'd relented on letting him go out for Halloween, with the condition that he take his sister with him. After much moaning and groaning, he'd agreed. But only after negotiating to get a half hour after that with his buddies. Her son was getting good at this grown-up business.

"Please tell me your sister isn't going to freak out when she sees you."

Ethan almost smiled, then caught himself. But his eyes still twinkled with humor, making her heart swell.

"Chill, Mom. Lily helped paint the blood on me."

Oh, goody.

"That doesn't make me feel a whole lot better." She reached out to ruffle his greased-up hair. He ducked away, but not before she saw another smile teasing the corner of his mouth.

"And your sister's costume is…?"

Ethan shrugged as if he had no idea what she was talking about, flashing her a playful grin. It had been a long time since she'd seen playfulness on his face, and her heart beat a little faster. Her boy was still in there, hidden behind that carefully constructed wall of his.

She knew Logan had probably helped, showing Ethan how to change the oil in Iris's old car, and how to check everything on Piper's compact. The two guys were already talking about how to fix the creepy lights in the basement, and Ethan told her just that morning that they'd "decided" on LEDs. He'd said it in a way that made him sound so grown-up and confident.

Ethan and Lily had insisted on surprising Piper with their costumes tonight. Susan and Roger had given Lily that pink butterfly costume, but Lily hadn't been thrilled with it. In a rare burst of brotherly affection, Ethan had offered to help.

"How upset can I expect your grandparents to be about Lily's getup?"

He slid her a sideways look. "A little. Maybe."

"Momma!" Lily appeared at the top of the stairs, hands on her hips and head held high. Piper bit back her laughter and gave her a bright smile after winking at Ethan. The only acknowledgment of the act was a slight nod of his head. It was enough, and it warmed Piper's heart all over again.

As Lily marched down the stairs, Piper took in her costume, which clearly had *started* as a butterfly. Ethan had strapped one of his old toy swords to Lily's waist, and had given her some sort of helmet. She was wearing boots. And an eyepatch. And butterfly wings that had been sprayed with silver glitter. She spread her arms out and smiled up at Piper.

"I'm a butterfly who got poisoned by knuckle raidation and it turned me into a superhero!"

It took a moment for Piper to get it. "Nuclear radiation?" Lily nodded enthusiastically, making the helmet rock up and down.

Ethan had outdone himself. Lily wasn't exactly a butterfly. But she wasn't going trick-or-treating as Deadpool, either, so Piper considered it a win.

They started at the Montgomerys' house. Piper figured it was best to get the kids' grandparents out of the way first, so she could relax for the rest of the evening. Susan was a lot less amused than Roger was, but it wasn't as bad as Piper had feared. Roger declared Ethan's zombie a "classic" and praised his originality with Lily's costume, so there wasn't much Susan could do at that point other than smile and take pictures.

Piper drove them back to their own neighborhood after that, and let them walk with the other kids while she watched from the corner. Ethan held Lily's little hand in his, and Piper was suddenly blinking away tears. Despite everything that had happened, the kids were doing okay.

They came back to her with their bags full, and she joined them for one last stop at the inn. She'd left Logan in charge of handing out candy at the front door. She conveniently *forgot* to tell him how crazy it was going to be, although he may have gotten a clue when she showed him the stack of ten-pound bags of candy sitting by the door.

She and the kids found him sitting on the steps of the Taggart Inn, leaning back against the porch post with his eyes closed. As soon as he heard their steps on the sidewalk, he'd sat up and reached for the candy like a robot.

"Relax." She laughed. "It's just us."

Logan gave Lily and Ethan fistfuls of candy, and then he and Piper went inside with Lily while Ethan jogged off to join his friends waiting on the corner. Within ten minutes, Lily was sound asleep on the sofa in the parlor. Piper accepted a glass of brandy from Logan and sat in the wingback chair, kicking off her shoes and tucking her feet under herself. She smiled at him as he sat in a chair opposite hers.

"How was your night?"

He choked on his drink and started laughing, then lowered his voice to keep from waking Lily.

"Oh, it was pretty much the way you think it was, you witch. Two hours of nonstop children screaming 'trick-or-treat' at me and demanding candy. It was like being robbed at gunpoint over and over. How many kids does this town *have,* anyway?"

She smirked. "It's a wonderful place for families."

"Yeah, I'm starting to get that." He rubbed the back of his neck. "I can see why your husband wanted to raise your children here."

The personal comment surprised her, but he'd been in her home. He'd seen the pictures of Tom. She stood to check on Lily, pulling a soft throw over her. As she returned to her chair, she looked over at Logan.

"Actually, we had no intention of living in Rendez-vous Falls."

"Really? Then how...?"

It should probably feel weird to discuss Tom with Logan, especially after that little moment they had Saturday after Ghostwalk. But it felt...okay. Not only because Logan was easy to talk to, but because lately she'd felt less heartbreak when thinking about Tom, and more gratitude that she'd had him in her life.

"I was pregnant with Lily when Tom deployed. I'd been through one deployment alone, and another when Ethan was four. Tom didn't want me dealing with an eight-year-old and an infant all by myself." She took a sip of her drink, staring into the amber liquid swirling in the glass. "I told him I'd have support from other families if I stayed on base at Camp Lejeune, but he was so worried, which wasn't like Tom. It was almost as if he knew something was going to happen."

Logan frowned. "He just didn't know it was going to happen to him." He shifted in the chair before meeting her gaze. "I'm really sorry."

"Thank you. The plan was for me and Ethan to stay with the Montgomerys, and I'd have Lily here in Rendezvous Falls. When Tom's tour was done, we'd go back to North Carolina or wherever the marines sent us."

There was a beat of silence. So many plans had been made back then. Logan stared at Lily asleep under the throw, his voice barely above a whisper.

"Lily said her father saw her once?"

It was the last time Piper had seen her husband alive. They were *giddy* with joy. They had their perfect family—a happy little boy and a sweet baby girl. Tom had told her he never knew there could be joy as deep as what he felt in that moment, with them all together. She'd teased him that Afghanistan was making him soft. They'd laughed. And then he was gone. Forever.

A hand landing on her arm made her gasp in surprise. She hadn't even seen Logan move to kneel at her side. His eyes were dark with concern.

"Christ, I'm sorry. I didn't mean to go digging so hard." His mouth twisted into a grimace of self-recrimination. "You're still grieving him. I shouldn't be…" He searched her face, and she realized she was crying. She quickly brushed the tears away, then looked into his eyes again. Her heart raced, then steadied. There was a tenderness in his face that made her feel surprisingly safe. This rambling man trapped in Rendezvous Falls until Christmas was the last person she expected to be opening her heart to like this. She shook her head, blowing out a steadying breath.

"No. *I'm* sorry." She rubbed her eyes, which were still overflowing. "It's not just about losing Tom. It's about losing who we were as a family. When Lily was born, our life was…perfect. And then it wasn't." She straightened in the chair and gave him a shaky smile. "I'm okay. He's been gone four years. I'm okay." A shudder went through her as she realized how true that was. Maybe not yet, but she *would* be okay.

Logan patted her arm, his voice rough. "Yeah, you are okay."

They stared at each other, with him still kneeling at her side, and Piper felt like she was falling into his golden eyes. With a start, she realized she'd leaned toward him as if pulled by a magnet. She gently moved her arm away, lost in confusion. What did it mean that she could talk about Tom with this man who made her feel like more of a whole woman than she'd felt since Tom's death?

Not sure she was ready to know the answer, she stood. Logan rose with her, his hand resting on the small of her back. That touch—the light feel of his hand—

made her want to lean into him again. And not stop this time. She looked up and realized he was thinking the same thing. She could see it in the heat of his gaze. Panicked, she stepped away, ignoring his knowing smile.

Whatever had happened just now was exactly what had happened the other night in the kitchen. Things just…stopped…when they got too close. It was dangerous. It was tempting.

She looked over at her daughter and inhaled. God, it felt like her first breath in hours. Her priorities fell back into their proper order. She was a *mom*. Logan was a guy who traveled the world. Actively embracing someone so…*temporary*…was not a responsible choice for her or her children. She looked back to Logan and smiled. "I'd better get my little superhero back home and make sure Ethan returns on time as promised." She leaned over and slid the blanket off Lily, who just mumbled something and rolled away from her.

"I'll get her." Logan gently brushed her aside and lifted Lily in his arms. The sight was enough to make her pulse go erratic all over again, and it took a moment before she thought to grab the blanket and tuck it around her daughter. Her *daughter*. Piper had no business reacting to this guy when she had a daughter. A son. A *family* that needed her full attention. But this man, cradling her child in his arms, and gazing down at Lily's sleeping face with something so close to awe… Well, it filled Piper's chest with warmth and affection. She huffed out a small laugh of disbelief. She was losing her mind.

"I suppose I should object and insist on carrying her myself."

He grinned, his eyes twinkling with humor. "But you won't because it's a long walk and she's heavier than she looks." He nodded toward the door. "Lead the way."

Piper tried to take Lily from him once they were inside her house, but Logan insisted on carrying her upstairs and to her room. They came back out into the hallway, and the space suddenly felt very small. Logan filled it, physically and in every other way possible. They stood for an awkward moment, watching each other in silence. Waiting to see who would make the first move. He had no way of knowing, of course, but they were standing right outside her room. He glanced toward the door, which she realized was…open. So, yeah. He knew exactly where they were. The four-poster unmade bed, with a pile of lacy pillows and a flowered bedspread, was clearly not Ethan's.

Their eyes met again, and his gaze went from warmly amused to flat-out heat. She was out of practice at this, but she knew heat when she saw it. His hand landed on her hip.

Logan's hand. Was on. Her hip.

She should move away. But she couldn't make herself do it. So they stood there. And then they were closer. How had that happened? Her hand rose and rested on his chest. She could feel his heart pounding rapidly under her fingers. In rhythm with her own. Her bed— her *bed*!—was right there…

"Mom!" The side door crashed open downstairs. She jumped away from Logan so fast her back hit the wall behind her. Holy shit, of all the stupid things! She'd just been thinking about pulling a man into her bedroom when her *children* were home! Maybe she was more out of practice at this than she thought, because that was about as stupid a thing as she'd ever done. Or almost done.

She couldn't even look at Logan. She turned away and called down to Ethan.

"Uh… I'm upstairs…changing…cleaning…" She gave Logan a wild-eyed look, but he was too busy biting his own knuckle to keep from laughing to help. What could she possibly say to keep Ethan from coming up here and finding a *man*? "I'm…shaving my legs!"

"Geez…gross overshare, Mom."

"Oh…ha ha…yeah." She couldn't even form a complete sentence, but her son didn't seem to notice. Logan, on the other hand, was shaking with laughter. She smacked his arm as she called back down to Ethan. "Hey…why don't you use the big TV for a while?" That would keep him away from the side door. "As…you know…a thank-you for being such a good big brother?"

"Okay. Cool."

Normally she'd never let him do that on a school night, but she was happy to give him permission because it moved him to the front of the house. Which meant Logan might get out without being seen.

And he did. Barely. He was out the door with a whispered goodbye. And a kiss. Logan leaned down and *kissed* her on the way by. On the cheek, but still. Before she could even react, he was gone. Her son would never know she'd had a man upstairs. She slumped against the wall by the door, her fingers on her cheek. If she had the heart attack she felt was threatening, it would serve her right for being so ridiculous.

Sneaking a man out of her house like a teenager. And wondering what it would be like to have him stay.

LOGAN YANKED SO hard on the bedsheet in Room Five that it came free from the other side. He let out a low streak of curse words. He'd been furious with himself for days. Of all the stupid, juvenile things to do, he'd made a move on Piper. In her *house*. Christ, what an idiot he was.

But damn it, she'd been standing there, all tender and tired and sweet. He could see her bed, rumpled and soft and inviting. Just like Piper. And he'd reached out and pulled her in. She hadn't resisted. In fact, she'd reached up and put her hand on his chest, setting his heart on fire. For just a moment there, she'd been thinking the same exact thing he'd been thinking. Until reality came crashing back in the form of her teenage son.

Ethan was a sharp reminder for both of them of why they were a bad idea. She had a family. A *complicated* family. And she sure as hell didn't want men in her house while her children were there. Now things were… weird. Piper wasn't avoiding him, exactly. But there was a new tension that hadn't been there before. Just when they'd settled into working together as a good team and having some fun, he'd blown it by caving to his attraction to her.

Shit, he'd even kissed her. On the *cheek*. What the hell was up with that high school move? Had he chickened out from kissing her for real? Or had that touch of his lips to her soft skin been exactly what he needed at the moment?

He finished making the bed and headed downstairs

to check the laundry. Piper was cleaning up the kitchen after breakfast. From here on out, every weekend was fully booked and the town would be hopping with holiday events, including house tours and some "Victorian Holiday" thing she'd tried to explain. He had to give this little town credit—they knew how to market themselves.

One of Iris's friends was coming in the front entrance when he got downstairs. She was one of the few he could put a name to right away, since he'd just seen her last week while visiting Gran. Helen Russo owned Falls Legend Winery up on the hill. They supplied the wine Gran set out for guests in the parlor every night. Two nights ago, he'd met her winery manager, Luke Rutledge, for a few beers at the Purple Shamrock. They'd met when Luke delivered a couple cases of wine to the inn. They'd shared a few laughs at the bar over small-town adventures. Who was in trouble for drinking too much. Who got caught in the wrong bed by his wife last week. Who flirted with the wrong girl and got their face slapped at the Shamrock last week. Turned out small-town gossip wasn't all that different from oil-rig gossip.

Logan had found himself telling Luke about the matchmaking fiasco with Kat Gifford. Luke had a good laugh over that, and confirmed the so-called book club Gran was part of had branched out into *creating* romance instead of just reading about it.

"Oh, hi, Logan!" Helen smiled up at him. She was around Piper's height, but her figure was more rounded. She had salt-and-pepper hair and friendly eyes that didn't appear to be scheming anything dangerous at the moment. "Iris asked me to pick up the winter planning book from Piper so she could review the calendar. I'm sure your grandmother knows that book by heart by now, but she's getting so restless being cooped up all this time."

"My grandmother's always restless."

Helen nodded, adjusting her purse strap on her shoulder. "That's for sure! That brain of hers never stops going. Is her fever down today?"

Logan nodded. The mild infection had slowed Gran's recovery a bit. "The doctor said the antibiotics are doing the trick. Fair warning if you're driving up there today—she's in a mood." Gran had nearly taken his ear off this morning on the phone when he suggested she needed to be patient. Helen laughed.

"When *isn't* she in a mood? I'd better get going. Piper said she'd have the binder ready for me on the parlor sideboard." Logan watched her walk away and almost asked her what made the book club think it was a good idea to match him and Kat. But he thought better of it. He'd already given his grandmother a lecture over the embarrassing episode. He went to the laundry room and took the towels out of the dryer.

The truth was, if he hadn't been her client, Kat *would* be his usual type. Sharp. Bold. Independent. Probably not afraid of a quick affair with no strings attached. Sounded like his perfect mate. He took the stack of still-warm towels and headed for the stairs. Funny how the only woman on his mind these days was a single mom in a ruffled apron with golden hair and sky-blue eyes.

Helen was back in the lobby, talking with Tracy Evans. Tracy was from LA, and was staying in Room Ten this week while she visited some friends. She seemed nice enough, if a little…out-there. She was a mix of edgy city girl and bohemian artist, with her tight, short skirts, black fingernail polish and strawberry-blond hair falling free down her back. This morning she had little braids running through it, pulled back and tied together with ribbon. Helen was talking to her about another of Gran's friends, Lena Fox, who was a local artist.

"Lena mainly does pottery, but she also does some amazing wire jewelry with crystals and stuff." Helen was admiring Tracy's chunky rings. "I'll give you her address…oh, hi again, Logan!"

He nodded toward them before moving on. "Ladies."

He got to the top of the landing and looked back to find both women watching him. Helen was leaning in close to Tracy and whispering. Tracy's eyes were on him instead of Helen. He smiled—*be nice to the guests*—then went back to work.

Later that night, he was just dozing off on the sofa when the business phone rang in Gran's apartment. He removed Mr. Whiskers from his stomach, which seemed to be the cat's favorite sleeping spot, and grabbed the phone. He was hoping it was Piper needing some help, needing him. But no. It was Tracy Evans in Room Ten. She said there was a strange noise in her room. Would he come check? Logan looked at the time. Almost eleven. Guests had to be kept happy, so he told her he'd be there in a few minutes, after he grabbed his toolbox.

He wasn't at all prepared when the door opened. Bohemian Tracy was gone. Tonight she was in a lacy blue robe that was loosely tied at the waist, falling open to reveal a very short, very low-cut matching nightgown.

Her hair was falling in shiny waves over her shoulders. She was wearing makeup. Not something he'd usually notice, but this was…a lot. Heavy mascara and apricot lips. At eleven o'clock at night. She did *not* look like a woman getting ready for bed. At least not for sleeping purposes. When Logan stepped in the room, he glanced around, wondering if maybe she'd brought someone up with her. But no. It was just her and a nearly empty bottle of wine. The door closed behind him, and he turned, his stomach falling.

Tracy was leaning back against the door in a film noir pose. All of her thick hair was cascading over one shoulder, and she very definitely batted her eyelashes at him with a come-hither look.

Aw, shit.

Logan cleared his throat loudly, making sure he sounded as businesslike as possible.

"You said there was a strange noise?"

She shook her head. "I thought there was something wrong with the radiator, but it's fine now. It's all warmed up and purring perfectly, don't you think?"

Yeah—no innuendo in those words at all. She was leaning against the door, blocking his only escape, in a pose that clearly said *do me.* He was trapped. With a guest who wanted a lot more service than he ever intended to give. Piper had never mentioned this situation in any of her many lectures on running the inn. The thought gave him pause. Had a male guest ever put *her* in this position? His fingers curled tightly, and then he shook them free again.

What the hell was wrong with him? Here he was with a beautiful, nearly naked woman clearly giving him an open invitation. And he didn't feel even a twitch of interest.

"Um…okay, Miss Evans. I'm glad it's all set. I'll just be going, then." He started to move forward, but she didn't budge. It's not like she could hold him against his will. But he had no way of getting out of here without going by her, and he was half afraid she'd jump him if given the chance. He chewed the inside of his lip, trying to think of a diplomatic way to extricate himself. "It's late, and I have a busy day tomorrow. I'm sure you want to get some sleep, too, so I need to go." *Right now.*

"Do you really need to leave, Logan? You could stay." She pushed away from the door and stepped toward him. Heavy perfume filled the air around her. He moved away, edging to the side and hoping for a chance to get to the door and escape. But Tracy was on to him, and came even closer. "Mrs. Russo told me you were here all alone, taking care of your grandmother. That's so sweet. She said you were single and didn't know many people in town. Same as me." Oh, boy.

He raised his hands, sidling toward the door. "Uh… I don't know what Mrs. Russo told you…" If his grandmother thought he'd been angry about Kat, just wait until he talked to her about *this*. Gran and her gray-haired biddies were messing around where they didn't belong. "Tracy, I'm not looking for…anything…right now. It's not that you're not beautiful. You *are*. But I can't…" His hand touched the doorknob and he let out a sigh of relief. "I'm flattered. Really. But I need to go. Right now."

And he did, leaving Tracy Evans standing in the center of the room in all her lace and glossy lipstick. She was a beautiful woman, if a little scary. Another place, another time…he might have accepted the invitation for a quick shag. But there hadn't even been a blip of a spark for him in that room tonight. None.

It was the complete opposite of what had happened in Piper's house, standing outside her bedroom, when he couldn't stop himself from touching her. From wanting her.

CHAPTER TWELVE

PIPER STOOD IN the hallway outside the open library door, listening. She'd just come back from visiting Iris and running a few errands for her when she heard Tracy and Logan talking about "last night." He wouldn't be so stupid as to sleep with a guest, would he? Her chest ached at the thought, which was silly. But as she listened, it became clear Logan *hadn't* done anything. He kept saying it wasn't Tracy's fault. That he just wasn't "in the market" right now. Funny…he'd seemed in the market the other night, when he tugged Piper close right outside her bedroom door. Tracy was rattling on, apologizing for acting so forward, saying she'd been drinking…asking for another chance. It sounded as if Logan had navigated a delicate situation at the inn last night.

Then Tracy said it was Helen Russo who'd suggested Logan was…available. Piper couldn't imagine nice little Helen Russo—who seemed to be the most levelheaded of Iris's book club—encouraging a *guest* to go after Logan. Poor Logan was trying so hard to let Tracy down easy, but she just wasn't taking the hint.

Piper looked at the small foil bag in her hand, which held the ring Iris had asked her to pick up. She'd dropped it at the jeweler for repair before her injury. Piper had an idea that was just crazy enough to work. She quietly slipped the emerald ring out of its velvet bag and put it on her left hand. Where her wedding band used to be.

"Look, Logan…" Tracy was still going on in the library. "I know last night was weird, but…"

"It's okay, Tracy. Forget it ever happened. *Please.*"

"But I don't want to forget! I know I came on too strong. I'd had some wine. But I felt a connection… didn't you? Last week, my psychic told me I was close to meeting the *one*. And then I saw you, and that lady said you were looking to settle down. I think…maybe we're fated to be together, you know?"

Piper shook her head in disbelief, wondering why Helen told Tracy that story. Logan's voice sounded pained.

"Tracy, you're a nice woman, and I'm sure you'll find 'the one' and make him happy. But I think Mrs. Russo gave you the wrong idea. I'm not…"

Piper put a bright smile on her face and swept into the room, sliding her arm around Logan's waist. He jumped, and she gave him a pinch of warning to keep quiet.

"*There* you are, sweetheart! I thought I'd lost you!" She flashed her smile in Tracy's direction. "Sorry to interrupt, Tracy, but I get nervous when my fiancé disappears on me."

"Your fiancé?" Tracy's face fell so far and so quickly that Piper felt a stab of pity for her, but she reminded herself that she was here to save Logan. He went still and silent at her side, looking down in wide-eyed confusion. There was a quick flicker of heat in his eyes when she looked up, and her stomach flipped. She pulled her gaze from his and answered Tracy, holding up her left hand and flashing the ring.

"Yes! It's all so new that I'm still in shock."

There was a rumble of laughter in Logan's voice as he reached out for her hand to examine the ring. "Yeah, me, too. Totally in shock."

His other arm wrapped around her shoulder, playing along with her game. As usual, his touch left her stuttering.

"Yes…um…shock. But we're…soul mates, you know? It was written in the stars. And here we are. Together."

She smiled up at Logan, just to really sell it, but as soon as their eyes met, everything shifted. She gripped the back of his shirt in her hand to keep herself upright. He must have felt her tremor, because he tugged her in close. Apparently he wanted to really sell it too, because he lifted his hand and traced his fingers across her cheek. Her lips parted, and his eyes went dark as night.

"Oh!" Tracy's voice made them both jump. They'd forgotten she was there. "Oh, I…had no idea. He didn't say…"

Logan cleared his throat. "Uh…yeah… I didn't want to make you feel bad, you know?"

Tracy held up her hand to stop him, color draining from her face. "I get it. I'm…happy…um…happy for you." She sounded as if she was trying to convince herself. She drew her shoulders back and gave them a tight smile. "I'll just go…"

She turned away, and Piper, despite the distracting sizzle under her skin everywhere Logan was touching her, felt sympathy for the woman.

"Tracy, did I hear you mention a psychic?" Tracy looked back and nodded. "You should visit Wolf Moon Crystals up on Route 14, south of town. I haven't been, but I've heard she does readings and sells all kinds of spiritual crystals and things." Piper said a quick prayer that Father Joe at St. Vincent's wouldn't learn of her recommending a tarot reader.

Tracy's smile relaxed. "Thanks. And congratulations."

"For wha..." Logan squeezed her shoulder and she caught herself. "Oh, yes. Thanks. We're not really making it public yet, because we haven't told our families. But when I heard his voice just now, I couldn't contain myself." She fluttered her lashes at Logan, and felt his body shaking with suppressed laughter.

Tracy left, closing the library door quietly behind her. Logan's arm was still heavy on Piper's shoulder. He held her hand with his other arm, twirling the emerald on her finger. She didn't move. There were no more witnesses who needed to be fooled. And yet...here they were. In the center of the library. Bodies close, staring at each other in silence.

The room smelled of lemon oil and old books. Until right now, she'd never thought of that as a sexy smell. She had a feeling it was a scent she'd dream about for a long, long time.

Logan broke the spell first, lifting his hand to cup her cheek. He frowned at his own hand, as if it had disobeyed him, and slid it behind her head to tug softly on her hair instead. His mouth slid into a crooked grin. "Piper Montgomery saves the day yet again. I'm glad you're such a quick thinker. It's bad enough letting a woman down easy, but when she's a guest, it's all kinds of weird. The ring was a great touch."

They were facing each other now, and Piper wasn't sure how that had happened. She could barely breathe, too busy anticipating what was coming. Yes, that's what she was feeling. *Anticipation.* For the first time in years, she was nearly trembling with anticipation of a man's kiss. She blinked in surprise. She wanted Logan to kiss her. And from the soft heat in his eyes, he wanted that too. She tried to regroup.

"Your grandmother asked me to pick the ring up from the jewelers. I overheard Tracy pressing her case, and the plan wrote itself. Sorry about the fake engagement."

His smile faded, but the warmth deepened in his gaze. "I'm not."

Nervous laughter bubbled up. It had been a long damn time since she'd stood in the circle of a man's arms. "You should be. If you think I'm a taskmaster as an inn manager, you should have seen me as a wife…" Thick silence filled the room. *Damn it.* Of all the times to bring up her late husband. She shook her head sharply, chasing Tom out of it. "I mean… I… Damn it. I ruined the moment, didn't I?"

Logan studied her, his head tipped to the side. His hand slid back to cup her face again. His palm was calloused and hard, but the touch lit her skin on fire. His head lowered a little bit more, coming ever closer. His voice was as rough, and as incendiary, as his touch.

"That's up to you, Piper. Do you *want* this moment? Or do you want it to stop?" Closer now, his breath warm on her face. "Are you ready for this?" His eyes were right above hers, and she tipped her head back to maintain the connection. Did she just push up on her tiptoes? She must have, because her nose brushed against his. His arm tightened around her. They had full body contact now. She felt a quiver low in her belly. She was tired of fighting it. She let her desire blossom there, hot and needy. Was she a widow? Yes. Was she a mom? Yes. But she was also a woman—a role she hadn't played for far too long.

Her hands slid up his sinewed arms to rest on his rock-hard shoulders. Her own voice shocked her—low, sultry, and strong. "I don't know if I'm ready. But there's only one way to find out. Kiss me, Logan."

He groaned, his hand trembling on her skin, and she braced herself. But he didn't pounce. Instead, he swept his lips across her forehead. Then butterfly-soft kisses on her eyelashes as her eyes fell shut. Across the apples of her cheeks. The tip of her nose. The very corner of her mouth. She finally couldn't take it anymore, turning her head to find his mouth with hers, almost whimpering with need.

And still, he wouldn't be rushed. He held her there, lips pressed against hers, without moving a muscle. Her eyes swept open to discover him staring back. She could see herself reflected there, but beyond that, she saw Logan. His need was as strong as hers, but he was holding back. And that just wasn't going to do at all. Her hand moved higher, fingers digging into his thick hair and pulling him in. Her tongue brazened a route along his lips, and with a muffled curse he answered, kissing her hard.

His lips were demanding. Controlling. Capturing

her, but giving her the freedom to respond. And she did. Their heads turned and twisted together as their mouths connected, parting for snatches of breath, then colliding again. His tongue pushed past hers to be the first to claim foreign territory, and she surrendered with a sigh, holding him there until he growled again. Then it was her turn to push in, getting drunk on the taste of him. Drunk on this. Kissing a man. No, not just any man. On kissing *Logan*.

She tried to push up farther, to connect harder, and realized her feet were no longer on the ground. He'd lifted her into the air, and now they were eye to eye. Their mouths parted, breaths coming fast and heavy as they stared at each other. His hand was cupped on her behind, and he gave a squeeze before slowly lowering her to the floor, her body sliding against his. Her only thought, as crazy as it was, was that there were too many clothes. Too many layers between them. Her fingers moved to the buttons on his shirt, but he stopped her with a low laugh.

"Easy, girl. Remember where we are."

He kissed her again, more gently this time, as if trying to bring her down from her frenzied state. And it worked. His lips moved against hers slowly, his hands sliding up and down her back in a steady rhythm that slowed her heart rate. He was right. She needed to remember where they were. The library. At the inn. In the middle of the afternoon. One more kiss, and she stepped back. At least, she tried to step back, but in reality, she barely moved. Her naughty fingers were still in his hair. He raised his head and smiled.

"You okay now?"

Her cheeks blazed with heat. She'd reacted to that kiss like a desperate woman who hadn't been kissed for a very long time. Which was exactly what she was. Logan must feel like he'd just been attacked.

"I… I'm sorry." She tried to smile, but her mouth was trembling. "I'm a little out of practice…"

"Hey." Logan's fingers lifted her chin until their eyes met. "Do not *ever* apologize for kissing a man like that. And especially don't apologize for kissing *me* like that. Damn, Piper." He surprised her with another soft brush of his lips on hers. "You're fucking irresistible." Another kiss. "I can't stop." She closed her eyes and kissed him back, knowing just how he felt. His hands moved to her waist, and he set her at arm's length this time when he raised his head.

"I can't believe I'm being the practical one here, but…"

She nodded, her hands resting on his forearms. "We're in the library in broad daylight. With guests in the inn." She glanced down at her watch. "And my mother-in-law will be dropping the kids off any minute. Oh, god…" She stepped back, away from his touch.

His shoulders shook with soft laughter. When he saw her puzzled expression, the laughter got louder.

"I can honestly say that's something no woman has ever said to me after we kissed."

Her brows gathered. "That they have kids?"

"No, babe. That they have a mother-in-law."

She started to giggle. It was completely absurd. She was laughing with Logan Taggart. After kissing him. They'd *kissed*.

And she wanted to do it again.

LOGAN FELT LIGHT-HEADED, and the only logical explanation was lack of oxygen. Or being knocked on his ass by a simple kiss. He frowned. Nothing simple about *that* kiss. Piper Montgomery had just rocked his entire world with nothing more than her mouth on his. At first he thought the sensation was the result of all the pent-up chemistry that had been growing between them, building to that moment. But then…it got *better*. And *hotter*. And he got *harder*. So much so that he'd had to stop and catch his breath for a second, doing the multiplication tables in his head to get rid of the erection pressing on the zipper of his jeans. Like an idiot, he'd gone back and kissed her again. And he wouldn't have stopped if they'd been in a less public setting. Wait. Why was she looking sad? What had she been saying?

"That's it, isn't it? My baggage." She sighed. "I knew it would be a problem if I ever started dating again. Here I am bringing up my in-laws, as if you didn't know I'd been married before. Talk about a buzzkill…"

"Whoa, slow down." He gave in to temptation and took her hand, tugging her closer. "Look, I know you were married. And your in-laws are always going to be part of your life, because they're your children's grandparents." He tipped her chin up with his fingers. "Tom is their father. He was your husband. I get it." A rare surge of jealousy rose in his chest over a dead man. "Right now, all we've done is kiss. And that's okay." He kissed her forehead, figuring touching her lips would fan the flames again, and he wasn't feeling all that strong right now. "We're adults. There's no wrong choice as long as it's what we both want."

The problem, of course, was that Logan had no idea

what *he* wanted. Other than Piper in his arms. It was as simple—and as complicated—as that. Her eyes closed, long blond lashes resting on her cheeks. She blew out a breath and nodded.

"Right. Of course. Thank you." She shuddered and stepped away, laughing nervously. "But I have to clarify something." He was glad to see humor in her eyes again. "I will never refer to *that* kiss as 'all we've done is kiss,' because that kiss was…really something."

Logan nodded. Yeah. That kiss…those kisses…all of it. That was most definitely something. Before he could answer, and maybe ask her if they could do it again, the doorknob turned with a squeak. It was a tiny sound, but it seemed to echo in the emotion-saturated library. Piper dashed toward the window before the door swung open and Lily bounced in. Susan Montgomery was right behind her.

He'd given a nice speech to Piper, but the truth was she *did* come with…baggage, for lack of a better word. Any relationship with her, no matter how brief or casual, would be filled with complication. There were kids involved, and he knew diddly-squat about children. Yet here he was, catching Lily in his arms and swinging her high enough to jingle the teardrops on the chandelier, which made her giggle.

"Be careful!" Susan's voice had the same edge it had the last time they'd met. "She's a child, not a stuffed toy."

Lily answered for him. "But Gigi, Logan makes me fly!" Feeling extra playful, and just a little defiant, he flipped her upside down and swept her toward the floor before swinging her back up again. She let out a squeal. "Again, Logan!"

But he could see the thunderclouds gathering in Susan's expression. No need to create *more* complications. He brought Lily to rest on his hip. To his surprise, she slapped her hands on either side of his face and kissed him right on the lips, finishing it off with a big "Mwah!"

Before he could filter himself, he turned toward Piper, laughing.

"What is it with the Montgomery women today?"

Piper's burst of startled laughter was cut short by Susan.

"What does *that* mean?"

Piper straightened, quickly smoothing an innocent expression on her face. "Oh…uh…it's nothing, Susan. I let out a scream earlier when I thought I saw a mouse, so the Montgomery women are being very noisy today." Piper walked over to Logan, resting her hand on Lily's back.

Susan stared at the three of them standing there— Piper, Lily, and Logan. They probably looked like a little family, and she clearly didn't like it, judging from the scowl that passed over her face before she smoothed it away with a careful smile. And a jab.

"Lily's father made Ethan squeal like that when he was little. They played airplane all the time, didn't they, Piper? I'm sure Tom would have done the same with Lily if he'd had the chance." Her sharp eyes fixed on Logan. "Did you serve in the military, Mr. Taggart?"

Well played, Susan.

Logan shook his head. "I did not. I was working on

the rigs by the time I was twenty. But I have friends in the armed forces, particularly the coast guard."

"The coast guard?" She rolled her eyes. "My son was a *marine*."

Logan thought of his friend, Jack, who'd pulled people from rooftops during Katrina and from burning oil rigs in the Gulf. Jack lost his life trying to save some day-sailors whose boat ended up against the rocky coast of Oregon one stormy, icy night. He wanted to point out that dead was dead, no matter what the uniform. But Susan had lost her son. There was no dignity in poking at her wound. He cleared his throat.

"You must have been very proud of him."

Piper took Lily from his arms and walked over to Susan. "We were all proud of Tom, weren't we, Susan?"

Susan nodded, silent. Assessing. Piper moved toward the door, giving him a quick, worried glance. She spoke to Lily. "How was your day, sweetie? Why don't you tell Momma about it while I go make our dinner?" And they were gone, leaving him alone in the room that had changed everything.

The room where Piper Montgomery kissed him.

PIPER SAT IN the cozy booth at the back of the Purple Shamrock bar. Evie sat across from her, and Chantese had just slid in next to her. It was a very rare ladies' night out. Usually Piper refused their invitations, but she desperately needed some girl talk. And she needed to get away from the inn. It felt like her life lately had been reduced to her house, where there were always projects staring her in the face, and the inn, with its own lengthy to-do list. Next up? Christmas decorating. With Logan. *Great*...

"I'm thinking maybe you should have ordered tea instead of wine," Evie said nonchalantly, moving her own wineglass in slow circles on the dark table.

"And why is that?" Piper smiled at the bright orange streak in Evie's hair. It was a nice seasonal touch. Evie was such a free spirit, with her colorful hair and sassy tongue. She was also a responsible business owner and active, if unconventional, leader in the community. She'd just accepted a position on the prestigious Festival Organization Committee, which she loved referring to as the FOCers—with a hard *C*—just to scandalize the older members in the group.

"Well," Evie replied, "tea leaves might answer whatever burning questions you seem to have, staring into your wine like that. Wine is notoriously lousy when it comes to answers. Wine wants to hug you and convince you you're a good dancer. Tea will tell you what to do." Evie shrugged. "Or so they say. But don't you work at a place where you *serve* tea and crumpets?"

Piper smiled. "Sometimes a girl just needs a change of scenery," she said lightly. Because the scenery at the inn was...Logan. She ran into him at every damn turn, and she had no idea how to handle it after that kiss. And he seemed just as hesitant as she was. Regrets? Embarrassed? She wasn't sure. Of his feelings or of hers.

Chantese gave her a pointed look. "Really? I'm thinking the scenery has been mighty fine at the Taggart Inn since Iris's grandson arrived. He's a hottie."

"Shhh!" She looked around, but no one was near their booth. The bar was quiet, but that wasn't surprising on a Wednesday night. That was her only condition on joining her friends for a drink—it couldn't be on a weekend. The inn was too busy. "I'm here to *escape* the inn, not *talk* about him…I mean…it."

"O-kay." Evie pushed her glass aside and leaned forward. "You've officially piqued my curiosity. I barely met him at the tattoo studio. What's he really like?"

Piper closed her eyes in frustration, which didn't help, because all she could see was Logan. His arms around her. Kissing her. Hinting there could be more if she wanted it.

"What's *who* like?" Whitney Foster sat next to Evie, giving a little wave to Chantese and Piper. "Sorry I'm late. We're bracing for another busy weekend at the winery, and I lost track of time setting up the tasting room…"

Evie snorted. "Let me guess—Luke Rutledge was the real reason you lost track of time." Whitney flipped her dark hair behind her shoulder. Piper knew her, but not that well. Tall and willowy—and just as sassy as Evie was—she'd come to Rendezvous Falls that summer to help her aunt save the Falls Legend Winery, and ended up engaged to the winery manager. She'd opened her own bookkeeping firm here, and the business was quickly growing. Even Iris, never one to embrace change, said she might have Whitney do the inn's taxes this year.

Whitney's cheeks blushed deep pink. "I have no idea what you're talking about. We were just…working. And got…distracted…" She raised her hand and waved it to get the bartender's attention. The bartender handed a glass of red wine to a tall, dark-haired man in a flannel shirt. The man delivered the wine to Whitney with an amused gleam in his eye. It was her fiancé, Luke Rutledge. Luke put the wine orders together for the inn.

"Here you go, babe." He kissed the top of Whitney's head as he set down the glass. He glanced around the table. "How are you, ladies?"

Chantese stared at Whitney. "You two are so adorable. You can't even go out with the girls without bringing your sweetie along."

Evie laughed. "Hey, if I had a guy like that, I'd want him with me everywhere, too."

Whitney patted Luke's hand on her shoulder. "What can I say? But really, he came to hang out with some of the guys." She looked up at him and waved her hand. "Off you go. It's girl time."

He shook his head with a laugh. "Yes, ma'am. Have fun."

Whitney sipped her wine and watched Luke walk away. Then her eyes met Piper's, making her squirm in her seat.

"Okay, spill. What's *who* like? Who were you gals talking about?"

Evie put her elbow on the table and rested her chin in her hand, batting her eyes at Piper. "Piper was just getting ready to tell us how much she doesn't want to talk about Logan Taggart."

"Ooh, you mean Iris's grandson? Such a hottie."

Piper couldn't help but groan when Whitney used the same term as everyone else. "A hottie? Seriously?" She gestured between Whitney and Evie. "And aren't both of you women engaged? You're not supposed to be noticing hotties anymore."

"I'm engaged, not blind," Whitney answered over Evie's loud laugh. "And my own personal hottie is so busy with the grape harvest and winemaking and the new hours at the tasting room that I hardly see him these days. That's the real reason I made him come along tonight." She looked over her shoulder to where Luke was sitting, talking to the bartender. Father Joe Brennan from St. Vincent's had joined him, as well as another older man who looked familiar. Piper thought he worked in the wine business, but that described a lot of people in the Finger Lakes.

Evie gave a broad wink. "But I bet you see a lot of him these nights…"

Whitney sat back, brushing off her shoulder with her fingers in a gesture of pride. "Hell, yeah, I do. How about you? Where's *your* hottie this week?"

"Mark's in Nashville doing a mural on Music Row. He'll be home this weekend." Evie straightened and looked at Piper. "And Chantese is single, so we are all hottie-less women right now in urgent need of hottie news. Save us, Piper. What's Logan like? Any man with an entire ocean mural tattooed on his arm, complete with a lighthouse, has to be interesting."

Piper took a sip of her wine. "It's an oil rig, not a lighthouse."

Chantese slapped her hand on the table. "A*ha*! You've *seen* it." Now it was her turn to cup her chin in her hand and give Piper a stare-down. "Spill it, girl."

Piper narrowed her eyes at Evie. "And where did *you* see his tattoos?"

Evie held her hands up in defense. "I told you I saw

him at Kat's studio, remember? Seemed like a good guy."

Whitney nodded. "Luke said the same thing. Not about the tats, but he liked Logan. Logan helped him fix one of the pumps in the fermentation barn last week. I think they came down here for drinks after. Luke said Logan's a magician with machinery." Her mouth slanted into a suggestive grin. "I wonder what else he's a magician with?"

Piper straightened. Logan had magic hands alright. And magic lips, too. But she was here to *forget* that, not talk about it. "May I remind you that I am the mother of two children? No one's getting 'magical' with me." Although for the first time in years, she wished they were. "I don't have room in my life for any magic fingers, unless they're my own."

"Well, hot *damn*, girl!" Chantese pulled back, laughing loudly with the other two women. "And here I thought you were so prim and proper. Never judge a book, right?"

"What does *that* mean?"

"Come on, Piper. You're always so pulled together and focused on your kids and working on your house that I never imagined you…well…you know." She laughed again. "But to be honest, I guess I never look at a woman and imagine them doing that." Her laughter faded, and she put her hand on Piper's arm. "Honey, you know us moms *deserve* happiness just as much as the next woman, right? And I don't mean self-serve."

Piper's cheeks burned. She'd never in her life been in a discussion like this. Whitney raised her glass in a mock toast.

"She's right, you know. Maybe it doesn't mean as much coming from two women who don't have kids…" she glanced at Evie by her side "…but being a mom doesn't mean you can't have a life—and a little magic—with a guy."

Logan had said the next move was up to them. *No wrong choice…* The problem was, she'd already made her choice. She *wanted* to feel his embrace. To feel his lips on hers. Then she thought of how Susan almost caught them, and shuddered.

"You guys know my mother-in-law. Can you imagine her reaction to me dating someone? As far as she's concerned, I'm Tom's wife, and *only* Tom's wife. It's been hard enough getting her to accept my decision to buy my own house and raise my own children. If I bring another man into their lives…" She shuddered at the thought.

Evie nodded. "Susan's had a tough time, and I know she hasn't been easy on you. But you are a grown-ass woman, and those decisions you're making are *yours* to make. Not hers. She can't really expect a thirty-some-year-old woman to remain celibate the rest of her life, can she?"

"I'm thirty-six. And yeah, I'm pretty sure that's exactly what she expects."

"Oh, no, honey." Whitney tsked. "Don't let her keep you from a man like Logan Taggart. No one's saying you have to marry the guy. You said he's leaving after Christmas anyway, right?" She nodded. He'd been adamant that he had no fondness for Rendezvous Falls. "Use your imagination and, you know…get back in the saddle again."

"Get back…" Piper started to laugh. "You're saying I should use Logan for what—a one-night stand?"

Whitney sipped her drink. "Grown-ups do one-night stands all the time. That's what all those swipey phone apps are for. But you wouldn't be swiping right on some stranger. And I'm assuming you *like* the guy or we wouldn't be having this conversation."

"I can't believe we *are* having this conversation!" Piper reached for her purse. She'd promised Ethan she'd be home by ten. "I came here for a nice drink with my friends and a few laughs." She wasn't a woman who sat around in bars discussing her sex life. What if someone heard them?

Evie leaned forward. "Uh-oh. We hit a nerve. You *do* like him. And not just as a hottie. What's going on with you two?"

"Nothing. We're friends. Lily likes him. He's helped me at the house with a few things."

He kissed me…

"Whoa! What?" Chantese leaned over and dropped her voice to a hard whisper. "You two have *kissed*?"

Piper's eyes closed tightly. She'd had no intention of saying those words out loud.

Whitney looked around, lowering her voice. Piper was grateful for their discretion in a situation where she apparently had none. "Have you done more than kiss?"

Piper shook her head. "We just kissed once. It was… unexpected."

Whitney's brows gathered. "Are you saying he kissed you without your perm…"

"No! Nothing like that. I was trying to save him from

a woman…" she looked at Whitney "…a woman your aunt encouraged to come after Logan."

Whitney dropped her head back, staring up at the ceiling and groaning as she slapped her hand to her face. "Oh my *god*. Evie warned me the book club was at it again. I thought they'd give up after me. I'm so sorry." She lifted her hand and looked at Piper, waggling her eyebrows. "But please—tell us all about this rescue kiss!"

She glanced at her watch, then quickly told them the story. Mainly because she needed help working through her feelings about it. Should a thirty-six-year-old mother of two be feeling butterflies at a man's touch? Was that weird? Shameful? Silly?

"None of the above." Whitney answered when Piper had finished. "A hot man just kissed your socks off. Butterflies are the *least* of what you should be feeling."

Evie nodded in agreement. "And that hot man left the door wide open to more if you want it. Commitment-free. And I'm thinking you want it."

Piper stared into her long-emptied wineglass. Everything her friends said was true. And yet…

"I loved my husband."

"Of course you did," Evie reached over to her. "But I can't imagine Tom would want you to be sad and lonely. Don't let his memory keep you from trying to find a little happiness."

"Maybe think of it as an experiment." Whitney sat back, tapping her fingers on the table in thought. "I mean, you've got a nice guy willing to take things further than a stolen kiss. He's not staying in town, so there won't be any weirdness down the road—it's not like you'll bump into each other at the grocery store. As long as you both have the same expectations, why not see how things go? At the very least, you'll be feeling someone *else's* magic fingers instead of just your own." She winked. "And if you decide you're not ready to do it again, that's that. At least you won't be wondering *if* you're ready."

"I agree with Whitney," Evie concurred. "You're obviously hot for each other, so scratch the itch and see what comes of it. You deserve this."

"Hear hear," Chantese agreed.

Piper didn't answer. Just because her heart wanted something, that didn't mean her brain stopped spinning with all the reasons against it. Her children. The Montgomerys. A money pit of a house to deal with. The busy inn. And a first Christmas coming up that had to be perfect. Having a one-night stand with Logan Taggart did nothing to accomplish that. That's what her brain said.

But her heart was plugging its ears and la-la-la-ing loud enough to block any excuses.

CHAPTER THIRTEEN

"Iris, if you don't practice smiling once in a while, that scowl is going to become permanent." Rick Thomas slapped his cards down on Iris's bedside table. "And… that's gin."

"Well, shit, I can't play cards any better than I can walk." Iris dropped her cards and glowered at her friend. "And haven't you heard? It's terribly sexist to tell a woman to smile more."

Rick didn't shrink from her glare. "Right—the gay guy who marched for women's rights with a pussy hat on his head is a sexist. Good luck selling that one, girlfriend."

"Rick has a point," Helen said from behind him. She was sitting by the window, taking up the hem on a pair of slacks for Iris. Helen looked up. "We love you, honey, but you have been a little…salty…lately."

Iris tried to scowl at her, too, then realized she already had a scowl on her face. Hmm. Maybe they had a point. She let out a frustrated sigh.

"I'd like to see either of you stuck in a hospital for a month and see how you'd like it. I want to go home." Her voice cracked on the last word. God, she wanted to go home. She was tired of gray paint and mechanical beds she could never figure out. The other night she'd nearly folded herself up like an envelope when she pushed the wrong button on the controls.

Rick hesitated mid-shuffle. "We know you do, Iris. You live alone and they're not going to release you until you can handle day-to-day functions on your own."

"I'm not alone. Logan is living there."

Helen set her sewing in her lap and gave Iris an earnest look.

"And you want your grandson helping you out of bed and bathing you?"

Iris found she *could* scowl on top of a scowl after all, but Helen wasn't impressed. She just shrugged and returned to her sewing.

Rick finished the shuffle, dealing seven cards to Iris and himself. "I met Logan a few weeks ago, and he's a freakin' giant. I thought I was tall, but he's got me beat. I wonder how he feels living around all your dainty antiques."

Iris couldn't help a little smile. "That's what Piper's daughter calls him—a giant."

Piper had brought Lily with her on a visit the previous week, and all Lily could talk about was Logan helping her fly, and Logan decorating, and Logan helping them in a plumbing emergency. Iris huffed at Rick's other comment.

"Logan and his sister will inherit all those antiques someday—probably sooner rather than later at this point—so he may as well get used to living with them."

"Oh, stop with the sooner-rather-than-later nonsense, Iris." Helen cut the thread with her teeth and tied a knot to finish the new hem. "You feel lousy now, but you'll outlive us all. You're too stubborn not to. The doctor told you you'd be home by the holidays, so just suck it up and do the work and be grateful to have friends like us who put up with you." She stood and held up the navy-blue trousers. "There! You'll be styling in these."

Rick tossed a card and selected another from the pile. "Helen's right, you know. You're lucky to have us."

Iris took the jack of hearts he'd discarded. "You're supposed to be making *me* feel good, not yourselves."

Helen hummed to herself as she folded the pants and put them in the small dresser near the bed. "Your apartment might be the reason he seems to be spending a lot of time in the inn's library."

Rick chuckled. "Poor guy. It's the only room in that place with a hint of testosterone in it. Isn't that where you sicced the hapless guest on him?"

Iris groaned as she took another card. "I still can't believe you did that, Helen. A *guest*!"

Helen waved off the fuss. "Relax. I didn't know she was going to go all femme fatale, but nothing came of it. I just thought the book club might be going in the wrong direction with all the 'tough girls' you were picking. Don't you remember how far off base we were with Whitney?"

The book club's first matchmaking target had been Helen's niece, and Helen was right—they'd tried matching her with a fellow accountant, a college professor, and a medical tech. All educated professionals like Whitney. No one saw that Whitney was falling for Helen's rugged winemaker, Luke.

"That may be, but the point is to keep Logan in Rendezvous Falls. Hooking him up with a woman who doesn't even live here won't do that. And, as I predicted, a sweet young thing didn't interest him. I know my grandson." Iris fanned her cards out on the table. "Gin."

"Shit." Rick sighed. "I've got a hand full of face cards, too. That gives you the game. Again." Rick boxed up the cards and stood. "We've gotta run. We'll be back in a couple days for the book club meeting. Your room is becoming our official new meeting place."

"Oh, hell, I haven't read the book yet." Iris looked at the stack of books Piper had brought her yesterday. "What was it again?"

Rick walked over to the books and slid one out, handing it to Iris. "This one. Cecile keeps whining that we need to do another romance, so I picked an action novel where the two heroes fall in love." He winked. "With each other. I'm not usually a romance fan, but it was pretty damn good."

Helen nodded. "I liked it, too. Those guys were hot! Should make for some lively discussion on Friday. Iris, *you* should pick the next book."

Iris did her best not to scowl. She hated to think she might be here long enough to host the December meeting, but that damn infection had really slowed things down. The pain was easing, but physical therapy wiped her out. Helen was right, though—she was lucky to have these loyal friends. She nodded and smoothed her face as much as she could.

"I just finished a book by Grisham that was good. We could do that for the next meeting. It's there by the chair."

Helen picked up the book and read the back cover. "Ooh, this sounds great!"

"How is Piper?" Rick asked. "I heard she's not working at the insurance office anymore?"

"She's full-time at the inn for now." And maybe forever if Iris couldn't get back in shape after her accident. "I thought *Logan* would try to run the place, but he's not showing much interest." She chuckled. "But he did add a new breakfast to our menu—the Roustabout Scramble. Piper says it's been a hit, but it's very…robust."

Helen stopped packing her sewing supplies and looked up, thoughtful. "So, Logan and Piper are getting along well? Have you thought about…?"

"*No!* Piper has enough on her hands without us trying to fix her up with a drifter like my grandson. Besides, she has children, and I don't think he'd have the first clue how to deal with a child."

It's not like Logan was a child-hating ogre, but he'd always been adamant that there was no room in his nomadic life for children. She'd assumed it was because his own father had dragged him and his sister all over the country when he was a boy, uprooting them every year or two for some new *opportunity*.

"If you say so." Rick stood. "But if he and Piper are working closely together, in *bedrooms*…well, you just never know. That's a lot of temptation."

"Oh, for heaven's sake, they're two adults, not a pair of horny teenagers. I think they can make a bed without having the urge to jump into it together!"

Helen slipped her coat on. "Sorry, Iris, but I'm with Rick. The two of them are in close proximity every day, just like Luke and Whitney were. Things happen…"

Iris pushed hard against the table she'd been playing cards on, making it rattle as it rolled to the side. "Are you two actively *trying* to make this so-called scowl of mine permanent? Logan has no interest in Piper, and Piper has no interest in dating."

She and Piper used to spend a lot of time in the kitchen together, talking about cooking and life and kids. She'd become very fond of Piper over the past year, and she liked to think it was mutual. That was probably why she was more concerned about *Piper* being hurt if anything happened than she was about Logan. Not only that, but if Piper *did* get her heart broken, she might not want to work at the inn, and Iris hated the idea of trying to manage that place without the little blonde dynamo. She also hated the idea of losing Piper and her children from her life. It wasn't worth the risk.

Helen slid the strap of her bag over her shoulder, looking thoughtful. "You know, Iris, there was a time when *you* fell in love as a single mom."

Rick perked up, his eyes bright with interest. "Do I know this story? Because I don't think I do, and I need to."

It had been fifty years since Sam Adler had insisted he was willing to take on her young son and her messy existence. But Sam's life was in Virginia, and hers was in Rendezvous Falls. She wouldn't leave, not even for love. To this day, she regretted sending him away alone. It wouldn't be the first or last time she'd been too stubborn for her own good, but it was the most painful.

Helen's gaze didn't leave Iris's face. She knew she'd hit a tender spot. "I'll fill you in on the way home, Rick."

He started to protest, then followed Helen's eyes and

gave Iris a quick smile and wink. "Fine. In the car, then. Don't forget we have to stop for sidewalk salt. The weather's supposed to turn crappy next week."

Helen reached up to pat Rick's shoulder. "Yes, you old worrywart, we'll stop for salt. We don't need any more broken hips in our circle."

Rick looked back at Iris when they got to the door. "Don't be surprised if we miss a few days next week. There's a hell of a storm coming in—first big one of the season."

"For heaven's sake, Rick!" Helen gave him a shove. "You sound like an old man."

Iris chuckled. "Yeah, like an old man who doesn't remember how to drive in snow. It's not like we don't get snowstorms every single winter."

"Ha. Ha." Rick tugged his gloves out of his pocket. "*I* remember just fine. It's all the *other* idiots I worry about. The first storm is always the worst for people being stupid. Then they wise up for the rest of the winter."

After they left, Iris stared out the window. The bright blue skies held no suggestion of the snowstorm Rick mentioned. But this was upstate New York. Blink and the weather changed, especially this time of year, when winter was chomping at the bit to kick autumn to the curb.

Was there anything to Rick and Helen's speculation about Logan and Piper? Helen bringing up Sam's name made the whole situation seem…a lot more serious. It was a reminder that single moms *could* fall in love, after all.

She wasn't sure who was at the greatest risk. Her

grandson, who might find his devotion to life on the road challenged. Piper, who might have her heart broken while still having two children to raise. Or maybe the one at the greatest risk was Iris herself. Two people she loved could end up falling in love, which might be wonderful. Or disastrous. Two people she loved could end up being hurt, and she'd have to get them through the aftermath without losing them from her life.

"ALL OF THESE boxes are Christmas decorations?" Logan couldn't believe it. Piper had just gestured at half the attic and announced it had to be moved downstairs. He turned to her. "Are you sure?"

She was standing a careful five feet away. She'd been doing that ever since their kiss. As if she could avoid his gravity field by maintaining a safe distance. That was okay with him. As much as he'd like another try at kissing her, she seemed determined to avoid it. If she didn't want it, he didn't want it. At least that's what he kept telling himself. Because really? He wanted it.

His resolve had evaporated a few minutes earlier, though, when she walked up the wooden stairs to the attic right in front of him. He'd known it would be a challenge, but ladies first and all that. She was wearing a bulky blue sweater that thankfully hid a lot of her tempting curves. But she wore it over leggings that looked like skin-tight jeans. And little ankle boots that had chunky brass zippers on the back. As he followed her up the stairs, all he could think was that he wanted to unzip them and work his way up her legs from there. By the time they reached the attic, he'd been hard. But that didn't last beyond her pointing to the mountain of boxes labeled Xmas.

She was tugging at a box over her head. "Yes, I'm sure. I didn't start working for Iris until after the holidays, but I was here when we packed it all up in January. We need to start hustling. It will be a combination of Thanksgiving and Christmas for a few weeks, but then it's red and green all the way. That's why I sent the kids to their grandparents' for a couple days." She nodded her head toward the window, where big, wet flakes of snow were starting to fall. "And it's perfect weather to put us in the mood for holiday decorating. The boxes are labeled by the room they go to. We'll do the shelf decorations first—Iris's little collections and stuff. Then we'll start putting up all the trees. Big trees downstairs, and a tabletop tree in every guest room. The only real tree will be in the lobby." It seemed like she was babbling—was she nervous? "We won't put that up until Thanksgiving weekend. But there's still a lot of work to be done. I mean, just look at all these boxes…" She yanked at the box again. Logan had no idea how heavy it was. He jumped forward to stop it as it tipped, and they both froze.

His chest was against her. Both their arms were raised, and her head was tipped back, giving her direct eye contact with him. He'd invaded her space, even if was for the noble cause of saving her from a box landing on her head. He cleared his throat and started to step away, reminding himself that he'd vowed not to talk her into anything. If she didn't want him, then… But wait— what was that look she was giving him?

That was *not* a get-away-from-me look. Her pink lips

parted, and her blue eyes darkened to cobalt. Did she…
did she just move against him? As if she needed *more*
contact? Leaving one hand on the box, he dropped the
other to her hip. She didn't move. His arm slid around
her waist, and she melted against him, her head resting
in the hollow of his shoulder, her eyes drifting shut. Her
arms dropped and her hands rested on his forearm, now
secure around her. He shoved the box to safety and put
his other arm around her.

She didn't turn, just stood there, her back to his
chest, eyes closed. The tension he'd felt simmering in
her since the kiss was gone, and she was soft and warm
against him. He wasn't sure what was happening right
now, but he sure as hell wasn't going to break the moment by asking. He just stood there with her in his
arms, waiting for her to make the next move. Damn,
she felt good.

Damn, *he* felt good. Peaceful. Calm. Yet still…a ripple of anticipation ran through him. Was it possible
she *wanted* to explore this—whatever it was—between
them just as badly as he did? His embrace tightened,
and she let out a catlike purr, moving her butt back and
forth against his jeans. Oh, yeah. Piper Montgomery
wanted more. His hand slid across her stomach, his fingers light against her. Tentative. Ready for her to stop
him. But she didn't.

There were ten thousand reasons not to do this. But
he couldn't think of a single one right now. He flattened
his hand on her abdomen, then lowered his head and
pressed his lips against her hair, breathing out her name.
Her eyelashes fluttered, then closed again.

"Logan...just...just hold me for a minute, okay? It feels so good to be held like this..."

He brushed his mouth across her hair again. "I'll hold you for as long as you need me to." He'd hold her forever if she asked. He wasn't sure how long they stood there, unmoving. He didn't care.

She finally let out a sigh. "I don't know if I'm ready for this..."

She moved her butt back and forth against his jeans again, making him hiss out a breath.

"There's only one way to find out." He slid his hand lower, and her legs parted to give him better access. He found his mark and cupped her in his hand. *Perfect fit.* The thin layer of knit leggings wasn't enough to dim the sensation for either of them. He spoke against her ear. "Just remember we can stop anytime." His fingers pressed against her. A little furrow appeared between her closed eyes. "Just say the word and I'll stop..." He hoped with every beat of his heart that she wouldn't.

Her whispered reply made his blood pound in his ears. "I trust you, Logan. Don't stop."

Her words were a gift. And a curse. Sure, she could trust him to make her feel good. But what if she wanted more? She moved against him again. *Shit.* He couldn't worry about that now.

His fingers started stroking, finding the sweet spot through her clothes and pressing until she made a sound that was half groan and half plea.

"Yes...right there...oh..."

He kept moving, kept applying more pressure, and she kept whimpering and twisting in his arms. Finally she cried out and shuddered against him. Rosy splotches appeared on her cheeks beneath blond lashes. She let out a long, shaky breath and let her whole weight rest in his arms. He kissed the top of her head as she came back to earth. Her eyes fluttered open. She was usually the one in charge, but right now she looked completely unmoored.

"It's okay," he smiled. "I got you. Just breathe."

Her eyes went wide as reality hit. She moved against his arms and he released her, even though everything in his body was begging her to stay put. She didn't move far, just a step or two, turning to face him. Those rosy spots on her cheeks were deep scarlet now, and she quickly covered them with her hands.

"What…oh my god… I can't believe… I…"

Logan chuckled. "Breathe in and out. Nice and slow. It's okay."

"It's *not* okay! I just…you just…" She stared down at the floor. He had a feeling she was working herself into a panic. "I can't believe I just did that. In the attic. I'm so sorry. You must think I'm…"

"Hey." Laughter gone, he stepped forward and gently tugged her hands from her face. "Look at me, Piper." He waited until she finally looked up. His chest tightened. Was that shame he saw in her eyes? "Neither one of us has a damn thing to apologize for. The moment was right, and we took it."

"I'm a *mother*."

"You're a *woman*."

She threw her hands up. "Yes, I know. People keep reminding me!"

He cupped her face in his hands and smiled. "If I

did my job right, you should be a very *satisfied* woman right now."

She huffed out a nervous laugh. "You did your job very well, Logan. But I can't believe I let that happen. In the middle of the afternoon! I mean, what if..."

He lowered his head and kissed her to stop the panic attack she was trying so hard to have. Judging from the way she pressed up onto her toes to kiss him back, she wasn't objecting. His arms slid around her, cupping her buttocks and pressing her against his hardness. He raised his head and looked into her eyes. Eyes full of invitation. And hesitation.

"What if *what*, Piper? What if someone comes all the way up to the attic and finds us? What are the odds of that happening? There are only two rooms booked, and you know damn well those two women are more interested in each other than whatever we're up to. And they told me at breakfast they were heading south to the museum in Corning. We won't be seeing them until tonight, especially in this weather." He kissed her again. He was losing all good sense and He. Did. Not. Care. "You just said your kids are gone for a few days. Iris sure won't be interrupting us." Another kiss. "It's the first real snowstorm of the season, and the odds of anyone just dropping by are pretty slim. So if you want me to do that thing again..." He slid his hand down her behind and gave it a squeeze.

She dropped her forehead against his chest and shook it back and forth. "This is crazy. We can't..."

"We *can*. If we want to."

He waited. Not patiently, but he waited. He wouldn't make a move without knowing that she was fully on board. She was still looking down, head against him, talking to their feet.

"I want to. But Logan…it's been…years. I'm afraid I'll be needy. Or frantic. Or just really rusty." He wanted to argue, but she had to work this out for herself. "A lot of my what-ifs are about *me*. What if I freak out? What if I'm not good at it anymore? What if I really like it? I still have two children. This isn't being responsible…" Not liking the direction her self-talk was taking, he put his fingers under her chin and lifted it so he could look her straight in the eye when he spoke.

"I *want* you to be needy." The corner of her mouth twitched upward as he spoke. "Frantic is good, too. I think you just proved you're not rusty. If you freak out, we'll stop. And the fact that you have two kids doesn't stop me from getting a hard-on every time I look at you."

She laughed at that, as if shocked at his admission. He knew how she felt—it was a shock for him, too. Her voice steadied.

"So…what exactly are we talking about here?"

Logan wasn't sure how they'd gotten to this place, but holy hell. He was holding Piper Montgomery in his arms, ready to drop to his knees to beg her to have sex with him if he thought it would work. In the middle of a snowy afternoon. He didn't want to wait for tonight. He didn't want to wait until they left the *attic*, but it was a little chilly up here for what he had in mind. He traced his fingers across her cheek.

"We're talking about you and me spending the afternoon having guilt-free, worry-free sex. Like the two adults that we are."

She chewed on her lip as she considered, then nodded, her eyes bright with the thrill of doing something so adventurous.

"Okay. I'm in. But...where?"

"We'll go down to my bed..." He paused. Could he make love to Piper in Gran's apartment? "Or over to your place..." Piper's expression fell. No, that wouldn't work, either. Then her brows shot up as if she'd had an idea. He hadn't thought her cheeks could get any more red, but they did now.

"Well...you know...there *are* vacant rooms right below us." She flashed him a quick, proud smile. "Each one of them has a bed. And the master key is in my pocket."

He lifted her in the air and laughed as he kissed her. "You bad, bad, *brilliant* girl."

CHAPTER FOURTEEN

OH MY GOD. Oh my god. Oh my god.

Piper's heart hammered as they left the attic, and all those holiday boxes, behind. What was she *doing*? How could she *do* this? She couldn't *really* do this, could she? Even if was her idea? No, she couldn't do it. Use a room at the inn for sex with Logan Taggart? There were so many things *wrong* with this idea. So. Many. Things. It was foolish. It was unprofessional. It was dangerous. She turned to him when they got to the base of the attic stairs.

"Logan…" She met his heavy gaze and her breath hitched. He didn't move as she searched his face. She had a feeling he'd be fine if she said "forget it" and walked away. And he'd be fine if she didn't. He was heading for South America right after Christmas. She probably wouldn't leave a ripple in his life either way. But here in this silent, empty inn, he wanted *her*. And she couldn't deny how much she needed to feel wanted. She tried her damnedest to remember again why this was a bad idea, but when she opened her mouth, there were no arguments to be found.

"Do you have a lucky number?" she asked.

His brows rose on his forehead. "I'm sorry?"

"Your lucky number? To pick a room?"

He chuckled low and soft. "Babe, whatever room you pick will be my new lucky number."

She swallowed hard. "Okay. Uh…probably the first floor. It won't be suspicious if someone sees us on the main floor, and we can hear the bell if someone comes in the lobby. And if we decide to…you know…do it again…the first-floor rooms don't rent out as quickly as the upper floors, so…"

"Piper." He shook his head, bemused. "Do you always think out your decisions this carefully? Even the ones about booty calls?"

"Booty calls?" She exclaimed it so loudly the words echoed in the hallway. She slapped her hand over her mouth, then lowered her voice to a hiss. "I've never had a *booty call* in my life!"

Logan's eyes went dark and hot. "You won't be able to say that after today. Let's go." His smile faded just a bit. "Unless you've changed your mind? Is that what all this babbling is about?"

She hesitated, then shook her head. "I'm…anxious. Nervous. But no, I haven't changed my mind. But… maybe we should set some parameters?"

He rolled his eyes. "Look, I know you like to have all your little ducks in a row, but we don't need parameters around *sex*. I got this, trust me."

"Not about the sex. About…after." She laid her hand on his forearm. "You've literally been around the world, so you've probably done this sort of thing a million times."

Logan barked out a laugh. "A million might be a stretch."

"You know what I mean." She waited for him to nod

in acknowledgment before continuing. "I *haven't*. I want you to know that I won't try to talk you into being my boyfriend. I know this is just…"

The corner of his mouth lifted. "A shag in the afternoon?"

She tried not to smile, but finally gave in. "I don't know if that sounds any better than a booty call. I want us to be on the same page. It's just sex…"

Logan put his hand over his heart and pretended to be pained. "I'm hoping it will be a hell of a lot more than 'just sex.' Look…" He reached for her hips, pulling her closer. He smelled like outdoors and spice and sweat and it was all a bit overwhelming. She focused on his words again. "I get it. No strings. You've got the kids and they come first and you don't want a boyfriend. It's all good. Whatever you decide is good, babe, but you're killing me right now. I want you so bad I can't think straight."

There was a beat of silence before she pulled away from him. His expression fell until she pulled her master key from her pocket and waved it at him.

"Let's see how Room Three feels."

The room was one of her favorites, with a dark blue Oriental rug covering much of the hardwood floor. It wasn't a large room, but it had a marble fireplace along one wall, surrounded by built-in bookshelves. The other walls had ivory wallpaper with a rich tone-on-tone design. The ceiling had elaborately carved crown molding. The striped drapes matched the blue-and-cream bedspread on the four-poster mahogany bed. While the drapes were open, the sheers beneath them provided a sense of privacy during daylight hours. It wasn't always a popular room with guests because of its small size and first-floor location near the lobby. But it had always felt like a cozy sanctuary to her.

Logan locked the door behind them, and all thoughts of sanctuary vanished with the heavy click of metal on metal. Now it was a room of…adventure. Of daring. Her chin rose. She was really going to do this. Going to make love to a man in that bed.

His hands rested on her shoulders from behind. "Excellent choice. This is much more my style than Gran's place." His head dropped and he brushed his lips across her ear, making her shudder. "But the most beautiful thing in this room is you."

She shook her head automatically. "You don't have to say that stuff. I've already said yes."

"Whoa." Logan straightened and turned her around. "I'm not trying to sweet-talk you into anything here, Piper. All that talk of booty calls and shagging was to lighten the mood. I *want* you. I want you because you're strong and funny and sexy as hell and yes, beautiful."

She started to roll her eyes, but stopped when she saw he was serious. She gave a short, startled laugh. "Give me a break. I'm an exhausted, overworked single mom who no longer wastes time trying to look beautiful for anyone." She lifted the hem of her old sweater, pilled and faded. "My outfit alone is proof of that. I don't even remember if I shaved my legs the last time I showered, which wasn't today, by the way, so be forewarned…"

"Damn, woman, are you going to talk this much all afternoon? Piper, you don't have to *try* to be beautiful. You are, from your heart right on out to the rest of you. I don't give a shit about when you showered.

Now stop stalling and overanalyzing everything I say and everything we do. If you wanna walk—walk." He put his finger on her lips. "But if you're staying—hush. And if you're really that unhappy about that sweater, feel free to take it off."

This was it. Moment of truth. Outside the windows, fluffy snowflakes swirled in the air, matching the swirling she felt in her stomach. Her eyes stung with a surprising rush of tears, and her voice cracked when she looked back up at him.

"I'm staying. But… I might need…a little help."

"What kind of help?"

Her cheeks puffed as she blew out a steadying breath. "I told you I'm out of practice…" Logan started to object but she raised her hand to stop him. "This isn't a pity party. I'm just stating facts. And to stand here and just strip in front of you…" Her cheeks flamed. "I know we said this is casual and all, but I'm not used to this. I might need some…"

And just like that, she was in his arms, warm against his hard body. He put his finger under her chin and tipped it up before placing a soft kiss on her lips. His voice was rough with emotion.

"Piper, are you saying you…" He kissed her again, tracing his tongue on the seam between her lips this time, then pulling back. "Are you saying you need a little more foreplay to get you ready?"

She pressed her thighs together and sighed at the heat that shot through her abdomen. Being ready was not the problem. So what was? He looked like he was ready to devour her right then and there, staring into her eyes with a slanted grin.

"Do you need me to seduce you, sweetheart? To take the lead?"

She chewed on her lip and nodded. Neither of them moved. How had he managed to understand something she couldn't even articulate herself?

His hands started to move, sliding up under her sweater and around to her back. He pressed one solid thigh between her legs, which parted for him. Her eyes closed as he rocked his leg up against her, and a little whimper escaped her lips. But the whimper didn't get far, as his mouth covered hers and his tongue pressed inward to claim her sighs as he kept grinding on her. His fingers had been the opening act upstairs, but this…she was practically riding his leg, and it was amazing. One large hand slid around to cup her breast over her plain cotton bra, and his thumb stroked back and forth once, twice—until her nipple was hard and aching. A tremor went through her, and she was shocked to realize she was ready to come again, just from his touch.

"Is this what you need, Piper?" He traced his kisses down her jawline to the base of her neck, pulling her body tighter against his leg with one hand and kneading her breast with the other. "Damn, you're like handling dynamite, ready to blow any second." He scraped his teeth across her shoulder. "Do it, baby. Let go. Blow up. Right…now." He raised his leg against her again and bit her skin, pinching her nipple at the same time. And she shattered in his arms, crying out.

Before she could get her bearings, she felt the mattress against her back. Logan was tugging at her sweater, muttering about needing to see her. She sat up so he could pull it over her head, then reached back to unfasten her bra. She glanced down at the well-worn garment and grimaced.

"Not very fancy…"

"I swear to God, Piper, if you don't stop talking and thinking and apologizing…" He ran his hand up her side to cup her face. "No more talking. No more thinking. Your job is to lie back and let me take care of things, okay?"

"But…"

He put his finger on her lips. "Do you still trust me?"

His weight pressed down on the mattress as he shifted to straddle her, still fully clothed. He waited as she considered his question.

"I trust you."

"Good. No more words, then." His expression sobered. "Unless you want me to stop. Then say 'stop.' But that's it. No other words. No other thoughts. Just sensation." The heat returned to his eyes, along with a spark of humor. "Nod if you understand."

She nodded with a shy grin. He reached beneath her to unhook the bra, then removed it.

"Holy…" Logan's voice trailed off as he stared at her breasts. She'd always thought they were a little small for her curvy frame, but she could tell Logan didn't think so. He stared for another moment, then yanked his shirt off over his head. She'd almost forgotten about the creatures swirling up his arm in colorful ink. Crashing waves with birds and the oil rig above and sharks, turtles, whales and more below. So many stories being told, but she couldn't make sense of them now. Because his fingers had just gripped the waistline of her leggings, tugging hard. So hard that she didn't even have to raise herself up for them to be down around her knees. He backed off the bed and stood. He stared down at her nearly naked body, then lifted one booted foot in his hand and grinned.

"I've been wanting to zip you out of these damn things all day." He unzipped the boot and pulled it off, tossing it aside. He did the same with her other foot. Then he finished peeling off the rest of her clothes, never taking his eyes off her. He left her feet against his chest, and they looked so small there. His hands moved to unbuckle his jeans, but he stopped abruptly, eyes snapping wide. "Shit, I don't have a condom…"

Without a word, she pulled her feet off of him and crawled across the bed to the nightstand. She opened the drawer, crossing her fingers that a guest hadn't used them all up. But no, there were three condom packets. She tossed them to a surprised, and obviously relieved, Logan.

"Seriously? My grandmother stocks the rooms with condoms?"

Piper just smiled and shrugged, not wanting to break his 'no words' rule. Iris told her she'd started stocking the nightstands with condoms years ago. She'd said she came of age on the cusp of the sexual revolution, and was an ardent supporter of safe sex. Whether that included sex with Iris's grandson, Piper couldn't say.

Logan chuckled and tossed the strip of packets on the bed near where she sat. "What am I saying? Of *course* my grandmother puts condoms in the rooms. Right next to the Bibles. That's her to a T. Remind me to thank her." When Piper's eyes went wide, he laughed. "I'm kidding. Now…where were we? Oh, yeah." His jeans hit the floor, quickly followed by his boxer briefs.

Piper's eyes went wide for a very different reason. It was all well and good to say size didn't matter, but…if it *did* matter, Logan had it. And he was clearly just as ready for this as she was. It was an effort to raise her gaze to meet his. He tipped his head to the side.

"Admiring or concerned?" he asked, making her blush.

She lifted a shoulder, sneaking another glance. "Both?"

Logan knelt on the edge of the mattress, crawling toward her. She fell back as he approached, and he moved between her legs. He traced kisses up the inside of her thigh, working higher and higher. She watched his progress as long as she could, and then her head dropped back against the mattress. She closed her eyes and gave in to the sensations coursing through her. Anticipation. Pleasure. Excitement. Her entire body trembled as his mouth got closer. She held her breath. Any second now, he'd be there.

But he wasn't. The kisses stopped. His movement stopped. Her breathing started. She opened her eyes to find Logan kneeling between her legs, staring at her.

"What?" she breathed, trembling with need. He stroked his hand up the inside of her leg.

"Did I do a good job of seducing you?"

"Oh my god, yes." Her body was humming like a tuning fork.

The corner of his mouth curved up. "Time for you to take some control back, baby. What happens next? Tell me what you want."

Her head fell back again, her eyes tightly closed. She sounded like she was begging. Because she was.

"I want you. I want you in me. Right now. Right *now*, Logan."

The mattress dipped and rolled, and still her eyes stayed closed. She was focused on the sensations moving through her like waves. The quivering buildup that threatened to overwhelm her. She whispered his name again, and he answered her with a kiss on her lips.

"Right here, baby. Right here." There was pressure, then it was gone. Pressure again, then gone. Her head rolled back and forth.

"Don't tease me…"

"Just making sure you're ready, honey. Just making sure…"

The next time she felt him there, she pushed her hips up and took him with a cry.

"Shit…" he hissed in her ear.

Neither of them moved. It did hurt a little. It had been a long time. But the hurt quickly melted into something entirely different. She moved, making him moan, and he sank into her. Slowly. Carefully. Filling her. He hesitated, then started rocking against her.

Colors exploded behind her eyelids. Bright, hot colors of friction and sweat and lust and satisfaction. Sweet, sweet satisfaction. She kissed his neck and they moved together in perfect rhythm, building and building until she couldn't hold on any longer. Her fingers twisted in his hair, his grunts barely registering. She called out his name as she came, and he silenced her cries with a kiss that drove as deep as his body was driving, until he finally let out a loud groan and joined her.

Piper didn't know how long they stayed there, without moving a muscle, just lost in the waves rolling through them. She slowly relaxed her grip on his hair, and his fingers eased on her buttocks. She'd probably have bruises. If so, she'd regard them as trophies. Medals for outstanding performance. She smiled against his neck. His head turned enough to brush his lips across her ear. His voice was rough and cracked.

"Wow."

She nodded in agreement.

"Yup."

"Is it okay if I just…stay here for a minute?" He twitched inside her. "I don't want this to end. Like… ever."

"I'm not going anywhere." She couldn't if she wanted to. She felt like she'd just melted into the mattress. Whatever that was—and lord knows it was more than just sex—it had blown her away. For all her assurances to herself that this was just a casual romp, there was nothing casual about her feelings toward Logan Taggart right now.

LOGAN PULLED IN a breath and held it, like he used to do back in his younger days after a long drag of weed— letting the vapors work their way into his bloodstream and waiting for that feeling of euphoria. Only now, it was the scent of Piper Montgomery he wanted to hold on to. Her usual fresh, clean scent mixed with the musky smell of the sex they'd just had was a high like no other.

He should move. He knew he should move. Hell, he was so much bigger than her, and here he was, just lying there. But damn, he didn't want this moment to end.

That was a new sensation, and he didn't know what to make of it. No way could he think clearly enough to figure it out right now. He moved and Piper winced.

"Shit. Sorry." He murmured, pulling away and discarding the condom. He sat on the edge of the bed for a moment, not sure what to do next. It was snowing more briskly outside, but the room was warm. And yet, leaving her gave him a chill. She must have felt the same. Her hand touched his bum shoulder. Her voice was soft. Tired. Longing.

"Come back. Just for a little longer."

Probably not a good idea when his head was still twisted and foggy. But then again, it was a chance to hold Piper in his arms, and who knew if that would happen again after today? He slid back onto the bed, pulling the covers up over them. She was like a heat-seeking missile, burrowing against him. He folded his arms around her without a second thought. It felt good. *She* felt good. Too good? Was there such a thing? Another question for a time when his head wasn't muddled with the intoxicating feel and scent of this amazing woman in his arms.

He wasn't sure how long they slept, but the room was decidedly darker when he woke with a start. A gust of wind rattled the windows. There was a phone ringing somewhere. In the lobby? Damn. How long *had* they been sleeping? He looked at the clock. It was almost five. Piper wasn't moving—still out like a light. Logan slipped out of bed as quietly as possible, then into his clothes, sans shoes and underwear. He padded into the hallway and out to the lobby, crossing his fingers that the women in rooms seven and eight weren't back yet.

Or, if they were, that they were upstairs. He glanced outside and stopped in his tracks.

Snow was coming down heavy and thick now, piling up on the steps and covering the parking lot. Now he hoped the women *were* back, and not out on the roads. The phone rang again. Speak of the devil, it was Milly Peters from Room Seven. She said she'd called three times, and he cringed. What else had he and Piper missed while they were sleeping? Milly and her friend in Room Eight—why had they even bothered with two rooms?—were staying at a hotel in Corning for the night because the storm was intensifying. He assured her they wouldn't be charged for that night and yes, their rooms would be kept for them to come back to the next day. He checked messages next, but there were only the earlier calls from Milly.

According to the weather app on his phone, they were now under a severe weather alert until the next night, with high winds and up to six more inches of heavy snow expected—something called "lake effect." The storm was coming down from the Great Lakes... Lake Ontario, to be specific. The inn was empty, and highly likely to stay that way on a stormy Tuesday night. Especially if he locked all the doors and turned off the Vacancy sign. He smiled. Piper said Ethan and Lily were staying with their grandparents, which meant they had the whole place to themselves. All night long.

He dashed to Gran's apartment long enough to feed the cat and grab a bottle of wine and two glasses before heading back to Room Three. Piper was sitting up in bed when he walked in, her cell phone in her hand. Her hair was mussed, although the ponytail was still intact.

Amazing it had lasted through all their activity earlier. He nodded at her and set the wine on the nightstand.

There were spots of color high on her cheeks, and she was holding the sheet up over her chest. Not exactly logical, since he'd thoroughly explored that region just a few short hours ago. Her lips were still kiss-swollen and thoroughly distracting. Like right now—they were moving, and he hadn't heard a word she was saying.

"I'm sorry, what?"

Her brows furrowed. "I *said* I can't believe we slept so long. Lily called and the phone scared me half to death." She sat up straighter. "Oh, god, did our guests get back?"

He shook his head. "They're staying in Corning tonight. The roads are bad—the snow is really coming down out there. Is Lily okay?" *Please don't let Lily and Ethan come home tonight...*

She smiled. "She's fine. She was worried about me being alone in the storm. I told her you and I were decorating for Christmas so the snow was perfect. I talked to Susan, and they'll keep the kids until Thursday afternoon as planned." Her eyes widened when he opened the wine and filled the glasses. "Wait. We really do have to decorate, you know. Besides, what if we get a surprise guest? We can't come running out of here half-dressed to greet them."

"We won't be getting any guests tonight."

"How do you know…" Her eyes narrowed. "Logan, did you turn off the Vacancy sign? Iris *never* does that unless we're full…"

"I'm pretty sure Iris never does *this* either." He gestured to Piper under the covers. "At least not in recent years." Her cheeks blushed pink again, and she shook her head.

"This is crazy. We can't stay all night…"

"We passed crazy a while ago, so there's no sense worrying about it now. And we *can*. Trust me." He sat on the edge of the bed, reaching over to take her hand. "Unless you don't want to?"

He'd never been the kind of guy who thought sleepovers were a good idea. Inviting a woman to spend the night could lead to…misunderstandings. The best way to avoid commitment was to avoid the *illusion* of commitment. And asking a woman to *stay* was flirting with that danger zone.

Piper stared at her small hand in his, thoughtful and silent. He was sure she was going to talk herself out of something as risky as spending the entire night together. And that might be best—for both their sakes. He was generally a go-with-the-flow kind of guy, but there was something prickling under his skin right now. He *wanted* to spend the night with Piper. Have dinner with her. Even hang the stupid Christmas decorations with her. He'd do whatever it took to be near her.

Meanwhile, Piper seemed to be having an equally heavy internal debate. Her eyes were distant and her expression serious. In fact, she was almost scowling at their hands now. She'd moved into that murky overanalyzing zone again. He squeezed her hand and released it, holding out a glass of wine.

"I'll tell you what," he said with a false sense of cheerfulness. "We're in no hurry." That wasn't true. He was eager to feel her in his arms again. "We've got all night. Think about that, Piper. All night in an empty inn. We've got enough time to eat, drink, decorate *and* make love in all twelve rooms if we want to."

She took the wine, giving him a crooked grin. "No way am I making twelve different beds tomorrow morning. If we do this, it's Room Three or bust."

He looked around the small room. It didn't have the froufrou floral motif that a lot of other rooms had. The furniture, especially this big bed, was more sturdy than fragile. And it was neutral territory. Not Gran's place. Not Piper's place. There was no sense creating memories where they lived. He tipped his head toward the fireplace.

"Is that thing functional?"

She took a sip of wine. "Yes. Why?"

"Well, if this is our room for the night, I think a fire would be a nice touch later." He reached for the other wineglass, then scooted to sit next to her, leaning back on the headboard. She moved closer, but her fingers still played with the bedding, holding it up. "Are you cold? Should I start one now?"

She shook her head. "No. Why did you think that?"

He made a point to look at her chest before answering with a crooked grin. "You're hiding under the covers. Since I've already seen and enjoyed everything you're covering up, I thought you must be trying to stay warm."

Color rose on her face. She clutched the covers tight. "I guess you're right. I wasn't prepared for this. For... what to do after. It's not like I'm some nubile twenty-year-old looking to show off my flawless body. I won't be sexting you any nude selfies of a body that's given birth to two children..."

The sheet slipped down slowly, revealing one perfect

breast. Maybe he should have told her to stay covered after all. No way he could concentrate now. Not with her nakedness revealed and her warmth soaking into him. He set down the wineglass, then took her glass and put it on the nightstand next to his.

"Your body looks pretty damn perfect to me. And you can sext it to me anytime."

Piper let out a startled laugh. "That's a hard no."

He pulled her closer, tracing kisses down her neck as she melted against him. "Understood. We'll just have to make some unforgettable memories, then. So I can picture you in my head. Let's start right…here…" He cupped her breast, lowering his head to take it in his mouth. Piper gave a startled cry, then buried her fingers in his hair and held him there. As if he needed any encouragement. He only removed his lips long enough to yank his shirt over his head and ditch his jeans. That took approximately five seconds and was still far too long to be away from her. He crawled under the covers, and she moved into his arms as if she'd had the same exact thought.

He'd told her earlier she felt like he was playing with dynamite, and it was true. She was dangerous. Dangerous to his ability to think clearly. Dangerous to his control over his own body, which craved her like a drug. She writhed under him, pleading for more. He grabbed for a condom. Dangerous or not, he needed…no…he *wanted* her. Not need. He didn't do need. But as he slid inside her again and heard his name on her lips, a tiny voice in his head whispered… *Liar*.

It was fast. Faster than he'd wanted, but it couldn't be helped. Slowing down with her would require con-

centration, and that ability had vanished when Piper
wrapped her legs around his waist and pulled herself
up to capture him. No sane man could concentrate after
that. He tugged the tie out of her hair. The thick blond
waves felt soft in his hands, like spun gold. He wrapped
his hands in it, as he rode them toward the inevitable
climax. They hit it together this time, both calling out
a jumble of words and cries as they clung to each other.

Holy *hell*. This little momma was the sexiest woman
he'd ever been with. He pulled her tight against him as
he fell to the mattress. A dangerous woman.

What scared him the most was that he didn't know
how he'd ever have enough of her.

CHAPTER FIFTEEN

PIPER LAY IN the warmth and security of Logan's arms and tried not to freak out. How many orgasms was that? Three? Four? Or was it just one long orgasm that started the minute his fingers touched her in the attic? Magic fingers. She pressed her back against him. Magic man.

He kissed her head. "Gotta give me a minute, babe."

"That wasn't what I…" Oh, who was she kidding? Of *course* that's what she was thinking about. Because this man made her feel a whole universe of emotions she wasn't at all prepared for, and she wanted to explore each and every one of them.

But they couldn't just keep having sex all night, could they? A soft sigh escaped her. It sure was a nice thought. She could see outside, where it was almost dark and the snow was coming down more heavily again. It looked like a Christmas snow globe. November could be like that—warm and sunny one day, snow and ice the next.

She rolled over to face Logan, not surprised to see him watching her with amusement and heat flickering in his eyes.

"Yes?" His voice was rough and gentle all at once.

"I told Lily and Susan that we were decorating. I'll have a lot of questions to answer if we don't do *some-*

thing." He pulled her in and kissed her. The man knew how to kiss, that's for damn sure. Every time their lips touched, her thoughts scattered. "Mmmm…"

Laughter shook his chest. "You like that, huh?"

"Very much." She kissed him back. "But we really have to…"

He squeezed her tight, then released her with a quick kiss on her forehead. "I know. We have to be grown-ups for a few hours. Let's make a deal. We'll bring some boxes down and get started." He winked at her. "Started on decorating, that is. With our clothes on." She gave him a pouty face and he laughed. "Hey, I'm happy to stay here."

"No. We have to at least get the pine garland up on the banister and decorate the lobby." She looked up at him and waggled her eyebrows. "But there's nothing saying we can't come back here later."

He pretended to think it over. "That's true. After all, the bed will have to be made in the morning regardless of whether we use it just for the afternoon, or all night long."

"Exactly!" She couldn't believe she was lying here naked with a man, much less laughing and making plans to come back later to get naked again. There was something about having the inn empty and silent around them, with the snow hushing all other sounds and reminders of life from outside, that made this feel…magical. She couldn't get that word out of her head, and it wasn't just about his fingers. *Magic.* She ignored the whispering voice telling her that magic wasn't real.

"So that's the plan, then." Logan sat up and grabbed

for his jeans. "Boxes. Dinner at some point. And back to Room Three later. Works for me."

She sat up on the opposite side of the bed. "Not much else to do with this weather."

He glanced over his shoulder at her. There was a glint of humor in his eyes. And of desire. It was a heady combination that made her belly tighten. His voice was laced with warm laughter. "I'm gaining a whole new appreciation for snow."

They didn't break for dinner until a few hours later. She expected it to be weird, doing something as mundane as dragging boxes out of the attic so soon after making love for the first—and second—time. But it was surprisingly comfortable working with Logan. Probably due to his ever-steady demeanor. Mr. Unruffled.

They talked as they worked. Logan told her about the places he'd been. The sights he'd seen. She felt boring compared to his adventurous lifestyle. He described being chased in some jungle by locals who didn't want the oil company on their land. Of having a transport boat capsize during a sudden storm, dumping six men into the Gulf of Mexico as lightning traced across the sky. He said it all so matter-of-factly.

She asked how many places he'd lived as an adult, and he'd just shrugged, wrapping a fake pine garland around the bannister. "I lost count a long time ago. I go where the work is."

"What about friends? Putting down roots?"

He shook his head. "I don't do roots. I go to a place for work, not for socializing."

"And you don't get lonely? It doesn't bother you to not have an actual home?"

He stopped and considered the question, then shook his head. "I didn't say I don't have *any* friends, but they tend to have the same lifestyle I do. And I never had an 'actual home' growing up, so no. It's never bothered me." He looked up the wide mahogany staircase. "I guess this old Victorian museum is the closest I had to a home, but even this place was always temporary."

"Does *anything* ever bother you?" He seemed just as surprised by her question as she was. But it did seem that he was perpetually just…mildly amused…by life, no matter what was happening. Piper both admired and resented his ability to be so levelheaded all the time.

He shook out another length of garland, avoiding her eyes. "Do things bother me? I guess. But I don't waste a lot of time on it. Everything passes. And if it doesn't, I do. I don't hang around one place long enough to be invested in stuff."

Piper frowned. "So basically, you don't care because you won't be hanging around long enough to be personally affected?"

He straightened and turned to face her. "That sounds a little harsh. But not completely wrong. I don't form a lot of…attachments." The corner of his mouth turned down in concern. "You're not looking for attachments either, right? We were clear earlier. Does my not getting bothered bother you?"

She stepped back, not prepared to be challenged, and not sure why she'd even brought it up. "Uh…no. We're good. No strings." She did her best to sound flippant. "You can do a different town every week for all I care."

And there was the crooked, vaguely amused grin that got to her every time. "And yet, you asked."

Her cheeks heated up. "Sorry. I guess I've been a parent for so long that it's hard to conceive a lifestyle like that. Where you just pack up and go whenever you feel like it. Where you don't feel a sense of responsibility for someone else." What would that be like?

He gave a casual shrug, but she saw a bit of doubt reflecting in his eyes. "I felt a sense of responsibility for my grandmother. That's why I'm here."

"But you're not staying."

"I never stay, Piper."

He went back to working on the bannister, his face carefully blank. Unruffled as always, as if he hadn't just said something important. Was he warning her off? Or just stating a fact?

I never stay, Piper.

After a stretch of awkward—at least on her part—silence, Logan started asking questions about her favorite holiday movies, and the conversation gradually slid into their usual banter. As if they hadn't made love that afternoon. As if he hadn't told her he never stayed.

They ate a late dinner in the kitchen. He panfried some steak while she put together a spinach salad with crumbled bacon and vinaigrette dressing. He fetched the wine from Room Three, and they ate at the kitchen table. She did her best to remind herself that temporary was exactly what she'd wanted. So this was good. A nice guy. A temporary guy.

The snow was still falling heavily outside, making the world look clean and soft. An occasional vehicle went by, slowly and carefully, but the snow hushed the sound so much that it was like watching a silent movie as they passed. They were in their own little bubble here, and it was a very nice bubble. It was a bubble where the worries of the world, even those in that pink house of hers barely visible across the lot, felt far, far away. She sat back in her chair and sighed.

"What a day." She resisted leaving the bubble by avoiding anything deeper than that simple—and complex—truth.

"In a good way, I hope?" Logan emptied his wineglass, appraising her over the rim.

"Yes, good. Surprising. But good." She stretched, wincing. She'd used muscles today that hadn't been used in a very long time. And she'd used them very enthusiastically. "I'll be paying for it tomorrow—I ache in some new and unusual places."

"Yeah?" There was a glimmer of laughter in his eyes and playfulness in his tone. "Too many flights up and down the stairs?"

She shook her head, chewing the inside of her lip to keep from giggling. "No, I don't think that's it."

"Were the boxes too heavy?" He stood and carried their plates to the sink.

"Oh, please. You wouldn't let me carry any box that weighed more than a pound, so I don't think that's it."

He was behind her chair now, his hands on her shoulders, thumbs kneading her back and forcing a sigh from her lips. He wasn't done teasing. "Were all those garlands too much for you?"

A low moan escaped as he rhythmically massaged her neck. She had to work to form actual words.

"Nope. Not it."

"Hmm. I wonder what it could have been. Do you have a fever?" He leaned over and pressed his lips to her forehead. "No, you don't feel feverish…" She tipped her head back so she could look up at him. He took advantage of the easy access and kissed her lips. "In fact, you feel downright perfect. And these lips remind me of what might have worn you out."

She smiled against his mouth. "Really? What's your guess, then?"

He tugged Piper to her feet and turned her to face him.

"It's hard to say. But… I keep thinking of that old phrase…"

"And what old phrase is that?" She pressed against him, and he wrapped his arms around her, lowering his head and his voice.

"Sometimes the best cure for something is the hair of the dog that bit you."

A laugh bubbled up in her throat. "Is that right? You think I'll feel better if I do the same thing again?"

He spoke against her lips. "There's only one way to find out…"

She followed him out of the kitchen, and he hit all the light switches on the way to Room Three. Decorating was done. A long night stretched before them, and she was as eager to greet it as he was.

Who *were* they right now? A man and woman who'd burned up the sheets this afternoon. A man and woman being relaxed and efficient as they decorated together. A man and woman being flirty and funny over dinner. A man and woman who—judging from the fire in Logan's eyes—were about to ignite those sheets again.

Whoever they were? Piper liked them. A lot.

THE FIREPLACE IN Room Three was burning low at one o'clock in the morning. But it was still enough to move warm flickers of light across Piper's skin as Logan watched her sleep. She was on her stomach, face turned away from him, arms splayed, as if she'd just fallen there unconscious. He smiled to himself. She pretty much had.

It was still snowing like hell outside when they'd drawn the curtains earlier, which was why he'd started the fire. They'd watched the flames for a while before slowly, tenderly making love. And then again. And... again. No wonder she was limp and lost to sleep right now. He should be in the same state, but he felt oddly energized.

He hadn't been with anyone in a while, what with being on the rig, injuring his shoulder, then driving up here last month. And even before that, he hadn't sought out female company all that often. It had basically been on a when-needed basis. Just the occasional one-night stand. Sometimes they didn't even make it back to her place or his place for a real bed. They'd make use of a bathroom wall or a back seat, give each other a quick release, then move on. No strings attached, by mutual agreement. Just the way he'd always liked it. Commitment meant someone expecting you to stay in one place, and his job didn't give him that luxury. He frowned at the fire.

Ted was living proof that wasn't true. He and Lori had lived in Mobile all their lives. Lots of guys on the rigs were locals. Or outsiders who'd moved there and put down roots, bought houses, started families. But roots weren't Logan's style. Never had been.

Rent a place. Don't keep a lot of possessions. Always be ready to pack up and go to the next place. The next job. The next woman. He watched shadows dance across Piper's back. This was one woman he might have a really hard time walking away from.

In the past, that kind of thinking would be enough to have him up and getting dressed, slipping out without a word, never to return. Instead, he moved closer and curled his body around hers. She let out a small moan of *don't wake me* mixed with *that feels nice.* He rested his leg over hers, eager to make contact with as much of her as possible. Then he buried his face in her hair and closed his eyes. He should be running. But he couldn't. Not yet. Not tonight.

The sound of a log tumbling woke him with a jolt. He blinked at the clock on the nightstand. Four o'clock in the morning. Piper was by the fireplace, stoking the coals and putting a fresh log on. Her hair fell over her shoulder, glowing like liquid gold in the firelight. She'd pulled on her sweater, but that was all. When she bent over, most of her ass was exposed, and it was one hell of a sight to wake up to. She glanced back at him and grimaced.

"Sorry. I was trying to add a log and made a mess. I can't move it on top of the coals to get it started…"

Logan slid out of bed and crouched at her side, taking the metal poker from her hand. He prodded the log back up where it belonged, then used the small shovel to push the hot coals away from the front of the hearth before drawing the chain link curtain closed again.

Piper sighed. "You make it look so easy. Were you a Boy Scout, or is it just a man thing?"

Being so close to the now-crackling flames felt good, so Logan sat back on the floor, leaning against the upholstered chair. He held open his arm for Piper to join him, and she quickly crawled over and tucked into his side. They both stared at the fire for a moment before he answered her question.

"I was never in one place long enough to join the Scouts or anything else as a kid. But my dad liked to take us camping." He gave a humorless chuckle. "At least, that's what he called it—camping. Sometimes it was just surviving. Sometimes all we had was that stupid old motor home."

That tan Winnebago was pretty tiny for an adult and two kids on a full-time basis. Every inch of the brown-and-orange-plaid interior was utilized for something. And some things did double duty, like the dinette that converted to a "bed" for Nikki at night. He and Dad often had their morning coffees outside so Nikki could sleep.

Piper looked up at him in surprise. "You and your dad lived in a motor home? Really?"

She made it sound like some grand adventure, which it rarely was. He seldom talked with anyone about those years with Dad. But there was something about having Piper snuggled up to him that made him let down his guard.

"Sometimes. Usually it was for just a month or so after we hit a new town. Then he'd try to find a house or apartment to rent."

"What did your dad do for a living? Iris doesn't talk about him much."

"What did he do? He dreamed. A lot." He stared into

the fire for a moment, lost in memories. Not *all* of them
were bad. "Brian Taggart was always looking for the
next big thing, forming partnerships with people he'd
just met. Or never met. A fishing boat in Oregon. Gold
mining in Alaska. A casino in Oklahoma. Building a
retirement community in Yuma. A dinner cruise boat
in Boston. A hotel in Key West." Logan felt weary just
reciting all the places they'd been. "Some of them were
successes. Most weren't. Even the good ones weren't
enough to hold him. He was always chasing something
bigger. With my sister and me in tow."

"What about your mom?"

Logan stilled. He *never* talked about Mom in any
detail. He never knew how to handle the rush of emotions waiting to flood over him whenever he dusted off
those memories. "Mom got tired of it all early on, and
stayed in St. Louis when Dad got the job in Yuma. She
let us go with him 'just for that summer.'" He raised
his fingers in mock quotes. "Then she found a new guy
with his own kids and she wasn't all that interested
in having us come back to complicate things. Told us
we'd have more fun with Dad, and sent us away. She
might have been right, but…"

Piper's voice was soft and knowing. "But that didn't
make it hurt any less."

No, it didn't. Piper didn't push him. Her legs were
curled under herself, her shoulder under his arm, her
head on his chest. She was warm and silent. Comforting
without saying a word. Everything about his mother's
memory hurt, but the pain was buffered somehow by
Piper's presence.

He hadn't thought about that awful day in years.

He'd been seven or eight, and Nikki was a year younger. They were standing by the dusty motor home parked in front of Mom's boyfriend's house. It was a hot August day, and the sky was bright blue, dotted with thin white clouds. He'd been so full of hope that day, excited at the thought of having his own room and going to school and being part of a normal family. But there was no room for Nikki and him in Mom's new life. And no welcome in the boyfriend's eyes. Mom gave them each a distracted kiss and hurried them back into the motor home. Dad had just nodded in acceptance, but Logan saw the anger that tightened the cords in his father's neck. Nikki cried. So did Mom. But she never left the boyfriend's side as they drove away. It was the last time they'd seen her.

"What happened?"

He shifted his weight, ready to be done with this, but Piper put her arm around his waist and held on. She looked up into his eyes and waited. Well, shit. He'd gone this far—may as well finish it.

"There was a car accident six months later." He blinked away. "Ironic, right? We were the ones living on the road, and Mom was the one who died on it."

"I'm so sorry…"

He shook his head sharply. Tension was making his skin feel tight. Here came that wave he'd dreaded. Anger. Loss. Regret. All of it. "It was a long time ago."

Piper sat up, fixing her sharp blue eyes on his. "I lost my mom as an adult and it was hard. You were just a little boy, Logan. Not much older than Ethan was when Tom…"

She stopped abruptly, her brows gathering. Things

were taking a much heavier turn than either of them wanted right now. He gave her a light kiss on the forehead before he spoke.

"I'd like to talk about him…about what happened… but not now. Not tonight. Not in the dark. Not…"

She flashed a quick, slanted smile. "Not when you're naked?"

He looked down and started to laugh. It hadn't even occurred to him that he'd crawled out of bed to join her without putting any clothes on. "*Definitely* not when I'm naked. Let's save the rest of our soul-baring for the daylight hours."

"Agreed. But just so you know—I like this. I like having a grown-up conversation with a man without feeling like I have to impress you or anything. I mean…" Her mouth twisted as her head tipped to the side. "It's not like we're dating or anything. I'm not nervous about impressing you or what's going to happen next, because we've already…"

"Already had a booty call?" He tugged her across his lap, groaning at the feel of her bare bottom settling on his thighs. "Are you saying we've gone at this backwards? We did the deed and *now* we're getting to know each other?" He buried his hands in her hair, fluffing it so it fell wild around her wide blue eyes. Her cheeks flushed with color, and her soft lips parted. Damn, what this woman did to him. "Are you scandalized by our behavior, Piper?"

"I was going to say we already know each other. You rescued me from a kitchen flood. I rescued you from an overzealous admirer. You've met my children. But yes…" The corner of her mouth lifted. "I suppose

I *should* be scandalized. I am sitting on a naked man's lap, after all." His body stirred underneath her, making her giggle. "Are you thinking scandalous thoughts, Logan?"

"When your hair is loose like that, and your lips are soft and pink like that, and you're sitting on my lap with nothing between us?" She leaned forward and pressed those lips on his, making his erection twitch again. "Yeah, all my thoughts are pretty scandalous right now."

She sighed against his lips. "Logan, what are we *doing* here?"

"Uh-uh-uh. Those thoughts have to wait for daylight, remember?" He lowered her back until she lay on the rug beneath him. He had no fucking *clue* what they were doing, but he knew talking about it might spoil it. So he kissed her long and slow, until she started squirming against him, and then he kept on kissing. She was pulling him into her web one kiss at a time.

She may not realize it—she may not even *want* it—but she was pulling him in just the same. His hands slid down to lift her hips until they rested on his thighs. It was a good thing his arms were long, because he was just able to reach the roll of condoms he'd brought in earlier. He'd found Gran's supply for stocking the guest rooms after dinner, and had helped himself. Piper watched, silent, as he tore one from the package and rolled it on. He rose to his knees and lifted her legs, wrapping them around his waist.

Nope—he had no clue what they were doing. He only knew he wasn't ready for it to stop anytime soon.

CHAPTER SIXTEEN

PIPER PANICKED WHEN she opened her eyes and saw daylight. Bright, sunny daylight. *Breakfast at the inn! Kids to school!* She sat up. *Where the hell am I?* Awareness finally dawned. She was alone in Room Three. Her hands covered her cheeks in horror. It wasn't a dream. She'd made love to Logan Taggart. Many, many times. Twice on the floor! She scurried out of bed, grabbing at her clothes and trying to think straight.

Okay. Okay. It was an aberration. The snowstorm was to blame. The empty inn. That moment of intimacy in the attic when she'd begged him to hold her. Then down to this room—the room that was *her* idea. She stopped moving, clutching her clothes to her chest and staring at the bed. For years now, she'd wondered if she'd ever want another man, if she'd ever allow another man to caress her, to make love to her. Would she be consumed with guilt? Shame? Would her love for Tom keep her from ever experiencing pleasure with someone else?

Her skin tingled with a flood of heat. That had *not* been a problem last night. But how did she feel about it now? She'd never once thought about Tom while in bed with Logan. Did that make her disloyal to her husband?

Tom. The man she'd married fifteen years ago.

They'd had a wonderful life together. If he'd lived, she'd *never* have wanted anyone else. She sank down to sit on the edge of the bed, blinking quickly to beat back tears. But Tom *hadn't* lived. And she had. It felt so good to feel a man's arms around her again. A man's mouth against her skin. To have an intimate conversation by the fire. Didn't she *deserve* a night like last night?

Her chin rose. Yes, damn it, she did. But what now? Last night—or rather, early that morning—she'd asked Logan what they were doing, and he'd quickly distracted her with more sex. To be fair, he hadn't had to work very hard, either. There was a sweet, soft ache between her legs to remind her how enthusiastically she'd participated. But today was a new day. And reality, as intense as the sunlight glinting off the snowbanks outside, was knocking at the door. Tap. Tap. Tap.

She jumped to her feet when the door opened behind her. Logan came in, carrying a tray with two coffees and a plate of pastries. He looked at the bed, then to where she was standing, covering herself as if he hadn't seen it all already. As if he hadn't already kissed every inch of her. And, typical Logan, he seemed as cool as ever—apparently not struggling with *any* of the worries she had.

"Good morning, sleepyhead." He walked to the chair by the fireplace, setting the tray on the small table there. She was frozen in place, feeling at a disadvantage, naked and flustered. Logan, however, appeared freshly showered, fully dressed and ready to start the day.

"How long have you been up?" Her voice sounded like an accusation, but Mr. Laid-Back just smiled.

"Long enough to make coffee, shovel the front steps,

shower, feed a pissed-off cat and grab a robe from Gran's closet." He nodded toward the bed, where a lavender robe lay across the corner.

She slipped quickly into the fuzzy chenille robe, her back turned to Logan in an illogical display of modesty.

"Thanks for the robe. And the coffee." She walked over and picked up a mug. "I'm sorry I slept so long…"

"We didn't exactly get a lot of sleep last night. And when we weren't sleeping…well…" He winked at her playfully. She wasn't sure if she was ready to be flirty this morning. Today was reality.

"Yeah, I remember." She sat in the chair, glancing over at the bed. The sheets were in a tangle. The bedspread was on the floor. What day was it? Wednesday. This room wasn't reserved until Friday night, so she had time. Time for what, exactly? She looked at Logan, and his expression hadn't changed. Relaxed, amused, satisfied. *Satisfied?* She had to be imagining that one. Her eyes narrowed on him. Nope. That was a satisfied gleam in his eye. She straightened in the chair. Was it possible an out-of-practice widowed mom had rocked this gorgeous man's world as much as he'd rocked hers? His smile deepened.

"What are you thinking about, Piper? 'Cuz whatever it is, it's putting some very pretty color on your cheeks."

She went to take another sip of her coffee, closing her eyes and trying to appear as cool as he was. But her hand trembled at the last moment and gave her away.

"Never you mind," she said primly. "I'm not going to feed your ego this morning. I'll get dressed after coffee and run over to my place to shower and change. Then you and I need to get busy."

His brows rose. "Yeah? I'm game."

She rolled her eyes. "Not *that* kind of busy. We have to get this place decorated before the weekend guests start arriving. We can't have boxes everywhere." She picked up a blueberry pastry and started to stand, but Logan put his hand on her shoulder before she could.

"Sit still and relax, Commander. Enjoy your coffee. I'll bring the rest of the boxes down and sort them while you're at your place. Between the two of us, we'll make good time. And if you're really nice to me..." he bent over, tipping her chin up and kissing her tenderly "...we can come back to Room Three later."

"I need to clean this room and get it made up." Her protest sounded weak to her own ears. He just shook his head and kissed her again.

"It's not booked until Friday. I checked. We have two doubles arriving today, but their rooms are ready and they're up on the third floor. And your kids aren't home until tomorrow, so there's no reason we can't come right back here tonight." He frowned at her. "Unless you don't want to?"

She stood, walking to the window and staring at the snowy parking lot. She'd have to call the plowing service and make sure they got here this morning. And she should check the pantry to see if she had all the foodstuffs she needed for the next couple of mornings. And vacuum. She had to vacuum upstairs and in the parlor. And decorate. So much decorating. After all that, she'd be too exhausted, and hopefully too smart, to come back to Room Three.

Strong arms circled her waist from behind, interrupting all those Very Important Plans. She leaned back against him as if it was the most natural thing in the world. His lips grazed the top of her ear.

"So is it only in the daylight that you overthink things so hard?"

It took a moment to register his words, because she was too busy registering what his closeness was doing to her.

"I don't know what you mean."

His chest vibrated with suppressed laughter. "Liar. You're making a mental list of all the reasons we shouldn't come back here later, when there's only one reason that matters. Do you want to, or don't you?"

She shook her head. "It's not that simple."

"Actually, it is. But go do what you have to do, and you can tell me what you want later. Just do me one favor?"

She stepped away, trying to settle her thoughts before granting Logan any favors. "What kind of favor?"

"Leave this room just as it is. I like the thought of it all sex-rumpled and ready for more if we decide to come back. Deal?"

She felt a wash of heat at the thought of this room being *sex-rumpled and ready* all day. It was silly. Scandalous. Not the behavior of a respectable single mother. She looked up at Logan, having no doubt what her answer would be.

"Deal."

Logan was right about them making a good team. By lunchtime, they'd accomplished far more than Piper expected. He was clearly capable of being more detail-oriented than his laid-back attitude let on. That shouldn't have been such a surprise, since he *was* an engineer. But she still found herself impressed by the way he'd orga-nized and prioritized tasks.

Logan offered to assemble all of the artificial trees in the public spaces downstairs so that she could come behind and decorate. It was a little out of her preferred finish-one-room-at-a-time approach, but she had to admit she and Logan were each work-ing to their strengths. He was big-picture. She was fuss-over-details. And it gave them a little space for a few hours, so she could bring her overactive libido back under control.

Logan had flipped some unknown switch inside of her yesterday. She'd just spent the night—and was se-riously considering another!—with a man so wrong for her it wasn't even funny.

He was a heavily tattooed devil-may-care drifter who'd come into town wearing a ponytail and rid-ing a motorcycle. Definitely *not* the kind of man a re-sponsible mother of two should consider for anything other than…well…exactly what she'd used him for. She frowned as she moved the stepladder into the library to start decorating the tree. Logan was whistling to him-self in the dining room. She wasn't *really* using him, was she? She unpacked the top layer of ornaments in order to get to the angel tree-topper. No, they'd both gone into yesterday's events with their eyes wide open.

Logan hadn't hidden the fact that he was only here temporarily. That he was eager to leave Rendezvous Falls behind and move on. The snowstorm had created the perfect opportunity for some very grown-up fun. She stretched. Yes, that *had* been fun. And there was a possibility of more fun tonight, since the kids were still with Susan and Roger. Part of her said a second night might complicate things. But another voice whispered this might be her last chance to have a wild night of sex for a very long time. Tender, sexy tattooed bikers didn't drift into town all that often. If they did, they certainly never looked her way. A temporary relationship was all she was willing to consider as long as she had young children at home. Ethan and Lily didn't need her bringing men into their lives.

The stepladder wiggled a little as she moved higher, stretching to make sure the angel was sitting straight on the tree. Everyone kept insisting Piper was a *woman* as well as a mom. Okay. She'd be a woman with Logan while he was here. Hopefully her stolen time with him would satisfy any itch she might have for the next four or five years. Then again, even if she had an opportunity with another man, would anyone else be able to make her feel the way Logan did with every touch, every smile, every kiss, every...

A strong arm wrapped around her waist and pulled her from the ladder with a Viking-like cry of victory. She squealed in surprise as Logan swung her around the room and tossed her in the air to get her turned around to face him. He was grinning up at her with a hungry look in his eye and gold tinsel wrapped around his neck like a scarf. She couldn't help laughing down at him. *Really* laughing. Her heart skipped around in her chest. God, when was the last time she laughed this hard? Laughed because *she* was having fun? Not watching someone else's fun, but *feeling* it in her own bones again.

The feeling was a happy shock to her system, and

she couldn't stop, especially when he nearly bonked her head on the library's ceiling fan.

"Oh my god. You really *are* a giant!" She reached down to put her hands on top of his shoulders. "A big, crazy giant who's going to give me a concussion!"

He laughed again, giving her another little toss before letting her body slide down his until they were eye to eye. The gold flecks in his brown eyes were on fire with a light that was more than just laughter. "I can think of something I'd like to give you right now, and it's definitely not a concussion. But it might be big and crazy. I think it's time for a little Room Three, don't you?"

She giggled. No, this man had definitely not factored into any of her plans for a perfect holiday. But if they only had one more night, why not take the leap? It was only a *little* dangerous. She dipped her head and gave him a quick kiss.

"I'm all for a booty call, but do you think we've done enough work to deserve a break in the middle of the day?"

"First, yes. Yes, I definitely do." He nodded enthusiastically. "And second, we deserve this whether we've done the work or not. Because you and I are awesome together and I can't wait any longer…"

She stopped his words with a kiss, her hands cupping his face. He let her slide to the floor, but the kiss never broke. His arms moved around her, his hands gripping her butt cheeks and tugging her close against him. *Yes, please…*

A sound registered from somewhere, breaking her concentration. She pulled her head back.

"Was that the door? Is someone here?" She pushed her hands against his chest in a panic to put space between them. Had Susan brought the kids? Her hand went to her hair. Logan had convinced her to skip the ponytail for today, but would Susan know what they'd been up to if she saw Piper's hair free and mussed from that swing through the air? Her heart started racing in panic.

"Easy." Logan's voice was amused as he tugged the tinsel from his neck. "I didn't hear anything. But I'll go check."

She nodded, fingers over her trembling lips. "I'm really not cut out for this kind of thing."

His right brow arched high. "I beg to differ. You are *perfect* for 'this kind of thing,' babe." He patted her cheek. "I'll be right back." He was back in just a few minutes, shaking his head. "The driveway's been plowed and the mail arrived, but we're all alone." He held up a finger to stop the objections she started to raise. "And if the women get back from Corning, they don't need us to be waiting for them. They already have keys. Tonight's guests aren't due until after four, which gives us more than enough time for a quick little shag and maybe even more of the decorating you're so fond of before they arrive." He'd walked closer with every word, until his chest brushed against hers. His fingers combed her hair back, then lingered there on her neck, making her tremble. A slow, sexy smile spread on his face.

"So, is it Room Three, Piper?"

A million reasons to say no. And still, she heard herself saying the opposite.

"Yes. Room Three."

It HAD BEEN, without a doubt, the best thirty-six hours of Logan Taggart's life.

No contest.

He flipped the thick blueberry pancakes on the griddle and glanced at the pan of blueberry compote Piper had bubbling in the pan on the next burner. A hearty breakfast for a couple of people who'd been working and sexing a *lot* since Tuesday afternoon. He grinned to himself. Yup, lots of sexing. Of course, the breakfast was also for their guests, because the real world had finally invaded their snowbound privacy yesterday. The women had returned from their Corning adventure in the afternoon. Two couples from Albany had arrived last night as planned, and were booked through the weekend for the holiday craft festival.

The arrival of outsiders had altered his and Piper's activities slightly, but not much. They couldn't run around the inn half-dressed and barefoot like they had that first night when the snow was coming down and the doors were locked tight. Yeah…that was fun. He turned down the flame under the compote before it burned. But even with four rooms occupied last night, no one had been staying on the ground floor. Once the guests were settled in, he and Piper still had plenty of privacy in Room Three. And they'd taken advantage of it, spending their second night together in a tangle of sheets, with a fire stoked in the hearth and a bigger fire stoked inside of Logan.

If someone had told him before that week that he would use the words "best ever" to describe hanging holiday decorations in his grandmother's inn with a bossy little mom of two… Well, he'd have laughed himself hoarse at the thought.

But the decorating wasn't the fun part—although he'd enjoyed it far more than expected. It was the breaks they'd taken every few hours to go back to Room Three that were memorable. He smiled to himself as he moved the pancakes to a warm platter. One minute they'd been working hard, then he'd swept Piper off the ladder in the library and…off to Room Three. Do a little dusting in the dining room before setting out Gran's snowman collection, then just one look into Piper's eyes and… Room Three, please. Shovel the the porch together, laughing and throwing snowballs, and just like that. Room Three.

"How's it coming in here?" Piper came up behind him and checked the compote. "Smells delicious."

Logan leaned over and kissed her. "*You* smell delicious. And look delicious, too."

She glanced down at the ruffled cotton apron that covered her simple top and jeans, then squinted up at him with a smirk. "Really?"

"It's not the wrapping that counts, babe. Every time I see you, I see you naked under me on that four-poster bed, with the fire in the hearth behind you." Just saying the words was enough to turn him on. From the way her pupils went wide and dark, they had the same effect on her. She gave herself a little shake and poured the blueberry sauce into two separate pitchers.

"We have two tables of hungry guests waiting. Can you bring the pancakes?" She nodded at the platters. "By tomorrow, the place will be full for the weekend." She turned away, carrying the sauce, and looked over her shoulder. "Including Room Three."

She made it sound very…final. And Logan, who had a job waiting in South America, didn't like it. Logical or not, he hated to think of them coming to an end. It was inevitable. But it didn't have to happen *now*.

They served breakfast and chatted with their guests for a few minutes. Piper suggested things to do around town now that the roads were clear and dry. She was quite the expert on all things Rendezvous Falls and the Finger Lakes area in general, rattling off restaurants, wineries, local and state parks, the best places to park for the craft fair… She knew it all.

After breakfast, she started washing the pans in the deep stainless steel sink. Outside, the snow was melting wherever the sun hit it. The world was intruding on their little adventure as surely as the grass was reappearing in yards around town. He put away the pancake mix and started cleaning the stove. Even with the silence, the two of them had a comfortable rhythm. It was nice. It was yet another one of those unfamiliar territories for him—being with a woman day and night like this. He'd had a few live-in lovers through the years, but none who felt like this. None had felt this easy. He walked over with a towel to help her dry the pans and glanced at her behind, round and inviting under those clothes. None that filled him with this constant, restless desire to pull them into a corner and kiss them senseless.

Piper squeaked when he wrapped his arm around her waist and did just that—tugged her into the corner by the window and kissed her coffee-and-blueberry-flavored lips. She quickly melted against him, then pulled away, shaking her head. Her eyes were sad, but determined.

"We have to stop." He tried to pull her back in, but she braced her hands on his chest. She stared straight ahead, avoiding his eyes. "I'm serious, Logan. This week…the past two nights…it's been…incredible." She finally looked up through long blond lashes. "*So* incredible. But it's time to get real. Not only are we going to have an inn full of people, but my children are coming home today. It was fun. But it's over. It has to be. Duty calls, and all that."

The word *over* didn't compute for him. Luckily, it didn't seem to compute for her, either. She sounded like she was trying to convince herself as much as him. She was saying what she *should* say, rather than what she *wanted* to say. And that was the key—what did they *want* to do? He knew his answer.

"I get what you're saying. Business. Real world. Kids. Blah, blah, blah." He tipped her chin up with his fingers. "But those things don't have to mean it's over. They just mean we need to be more…creative."

Instead of melting the way he'd hoped, her voice went frosty. "The fact that you just used 'blah blah blah' and my *children* in the same breath tells me that you are not getting it at all." She stepped back, twisting the dish towel in her hands into a knot. "Ethan and Lily are my number one priority, Logan. I am *not* complicating their lives any more than they already are by getting involved with a man." She turned back to the sink and started drying the griddle, then set it down and turned to face him again, her hands braced on the sink behind her as she leaned back. "Look, I didn't think I'd ever desire another man after losing my husband. Ever. You showed me I could. It's a big step for me, and I'm grateful. But…"

A flash of anger—or hurt—shot through Logan. "You weren't some charity case, for god's sake. I don't want you to be *grateful*. And I sure as hell don't want you saying it's *over*!" He jammed his fingers through his hair and blew out a sigh, lowering his voice. "I know your kids come first. I didn't mean it to sound otherwise. I'm just saying you and I can find a way to get together, even it's just stolen moments…"

"I wish I could see that working. I really do. But one mistake and…" She shook her head. "I don't know…"

He should let her walk away. It wasn't his style to beg anyone to be part of his life. But this was Piper. It was different with her.

"We're good together, Piper. We're really freakin' good together." The corner of her mouth lifted, giving him hope. "Let's not throw that away yet. We'll be careful. No one needs to know." He walked over and cupped her face in his hands. "But if I have to hang around this frozen, godforsaken town and sip tea in my grandmother's Victorian mansion for another month, at least give me the hope of a few more Room Threes."

She gave a surprised snort of laughter, shaking her head but not denying him. "So let me get this straight— you weren't taking pity on *me*, but now I'm supposed to take pity on *you*?"

"If that works, sure." He tipped his head and gave her his best puppy dog eyes. "Feel sorry for poor me, sleeping alone in Gran's apartment, with no one to keep me warm…"

She patted the back of his hand with a smile. "I have children, remember? I can't do sleepovers when they're home."

Logan nodded, but he couldn't help thinking that was a damn shame. Sleeping with Piper had been one of the nicest surprises of the past two nights. He tended to be a bed hog, restless and sprawling. But with Piper by his side, he'd been settled and peaceful as long as she was in his arms. And he'd made sure she was in his arms all the time.

Piper's expression sobered, and he knew she was trying to be logical again. He hated when she did that. So he kissed her. Right there in the kitchen. Where they could be caught at any moment. He folded her into his arms and kissed the living daylights out of the woman. And she kissed him right back, moaning softly and wrapping her arms around his waist.

She finally pulled away with a low laugh, smacking him lightly on the chest. "You need to stop doing that. I can't think when you pounce." She arched a brow at him. "And I know that's exactly why you do it."

He shrugged, splaying his hands in innocence. "It's not the *only* reason I do it. It's not my fault you're so damn irresistible."

She turned away and picked up the dish towel. "Yeah, I'm irresistible, alright. With a four-year-old chatterbox attached to my hip and a mad-at-the-world teenager making my hair go gray. Not to mention an old house falling down around my ears and former in-laws trying to run my life." She glanced over her shoulder at him. "Real life comes back today, Logan, and it's going to make me a lot less irresistible. Trust me."

He stared at her back as she dried the pan, apron tied around her waist, jeans dusted with pancake flour. She couldn't make herself less irresistible to him if she tried. His little momma, working hard. Last night, she'd cried out his name as she wrapped her legs around his waist and held on for a ride that left them both sweaty and spent. Both images turned him on. He'd want her, no matter what. He *did* want her. No matter what. He walked out of the kitchen without another word, stunned at his realization.

Piper Montgomery couldn't do anything to make him stop wanting her. She'd pulled him in, literally and figuratively, and he'd willingly fallen. Not just for the sex. For the woman.

CHAPTER SEVENTEEN

"A BOOTY CALL?" Iris scoffed, doing her best to ignore the way her heart just skipped a beat at the scene Helen just described. She sat up on the edge of her bed and reached for her blue slacks nearby. "You expect me to believe that Piper Montgomery suggested a *booty call* to my grandson in the inn? At lunchtime? That's impossible!"

Helen lifted her shoulder. "Say what you want, Iris, but I know what I saw. *And* what I heard." She paused. "Do you need help dressing?"

Iris swatted Helen's hand away. "No. I do *not* need your help. It's just…" She blew out a breath. "Pants are the hardest, you know? I can't pull them up while my ass is on the bed. But when I stand, I need to hold the walker for balance. And I need both hands to pull up the pants! It's tough as hell to do both."

She set the trousers on the floor and put her feet into the legs, then moved them up over her knees. She'd worked out a system that limited her vulnerability, but any level was too much for Iris.

Vickie Pendergast was sitting in the corner chair, ignoring Iris's dressing dilemma and focusing on Helen's story. As always, she looked flawless. Vickie's champagne-colored hair was carefully styled, and her Coach bag was on the floor near her feet. It was Vickie's special talent, but today Iris found it annoying. It wasn't fair that her friends were living their normal lives and she was trapped here in rehab. Vickie smoothed her hands down her wool sweaterdress as she crossed her legs and leaned forward.

"Iris, you kept saying Logan wouldn't *want* someone as sweet as Piper. Why have we been trying to fix that boy up with biker babes all this time?" She gave Iris a pointed look. "Then again, maybe little Miss Booty Call isn't as sweet as we thought."

Iris was just beginning to stand, so she couldn't flip her middle finger Vickie's way. She let her tone do the work. "Don't be ridiculous. I don't know what Helen *thinks* she saw or heard…" She was on her feet now. She took one hand off the walker and grabbed for the pants. This was damned embarrassing, even if Helen and Vickie were two of her closest friends. She yanked the pants high enough that she could sit back down to fasten them. She blew out a sigh of relief, then flashed Helen another dirty look. "You were just wrong, Helen. That's the only explanation."

Helen didn't answer right away, watching as Iris zipped her trousers and fastened the belt. "Wouldn't pants with an elastic waistband be easier?"

Iris shook her head. "I'd need *two* hands to pull elastic pants up, unless I order them two sizes too big, and that's not happening."

"What about sweatpants?" Vickie asked, apparently deciding Iris wasn't humiliated *enough* that morning. They're looser and…" Her voice trailed off when she saw Iris's expression, and then she tried to defend the idea. "Lots of seniors wear them…"

Iris scowled at Vickie.

"You have known me for forty years. Have you ever once known me to wear *sweatpants*?"

Vickie straightened, fussing with the gold bangles on her wrist. "Well, excuse me for wanting to make things easier for my friend. I'm not suggesting you wear them to church, you old grump. But around your apartment or here at the center? What's the big deal?" She turned to Helen, knowing just how to push Iris's buttons. "So tell me about Piper and Logan's booty call again—every little detail."

Helen sat on the end of Iris's bed, curling her feet up under herself. She was in her early sixties, short and not so slim, with a quick, easy smile. Helen had been through some tough times since her husband died a few years ago, but she was much happier now that her niece had moved to Rendezvous Falls that summer, and was now planning a wedding. Helen's dark eyes darted to Iris, then back to Vickie, probably figuring she could outrun Iris if the need arose.

"Like I said," Helen started. "I stopped by the inn Wednesday after the snow stopped." She looked at Iris. "*You're* the one who asked me to check on things. To make sure the lot was cleared, and that Logan and Piper had the inn ready for this weekend. I saw Piper in the library, decorating the tree. I didn't want to startle her while she was up so high on the ladder, so I waited in the hall. I didn't even know Logan was in the room until he ran over and grabbed Piper right off the ladder. Scared me almost as much as he scared Piper!"

Iris scowled, as irritated with her grandson as she

was with Helen. Damn that Logan for messing around with Piper. But maybe that's all it was? Horseplay?

"Helen," she said. "Logan was just being a guy and messing around. After all, they'd been basically snowed in there for two days and he was probably bored…" Wait. Piper told Helen on Monday that she was sending the kids to the Montgomerys' for a few days so she could focus on decorating the inn. So Logan and Piper had been *alone* together at the inn during a snowstorm. *No.* There was no way Piper, a responsible single mother, would have a fling with a guy like Logan.

Then again…there was a time when *she'd* been a young single mom. And she'd had a wildly passionate affair with Sam Adler. Was it really so crazy to think Piper might do the same?

She looked up to see Helen and Vickie both smiling at her. "What?"

Vickie laughed. "Oh, come on! You just said it— Logan and Piper were snowed in together. All sorts of things could have happened."

"Exactly," Helen said. "Sure, they were laughing when he grabbed her and swung her around. But I know the difference between horseplay and foreplay. Trust me, once she started sliding down the front of him, there was nothing funny about it. I almost needed a cigarette just from *watching* them." Helen pretended to fan herself, earning another laugh from Vickie and scowl from Iris.

"Okay, okay." Iris waved her hand. "So they flirted a little. Christmas decorating probably put them in a…a happy mood. That doesn't mean…"

"Iris, that kiss was more than playful and flirty. It

was *hot*. And it was definitely not the first time they'd done it. They were very…familiar…with each other."

Iris shook her head in frustration. "I'm going to wring Logan's neck. I told him when he got here to stay the hell away from Piper."

Helen patted Iris's leg gently. "I know you've become very fond of Piper, but she may not be quite as vulnerable as you think. She's the one I heard mentioning a *booty call*. That's when I figured it was time for me to leave."

Vickie studied the rings on her fingers. Three husbands had netted her a nice jewelry collection. "Good thing Cecile isn't here today. She'd have us picturing them doing it in the lobby, like in one of those romance novels she enjoys so much."

Helen laughed. "I do wonder about Cecile and Charlie sometimes. She has an interesting approach to… romance."

"I just can't believe it…" Iris breathed.

"What? That Cecile and Charlie might have a red room of bondage?" Vickie snorted. "I'm not so sure they don't…"

"Not that!" Iris rolled her eyes. "Charlie can tie up Cecile eight ways from Sunday if it makes them happy." She stood and moved slowly toward a chair near the window. Her physical therapist told her she needed to walk around the room every few hours. She ignored the way Helen hovered behind her every step. It didn't hurt as much as she expected as she sat. Maybe she was making progress after all. She looked up at Helen, who quickly busied herself checking out the plants by the window.

Vickie gave her a sharp look. "I can't help thinking of Sam…"

Iris stopped her from saying another word. "That was different. Sam and I were just two passing ships…"

Vickie stood, her bag in her hand. "Iris, that man asked you to marry him."

Yes, he had. The pain of saying no was still sharp in Iris's heart fifty years later. She'd loved him, but she couldn't set her responsibilities aside for love. And Piper wouldn't, either.

"The only thing I couldn't figure out," Helen said, "is why they were talking about Room Three? Is that a special room or something? Do you think that's where… Oh. Wow. Yeah." Helen leaned back against the windowsill and chuckled. "Iris, they used one of *your* rooms for their booty call!"

"Stop saying that!" She put her hands over her face. Her grandson and Piper spending time together in one of her guest rooms…it was just so absurd. Her shoulders started to shake. What else could she do but laugh? She dropped her hands to her lap and looked at her friends. They quickly joined her in laughter, eventually getting so loud that a nurse stuck her head in the door to shush them.

Vickie pulled tissues from her bag and handed them around so they could dry their eyes. "So now what?"

Iris dabbed her eyes and sighed. Now what indeed.

LOGAN REACHED DOWN for the last of the basement light fixtures, and Ethan set it in his hand.

"Thanks, kid." He looked down from the stepladder. "You want to wire this one?"

Ethan's eyes went wide. "Really?"

"You've watched me wire seven of the things. You

should have it by now if you were paying attention."
Logan stepped off the ladder, handing the light back
to Ethan. "You got this."

Ethan went up the ladder, balancing one end of the
long light base on his shoulder the same way Logan had
been doing as he started twisting wires together. The
breaker for the basement was turned off, so there wasn't
any danger. Logan stopped him a few times to give him
advice on how far back to strip the plastic covering and
how to twist on the wire caps so the wires made good
contact. The boy fumbled a little with the screwdriver,
but he got the light secured in place.

Logan nodded. "Good job. Pop the bulb in and let's
light this place up." Ethan put the slim LED bulb in
and hopped off the ladder. Logan nodded toward the
electrical box near the base of the stairs, and Ethan
walked over and flipped the switch.

The boy started to laugh. "Mom can't complain about
it being dark and scary anymore!"

Maybe they should have cut the number of lights down
to six. This basement was as bright as an airport landing strip now. But with LEDs, it wouldn't cost much in
electricity. And Piper would feel safe coming down here.

"Definitely not spooky." He called out when Ethan
moved to head up the stairs. "Whoa! Where do you
think you're going?"

The boy looked up at the lights, then over to Logan.
"What? We're done."

Logan gestured to the snippets of wire and plastic on
the floor, and the pile of boxes and packaging. "We're
not done until everything's cleaned up and put away.
Grab a trash bag and let's get to it."

Ethan groaned, but he did as he was asked. They worked in silence until Logan grabbed the broom and started sweeping. That's when Ethan blindsided him.

"Are you and my mom...dating now or something?"

Logan wasn't prepared for the question, especially since it had only been a week since the snowstorm that brought him and Piper together. They hadn't had more than a few stolen kisses—and some heavy petting sessions—since the kids returned from their grandparents' the previous Thursday. And one fast morning shag against the wall in the laundry room over the weekend, when neither of them could go another minute without being together. They hadn't even taken the time to undress. Just unzip, adjust, and...connect. Quick, hard, and hotter than hell. And still, not enough to satisfy. As he tried to figure out how to answer her son, he wondered if he'd ever have enough Piper Montgomery to satisfy him.

"Um...has your mom said anything?" So many ways for this conversation to go wrong and upset Piper in the process. Had Ethan had the bees and the birds talk yet? He was thirteen, so he hoped so. But the kid didn't have a dad.

Ethan shook his head, kneeling on one knee and holding the dustpan for Logan. His tone was neutral, but almost too much so. He wasn't making eye contact, but then again, this was Ethan and Ethan didn't do eye contact often. He lifted one shoulder. "No. But you seem into each other, and... I don't know. My grandmother thinks something's going on. And you're over here doing all this stuff..."

He'd hung the new dining room light two days earlier, with a little help from Ethan, who'd been hanging around in the doorway and had jumped in as soon as Logan asked. They moved the dining room table and chairs back into place when they were done. As a thank-you, Piper had asked him to stay for Chinese takeout with the kids. He'd thought it would be weird, sitting at her table with her children, but it hadn't been. Lily had everyone giggling at her attempts to pronounce Logan a master "leck-tishon"—the closest she could get to *electrician*. Yeah, even Logan had giggled. What was up with that?

After dinner, Piper had a wallpaper stripping party in the kitchen, where Lily sprayed white vinegar on the paper, and the others used scrapers to get the sticky stuff off the walls. A grumbling Ethan lasted less than an hour before begging off to do "homework." Logan figured that was a lie, and Piper confirmed it. But she'd explained that it was a big enough deal Ethan had helped in the dining room, and she didn't want to push her luck. Logan swallowed hard, really wishing Piper was here to navigate talking to her son about them. He looked up and realized Ethan was still waiting for an answer.

"Well, Ethan, sometimes men and women are just... friends. Like your mom and me. And as a friend, I'm just trying to help her..."

"Why are you using that weird human from *Sesame Street* voice? I'm not a kid, you know. I know how it works between men and women." Ethan brushed a shock of hair from his eyes, then quickly looked away. "Dude, if you're into her, just say so. It's not like I care."

Logan might not know a lot about teens, but that last line felt like a trap he did *not* want to step into. "What exactly do you think you know about how 'it works' between men and women?"

Ethan tied the trash bag and started up the stairs. "If you're asking me if I've had 'the talk,' my grandfather already put me through that torture, so you can skip it. You didn't answer my question."

Logan barked out a laugh, wondering how Piper kept up with her son. One minute he was a sulky little boy, and the next he was sounding like a man. "Actually, I *did* answer your question. I said your mom and I are just friends. Feel free to tell your grandmother I said so." Agitation nudged at him. He didn't like Susan talking to Piper's children about their relationship. This was why he'd made a point to avoid single moms—too many people watching and judging and complicating things. He took the trash bag from Ethan. "And remind her that I'm outta here after Christmas, so she doesn't need to worry about us."

The boy's eyes clouded for a moment, and then he shrugged and headed outside with the trash bag. "Whatever, man."

Later that evening, Piper knocked on the door to Gran's apartment. She'd sent a quick text just minutes before, checking to see if she could stop by with a thank-you gift for her glowing basement. He'd jumped up to pour a couple glasses of wine, hoping he could convince her stay a while. He was craving uninterrupted time with her. He looked around Gran's apartment. There was nothing in this place that said "sexy rendezvous." Nothing that said a man *lived* here, much less wanted to seduce a woman here. Unless perhaps the man and woman lived in 1892. Mr. Whiskers sauntered into the living room and meowed at him in agreement. Two males trapped in a time capsule.

Piper smiled up at him when he opened the door. She was wearing snug jeans and a fluffy pink sweater, with those damn zippered ankle boots. She was holding a platter of cookies in her hands.

"Are you going to stare at me all night, or let me in?"

"Is it okay if I do both?" He took the platter and moved aside for her to come in. "Welcome to my very manly abode." He set the cookies on the console and pulled her into his arms. She didn't argue, pressing up against him with a light laugh.

"Don't let Iris hear you dissing her antiques like that. She worked hard to put this collection together. A few of these pieces are worth a bundle."

His nose wrinkled. "I'm sure that's true, but it's so not my style. I prefer Room Three."

Her eyes went warm and she slid her arms around his waist. "Room Three *is* nice, but we can't take those kinds of chances without an empty inn and a snowstorm to keep everyone else away."

He had a sudden and fervent desire for more snow. Lots of it. Then he thought about Ethan's questions earlier. About the way Piper felt right now, in his arms and up against his body. His brain was caught somewhere between what-are-we-doing and make-love-to-her-you-idiot.

"Look… I don't mind stealing moments with you, Piper. I get it. It's fun. It's adventurous." He kissed her lightly. "But… I don't want to have to wait for snowstorms. I don't want all our moments to be stolen ones."

She blew out a quick breath, settling back in the

circle of his arms. "Are you saying you want to make this..." she gestured between them "...whatever we're doing...you want to make it official? Like, public-knowledge official?"

He brushed a strand of hair from her face, not sure how to answer. "I'm not saying we have to announce we're going steady or anything. But it would be nice to see you outside of these walls. Without having to keep my hands to myself."

She considered his words, frowning. That wasn't a good sign. She pulled away, walking over to the dining table and picking up a glass of wine. She stared into it as if looking for answers and finding only questions. "Is that what we're doing? Going steady? In a relationship? Boyfriend and girlfriend? How serious do you think this is going to get, Logan?"

He had no idea how to answer. "Can't we figure that out as we go? Take it a day at a time? No strings..."

"No strings?" She looked up at him, her brows furrowed. "You don't think we've already created strings?"

Yeah, they had. Of course they had. Strings slicing right through the center of his heart. He scrubbed his hands down his face.

"I don't know. This is uncharted territory for me. I feel things for you that I haven't felt before, but you know I'm not staying. I've got..."

Her eyes went soft and sad. "You've got South America. And I have two kids."

"Look, I've never in my life stayed in one place for long. Not as a kid. Not as an adult. I wouldn't be any good at it. I wouldn't know where to begin." He started to turn away, but her hand on his arm stopped him.

"This is uncharted territory for *both* of us. Maybe we should stick to that one-day-at-a-time plan a little while longer." She stared up at the ceiling, lost in thought. "I don't know. Maybe it doesn't matter who knows, as long as we don't let the kids know we're serious."

He should probably tell her it was too late for that, but before he had a chance, her eyes lit up and she gave him a bright smile.

"I know! SYAC!"

He wondered if she was pulling a Lily trick, trying to pronounce some word he should know. But damn if he could come up with a guess.

"Sigh-ack?"

"See You After Christmas. S-Y-A-C. The SYAC party! We get to go this year!"

He turned his hands up in surrender. "I have no clue what you're talking about."

She rushed to explain. "The local business owners and employees throw a legendary party at the Purple Shamrock every year before the holidays hit." She took a quick sip of wine. "This is my first year being invited, since I'm working at the inn. Which means *you* can come, too. Which means we can go together. It's next week!"

He'd been to the Shamrock a few times, usually with Luke Rutledge and a few of his pals. The thought of tugging Piper out onto the dance floor there made him smile.

"Okay, I'm in. But I still don't get where the name came from."

"My friend Evie from the diner said it all started as a joke. Once they started doing the Victorian Christmas thing every weekend from Thanksgiving to Christmas twenty years ago, the shops and restaurants were so busy that the workers could never get away for holiday parties on the weekends, and they were too exhausted anyway. So they started jokingly saying 'see you after Christmas' when they saw each other, because that's what it felt like." She walked to the sofa and ran her fingers down Mr. Whiskers's back, making him arch high and purr. Logan wasn't proud of it, but he was jealous of the damn cat. "Someone came up with the early, mid-week party idea, and now it's a big shindig where everyone lets down their hair before the holiday madness." She gave him a playful look. "And there's a very strict no-gossip rule. What happens at SYAC *stays* at SYAC."

He couldn't keep away from her another minute longer. He walked over and kissed her. "So if we get carried away and act like boyfriend and girlfriend there…?"

She kissed him back, so deeply he almost forgot he'd asked a question until she pulled away to answer. "We can act any way we want to. Interested?"

Oh, hell yeah. He was interested. Interested in SYAC. Interested in *her*. He didn't need words to reply—his mouth and hands did the trick. Her head fell back to give him better access to her neck and shoulders, and she whispered the sweetest words he could imagine.

"I've got an hour before I have to be home…"

He didn't hesitate, grabbing her hand and leading her to his bedroom. Froufrou be damned, if Piper was willing, he'd make love to her in an *actual* museum, so this place would do just fine.

CHAPTER EIGHTEEN

PIPER STUDIED HERSELF in the small mirror by her side door and blew out a long breath. She was doing this. She was going out—in *public*—with Logan Taggart. Together. With other people. He was picking her up and everything. She pushed a loose strand of hair behind her ear. This was it. A *date*.

She hadn't gone on a date since college. She glanced at the pictures on the refrigerator. Since Tom. *I can't do this.* No, she *could* do this. Because it wasn't a "date." That was a silly word. She and Logan were friends. Intimate friends, but still…friends. They were going to be with other friends. As…friends.

Not a couple. Not a date. Not as boyfriend/girlfriend. Just two adults who happened to be going to the same place. As friends. Where there'd be drinking. And dancing. Together.

Oh, God—what am I doing?

She covered her face with her hands, hoping it would have the same effect as breathing into a paper bag in stopping the panic attack she felt coming on. There was a sharp knock on the door and she cried out in fright. At this rate, she'd give herself a heart attack before she ever had a chance to make it to the dance floor.

Logan was leaning against the doorjamb, all denim

and cotton and leather and deliciousness. His eyes scanned her quickly and seemed to approve of her skinny jeans, dark red knit top, and high-heeled pumps. The cherry-red shoes seemed to be his favorite, since his gaze stayed on them so long she had to clear her throat to get his attention.

His eyes were heavy-lidded and full of hunger when he looked up. She was tempted to grab him by the front of his shirt and drag him upstairs. Screw the party. But Lily's giggle from the front room was a reminder that her children were home, and they were doing this thing tonight as *friends*.

Piper snatched her jacket from the back of the chair, covering up before either of her children saw her low-cut top. Logan gave a low laugh.

"Too late to cover up, babe. I already saw everything."

"Shhh!" She looked over her shoulder, but they were alone in the doorway. "You can't call me that here."

"Then come outside and climb into this battleship my grandmother calls a car, where I can call you whatever I want."

She laughed, then slapped her hand over her mouth. Too late. Lily came running down the hall and into the kitchen.

"Hi, Mr. Logan! Are you going to the party with Momma?"

Before he could answer, Ethan sauntered in the room, heading for the refrigerator after giving them a carefully disinterested glance. "They're going on a date, Lily."

"Ethan! We are *not*!" Piper knelt to give Lily a quick

hug. "Mr. Logan and I are just riding together to see some friends, okay?"

Lily nodded, nowhere near as concerned over the concept of dating as Piper was. She ran back to the living room with a wave.

Piper stood, expecting Logan to be amused at the close call. Instead, he was watching her son, and there was worry in his eyes. Ethan spoke before she could ask about it.

"Well, go do your thing, guys. Which I'll try really hard not to think about."

It didn't occur to her until they were almost at the Purple Shamrock what Ethan meant.

"Ethan suspects something." The back of her head hit the headrest. "What are we going to do?"

"Suspects what, exactly? We're not Bonnie and Clyde running around the countryside murdering people. We're a couple of adults doing adult things, such as going to a bar." He glanced over at her and shook his head. "I don't like you acting as if we're doing something wrong."

"Logan, we may not technically be doing anything wrong, but getting my children involved in this *would* be wrong. I don't want them hurt because of us." He started to object, and she waved her hand at him. "I know, you think I'm overthinking things. But I can't let Ethan and Lily pay a price for my actions."

"What kind of price would they have to pay?"

"The kind of price where they think you're going to stay, and then you leave." It was already going to be hard enough for *her* to watch him go. "They've had enough loss in their lives."

Logan considered that, pulling into the rapidly filling parking lot at the Purple Shamrock. He turned the car off and sat for a moment before reaching for her hand. "Fair enough. We'll be careful where the kids are concerned." The corner of his mouth rose. "But for tonight, there are no children to worry about. What happens at SYAC stays at SYAC, remember?"

She laughed, letting go of as much tension as she could. "Let's do this."

The bar was packed, and so was the dance floor. Many of the people she knew, at least enough to say hello to. But Logan was a new face, and everyone—especially the women—gravitated toward him. He only had eyes for her, though, pulling her onto the dance floor when things got too crowded at the bar.

Their first few dances were fast and loud, and she discovered laid-back Logan had some moves. They laughed a lot, and she started thinking Logan's nothing-bothers-me attitude was one she should learn from. Not worrying felt good. As the night went on, they moved closer and closer to each other. By the time a few hours had passed, they were pressed tight against each other, swaying slowly to Ed Sheeran while Logan whispered dirty suggestions in her ear. She swatted at him, giggling and blushing as they headed back to their table where Luke, Whitney, Evie and her fiancé, Mark, were waiting.

Piper had missed this. She hated being the third wheel at get-togethers where everyone else had a partner and she was left to find a free chair somewhere, inserting herself in conversations, feeling like the odd one out. But today? Today she was half of the Logan and Piper couple. And it felt really good. As if thinking the same thing, Logan put his hand over hers and gave it a squeeze. Her smile deepened, and they started leaning toward each other.

"Oh my god, look at these two!" Evie crowed. "They're all mushy for each other. It's too cute!"

Mark, a quiet artist who'd come back to town that summer to paint a mural and win his high school sweetheart back, nudged Evie with his elbow. "We're still mushy for each other, aren't we? And Whitney and Luke, too."

Luke grimaced. "I am *not* mushy."

Whitney laughed, smacking him on the arm. "Liar! You're the mushiest of them all. When I was sick last week, you made me homemade chicken soup and snuggled with me when I had chills so bad the bed shook."

Luke leaned in for a quick kiss. "That's not being *mushy*. That's loving someone."

Piper was just about to say something about how sweet that was, when Logan spoke up.

"I am *not* in love."

The table went silent. Not as silent as Piper's heart was, which wasn't even moving. Logan's eyes went wide as he realized what he'd said. Whitney spoke before he could, her eyes narrow with suspicion. And annoyance.

"That sounded pretty emphatic, Logan. Are you trying to convince us or yourself?"

He looked at Piper, and she forced a smile on her face, patting him on the arm. "It's okay. No strings, right?"

"That's not what I meant. I just…"

Evie saved the moment from getting any heavier. "Love or not, that was definitely a mushy look between you two. So you may as well own that much."

Piper was surprised to see a splotch of color on Logan's cheeks. Was he blushing? His eyes never left hers when he answered.

"This woman makes me soft in the head, and if that's what mushy means, then I'll definitely own it."

That was nice, but she couldn't help wondering if he'd just said it to make up for not being in love with her. They left shortly after that. He parked Iris's Buick by the garage, and they both sat there, neither one making a move to leave the car. Logan reached over and took her hand.

"I don't know why I said that about…love." He dropped his head. "I know I hurt you. I'm sorry."

It *had* hurt. A lot more than she'd expected. She did her best to sound nonchalant. "Don't worry about it. You declaring your undying love for me was never part of the deal." She gave him a bright smile to really sell it before she opened her door. "It's fine."

She walked away before he could make it around the car to kiss her good-night. He called her name, but she kept walking. Maybe this was exactly what she needed. A man who made her laugh. A man who set her skin on fire with his touch. A man who made her feel like a woman again. A man she would only have for a little while. That should be enough. But deep in her heart, for the very first time, she realized…it wasn't.

He may not be in love with her, but she was falling hard for him. She was falling in love with Logan Taggart. Instead of filling her with joy, the thought filled her with dread.

I never stay, Piper.

LOGAN WAS HELPING Piper finish painting her hallway the weekend after Thanksgiving when Ethan came thumping down the stairs. The boy took one look at him, then turned away without saying a word to pour himself a glass of milk.

This was a new thing, Ethan's cold shoulder treatment of Logan. Piper said things had been tense at Thanksgiving dinner, with Susan dropping snide comments about Logan and Piper and Tom and people "inserting themselves in other people's lives." While it seemed to go over Lily's head, Ethan had clearly soaked it up.

Piper straightened, pushing up the sleeves of her paint-spattered sweatshirt. "Good morning, son!" Her cheerfulness sounded forced. "How are you today? By the way, I'm fine, and Logan here is fine, too. Thanks for asking."

Ethan studied them over the rim of his glass as he drained it. He set it in the sink and started walking away.

Piper glanced at Logan, then called out to her son. "Ethan, lose the attitude and be polite to our guest. Especially when he's here to help us."

Ethan kept walking, and Logan had had enough. His voice was sharp, but damn it, he wasn't going to have Piper treated like that.

"Hey. Your mother's talking to you."

Ethan froze. Piper did, too, before rushing to defuse the situation. "It's okay."

Logan frowned. "No, it's not." He spoke to Ethan again. "You need to show your mom some respect, man."

The boy turned slowly, his face red. "I don't need to do anything, *man*. You're not my father, you're just my mom's boyfriend."

Logan stepped forward, but Piper grabbed his arm, her fingers biting in.

"Don't, Logan. He's looking for a fight." She turned to Ethan. "And you? You're grounded. Again. For ignoring me and being rude to Logan."

Ethan glared at her. "So you're taking *his* side over mine? Nice, Mom." He stalked away, and it took every ounce of willpower Logan had not to go after him. But Piper's fingers were still dug in.

"Let him go. It's normal for teenage boys to act out. He's asserting himself, and the counselor said…"

"I don't give a damn what the counselor said, Piper." He pulled away. "You're the parent, and the kid owes you some respect."

She nodded. "And he'll give it to me, when he's calmed down and doesn't have an audience he's trying to impress." She reached down to run the paint roller in the tray, getting back to work as if nothing had happened. "He's not used to seeing a man in this house. And Susan's putting nonsense in his head. I'll deal with him—and with *her*—in my own way. In the meantime, let's get this hallway done so I can hang the pictures of the kids I just had framed. I want them up for Christmas."

Logan marveled at how her son's angry words seemed to roll off her back. *Now* who was the one who never got bothered? That was supposed to be *his* role, but it seemed they'd traded places.

It was unusual for him to feel this sense of protectiveness toward a woman. He not only wanted Piper to be happy and safe. He *needed* it. He needed her. He needed this bubbly, tough little woman who was making him lose sleep every night as he lay awake, reexamining everything in his life.

Was he in *love* with Piper Montgomery? Was it possible to fall in love this quickly? This completely? He glared straight ahead at the wall. What did he know about love? He'd never seen it in action. His grandparents divorced. His parents separated. His mother died. His sister was as much a wandering soul as he was. And let's face it, life on the oil rigs wasn't always conducive to good marriages, and oil rigs were his life. It meant a lot of time apart, and many relationships didn't survive it. But Ted Prescott's had. He and Lori had a partnership that really worked. Logan started painting again, as Piper hummed to herself at his side.

Could Logan and Piper have what the Prescotts had? Maybe. If it was just them. But it wasn't. It was Lily and Ethan and the Montgomerys and Gran and… The image of all those faces, all those expectations, quickly cooled the heat in his veins. Piper was great. Maybe he *did* feel something. But long-term? She deserved better than a guy who never stayed.

To remind himself of that, he called Ted the next day, checking in on the South America job.

"Things are a little dicey down there politically, but

the last I heard, the job was still yours. If you want it." Ted cleared his throat and continued. "But before you say yes, I was going to call you about a business proposition that a couple of roustabouts like us might be able to run."

"What kind of business proposition?"

"Crown Arctic Oil called a few weeks ago and asked for my input on a new system they're thinking about using to refit an older rig. It was like the one we used in the Philippines—remember when we retrofitted that ancient beast five years ago and almost doubled the oil output? I guess word got around."

"O-kay...and...?"

"Aaaand..." Ted laughed. "They want to pay us. A lot. As *advisers*."

"Us? They called *you*." Logan didn't know where Ted was going with this.

"It was *our* idea, man. And if *Crown Arctic* will pay us, maybe other companies will, too. We can advise on a hell of a lot more than just that retrofit. Between the two of us, we've pretty much seen it all. It was Lori's idea to set up a consulting company. There'd be travel, but a lot of it could be done online and by phone, with a few trips here and there. Decent money *and* a half-way normal life."

"Sounds too good to be true, Ted." Like one of his father's schemes.

"All I'm asking is that you think about it. In the meantime, help me out with the Crown Arctic deal. We'll look at the schematics, and head up there after the holidays, before you commit to that other gig."

"Fun time to go to Alaska."

Ted guffawed. "I know, but it should only be a few weeks. And your grandmother should be good by then, right?"

Probably. But did he really want to chase a whole new career? "Jesus, I'm turning into my father."

"What does that mean?"

"Nothing, Ted. Sorry. I'll...umm... I'll think about it, okay? Things are up in the air right now, but have Lori send whatever she put together and I'll look at it."

CHAPTER NINETEEN

PIPER WASN'T SURE she would have survived until December without Room Three. She looked over to where Logan was stoking the fireplace. It wasn't just sex, although they did enjoy that as often as possible—in Room Three, in Logan's room, and sometimes a quick meet-up in the laundry room. But Room Three, when it was vacant, became their place to curl up by a fire and enjoy coffee together in the mornings when their work was done. Before Lily arrived home from preschool. When they could pretend they were just two single, unencumbered adults who were free to enjoy each other's company. They could hold hands in here, or even cuddle together on the floor, staring into the flames. Falling in love. At least, that's what Piper was doing. She couldn't tell with Logan.

He scooted across the floor after closing the fireplace screen, pulling Piper into his arms and holding her tight. She wrapped her arms around him and returned the hug, burying her face in his sweatshirt and taking in his sweaty, salty, earthy scent. He kissed the top of her head.

"So family dinner was really bad, huh?"

"The worst." Her words were muffled by his shirt.

"Susan did everything but brand me with a scarlet letter."

"I don't get it. You're a grown woman. You deserve to have a life, Piper."

She looked up, snuggling into the crook of his arm. "Apparently not. Susan wants me to stay 'loyal' to Tom forever, even in death."

"That's some bullshit right there. Let me talk to…"

"No! Oh, god no. Let things calm down first. I can't handle any more drama. Lily's already upset and thinking she did something wrong because Gigi and I argued. As usual, I have no idea where Ethan's head is at."

Dinner at the Montgomerys' the night before had been a disaster. Susan had already been dropping not-so-subtle hints about her disapproval of Logan in Piper's life since before Thanksgiving. Piper had been trying to dance around the comments without getting into a confrontation, but that plan went up in smoke at the dinner table last night. Lily announced to everyone that she saw Logan and her momma kissing on the front porch. Lily thought it was funny that Momma and Mr. Logan kissed. She was definitely the only person at the table who felt that way.

Ethan had looked back and forth between Piper and Susan as if his loyalties were torn. She hated that he felt he had to take sides. He finally left, retreating to the Montgomery living room with his game console. Lily had moved closer to Piper's side. Roger had cleared his throat four or five times, but didn't say a word. He was Switzerland.

Susan, however, had found plenty of words to use. She suggested it "too soon" for this sort of thing. That it was "clearly upsetting the children." She suggested Piper was disrespecting Tom's sacrifice—whatever that meant. Piper had taken it for as long as she could, and then she'd slapped her hand on the table.

"Tom's *gone*. What do you want from me?"

Susan's eyes narrowed. "I know he's gone. There isn't a day that goes by that I don't remember. But it seems you've been able to move on."

"Yes, I have. After four years. It doesn't change what I felt for Tom, but Tom's not here." She'd taken a deep breath at that point, to keep things from going completely off the rails. "Susan, you have to stop trying to run *my* family. Logan is a really good man. He's great with the kids. And he's not trying to replace anyone. He's his own man."

She sighed against Logan's chest as she recounted the conversation, and he started rubbing her arm and back.

"Jesus, you're tight as a drum. Relax, baby. We'll figure it out. Just give it time, okay?"

"Seriously, Logan, how are you so calm all the time? Sometimes it's annoying as hell."

He chuckled. "It's just how I am. Stuff tends to work itself out, and if it doesn't…"

"If it doesn't, you move on."

He paused. "Well…yeah. But I'm here now, Piper. The cat's out of the bag, so let's just see where it takes us."

She pulled away far enough to look straight into his eyes. "But what *are* we doing? Before I get my children any deeper into this—before *I* get any deeper—I need to know that."

He stared into the crackling fire. When he finally spoke, his voice was low and rough with emotion.

"Piper, I…I think what we have is special. Maybe it's *love* special. I don't know. I have zero frame of reference for what love feels like, so I honestly don't know." He jammed his fingers into his hair above his forehead. "I don't want us to stop. I don't want us to have to hide what we're doing. I want to be able to hold your hand in public and kiss you in front of your kids."

"But you can't promise me you'll stay."

"Is that what you want from me? A promise?"

She had no idea what she wanted. No, that wasn't true. She wanted it all—a life with Logan and a happy family. It just felt like an impossible dream right now. "I don't want to disrupt Lily's and Ethan's lives by announcing that Mommy has a boyfriend." His brows lowered at that word, but she pressed on. "It's my job to keep their lives stable and…dependable."

"First, Lily made sure everyone knows you have a boyfriend. And second, are you saying I'm not dependable?"

She pulled back again, straightening and shrugging his arm off her shoulder. "Are you saying you're staying in Rendezvous Falls?"

His mouth opened, but his silence was deafening. How many times had he told her that he wasn't good at staying? That, in fact, he'd *never* done it? She gestured toward him.

"I rest my case."

"That's not fair." She wanted him to say he loved her. She wanted him to say he wasn't leaving. But he didn't do any of those things. He couldn't even look at her. Instead, he looked out the window over her shoulder. She shook her head.

"Let me ask you something. Have you never had a serious relationship because you don't stay anyplace long enough for one to grow? Or do you keep *moving on* to make sure you don't form any relationships at all?"

He frowned. "That's a chicken-or-the-egg question, and I don't know how to answer, Piper. I just…move on. I can tell you one thing." He put his finger under her chin and tipped it up to kiss her lips. "I've never thought about staying as much as I have with you. Is that love? I don't know." He kissed her again. "But if you want us to play it cool, I'll do that."

He kissed her again, deeper, stronger. She loved this man. But he couldn't say the same to her. Was he worth the risk? He pulled her onto his lap, his hands moving up under her sweater.

For now? Yes. Yes, he was.

"WHY IS THE armchair over there?" Gran moved her walker into the library, her frown deepening. Logan and Piper had been giving her a tour of the downstairs rooms at the inn after her arrival home an hour earlier. Piper jumped to answer this question, which was approximately number five hundred fifty as far as Logan could tell.

"There's more light for reading with it closer to the windows, Iris."

His grandmother stared hard at the offending chair, then, apparently unable to come up with an argument, turned her attention to the bookshelves.

"Where are all the books? There should be more than that. One whole shelf is nearly empty."

"I'm sorry, Iris. I haven't had a chance to put the books back that you had at the rehab center. I'll do that today…"

Logan shook his head. "It doesn't need to be done today. Gran, isn't it time for you to give this inquisition a rest, along with that new hip of yours?"

Gran's eyes turned icy. "This isn't a damn inquisition! This is *my* business, and I need to see that it's still the way I left it."

He saw the color rising in Piper's face, and Logan bristled. He put his hand on Gran's walker, leaning lower to look her straight in the eyes.

"That's enough. You know damned well the inn is fine. And that's what's got you so cranky, isn't it? Piper's had this place running like a well-oiled machine for weeks, so knock it off and thank her."

Gran's eyes widened for a moment, then softened as she started to laugh. "Well I'll be. You've got a little of me in you after all, boy." She turned to Piper. "He's right. It pisses me off, but he is right. The Taggart looks great, and I know you're a lot more responsible for that that he is." She rolled her eyes his way, but he didn't take the bait. "Thank you, Piper."

She nodded. "You're welcome, Iris. I love the place as if it was my own."

Gran looked between him and Piper, nodding and muttering under her breath. "Maybe it will be someday."

Piper looked up at Logan in shock, but he was as much at a loss as she was. Before either of them could question the comment, Gran's book club buddies came through the door. Helen and Cecile both had casseroles, while Vickie and Rick carried wine bottles and grocery bags loaded with stuff. Another woman followed with a silver platter loaded with fancy cookies. Did they think Logan wouldn't feed his own grandmother?

Piper stepped to his side as Gran and her friends headed back to the apartment.

"It's a small-town thing. Food is the answer to all social situations. It's the official symbol of welcome home, get well, sorry for your loss, and happy birthday. When we lost Tom, I thought Susan and Roger were going to have to buy a second refrigerator to hold all the food people brought." The door to Gran's apartment closed, leaving the two of them alone in the hall. Piper started to turn away, but he stopped her.

"I'm glad Gran's home, but it does complicate things a bit. I have my own room, but it'll be tricky sneaking you in and out. I guess we'll need to sneak down to Room Three more often."

But Piper shook her head. "It would be way too easy for Iris to find us there. She's getting around pretty well, and she has a master key of her own." She looked up through her lashes, her blue eyes suddenly sad. "I think we have to take a break for a while, and that might not be a bad thing."

He knew she was thinking of her former in-laws and their...at least *Susan's*...resistance to Piper and Logan being together. "Is Ethan still giving you trouble?"

Piper shrugged. "I don't know if I'd call it 'trouble,' but he's a little more moody than usual. And his *usual* is pretty damn moody. I'd say they just need time, but honestly, our time's nearly up anyway, isn't it?"

"What do you mean?" But he knew. Gran was home and seemed pretty mobile. Christmas was just a couple weeks away. He had a job to get to. All he had to do was decide which job that was. South America and a long goodbye? Or try the consulting gig with Ted and see if he could make it work? If he could have more time in Rendezvous Falls between consulting trips, he'd have more time to see where things were going with Piper.

She went on her tiptoes to kiss his lips. "I think our little adventure is coming to an end. Let's not pretend it wasn't always going to."

His arm went around her waist, holding her there so he could kiss her more deeply.

"What if it didn't have to?"

She went still in his arms. "What are you saying?"

He lowered his face into her thick hair and sighed. What *was* he saying?

"I'm saying this place…" He pulled back enough to see her eyes. "And the people, are…making me think about things. Differently." This wasn't how he'd planned this conversation. Who was he kidding? As usual with everything else in his life, he *hadn't* planned this conversation. But he was in it now. "I'm thinking that maybe…"

"Hey, you two!" Cecile's voice echoed in the hallway. Piper jumped back, pulling out of his arms and irritating Logan. He wanted them to *stop* having to jump apart all the time. Cecile didn't say a word about their embrace, though. "Our friend Jayla Maloof just got back from a trip to Europe, and she made a huge batch of Mediterranean cookies and treats. Come join us!"

Cecile disappeared, and Piper looked up at Logan.

"There's no sense trying to say no. They'll badger us until we go, and it *is* Iris's first day home." She walked away, then stopped when she saw he wasn't following. "What were you trying to say?"

He shook his head. "I'll tell you later. When we're alone."

She laughed. "Good luck with that. Alone time is going to be rare."

LOGAN WAS OUTSIDE shoveling heavy, wet snow from the front steps that evening when his phone rang. He had a decidedly adversarial relationship with this lake effect snow nonsense, which seemed to sweep in out of nowhere. Two hours earlier, the sun had been shining. He cursed under his breath as he yanked his gloves off and fished the phone from his pocket. Seeing Piper's name on the screen took away all his grumbling thoughts.

"Hey, babe. Is Lily asleep already? I'm just shoveling..."

She talked over his words. "I'm stuck."

"Stuck home? Is Lily sick or something? Is Ethan...?"

"No, I mean I'm *really* stuck. In a ditch. I had an accident."

He set the shovel against the porch rail, looking over to her house. Her car was gone. "Where are you? Are you okay?"

He was already headed inside for the keys to Gran's car when Piper let out a long, shaky breath.

"I...I think so. My wrist hurts. And my shoulder. I can't get the door open. And the battery's almost dead on my phone. I was going to pick up some Christmas decorations from Whitney and Helen for the Christmas pageant, and there were some deer, and…the car just started spinning…and… Logan, make sure the kids are okay…"

And that was it. The call went dead. Cursing, Logan called back, but nothing. He threw the garage door open so fiercely, it was a surprise it didn't shoot right off the rails. Logan closed his eyes and stood there for a second. He was the cool, calm, collected one. The one everyone turned to in a crisis precisely because he *didn't* waste time imagining fifty different scenarios. He focused on what he knew and saw, and he dealt with it. So why was he envisioning the worst possible outcome now? Why was he picturing Piper in a crumpled car? Alone. With no way to call for help. He turned away from the garage and started jogging to her house.

Make sure the kids are okay…

He pounded on the side door, then opened it, calling for Ethan. The teen came down the stairs, a gaming console in his hand.

"Try knocking, dude."

Lily prevented Logan from saying something he'd regret. She was yelling his name from the top of the stairs. "Logan! Are you taking me to dance class tonight? I don't want to be late."

"Your class isn't until later," Ethan said. He got to the bottom of the stairs and looked out the window, where darkness was settling in along with the snow. "Damn! What time is it? And where did all that freakin' snow come from?" He walked into the kitchen and picked up an orange from the basket on the counter. "I hope Mom's bringing pizza home, 'cuz I'm starving."

"Have you heard from her?" Logan had to keep reminding himself to stay cool. Scaring the kids wouldn't help anyone.

"Nope. She probably got yakking with Whitney. I gotta get back to my game. Told the guys to wait for me, but they're assho…" He glanced at Lily standing in the doorway, wearing a head-to-toe pink leotard. "They've probably already started again, which means they left me for dead." He turned to go. "Later."

"Ethan." There must have been something in his voice, because the boy stopped and turned *without* rolling his eyes or sighing.

"What's going on?" Ethan finally picked up on Logan's tension.

Before answering, Logan looked over at Lily, all bright and hopeful. Her hair was pulled up into a bouncing ponytail high on her head. It made him think of Piper. Of how she'd want him to handle this. Logan crouched down.

"Hey, munchkin, why don't you go get your bag ready for rehearsal." He tugged at her ponytail. "And find a nice warm sweater to wear, okay? The weather's kinda cold."

"I don't wear sweaters to rehearsal, silly! I'll be too hot."

He willed his voice to stay calm. But it was Ethan who sent Lily scampering.

"He said get a sweater, so get one from your room. Now."

She didn't show any sign of recognizing the tension swirling around the kitchen. She turned and waved her hand in the air. "Fine. I'll get a sweater. But I think it's unness-airy."

As soon as they heard her feet on the stairs, Ethan asked. "What's happened?"

"Your mom had a little accident. She's okay, but I'm going to get her. I want you to take Lily over to the inn and stay with my grandmother. She'll get dinner for you both. I think I smelled her famous chili earlier, which means she'll have plenty to share. Then stay there until your mom and I get back."

"At the inn? No way. We'll wait here..."

"Ethan. Stay at the inn."

"You're not my..."

Logan slammed his hand down on the counter so hard the cutting board bounced up in the air. He pointed at a now-pale Ethan.

"I don't have time for this asinine power struggle right now! Man up and take your sister to the inn where there are people and distractions and *food*." He sucked in a breath and lowered his voice. "Please, Ethan. Just do it. We're wasting time arguing when I could be..." Looking for the woman he loved. He headed for the door, figuring Ethan was going to do whatever the hell he wanted. He could have Iris send food over and let Piper deal with Ethan later. "I'll call you when I know anything."

Logan was almost out the door when Lily reappeared.

"Logan! You gotta to take me to rehearsal!"

Her brother took her hand. "Pretty sure class is canceled, Lily. It's snowing." As Logan left, he heard Ethan continue. "You and I are going to have dinner with Miss Iris, okay? Mom will come get us later."

Logan gave Gran a quick rundown of the situation

before heading back to the garage and praying the old Buick would get him through the snow.

It was touch and go for the first few miles as he adjusted to how the big coupe handled on the conditions. But the car was so damn heavy that it didn't get shifted around in the ruts much. In fact, the combo of the weight and front-wheel drive allowed it to cut its own path with authority—even in this nasty crap-storm of giant wet flakes that turned to thick slush and ice on the pavement. It was sloppy and slippery and messy. He didn't have to worry about a lot of other drivers as he headed out of town and up the hill.

He called Whitney Foster as he turned up Falls Road. He was hoping Piper somehow got out of the ditch and made it to the winery. Whitney answered. He put her on speaker so he could leave the phone in the cup holder and his hands on the wheel. The car had some sort of traction control that helped it maintain forward motion when the slop turned slick, but the heavy snow still tried to pull the vehicle sideways.

"Logan?" Whitney's voice was tinny on speaker, but he could still hear the fear in it once he told her he didn't know where Piper was. "Luke is almost back from Penn Yan, coming up over the hills. I'm texting him to not stop here. To head straight down toward you. He'll be on the lookout for tracks or...anything. Between the two of you..."

"Sounds good. I'm just coming up the hill now. Roads are a mess."

"I'm sure she's fine, Logan. Are the kids...?"

"They're with my grandmother."

"Perfect. Logan, I'm sure she's okay." He heard the

need in her voice. The need for reassurance. He gripped the wheel and bit back a curse as the car dove for the edge of the road again. He did his best to sound relaxed.

"Oh, yeah. Probably mad at herself for forgetting to charge her phone. I'll get an earful when I find her."

Whitney laughed, but it was a tight, tense sound that didn't match her words. "Ha! You're right. Careful she doesn't blast you with friendly fire." She paused. "Call me, Logan."

"Will do."

Darkness was settling in. With the snow in the air and over the road, everything was charcoal gray and blurry. He couldn't go quite as slow as he wanted to, because the big car needed a little momentum to push uphill through the slush. If he slowed too much, the tires would just spin on the instant ice that formed under them and he'd be stuck.

The radio was off, in that weird way that people turned the volume down to concentrate better in bad conditions. He could hear the snow slopping under the car. He could hear his own heartbeat pounding in his ears as if a hard-rock drummer was driving the pace. This right here was why he didn't get attached to places and people and…women. When he stayed on the move, he didn't give himself time to feel this kind of terror in his chest. Had he seen tragedies on the job? Sure. It was sad. Distressing. Upsetting. He'd even shed tears or heaved his guts over a few.

But he'd never felt like this. Like his *own* survival was at risk. No, it was worse than that. He'd had his own life on the line plenty of times. But this deep terror in his chest? He'd never cared enough for anyone to feel that. He'd never loved someone this hard. This completely. So much that the thought of losing them tore at his heart like a chainsaw. Maybe he'd been better off as a rolling stone, because this feeling right now? This feeling sucked.

He turned on to Lakeview Road, knowing he was only a few miles from the winery. Had he missed her in the swirling snowflakes? Then he saw it. A circular swirl of tire tracks in the center of the road, and two taillights sticking up in the air at an odd angle. The Buick bucked a few times as he hit the brakes, but the traction control kept it straight. He started the hazard lights and jumped out with the flashlight in his hand, yelling Piper's name.

Once he reached the car, he saw the force of the impact had crumpled the corner of the hood. He got to the driver's door, sweeping snow away. His knees nearly buckled when he heard her voice.

"I'm okay! I just can't get the door open…"

He grabbed the door handle, but it wouldn't budge. "We're going to get you out of there, okay? But I need you to look at me. Let me see that beautiful face, babe."

She was still, but then her hands moved to the steering wheel, and she pushed herself back against the seat. She seemed to be doing a silent self-assessment, staring straight ahead and taking a deep breath before turning to the door. The side of her face had some friction burns from the airbag, but her eyes were clear as she gave him a thin smile. He took what felt like his first full breath of air since getting her call.

A dark pickup rolled up from the other direction,

coming to a halt by Gran's car. Luke Rutledge lowered the window. "Logan! Is she okay?"

Logan waved back. "She's fine, but I'll need some help getting the door open. Call Whitney and have her call my grandmother—she's got the kids." When he turned back to the car, Piper was pulling on the door handle.

"Don't worry, babe. We'll get you out."

"The kids…"

"The kids are fine. They're with Gran at the inn."

"It happened so fast…" She was looking straight into his eyes now, a large tear moving slowly down her cheek. "I was being careful, but the deer…they were right there in the road when I came around the corner… I hit the brakes too hard. The car spun. So stupid…"

"It's okay, babe. It was an accident."

"But my car… I can't afford a new car… Christmas…"

"That's what insurance is for. Don't worry about it. You're sure you're not hurt? Do we need an ambulance?"

She shook her head. "My wrist is sore, but it's not broken or anything…" She flexed and moved a little. "I'll be sore all over tomorrow, but nothing feels serious. Can I get out now?"

Luke walked up with a crowbar in his hand. "We'll get you out one way or another. Looks like the car's totaled anyway."

Another tear escaped her eye, and Logan rushed to reassure her. "It's okay. Don't worry about it."

"Easy for you to say." Her smile deepened. "You came looking for me."

"Of course I did."

They didn't need the crowbar. Between the two men, they were able to pull the door open and let Piper out. Logan wrapped his arms around her and held her tight, as much for his own warmth as for hers.

The past half hour had terrified him more than he'd ever been, which was saying something after twenty years on the rigs. But it also sorted things so cleanly and clearly in his mind that he was nearly dizzy from the sensation. It was like lock pins tumbling into place with such precision that his future went from foggy to crystal clear in the length of a heartbeat.

"The kids...they haven't eaten yet. What time is it? Lily has rehearsal..."

That was his Piper. Always thinking of others first, even after a freakin' car wreck.

"Easy, Momma Bear. Gran had a big pot of chili going, so they're fed and safe. I don't think Lily's class happened with this weather. Don't worry..."

"It's my *job* to worry, Logan. I'm all they've got."

He realized that just because *he* could now see their futures with HD clarity, that didn't mean Piper could yet. That was up to him.

"No, you're not, baby. They've got me. *You've* got me. We're gonna make this work. I love you, Piper." And just like that, he knew. He loved her. He loved Ethan and Lily. He was going to make them a family again. He leaned in and gave her a gentle kiss, doing his best not to jostle her. He saw Luke walk away out of the corner of his eye. He was pretty sure he heard him laughing as he did.

"Logan...slow down." She pulled back, looking at

him in confusion. That wasn't exactly what he wanted to hear after declaring his love.

"We'll be a *family*, Piper." He was in such a hurry to help her see how everything was solved now. How the answers were all right there, in his love for her. He had to lean forward to hear her next words.

"We're already a family. The kids and me."

"Well, yeah, but now we'll be one together. I'll be their dad…" He knew it was a mistake the instant he said it, even without seeing the way her body recoiled. "I don't mean it like…"

Maybe it wasn't the best timing on his part to declare his love to a woman who'd just stepped out of a wrecked car. But he'd have another chance. He'd make it right. Because he loved this woman.

"Logan, call the Montgomerys. They can take the kids so Lily doesn't freak out seeing me all banged up."

"Honey, I'll take care of Ethan and Lily."

She shook her head. "No. They're family. They'll know what to do. Please, call their grandparents."

She walked to the car without looking back.

…they're family…

He had some bruises, too. All over his heart.

CHAPTER TWENTY

PIPER'S SHOULDER HURT, but that wasn't what had her pacing the house in the wee hours of the morning. She simply couldn't sleep. The seat belt had left her shoulder black-and-blue. She had a slightly sprained wrist. And a totaled car. Damn it. Even with insurance, getting another car would wipe out her emergency fund, because she'd opted for a higher deductible to save on the monthly payments.

She stopped in the living room, staring at the pictures of Tom. Their wedding photo was hanging by the door. And their last family portrait, with Lily so tiny in Tom's arms and Ethan's goofy little-boy smile, was over the sofa. Silent reminders that she'd had her chance at love. And she'd made the best of it.

She turned on the light and looked at Tom's handsome face, all chiseled and tough. A marine's marine, his buddies called him. A walking military recruitment poster. A loving father. A skilled and tender lover. A dear friend. A casualty of war. And his death made her a casualty, too.

And then Logan Taggart came along. Unruffled and amused by life. The man who *never* stayed. She thought he'd be safe as her first venture into dating again, because he was so temporary. The man certainly had no intention of staying at his grandmother's inn any longer than necessary. But tonight…tonight he'd found her in the storm. She'd been so happy. So relieved. So secure. And then he'd told her that he loved her. Loved her children. *Tom's* children. He said he wanted them to be a family. He said he wanted to stay. It was everything she'd wanted.

And she'd panicked harder than when her car had spun out of control.

Lily had adored Logan from Day One, but Lily adored everyone. Ethan had moments when he and Logan had bonded, and moments when resentment oozed from the kid's pores. But then, Ethan was kinda like that with everyone. Would they want a "new daddy"? Was that fair to them? Was it fair to Tom? She looked away from the portrait, but her late husband was everywhere in this house. In her life.

I love you, Piper.

Logan's voice echoed through her head. Had he meant it? Was it just something he'd blurted out after finding her? Was it possible that he'd finally fallen, too? She shook her head.

Seriously—did she really think he'd give up his lifestyle…his *identity*…to take on not only her, but her family? She looked around again. *Tom's* family. She didn't even want to think about how that would go over with Susan. She settled on the sofa and closed her eyes, willing her brain to stop spinning so she could rest. For the most part, it cooperated. Except for the tender, almost desperate, words she'd heard tonight.

I love you, Piper.

"I'M TELLING YOU, that girl's raising the gate."

Lena set her e-reader in her lap with a sigh. "Iris, what does that even mean? What gate? And why is she raising it? Is this some *Game of Thrones* reference?"

Rick chuckled. He was sitting in his favorite wingback chair by the fireplace in the library. "I'm having a hard time imagining Iris watching *that* show, but think about it. In any of those medieval or fantasy movies, when the enemy attacks, the people in the castle raise the gates to protect everyone inside the walls."

"And you think Piper is raising the gate because…?" Helen tipped her head to the side in curiosity.

"Because she's feeling attacked!" Iris gestured angrily. "Logan told her he loves her and she panicked. Now she's upset and he's confused and…" Iris's shoulders fell. "They're all coming at her—the Montgomerys, Logan, the holidays…" She knew the signs. She'd been there once herself. Piper had told her just this week how Susan was hassling her about Logan. "She's under too much pressure, and she's going to lock everyone out if we don't do something."

"Hang on." Lena reached for the cup of tea on the table by the window seat where she'd curled up with a pile of pillows, her long velvet skirt draping to the floor. Iris wasn't sure if she looked like an elegant hippie or a sloppy Victorian. "Unless *we* do something?" Lena asked. "What are *we* supposed to do? And I'm still not clear on the gate-raising metaphor."

"Lena, when Jerome died, what was your first priority?" Iris asked.

Lena blinked. "DeAndre and Lissandra, of course."

"Exactly. To the exclusion of all else, including other men, right?"

Lena's eyes widened. "Well, I wasn't looking for another man, so…"

"But what if another man *had* come along? One who loved you and loved your children? One you thought you could love, too?"

Lena set her tea down and got a faraway look in her eye. "One did, actually."

"Really?" Cecile nudged Helen at the tiny breakfast table where they sat. "Do tell!"

Iris was as surprised as anyone. She'd never heard Lena mention any man other than her late husband.

"He…it…it just wouldn't have worked. He was white, and his family was dead set against him marrying a black woman. Especially a black woman with two little black children. Neil didn't care, but they were determined to make things ugly. And Jerome's mother was furious that I'd even *think* about another man besides her son, much less bring that man into my house with her son's babies." She stared at the floor, her voice low and sad. "It was just too much, you know? I had this new reality I was trying to adjust to—two kids with no daddy—and all the damned drama was…too much. It wasn't fair to my babies. Or to Neil, for that matter. So, I…" She looked over at Iris and smiled sadly. "I guess I raised the gate to protect my family."

"Exactly." Iris nodded. "That's what I'm saying."

Vickie crossed her ankles gracefully and sipped her wine, giving Iris a mischievous grin.

"You mean like you did with Sam Adler?"

Sam was the one she'd let get away. She straightened, determined not to let Vickie know she'd hit her mark.

"Yes, like Sam. But I had the inn. I had a son who was stressed out over the divorce and who hated moving into this big old place. I had friends and family with a hundred different opinions on how I should behave. And along came Sam. My very own Paul Newman." She smiled as an image of dusty-blond hair and steel-blue eyes came to mind. "He loved me. And I loved him. But he wanted to sweep us all off to his home in Virginia. His family had a business there. He had a beautiful farm Brian would have loved. But I'd already started my own dream *here*." She looked around the library, smiling at the memory of what a disaster this place had been when she bought it. "My friends didn't want me to go."

Vickie raised her hand, her expression carefully innocent. "For the record, *I* wanted you to go."

Everyone laughed, including Iris. "You *always* want me to go." Her smile faded. "But my ex-husband was being such a bastard. I was being pulled and pushed and pressured. Brian was acting out, and one day he fell down the stairs and broke his arm. It was an accident, but everyone, even Sam, was coming *at* me, telling me what to do and how to feel. And it felt like it was me and my son against the world."

Lena nodded. "Yeah, that's how I felt, too."

Rick frowned. "So both of you gave up a second chance at love because of your kids?"

"No," Lena answered. "It wasn't just the children, although they were a big part of it. It was everything put together. No offense, Rick, but you have no idea

how much pressure women are under to be so fucking *perfect* all the time." The other women nodded in
agreement. "Especially when it comes to being a 'good
mom.'" She made air quotes around the words with her
fingers. "Not only does everyone on the planet have an
opinion on what a perfect mom looks like, but as single moms, our own children are looking at us with so
much…*need*." She shrugged and raised her hands. "And
when Momma Bear takes over and closes that gate, no
one's gettin' in to mess with that little family unit. Because we're tired and we're stressed and we can't deal
with One. More. Damn. Thing. Not even love."

The room was silent. Finally Rick blew out a long
breath.

"Well, that's just sad as hell, ladies."

Cecile nodded. "It *is* sad. But both of you are saying
that people telling you what to do just made it worse. So
how are we supposed to stop Piper from wrapping her
wings around that family like a mad momma goose?"

Iris slumped back in her chair. After a few minutes,
Helen spoke up.

"I think I know *one* way we can help." She was staring out the window. "We can't tell Piper what to do, but
what if we can get everyone else around her to back
off?"

"What are you talking about?" Iris asked.

Lena looked outside, too, and gave Iris a wicked
smile.

"Oh, that might just work. Susan Montgomery just
pulled up over at Piper's house. What do you say we
bring her in here for a little chat?" Lena snapped her
fingers at Rick, who started to laugh.

"Are you snapping those fingers at *me*? For wha... Oh, I get it. I'm supposed to be the runner, eh?" He stood. "Fine, but you ladies better know what you're doing."

Iris fluttered her eyelashes at him. "Don't we always?"

He barked out a laugh. "More like never, but I'll be your errand boy."

Iris brushed a few crumbs off the tea table and reached for her cane. She hated the damn thing, but it was far better than the walker that made her feel caged. She heard the front door open, and she stood. Rick and Susan came into the parlor as Iris was taking a seat by the fireplace. It was the largest chair in the room, and she chose it for its strategic influence. Susan could be a pompous pill, so Iris needed all the power moves she could find. She was fighting for her grandson's happiness here.

Susan seemed baffled at why she'd been called over to the inn. Rick was going on about how much they'd missed her, as if she'd ever attended more than two book club meetings over the past thirty years. He showed her to the chair he'd been using, then parked himself next to Lena on the window seat. They chatted about the holidays and the weather and the upcoming holiday home tours. They laughed about the hideous renovations old man O'Keefe was doing to his midcentury modern home, in a vain attempt to make it look more Victorian. The entire time, Susan's eyes kept darting to the door. As Helen served everyone tea, Iris figured it was time.

"Susan, dear, what exactly is your problem with my grandson?"

Susan froze, her teacup halfway to her lips. Then she continued to drink, unruffled. It was Rick who choked and sputtered in the corner.

"Iris…" he scolded.

Susan shook her head. "It's alright, Rick. Iris likes the shock-and-awe approach. She's famous for it at the business association meetings." She looked back to Iris, her dark eyes calm and assessing. "My so-called problem with your grandson is that he's inserted himself into *my* son's family, where he doesn't belong. Let him find some other woman, Iris."

"So you're saying Piper needs to remain celibate for what…fourteen more years until Lily's out of high school? Or is that too soon for you? Maybe you don't want another man walking Lily down the aisle or playing with her children someday? So Piper stays alone forever." Iris leaned forward. "That's how you want to honor Tom's memory?"

Susan's face paled. "Of course not. But I certainly don't want her bringing men in and out of the house while the children are young."

She waved her off. "Piper isn't bringing *men* in and out of the house—*her* house—and you know it. It's one man, and he's a good man. Don't you care about Piper's happiness?"

Susan's mouth went thin. "I don't see how my family is any of your concern, Iris."

"Logan is *my* family."

Susan huffed. "So what, we're going to be the Hatfields and McCoys now?"

"Okay," Lena stood, moving between where the two women were seated. She gave Iris a hard look before turning to Susan. "What's your relationship with your Piper these days?" Susan looked away, not answering. Lena nodded. "I thought so. I'm guessing you're seeing less of your grandchildren than you'd like, right?" She turned to Iris. "And how long do you think Piper's going to want to work at the place where she fell in love with Logan? And how long will Logan stay, knowing Piper's right there and doesn't want him?"

Iris inhaled sharply. If Logan left, and Piper quit, she'd be finished in more ways than one. Lena pulled one of the side chairs over and sat, her elbows on her knees. "And Susan, before *you* start thinking that's a good thing, who's to say Piper will want to live next door to this place? Maybe she'll move closer to her dad in Texas. That's a long ways away, isn't it?"

Susan's mouth dropped open, but she didn't speak. Iris knew just how she felt. Lena smirked at them both.

"Okay then. I don't know Logan or Piper well enough to say if they belong together or not. But they sure as hell deserve a chance to figure it out on their own. Without interference from you."

Susan's expression was pinched and angry, but she didn't answer. Instead, she rose in silence and left the inn. Leaving them all wondering if they'd made things better or worse.

CHAPTER TWENTY-ONE

PIPER STOOD AT the sink at the inn, frying pan in hand, lost in thought. Or, more accurately, lost in no thought at all. Lily was drawing pictures of Santa at the kitchen table. The closer Christmas got, the more Piper's brain refused to function. The accident had made it worse. Not because of any injury. She was feeling fine now that a few days had passed. But now she had insurance to deal with, and Ethan and Lily were *both* clingy and on edge. She hadn't seen or spoken to Susan or Roger in a week, although she could have sworn she just saw Susan's car in the parking lot. The inn was busy, with everyone coming to Rendezvous Falls for the Victorian Christmas events, or just to visit family and friends.

It was good to have Iris back, but even that had presented another dilemma yesterday when Iris confessed she probably wouldn't be able to return to doing the same work she'd done before. Which meant she needed Piper to stay on full-time. Piper had never imagined being a full-time hospitality manager, cooking and making beds and vacuuming endlessly. Not to mention cleaning toilets. But Iris had offered her good money, and she really did enjoy the job.

"Hey." Logan's voice behind her filled her with warmth. And tension. He was at the top of her list of what-do-I-do-about-this issues. His hands slid around her waist and he tugged her back against him. She pulled away, nodding toward her daughter as silent explanation.

He hesitated, then removed his hands with a sigh. She'd been holding him at arm's length since the accident, and he was clearly getting frustrated. She could hear it in his voice, low enough that Lily wouldn't hear.

"She loves me, you know. She'll welcome me with open arms." He snuck a quick kiss to the side of Piper's neck after making sure Lily was still focused on her drawing. "The way you used to."

Piper set the pan in the rack and turned. She put her hands on his chest and gently pushed him back a step. "You don't know that. Logan the Giant who lives at the inn is one thing. Logan the guy who's taking her daddy's place? That's entirely another."

"She doesn't even remember her father…"

Piper stiffened, her eyes narrowing in anger. "*I* remember her father. And I'll spend the rest of my life making sure *she* remembers him." Her hand was over her own heart now. "That she knows him through me."

Logan's eyes closed tight. "I'm sorry. I can't seem to say the right thing this week. Of *course* she needs to know her father." He opened his eyes and fixed her with a dark, troubled gaze. "We can do this, Piper. We can make a life together, with the kids. I'm not saying there won't be bumps along the way, but we can do it if we try. If we work at it…"

She pushed away and walked over to Lily.

"Baby, can you go do your drawing in the library? You can sit in the window seat if you want." Lily was convinced the pillow-covered window seat was made just for her, so her eyes lit up.

"Really? Can I take the markers?"

"No, but you can take the big box of crayons from behind the reception desk."

"Yay! Thanks, Momma!" She bounced up, hugging her pad to her chest. "Hi, Logan! Bye, Logan!" And she was gone, leaving Piper and Logan alone in the kitchen.

She stared at him, wishing things could be different. Wishing life hadn't sent her *two* men to love. It sounded like a blessing but felt like a curse.

"Logan, we need to talk."

"Aw, hell. That's never good." He walked over and tipped her chin up to kiss her. "How about we don't talk and just kiss?" His lips brushed hers and she was easily lulled into following his plan. The kiss deepened, his arms folding around her until they were molded to each other. Her belly clenched in desire, the way it always did when Logan held her. But was that enough? He must have felt the moment she started to cool, because he released her and pulled out one of the kitchen chairs. "Okay. Sit. Let's have this talk."

They sat, and she stared out the window rather than get lost in his dark eyes. She needed to focus, and Logan tended to blow her concentration out of the water. She released a sigh and started, not even sure herself what words would come out.

"I'm not saying we're not worth the effort, Logan. But I don't think I can handle it right now. You talk about *working at it* like it's no big deal, but I'm worked out. I have my hands full being a working mom who owns a money pit of a house and has to figure out how to get a new car. I have to help my children navigate this new world of theirs. Yes, Tom's been gone four years, but that's a blink of an eye in kid-time. They're already struggling…"

"Lily's not struggling," Logan protested. "She's the happiest kid I've ever seen."

"You've never seen her after she's wet her bed or woken up screaming from a nightmare in the middle of the night. Her terrors come when the world is too quiet for her to ignore them any longer. If she can keep that bright smile on her face, the monsters can't come. You see the happy kid. But I'm her mother, and I see the monsters."

"Damn." He scowled at the table, his heavy brows low over his eyes. "I didn't know."

"You didn't *need* to know. It's not your job to know that stuff. It's *my* job."

His big hand covered hers. "You don't need to do that job alone, Piper. I can help…"

"How does it help me to have to bring you in the loop on all the things I'm dealing with? That's just… You'd become one more thing to deal with. And frankly, I don't think I can deal with one more thing. I honestly don't."

And there it was. The truth, out in the open and staring them both straight in the eye.

"What are you saying?"

"Logan, what we had was…" *Magical. Lovely.* "…special. I never thought I'd feel like this again. But it was always designed to be temporary. It was…greedy of me to think I could get away with falling in love again."

He squeezed her hand hard. "So you *do* love me?"

She finally turned to meet his eyes. "Of course I do. How could you doubt it? But that doesn't solve anything."

"Wait… I thought love solved *everything*?" He was only half kidding. She knew that because even though his mouth slanted into a smile, his eyes were desperate. Her heart skipped. Could she really do this to him?

"Only in fairy tales and romance novels, Logan." She shook her head. "I can't do this right now. I'm not strong enough."

"Can't do *what*?"

"I can't love you. I mean, I can't stop. I'll *never* stop. But I can't let myself try to make this work. Ethan's barely hanging on, Logan. If I bring you into our lives full-time, it's just one more shock he'd have to deal with."

The half smile was back. "I don't exactly think it would be a shock."

"Maybe not, but it would be a life-altering event. After more life-altering events than any boy should go through. I'm his mother. It's my job to protect him."

Logan pulled away. His posture was tight, his chin hard as stone. "Protect him from *me*? Seriously?"

"Not you, but…yes, you." Tears sprang to her eyes when he flinched from the words. "Damn it, Logan, our timing is all wrong. There's just too much… I can't do it to my family. As angry as I am with Susan, she has a point. The kids have been through enough."

She wasn't sure if it was her words or the mention of Susan's name that propelled Logan to his feet. His voice rose as he started pacing the kitchen floor.

"So now I'm something the kids have to *go through*? I'm some fucking trial they have to bear? That *you* have to bear? That's bullshit, Piper, and you know it." He jammed his fingers into his hair and growled in frustration. "I can *help* you bear whatever burden you think you have going on. Two heads are better than one, remember? We'd have two incomes, we'd have two vehicles. We'd be two parents…"

She shook her head hard back and forth, and his anger started to sharpen, along with the disdain in his voice.

"Oh, wait, that's right. They had two parents already, so that's that. They don't get to have a second dad because they already had one. You're not allowed to be happy because you were already happy once. They don't get to be a family because they…"

Piper was on her feet in a flash, poking him hard in the chest with her finger. "Stop it! Stop saying we're not *already* a family! We don't need a *man* to magically make us 'real.'" She glared up at him, not a bit cowed by the anger in his eyes. *Bring it on.* "Lily and Ethan need me, and I'm *all* they need!" She knew she wasn't making sense anymore, but she was too hot to care. "You think you're going to just swoop in and make us whole? What are you going to do about *Tom*? How are you going to solve the problem that makes you forever *second*? Can you handle being a second dad? A second husband? How's that going to play on your ego?"

They glared at each other in silence before he ground out a few words through his teeth.

"I was the second *lover*, and I didn't hear any complaints from Room Three."

Her breath sucked in with a hiss, and she slapped him. Hard. Hard enough to make her palm sting. Hard enough to leave a bright red imprint on his cheek. Time and sound and hearts stopped. They just stared at each other in sadness and shock.

He lowered his eyes first, his voice thick with emotion and regret.

"I deserved that."

"No…" she breathed. "No. You didn't. Neither of us deserve this. But here we are. Two people who fell in love at the wrong time. I can't do it, Logan. If you really love me, you'll understand that. I can't…" Tears clogged her throat.

"Don't say that. Not yet. I *love* you, Piper. I'll do all the work. I swear to God I'll do it all. I'll take your burden, not add to it…"

She bit her lip hard, and still couldn't hold back the sob. "I can't, Logan. I can't…"

She started to turn away, but somehow ended up in the warmth of his embrace. She sobbed against his chest, crying until she didn't think she had tears left in her. And still she kept crying, soaking his shirt. He held her, supporting her when her own legs couldn't. He didn't speak, just made murmuring sounds of comfort as he brushed his lips on her hair.

It made no sense. This man. Her feelings for him. None of it made sense. She had to put her family first. But walking away from him… Her sob got caught on a bubble of laughter.

"What?" He spoke against her temple.

"*You* were the one who was supposed to walk away." She burrowed her face against him, muffling her words in his shirt, but he understood. Of course he did. He was Logan and he loved her. Her heart hurt so much she almost couldn't bear it when he spoke, calm and strong in his sorrow.

"I was the one who was supposed to walk away, but you're the one actually doing it. Is that what's so funny?"

She shook her head against him. "None of this is funny."

"But it *is* ironic, babe. You're the one who sticks. I'm the tumbleweed. And here we are. I fought it like a feral cat. And now that I'm finally ready to commit, you're not." He put his fingers under her chin and tipped her head back. "But here's one thing you should know about me. I'm stubborn, and I don't quit." Her lips trembled, and he dipped down and gave her a quick kiss. "I won't quit on us. I'll give you space, but don't ever think I've quit. We can make this work, Piper. I know it."

She tried to smile. It was too good to be true. But she felt just the tiniest spark of hope in her heart. She lifted up on her toes to kiss him, and he tightened his arms around her and kissed back with everything he had. Deep and commanding. She returned in kind, trying so hard to believe in the possibility. Trying so hard to believe that this was enough. That their love might just be enough to outweigh the rest of the world. Her arms wrapped around his neck. That his love really could solve everything.

"Let go of her!" Ethan's voice cracked in anger, and his fingers wrapped around Logan's forearm, pinching and hitting to get him away from Piper. Logan released her immediately, putting his hands up and deflecting Ethan's wild punches as her son yelled. "You're not my dad! You don't get to kiss her like that! You don't get to touch her! She doesn't want you! She doesn't *want* you!"

LOGAN HAD NO problem protecting himself from Ethan's attack. But there wasn't an armor in the world strong enough to protect him from the pain and fear in Piper's eyes as she tried to calm her son. She wrapped her arms around Ethan, saying his name over and over until he stopped struggling against her.

"It's okay, Ethan. It's over. It's okay, sweetheart." For one quick moment, Ethan turned into his mother's embrace, but he quickly fought free, yelling at Piper now.

"You were *kissing* him! You were *kissing* him, Mom! What about Dad? Gigi was right—you *are* forgetting him. But I won't let you! I won't! He was my dad!" Ethan's face was blotched and red with anger. Wet with tears. It broke Logan's heart.

"Ethan, man, it's not…"

"Shut up!" Ethan screamed the words. "You shut up! You stay away from us!"

A small, frightened voice joined the fray.

"Stop fighting! Everybody stop *fighting*!" Lily threw her book on the floor and ran into the room, between Ethan and Logan, arms thrown wide. "Stop it! Stop yelling!"

Logan started to reach for her, but stopped when the girl recoiled, looking at him in wild-eyed anger.

"You made Momma cry! Gigi said you didn't belong here and I didn't believe her. But now you're making

Momma cry!" Her big eyes shimmered with tears, and her lips trembled. Her face twisted in a rage he never dreamed the child could muster.

You may as well have planted him on the surface of the moon. He had no clue what to say. What to do. Maybe Piper was right. Maybe he wasn't ready for this family business. But he couldn't give up just yet. He knelt on one knee.

"Lily, your momma and I were talking about..."

She came at him swinging, and landed a hard little fist on the corner of his eye. He stood, reeling from her anger. Her voice passed the scream level now, reaching a screech.

"I don't *care*! I hate this fighting!" She was still swinging, striking his legs with her tiny fists. Still in shock, he didn't dare reach for her. Piper quickly knelt and pulled her back. But she couldn't stop the words pouring out from the little girl. "I *hate* you! You made my momma cry!"

Ethan's voice cut in, angry and still cracking with hurt. "Logan just wants to make Mom and us forget Dad, Lily." He looked at Piper. "And *she's* letting him do it."

Logan shook his head. "No! That's not true. Your dad was..." He was going to say how good and brave and loving Tom was, but Ethan never gave him the chance.

"Don't you talk about him! He was *our* dad, and you didn't know him!" Ethan went to his sister and took her hand. "Come on, Lily. We don't need to listen to this guy." Logan dropped his head. Susan Montgomery had planted those seeds. But how could he fight it without bad-mouthing the kids' grandmother?

Lily looked at Piper with enormous tears sliding down her cheeks. "I don't wanna forget Daddy. The mermaids loved Daddy and I don't wanna forget him, Momma!"

Mermaids?

Piper took a deep, shaking breath.

"You're right, sweetheart. The mermaids loved Daddy, and so did I." Ethan's mouth opened, then snapped shut at his mother's glare. Ethan might be furious, but he wasn't stupid. Piper's voice broke when she stroked Lily's hair. "Logan and I are friends. But that has *nothing* to do with your Daddy."

"But Gigi doesn't like him! She told Ethan and me. She said he was an antelope." Piper managed a puzzled smile.

"An antelope?"

Ethan gave Logan a sullen look. "Interloper. Gigi said he was an interloper."

Logan thought about what Piper had said about their bad timing and realized she might be right. Maybe there'd never be a "perfect" time, especially if Susan kept up her campaign against him. But if he fought to be part of this family right now, he'd do more damage than good. To the kids. And to Piper. He didn't want that. He'd told her he'd wait. And he meant it. Maybe not until *perfect*, but at least until things settled down.

"Guys," he said, splaying his hands in a gesture of innocence. "Your mom and I are friends, and friends are good. But our friendship has some people…confused. So we're going to take a break." Piper's eyes went wide, but she stayed silent. "Because your mom loves you both more than anything in the world, and always will. You come first, and that's the way it should be. So she and I are going to cool it, okay?"

Lily was in Piper's arms now, clinging to her like she was a life raft. Her lower lip stuck out in a pout, and her face was soaked with tears. "And I don't want you at my Christmas dance recital. I don't want you anywhere. I h…"

"Okay, sweetheart," Piper soothed. "Calm down. It's okay, Lily."

Logan cleared his throat, which was thick with some emotion he couldn't put his finger on. Regret? Love? Anger? Frustration? Pain? All of the above?

"Okay, Lily. If that's what you want. I won't come to the pageant." Piper and Lily's faces were nearly identical—tear-shimmering eyes, trembling lips. He thought he'd said what Lily wanted. But the child's eyes narrowed even further.

"Fine! *Don't* come! I don't *want* you there! You make Momma cry and she forgets Daddy's mermaid, and… and… I *hate* you, Logan!" She buried her face against Piper's neck and started to sob.

He thought his heart had already taken all the pain it could handle, but this… What a fucking mess he'd made of everything, just by falling in love. No wonder he hadn't done it before now. Why would *anyone* open themselves up to *this*?

Ethan glared at Logan. "See what you've done now?" He stalked away, shaking off Piper's hand. Piper murmured words against Lily's hair, rubbing her back, then looked up at Logan. Her voice was tight.

"I tried to tell you…" She took a ragged breath. "A break is probably a good idea." She looked around the kitchen. He knew she was wondering how they could work together with all this between them.

"I'll stay out of your way." He hated the thought, but it was what he needed to do. "I'll give you guys all the space you need. For as long as you need."

Her mouth opened, then closed again. Finally she just nodded and turned away, with Lily still whimpering in her arms. After they left, Logan stood there, staring at the empty doorway, and wondered how he'd survive this *break* he'd so brilliantly suggested.

CHAPTER TWENTY-TWO

PIPER BLINKED BACK tears for the hundredth time. She pushed and pulled the noisy vacuum cleaner across the carpet in the downstairs hallway at the inn. Right outside Room Three. Logan said they were on "a break." It was what she'd wanted. Time to deal with her family. Time to get her kids settled and secure. Time to get ready for Christmas.

Stupid break.

No, it was a *good* thing. She couldn't put herself and her love for Logan before her own children. She vacuumed around the console table in the hall, leaning over to get under it as much as she could. It was selfish to think she could love again after Tom. Love so much that not seeing Logan was making her heart ache and her eyes leak at the most inopportune times.

This morning she'd served breakfast to a honeymooning couple from Buffalo, and just seeing their happiness and the tenderness in the way they touched each other and looked at each other... It was enough to send Piper running to the kitchen to cry into a dish towel. But she was doing the right thing for her family.

"Are you vacuuming that carpet or assaulting it?" Piper looked up to see Iris standing there, cane in hand.

One brow was high, and her mouth tweaked up into a smile. Piper turned off the vacuum.

"Sorry, Iris. Was I doing something wrong?" She looked down the hall, where there wasn't a bit of lint to be seen on the spotless rug.

"It wasn't the doing, it was the…um…attitude toward the doing. You looked like you were using that vacuum as a weapon. I just put a pot of tea in the parlor. Why don't you come sit with me? Before you frighten one of our guests." Iris was already headed toward the parlor at a surprisingly brisk pace on that last comment, making it clear she'd been giving an order, not offering an invitation. Piper sighed and set the vacuum in the utility closet. Iris obviously had something to say. All Piper had to do was get through the conversation without crying.

She put her head in the library to check on Lily on her way to the parlor. Her daughter was engrossed in a picture book about the animals of North America. She looked up with a smile before lowering her head again. Lily and Ethan had both been quiet since that blowup in the kitchen. But different kinds of quiet. Lily's silence was tentative and timid. She was anxious and jumpy. She'd had a nightmare the night before and woken up screaming, but she wouldn't tell Piper what it had been about.

Ethan's silence was angry and brooding. Not his normal "whatever" attitude. It was deeper, and he refused to talk with her about it. She could tell he was struggling, but she couldn't find a way to make him open up. Something had to give, because there was no way they could have a perfect Christmas with all that tension in the house.

"Piper?" Iris's voice came from the parlor. "Please don't make me get up again. PT wiped me out this morning."

"Be right there!" She looked at her daughter. Her heart. And smiled. "Want to help Momma make muffins later?"

Lily's face lit up. "Blueberry muffins?"

She nodded. "Blueberry and cranberry. And some oatmeal-raisin ones, too."

"Ew. You can make those by yourself, Momma. But I'll help with the others!"

"Okay. You stay here while I talk to Iris, and then we'll get started."

Iris was sitting by the window, and she smiled when Piper came in. "This weather is crazy. Snowstorm a few days ago, and sixty and sunny today. It's so nice Logan took his motorcycle out for a spin. For some reason, he doesn't like my car."

His name hit her hard, but Piper did her best not to show it. Maybe it was just Iris's way of saying he wasn't here, so she could relax. He'd done his best to stay out of her way, but the man lived here. They were bound to see each other in the halls or in the kitchen or, like last night, out on the porch as she left. His eyes always lit up when he saw her, but he stayed a safe distance away. Didn't say more than a few words of greeting. Then he'd quietly vanish. She sat at the tea table with Iris. Funny how it was always Logan who walked away and never her. As if she couldn't make herself leave him.

"Oh, you've got it bad, girl." Iris's voice echoed her exact thoughts, making a little laugh bubble up.

"What do you mean?"

The older woman just rolled her eyes. "Please. You've got the same kicked-puppy look that my grandson's been wearing all week. Why are you two torturing yourselves like this?"

And here came the tears. Piper blinked rapidly in a vain attempt to hold them back, but she gave up when Iris handed her a clump of tissues.

"It's a mess, Iris. And it's not Logan's fault. It's just... timing."

"Bullshit." Iris slapped the table with her hand, making Piper jump and the teacups rattle. "There's never a bad time for love to come into your life. And there's no good excuse to reject it. Love doesn't happen that often, Piper. Some people, like you, are lucky enough to find it more than once."

Piper nodded. "That might be true, but... I have two children who come first. Your grandson's a great guy, but he doesn't hold a candle to those two. He'll go back to an oil rig somewhere and he'll move on. That's what he's best at, right? Moving on?" The thought of Logan leaving made her chest heavy. But it was bound to happen. He wasn't going to hang around his grandmother's Victorian apartment forever. If only their timing had been different.

Iris snorted, and Piper realized she'd said that last sentence out loud. "And when will the timing be right? Next year? In three years, when Ethan's driving and pushing the boundaries of his freedom? In five years, when he's getting ready for college? In ten years, when

Lily's a hormone-fueled teenager herself? When they're both adults and, as you said, Logan's moved on? When is this mythical perfect time for a single mom to fall in love again?"

Piper was silent.

"That's what I thought. Well, I suggest you think on it. Because there is no time more 'perfect' than right now, so you might want to figure out how to make it work. And that's all I'm going to say about it."

Piper's voice dropped to a near whisper. "I'm doing the best I can."

Iris sighed, her smile fading. "I'm sure you are, dear. But best for whom?"

"Best for…" Piper struggled with an answer. For *everyone* made her sound too important. For her children made her sound like some saint. For herself was selfish. For Logan wouldn't be accurate, because he seemed just as miserable as she was.

Iris sat back, thoughtful. "I was once a single mother, you know. Not a widow, but still…alone with my babies in a rickety old house that was falling down around my ears after my husband left. So…a lot like you." She stared hard at Piper. "I let my second chance get away. I'd hate to see you do the same."

Piper stiffened. She couldn't let herself weaken. She'd made her decision and she had to stick with it. For the sake of her children. That was her job, and she should never have forgotten it in the first place.

Iris could scoff all she wanted, but this? This was *not* the time for her to put more pressure on her family. Piper was sure of it. So why did she feel so damn *sad* about it?

LOGAN WAS IN a mood. Maybe it was Piper-withdrawal. Maybe it was that nagging Taggart wanderlust of his starting to kick in. But he was definitely in a mood. Which made Ted's news all the more frustrating.

"What do you mean, the job's not there anymore?"

He paced across his room, holding the phone to his ear while keeping his eyes averted from the lace canopy over his bed. The bed where Piper and he had made love more than once. The walls of the Taggart Inn were closing in on him more and more with every passing day. There were more Piper memories in this old place than he could handle. Ted let out a sigh on the other end of the line.

"The whole region is on edge, Logan. Lots of protests and sabotage. There are rumors the government might even try to nationalize the oil industry. The company is cutting back to skeleton crews until things cool down."

So that was it, then. He may as well stay in Rendezvous Falls. It was like some huge cosmic joke. When he wanted to stay, Piper pulled the rug out from under him. Now that he didn't want it… "If not South America, how about the Gulf?"

Ted chuckled. "The snow's getting to you that bad, huh?"

"It's not the snow…" Logan couldn't help smiling at the memory of those days he and Piper had spent in Room Three during that snowstorm. "But there's nothing for me here."

"What about your lady-friend?"

Logan looked out the window at Piper's house. "Like I said, there's nothing for me here."

"Well, shit. I'm sorry to hear that. Lori and I were

looking forward to meeting the woman who might finally tame Logan Taggart." Logan didn't respond. "Right. Well…don't give up without a fight, buddy. Have you thought about that consulting business we talked about?"

He had. Back when he'd been thinking he and Piper would make a go of it, he figured between consulting and the inn—which Piper and Gran could run when he was away—he'd have a good living and enough variety to keep him happy. But happiness felt a long way away right now. "I don't know, Ted. I think I'm better suited for following orders on a rig rather than coming in and giving them as some adviser."

"And you think that shoulder of yours is better off working the rigs?" Logan just grunted, and Ted pushed on. "Do this one job with me. It's a few weeks freezing our asses off to get a boatload of money. If it's not your thing, don't do it again. But Logan, I'm not going back on the rigs. I'm getting too old for that life, and Lori wants me home, being a dad and a husband."

"I get it." And he did. For a few brief moments, he'd thought the same of being with Piper, Lily and Ethan. For a few brief moments, that had been all he'd wanted. He still wanted it. But she didn't.

He ended the call with Ted and went to join Gran in the living room. The apartment had shrunk since she'd moved back home. His small bedroom was his only chance at privacy, but the walls in there got close after a while. She was reading some magazine about old country houses, so he sat on the sofa and picked up a book himself. But he never opened it.

"If you don't stop scowling at my cat, he's gonna start taking it personally."

Iris looked at him over the top of her magazine. He'd been spending so much time in this apartment that he was starting to feel caged up and restless.

"Sorry, Gran. Feeling a little claustrophobic." He got up from the sofa, sending the orange cat running for cover.

"You know, you're going about this situation all wrong." She set the magazine in her lap. "You'll never win her back by hiding from her."

"She asked me *not* to try to win her back. She needs time. Space. Whatever." He huffed a laugh. "Great, now I'm starting to sound like Ethan."

"So you're just going to make it easy for her, then?"

He looked at her in confusion. "What choice do I have? It's what she wanted. We have a system. I take care of the third floor and the dining room. She takes care of the rest. Separate duties in separate areas."

They couldn't help bumping into each other once in a while, and it always created a tangle of feelings for both of them. He could see it in her eyes. Regret. Sorrow. Tension. And once in a while, usually when she first spotted him, a glimmer of familiar heat. Affection. Longing.

Gran, in her inscrutable way of messing with people, changed topics abruptly. "You gonna take that fancy consulting job?"

Logan lifted his shoulder. He'd told Gran about it last week. "Maybe. Keeps my hand in the oil business so I don't get too twitchy."

She raised her brow, noting the way he was pacing right now. "You mean there's a twitchier version of you?"

"Give me a break, Gran. I'm doing the best I can."

"Are you?"

"You sound like a damn shrink when you do that."

"Well, maybe you *need* a damn shrink, if you think you're really doing what Piper wants."

He threw his hands in the air. "What are you talking about? She *told me…*"

"Oh, for heaven's sakes, you're not an idiot. Love makes people stupid, but not *this* stupid." She gestured at him. "Suck it up and go after that girl before she raises that gate and locks it up for good."

His mouth dropped open. "Raises her *what*?"

"Bah," she said, waving her hand at him. "Never mind that. Just know that if she goes through this holiday without you, she might decide she doesn't *need* you."

"She *doesn't* need me, Gran. She's strong enough to do this on her own."

"Look, Logan, I can only beat around the bush so long waiting for you to get it." She grabbed her cane and stood. She was getting stronger and steadier by the day. She took a step forward and pointed at him. "Piper loves you. You love her. But you're both scared. One of you has to take the chance. And single moms don't take a lot of chances."

"You want me to go after her? To put more pressure on…"

"Don't *pressure* her. But be there. Remind her how much she loves you. Be the one who takes the chance." She patted his arm. "She's not the only one who misses you, you know. Lily's Christmas recital is coming up this week."

Logan's chest tightened. "Lily *hates* me. She said so."

The little girl's words were branded into his brain.

His grandmother laughed. "Children hate everyone at one point or another. Especially when things don't go their way. Your father threw that word at me when he was a boy. Pretty sure you and your sister did, too. If you want to take on those kids, you're going to need thicker skin."

But this wasn't about him.

"Lily's already having nightmares, and it's probably my fault."

Gran turned away, her cane tapping on the wood floor. "Lily's been having night terrors for years. But hey, you do whatever you think is best. Piper's got her hands full with both those kids, and doesn't need to be making *you* feel better on top of it."

And then she was gone. Leaving nothing but confusion—and a burning hot longing for Piper—in her wake.

CHAPTER TWENTY-THREE

PIPER AND LILY had a giggling good time making muffins together at the inn that afternoon. They made more of a mess than Piper would normally endorse, and it felt good to just…be a mom. By the time she finished cleaning up, Lily was asleep at the table, her head on her arms. Piper lifted her gently and headed for the door. The time wasn't far away when her daughter would be too heavy for her to carry like this.

The kitchen door swung open just as she got there. She was expecting Iris. Not Logan. He stopped abruptly. Then he did the worst possible thing. He smiled. And there were the tears Piper thought she'd tucked away for the day. She must have wavered on her feet, because he was there in a second, taking Lily from her arms. Lily never woke, just mumbled and snuggled close to his neck. So trusting. So secure. The way a father would make her little girl feel. The tears came heavier, and Logan drew *her* in, too, kissing the top of her head before whispering.

"Hey…easy…don't cry, babe. It's okay." He kissed her again. "Don't wake Lily. I didn't know you were in here, sorry."

She sniffled and stepped back, wiping her hand

across her face. He was too close. Too intimate. Too much. She reached out. "I'll take her."

"No. I've got her." He glanced at the clock. "Ethan won't be home yet. I'll carry her over to the house." He started to turn, then stopped and looked back at her. "If that's okay?"

She nodded. It was a bad idea—the *worst*—but how could she say no to this man she loved, holding her sleeping daughter so sweetly? They walked across the lot in silence. And into her house, which warmed immediately with his presence. He laid Lily on the living room sofa, then pulled the throw over her. He stood and faced her, looking as hesitant as she felt.

"I'd better head back. I know you don't want Ethan to see me here." He looked at the front window, then frowned. "No tree? I thought you were a get-it-up-early person?"

She bit her lip. She hated admitting she couldn't do something by herself. His eyes went soft.

"You don't know how to get your ten-foot dream tree in the door and set up, do you?"

"I may have to revise my plans a little, but I'll figure it out." She had no idea how.

He chuckled. "I don't doubt it, Piper. But you know I'm here for you. All you have to do is ask and I'm here."

"Don't...do that." She looked away. "I'm not ready for the friend-zone with you. It hurts too much right now, Logan."

He winced. "I don't know if I'll *ever* be ready for that." He turned away. "I'll just...go, then."

She nodded, arms wrapped around herself. Having him here was too sweet. Too painful. He didn't say anything more until he reached the door, staring straight ahead and not at her.

"I meant what I said, Piper. You call me, anytime, and I'll be here. Because I love you."

The flood of tears came the moment the door closed behind him. She was just getting herself composed again when Ethan came sulking through the same door. His backpack hit the floor with a thud and he went to move past her without even acknowledging her existence. And she'd had enough of it. She'd had enough of *everything*.

"I'm standing right here." She threw out her arms. "Am I invisible now?"

He gave her a sideways glance, barely slowing. "What's your problem?"

She grabbed his arm hard and fast, spinning him around. His eyes went wide when she shook her finger under his nose.

"*Enough*, Ethan. I'm your mother, and you *will* respect me."

He tried to pull away. "Hard to do after you were kissing some guy trying to break up our family, Mom."

"Your grandmother was wrong about that. Logan's done nothing wrong. And frankly, neither have I." Her voice lowered. "Like it or not, son, I'm an adult and I get to have my own life once in a while. I'm sorry if that hurt you and Lily, but that wasn't ever our intention. Logan is a good man."

"He's not my father."

"No, he's not. But he was our friend." *And I loved him.* "And your father would never want you to treat someone badly who went out of his way to help us the way Logan did."

There was a barely perceptible movement in the vicinity of his shoulder…an almost shrug? It was better than the sullen attitude he'd worn for days, so she pressed on.

"Your father would never want you to treat *me* the way you have lately."

The words hit their mark. Ethan's shoulders stiffened, then dropped in defeat. He looked up, his eyes holding more regret than he probably intended to show. "Prob'ly not."

Another tiny step of progress. He stared at the boxes of Christmas decorations stacked along the wall, sitting there until she was in the mood to put them up.

"Have you thought any more about going to your sister's recital?" Lily was going to be a ballerina angel in the community Christmas pageant at St. Vincent's next week, but Ethan had flat-out refused to attend. "This is important to your sister. I really need you to go. For Lily."

"No way."

"Ethan…"

Piper ground her teeth together so hard they hurt. Christmas was ten days away, and she would pull this all together, one way or another. People were going to have *fun*, damn it. Because it was freakin' Christmas, and that's the way it was supposed to be.

"Mo-m. I don't want to watch a bunch of little kids jumping around to stupid Christmas music." He turned for the stairs. "Besides, you only want me there so we look like some Christmas card family, and it's all so fake."

"What are you talking about?"

"Gigi and Poppa are gonna be there, and you'll be wearing that gross sweater that lights up..."

"Lily picked out that sweater, and she loves it." Piper tried to lighten the mood. "I'll have to turn it off during the recital, though, or I'll look like part of the show."

Ethan didn't see the humor. "It *is* a show. That's my point! Everyone's pretending all nicey-nice, when you and Gigi are still mad at each other. You freakin' cry every five minutes, and Lily's moping around like someone stole her teddy bear." He kicked one of the open boxes of decorations. "If you actually hang all this stuff, the house'll look like Santa puked in it."

"Ethan!"

"It's true! None of this stuff will make any of us feel better."

He was right, of course. "What *would* make you feel better?"

"I don't know. But it's *not* some stupid Christmas pageant." He stomped up the stairs. "I'm not going."

"With that attitude, it's probably best if you don't. You'd spoil everyone's fun." She probably shouldn't have said it. He hesitated for a second, then continued up without looking back.

"Whatever."

Piper went into the kitchen and proved her son right by crying yet again. And yes, she'd been doing it a lot lately. Angry tears. Sad tears. Tears that snuck up on her by surprise. Tears she basically scheduled every night before sleeping because she knew they were coming. Tears for her children. Tears for herself. Noisy tears that came with the urge to throw things. And, right now, the silent kind that sheeted across her cheeks without a sob.

Ethan wasn't wrong. No one was happy. Especially her. And she had no idea how to fix it.

It was ironic, really. She was the fixer of things. The planner. The "Energizer Bunny," as Tom used to tease. She grabbed a wad of tissues and sat at the table with a sigh. She was the one with all the schedules and to-do lists. But right now, she felt…frozen.

There was a Logan-sized hole in *all* of their lives. Hers. Lily's. Even Ethan's. In just a short period of time, no matter how much she'd tried to protect her family, he'd become part of them.

There was a soft knock on the door, and Piper groaned. *Now what?* None of the answers she could come up with would have prepared her to see Susan Montgomery standing on her front porch, holding a bouquet of red-and-white carnations tied in a festive Christmas ribbon. And…smiling. Piper just gaped at her, not equipped for another confrontation, but not sure how to respond to the affectionate expression on Susan's face.

"Piper, honey, we need to talk."

"Logan?"

"Jesus, Gran…why do you sneak up on me like that?" He wiped at the coffee he'd just spilled down the front of his shirt. "You're like a ninja, even with that cane."

"What cane?" He turned from where he'd been staring out the apartment window, and she raised her empty hands with a grin. "I'm free!"

"Is that wise?"

"The doctor said it's fine at home, as long as I have a wall nearby or something to balance myself with."

She gestured to the chairs scattered around the crowded room. "I'm never far from something to grab."

"Well…congratulations. And be careful." He looked to the window again. Thin, light snowflakes fluttered sparsely through the air. Ted had texted again that morning, looking for an answer on the Alaska job. He had no idea what he wanted to do, so he'd ignored the text. Hanging around here waiting for Piper's decision felt like a death sentence. It would have been better for his heart if she'd just said she didn't care at all.

"Logan."

"Oh, yeah…sorry, Gran. What did you need?"

"Vickie is here to pick up some Christmas decorations for the pageant tonight. I need you to carry them out to the car."

He was surprised she still had any decorations left, after he and Piper had emptied the attic… And just like that, he fell down the rabbit hole of Piper-thoughts. *Not productive.* Gran cleared her throat and he followed obediently, because she was Gran and disobeying her would only lead to an argument. He didn't have the stomach for any more arguments right now.

There were two shopping bags sitting on the reception desk. They were filled with new-bought tinsel garlands and weighed less than a pound put together. Even with a cane, he suspected Gran could handle them. And Vickie Pendergast was fit and healthy and standing right there, watching him lift the weightless bags. She was the fanciest of Gran's book club friends, always carefully put together. Today was no exception, in her trim corduroys and a blue sweater with a matching shawl.

"Such a gentleman!" Vickie exclaimed, more loudly

than necessary. "Thank you so much for helping us. I don't know *what* we would have done…"

Gran gave her a smack on the arm and hissed something that sounded like "…overkill, you off-Broadway hack…"

He went outside to where Vickie's Mercedes was parked, not three feet from the wide porch steps. She or Gran probably could have *thrown* the bags into the car from the front door, so he had no idea why they needed his help. He turned to ask, and saw both women staring across the parking lot toward Piper's house. Before he could stop himself, he looked too.

Piper's car was gone, but Roger Montgomery's SUV was there, with a huge blue spruce tree tied to the roof. Susan was unlocking the front door, but there was no way those two were going to get that tree in alone. He frowned. That really wasn't his problem, was it?

"Oh, look!" Vickie said, still using the singsong voice Gran had smacked her for earlier. "It's *Roger* and *Susan*!" She waved enthusiastically, even though neither of the Montgomerys was looking in their direction. "Susan said they were going to surprise Piper and the kids by decorating her place today while everyone's at church getting ready for the pageant. But look how big that tree is. Oh, my. How will they *ever* get it inside?"

Logan waited for Gran to light into Vickie, but instead, she was looking between Roger and Logan. There was a flash of something calculating in her expression when she agreed.

"And Roger had that shoulder injury last year, Vickie. He shouldn't be lifting. Logan, dear, you should go help him."

"What?" He stared at Gran. "They don't want *my* help. Besides, *I* have a shoulder injury too, remember?" He rolled his shoulder, surprised to realize it wasn't hurting so bad now that he'd been off the oil rig for a while.

Gran's expression hardened. "Since when have you refused to help people in need, young man?"

"Did you seriously just call me 'young man'? No. I'm not going over there. No way." As much as he resented his grandmother treating him like a teen, he knew he sounded like one right now. Instead of arguing, Gran's voice softened.

"They're just trying to give Piper the special Christmas she wanted. Susan and Roger are doing that for her."

Piper had apparently made peace with her former in-laws again. He was happy for her. For the kids. But it probably only happened because Logan wasn't in their lives anymore.

Vickie took Gran's arm. "We should get back inside. We don't want you getting sick, Iris." Vickie looked down at Logan. "How much are *you* willing to do for Piper?"

His mouth dropped open. He barely knew this woman, and he sure didn't need any lectures from her. But as her question sank in, all he could see was Piper, standing in her living room just a few weeks ago, bright-eyed and happy, pointing to where her "perfect" Christmas tree would go and telling him how she was going to decorate it.

He and she had finished putting new wallpaper up in the kitchen that very afternoon. She'd insisted the whimsical teapots and teacups in the design were "period authentic" for the house, and Lily said the teapot reminded her of a character in her favorite movie. Piper and Logan had finished putting the new hardware on the kitchen cupboards, which all worked properly after Logan and Ethan had adjusted the hinges. Logan had taught Ethan how to use wooden shims to level the doors.

They'd ordered pizza that night and played some crazy game of Lily's that involved getting whipped cream in the face. They'd all laughed themselves silly. After the kids went upstairs to bed, Logan had taken Piper to the living room sofa and...

"Logan?" Gran's voice cut in, stealing him from what was probably the best memory.

"Yes, Gran?"

"Go help them. If not for Piper, then do it for Lily and Ethan. I know you love them, so do this for them."

He chewed his lip, shaking his head even as he took a step forward. If he loved them, then he needed to fight for a place in their lives. And right now, the Montgomerys were the gatekeepers. If he could get past them, he might have a chance.

Gran's voice called out as he walked away. "Thatta boy." He was pretty sure he also heard her say "...worked like a charm..." to Vickie as they went back inside.

Roger looked up at Logan's approach. Then he *smiled*. Not what Logan expected.

"I should have known," Roger said.

Logan put his hands up in front of him. "I'm only here to help with the tree."

"Oh, I know." Roger started untying knots in the

rope holding the tree to the vehicle. "Iris said she'd have some muscle here to help this afternoon. I thought maybe she meant that Rick guy from her book club. But of course she planned for you to be here. Let me guess…" Roger looked back over his shoulder. "You had no idea either?"

Logan huffed out a short laugh. "None. She played us both." She and her meddling book club pals.

"Don't just stand there. Grab the base of the tree and head inside. If we're lucky, it'll fit in front of the window."

They wrestled the tree inside, where a shiny new tree stand was waiting. Along with Susan Montgomery. She seemed far less surprised than her husband was to see Logan, looking right past him to Roger without a second glance.

"I'll leave you boys to get that thing secured and put the lights on. I'm going to unpack Tom's Santa collection in the dining room."

Roger watched her walk away, his forehead furrowed. He took a deep breath, then let it out with a smile. "The woman still manages to surprise me once in a while. Come on."

Even Logan needed a stepladder to get the angel on top of the nine-foot tree once they got it in the stand. Then he started the strings of lights, passing them down to Roger. The guy seemed to have a system for putting the lights just right. If they weren't, Roger moved them. And moved them again. There was apparently an art to it that Logan didn't grasp. But he knew Piper would love it. She'd love the strings of colorful beads, too. And all the ornaments. Some were round and glittery.

Some were cute and fluffy—they'd definitely appeal to Lily. And there were a few sports ones mixed in for Ethan, who'd be unimpressed, or at least act that way.

Logan stood back to take a look as he and Roger finished. He wished he could be there when Piper saw it. He rubbed the center of his chest, which was just one big, dull ache. Being here hurt.

"It's beautiful." Susan's voice came from directly behind him, making him jump.

"Uh…thanks. Your husband did most of it. I should go…"

She reached out and touched his arm, stopping him cold. "Logan. Please." Her usual edge was gone. She sounded…tentative. "Can we talk?"

He started to refuse, then saw Roger behind Susan, nodding firmly up and down in some sort of signal to Logan.

"O-kay. But I do need to leave soon. I don't want Ethan to come in and…"

Susan waved her hand. "Don't worry about Ethan. Sit down. Please."

They all sat, Roger and Susan on the sofa and Logan in the armchair. He felt like he was about to be interrogated. There was a beat of uncomfortable silence, which Roger jumped to fill.

"The kitchen looks great. You did that, right?"

"Piper and I did, yes, sir." He hid a smile, thinking of Piper and all those online video tutorials she'd watched.

"Hell of a lot better than what was there." Roger looked at him. "You put up that new dining room light, too, right? And the basement lights? And you painted the hall?"

Before he could answer, Susan let out a harsh half laugh.

"Okay, dear, I get it. He's done a lot for Piper and the kids." Her mouth pinched. "I'm grateful. And I owe you an apology."

Wait. What?

She raised her eyes to meet his. "It's been brought to my attention that I may have been unfair to you."

Roger cleared his throat loudly. Susan looked over at him, then straightened.

"I was more than unfair. I was…harsh. I didn't want you here."

And she'd made sure no one else wanted him here, either. Including the woman he loved.

"Yeah, that message came through loud and clear. To everyone."

Anger rose in his chest. Being in this house, with so many memories of Piper, was like being cruelly teased. Like seeing a mirage while lost and thirsty in the desert, then watching the illusion vanish from sight. Susan's apology, probably coerced, wasn't going to fix a damn thing. He stood and moved for the door.

"Susan, I know this little setup was probably Gran's idea and she meant well, but enough, okay? Piper's got her tree. You've made your apology. It's a big freakin' Christmas miracle and everyone can be happy. But I have to go."

"Piper loves you."

Susan's words may as well have nailed his feet to the floor. He closed his eyes, squeezing them together tightly and trying his best not to lose it. One breath. Another. His throat was thick with emotion.

"I know that. I love her, too. But…"

Then Susan was standing at his side, and he was shocked at the compassion in her eyes. She lifted her hand as if to touch his shoulder, then dropped it nervously.

"Never follow a declaration of love with a 'but,' Logan. Because nothing can really stop love. Not even foolish mothers-in-law." She gave him a sad smile. "*Former* mothers-in-law, that is. I truly am sorry." She looked at the family portrait on the wall, her eyes shimmering with unshed tears. "My son loved Piper with every ounce of his being. And he would be horrified if I kept her from finding happiness now that he's gone. It's really hard for me to let someone else into Ethan and Lily's life, where *Tom* should be."

The woman had lost her only child. Logan thought of losing his mom—how alone he'd felt. How angry he'd been. How frightened.

"Susan, I will *never* let your grandchildren forget their father. And if I can ever win Piper back, I will be here for Lily and Ethan. I promise you that."

Her head bobbed up and down. She was pressing her lips together to keep from crying, and he could hear the little breaks in her breath. Roger came over and put his arm around her. She was nearly sobbing, but also smiling, as she drew in a deep gulp of air.

"I believe you, Logan. And don't worry about Piper. She's just afraid, like I was. Be patient. She'll come around."

He could only hope that was true. Logan headed for the door, but this roller-coaster day wasn't done with him yet. Ethan was coming up the steps.

CHAPTER TWENTY-FOUR

"Are you going to keep that angel to yourself or hang it on the tree?" Chantese stood at the bottom of the stepladder, looking up to where Piper stood, clutching a cardboard angel cutout. A tall green tree, made of construction paper, was taped to the church gymnasium wall. Paper garlands draped across it, still sticky from the little fingers still putting them together on the craft tables. She looked at the angel in her hands and sniffed back traitorous tears.

She thought of the tree she *didn't* have at home, and wondered how she'd get one. She also thought of the tree in the library at the inn, where Logan had snatched her off the ladder a few weeks ago and persuaded her to sneak back to Room Three. She smiled. He hadn't had to work very hard to get her on board with that plan.

"Earth to Piper?" Chantese started to laugh. "Girl, just call the man and put yourself out of this misery."

"I can't." She straightened and slapped the paper angel onto the wall. "You know that's over." She came back down to the floor and did her best to look convincing. "And it's fine. It's best. For everyone."

Her friend just shook her head, her long, thin braids swaying. "Keep telling yourself that, sister. *You* may believe it, but trust me, no one else does."

She felt a flare of resentment. Everyone had an opinion. "I need my friends to *support* me. Not give me some bullshit lecture, okay?"

"Ah, the tree looks lovely, ladies." Father Joe had walked up behind Piper. Perfect timing. "And so much in the spirit of the season with all the little ones around." He gave her a knowing look that made her blush. He'd definitely heard her just now. "Just like our attitudes and speech, eh?"

"I'm *so* sorry, Father Joe. I forgot where I was. I mean, not that I curse like that everywhere else. I *don't*!" She was probably going straight to hell for lying to a priest. "And certainly not around children. I just...got upset. Not that I swear when I'm upset, and I don't get upset that often, but..."

Joe chuckled softly, his Irish brogue thickening. "Relax, child. I was just goin' on with you. No one more than three feet away heard you, and that wasn't the Lord's name you were tossing around, so you're fine in my book. The holidays can be stressful, especially for a single mom such as yourself." The priest looked around the room. "I see Lily, but where's your boy, Ethan?"

Piper pressed her fingers to the corners of her eyes to stem the tears. "Probably at home playing some video game. I'm afraid he's not very into Christmas this year, Father."

Chantese's son, Malcolm, came running over, and she excused herself to escort him to the restroom, leaving Piper and Father Joe alone in front of the paper tree. He tipped his head to the side and studied her for a moment. Then he took her arm and tugged her farther into the corner and away from listening ears.

"Are *you* into Christmas this year? You don't seem yourself, lass."

She bit her lip hard to keep from crying, but when she shook her head, she knocked some tears free. She inhaled sharply, hanging on to what little holiday spirit she could find.

"I'm trying, Father Joe." She wiped her cheek quickly. "But nothing's going right. The kids are *so* unhappy. I promised them this big, perfect Christmas, and it's just not happening."

He gave her a warm, knowing smile. "So you think your children are unhappy because you aren't giving them this so-called perfect Christmas, then?"

Her shoulders fell. "No. They're unhappy because I've made such a mess of things. I moved them into a house that's falling down around our ears. And it's *pink*, which Ethan hates just on principle. But then again, Ethan hates everything these days. Including me."

"I'm guessin' you know that's not true."

She huffed out a laugh. "Not according to him. His dad's gone. I moved him out of the home he'd known for four years. I work. His grandparents and I are at odds." Although she honestly didn't know where they stood after Susan's surprise visit and even more surprising apology a few days ago. Piper wasn't quite sure she trusted it. "And then I *really* screwed things up by dating someone."

"Logan Taggart, yeah?" Fresh tears came at the mention of his name. She hadn't noticed until now that Joe had eased her into a quiet hallway for privacy. He handed her a tissue. "And Logan wasn't a good man? He did something bad?"

"No!" Piper bristled in his defense. "He was *wonderful*. Lily adored him. He was patient with Ethan, which isn't easy. And I…" She paused, her voice softening. "He was wonderful, Father Joe. A really good man."

"I see. He left you, then?"

Her throat clogged with tears, and she knew an ugly-cry was looming.

"No. He didn't leave me. I asked him to stay away."

"But why?"

Good question…

"It was too much, Father. For everyone. For *me*. It's not fair to the kids for me to…"

"To fall in love?" His words were soft, but still had the effect of a full body blow.

She pulled herself together, wiping her cheeks with the back of her hand and sniffling loudly.

"I'm sorry, Father Joe. I can't talk about this right now. Thanks for asking, and I'm sorry I cursed in church…"

Joe laughed. "You cursed in the *gymnasium*. I give you absolution on that one." His laughter faded. "Piper, you say you want this 'perfect Christmas,' but the only ingredient needed for that is love. That's what Christmas is all about. And here you are, barring the door *against* love. Do you really think it's best for your children…?"

Anger stiffened her spine. "If one more person tries to tell me what's best for *my* children, I am going to lose my shit, and I don't care *where* I'm standing or whether

I get absolved or not." She went to brush past him, her voice cold. "Excuse me, Father."

His voice was calm. Steady. Everything she wasn't.

"Piper, I'm not telling you anything you don't already know." She stopped, her back to him, but unable, even in her anger, to just stalk away from a *priest* while he was speaking. "I saw you at the Purple Shamrock with Logan. I saw the way you looked at each other on the dance floor. I saw love there. If there's one thing I've learned in my line of work, it's that love always wins."

She stood there, absorbing his words and wondering if it was really that simple. But Father Joe didn't say it was simple. She finally nodded, thanking him and walking away.

Lily looked sad and lonely at the craft table, gluing felt antlers on holiday decorations by herself while the other children were giggling and talking all around her. Lily had been sad since the argument at the inn, when she'd seen them all fighting with each other. When she told Logan she hated him. That word was tossed around pretty easily by angry children. She'd heard it from Ethan often enough. But could she really consider bringing Logan back into their lives if Lily no longer liked him? On top of Ethan's brooding resentment? She swallowed hard. Her responsibility was to her children first.

Chantese appeared back at her side. "Malcolm's grandmother just brought him something to eat before the pageant. She'll watch him for a bit. Evie's holding a table for you and me at the diner. You look like hell. You need to eat something."

"Gee, thanks." But Chantese was right—Piper hadn't been eating. Or sleeping.

Their booth was near the front windows, usually Lily's favorite spot. She was always such a people-watcher. But not today. She sat slumped forward, moving her mac-and-cheese around on her plate without actually eating any of it. Evie was talking about the tree-lighting ceremony coming up that weekend, and she leaned forward to ask Lily if she was ready to talk to Santa Claus, who'd be arriving on a fire truck.

Lily shook her head, her voice low. "I ruined Christmas."

Evie and Chantese gasped. Piper put her arm around Lily and hugged her tight, kissing the top of her head.

"Sweetie, Christmas isn't ruined …"

"It *is*!" Lily cried, struggling to pull away, then collapsing in tears against Piper. "It's all my fault! I told Logan I hated him, and now he's mad at us. I *ruined* it!"

Her skin went tight with guilt and horror. "Oh, baby, he's not mad at us…"

"Then why won't he talk to us?" Her voice was muffled against Piper's sweater. "Why doesn't he come over to our house anymore? Why is he going away? It's all because I yelled at him. I ruined everything."

"Going away?" Piper ignored the expressions on her friends' faces, which had morphed from sadness for Lily to uh-oh looks for her. The thought of him leaving went straight through her heart. He'd said he loved her and she thought maybe…

"I heard him tell Miss Iris. He's going to Laska. Is Laska a long ways away?" Lily looked up, her eyes shining with tears. Piper knew the feeling. But why was Logan going to Alaska? What happened to South America?

"Yes, honey. Alaska is a long ways away. But he's not leaving because of you. He was always going to leave." She swallowed hard. "Christmas is still coming, and it's going to be wonderful! You're dancing tonight, remember? Won't that be fun? Then we'll…"

"Stop it, Momma!" Lily threw herself into the corner of the booth and crossed her arms, glaring at Piper. "We don't even have a *tree*! Ethan said it's stupid and he's right. All you do is cry. This is gonna be a *lousy* Christmas, and it's all because I made Logan not like us anymore."

Chantese reached over and took Piper's hand as she spoke to Lily.

"Baby, there's no such thing as a lousy Christmas. Your momma would never let that happen. Evie and I will come over this weekend and we'll put up so many silly decorations that it will look like you live at the North Pole."

Piper did her best to smile, but her mouth trembled. "It'll look like Santa puked all over it."

Lily giggled. "Not exactly what I was going for," Chantese said with a laugh. "But okay."

"Really, Momma? Are we decorating this weekend?"

The only way she'd have the time and energy to do all of that would be if she asked Iris to have Logan take care of the inn, which was fully booked this weekend. She hated to do it, but she knew he'd agree. Because he loved her.

"Momma, can Logan come help?"

Piper sucked in a sharp breath. "Oh… I don't know.

He'll be pretty busy at the inn." And packing for Alaska.
She glanced across the table. "But we'll have lots of
help." She knew she was going to have to swallow her
pride in order to give her daughter a dream Christmas.
"I bet we can get Gigi and Poppa to come over, too."

Lily grew serious again, holding up her pudgy little
forefinger in warning. "But no fighting, Momma. No
more fighting with Gigi. It's not nice."

Piper nodded in agreement. Her truce with Susan
was new, but she had to hope it would hold.

"No more fighting, Lily." She held up two fingers
like a pledge. "I promise."

ETHAN WAS STILL GLARING, but at least he was glaring
at the kitchen table now instead of at Logan. He was
pretty sure the kid left burn marks on his skin when he
first came into the house and saw him. Logan had at-
tempted to exit past him, but Susan Montgomery called
him back.

So Logan turned back. Quite the day he was having,
thanks to his grandmother's do-gooder efforts. Ethan's
eyes went wide at the holiday transformation inside the
house. There were very few inches of space that weren't
somehow embellished in gold, red or green.

Roger was the one who'd gently tugged the boy into
the kitchen and sat him down, along with Logan, and
encouraged Susan to repeat her apology. It wasn't any
easier for the woman the second time around, but she
did it. And now Ethan was attempting to bore holes in
the table with his eyeballs. His voice was low, with a
touch of sullen. Basically...normal.

"So now you *don't* think Logan's trying to replace

my dad? You think it's okay for Mom to date the guy. Any guy." He scowled. "You think *Dad* would be okay with that."

Susan blanched. "I didn't say that…"

But Roger talked over her. "Yes."

She stared at her husband, and her expression softened. "Your grandfather's right. Your dad would want your mom to be happy. He'd want all of you to be happy."

Roger nodded, leaning across the table toward his grandson. "Do you remember when your Momma was pregnant with Lily?"

Ethan frowned. "Yeah. Sort of. Why?"

Logan found he was leaning forward too, wondering where this was going.

Roger glanced at Susan, whose eyes had gone shiny, then continued. "You were worried about this new family member coming along and taking up Mommy and Daddy's time, remember?" Ethan barely shrugged, looking everywhere but at anyone's face. Roger smiled. "You *do* remember. Do you remember what your father told you?" Another nearly invisible shrug. But Roger pushed this time. "Tell me what he said, Ethan."

The silence stretched on in the kitchen. Logan glanced at his watch. The Christmas pageant was starting in less than an hour.

"He said love was like elastic." Logan's head rose at Ethan's words. The boy looked at his grandfather, who nodded at him to continue. Ethan glanced in Logan's direction, but the glance didn't stick. Instead, he stared back to the table. But the anger was gone from his face. "He said love was like elastic, because it…it stretched. It could look one size, then stretch to another. He said love was *better* than elastic, though, because it stretched forever and never broke. It just kept stretching as much as needed." The edge of Ethan's mouth twitched. "He said it stretched as much as Mom's belly was stretching with Lily."

Susan dabbed at her eyes with a tissue. "Your father loved you so much, Ethan. He loved your mother. And she…" She looked at her husband. "And she loved him back."

Logan couldn't sit there any longer. This was a family moment, and this wasn't his family. He started to stand, but Susan reached over and held his arm.

"No. Stay. This is where you come in." She looked back to Ethan, but didn't release Logan's arm. Her mouth trembled. "Ethan, your mother's love expanded to include Lily without loving you any less. So I suppose it can expand to include Logan, too."

It wasn't the most ringing endorsement he'd ever heard, but it was a big step on Susan's part. She was basically accepting his presence in Piper's life. And encouraging…well, that might be too strong a word. She was *suggesting* that Ethan might do the same. Logan and Ethan stared at each other in silence across the table.

Ethan's eyes eventually dropped. He lifted his shoulder yet again.

"Yeah, maybe."

Logan's chest swelled. A *maybe* from Ethan was huge. It was several steps up from *whatever*. It was progress. But it was still just one small victory in a much larger battle. Piper still thought Logan was a threat to her family's stability. Lily still hated him.

"Son, you should get ready for the pageant." Roger patted Ethan on the shoulder, but Ethan pulled back.

"I told Mom I'm not going. It's stupid. She bought me a red-and-green-plaid shirt with little Christmas trees on it, and she expects me to wear it."

Both Susan and Roger started to protest, but Logan waved them off. He remembered enough about being a teen to know that arguing with Ethan wasn't the way to change his mind. Logan nodded at the Montgomerys, hoping they'd trust him to handle this.

"He's right. It *is* stupid. And that shirt sounds gross."

Ethan, in a rare caught-off-guard moment, looked up in surprise. "What?"

"You're right, man. Bunch of little kids singing silly songs. Who needs it?"

"But… Mom wanted me to go. She bought the shirt special."

"Well, sure. She's into the whole perfect family Christmas thing. But *you* don't need to fall for it. You're smarter than that."

Ethan considered that for a moment. "But won't Mom be upset?"

Logan shrugged. "You already told her you weren't going, so she won't be expecting you." He sat back and crossed his arms, doing his best to summon up an Ethan-like expression of disinterest. "Lily will be looking for you, but she'll get over it, right?"

Ethan's brows lowered. "That's harsh. She's only four."

"Well…what are you gonna do? Stay here and play *Game of War* with your buddies online, or go watch a stupid pageant?" He fixed a hard stare on the kid. "It's your choice."

Ethan scowled, knowing he'd been cornered, then stood. "Fine. I'll go change my shirt." He glanced at Logan, a grin tugging at the corners of his mouth. "Mom's wearing a sweater that lights up."

Of course she was.

The Montgomerys headed to church while Ethan was changing, because Susan had volunteered to help with refreshments or something. Logan assured them he'd get Ethan there.

The short car ride to church was quiet. This day had turned Logan inside out and upside down, and Ethan was probably feeling the same way. Susan hadn't exactly embraced Logan, but she'd laid down her battle sword.

"You aren't coming in?" Ethan looked at Logan when he pulled the car to the curb in front of the church hall. Piper would be thrilled to see her son at the pageant. But would she be thrilled to see *Logan*? That might be pushing his luck, and he couldn't afford to blow this.

"No, man. I don't want to blindside your mom in the middle of Lily's big night. Bad timing." He was still terrified she wouldn't let him back into her life. "You go on inside."

He watched Ethan jog into the building. A colorful minibus from the local senior center slowly off-loaded its passengers in front of him as he waited to leave. Seemed like the whole town was pulling into the lot at once. He was just starting to drive away when he heard his name being…*screamed.*

It was Lily, dressed like an angel, running full bore for the car. And the busy parking lot.

CHAPTER TWENTY-FIVE

PIPER HAD BEEN absorbed in trying to attach the sparkly halo to Lily's fine hair when she looked up and saw Ethan. She nearly choked on the bobby pins she had in her mouth. Her son was not only *there*, but he was wearing the Christmas shirt she'd bought for him. The one he swore he'd never wear, even at gunpoint. And... he was *smiling*. Sort of. No, that was definitely a smile.

It wasn't until Lily started jumping up and down and clapping that Piper came out of her stupor and embraced Ethan. And he embraced her back! She was sure she felt his hand briefly touch her shoulder. That counted as a hug. For the first time in over a week, the tears on Piper's cheeks were happy ones.

"Ethan! What are you...? I'm so glad you came." She held him at arm's length. Good grief, she kept forgetting her son was almost as tall as she was.

He looked down and tugged on Lily's hair. "I had to see this munchkin try to dance."

"Hey!" Lily swatted his hand away, giggling. "You just wait. I'm gonna do a stupen-pundulos twirl!"

"I think you mean *stupendous*." His eyes had a spark of amusement he couldn't hide, no matter how much he tried to be low-key.

"Honey, I'm so happy to see you here." Piper couldn't

stop smiling. "Who did you catch a ride with?" Roger and Susan were already here. They'd greeted her and Lily a few minutes ago.

"Logan brought me."

Was Logan *here*? She started looking around, but Ethan shook his head.

"He didn't come in. He didn't think you'd want…"

Lily looked around Ethan's legs, doing the same frantic search Piper was. "Where is he? Is he still mad? *LOGAN!*" And she was gone in a flash, darting straight for the incoming crowd and disappearing into the winter coats and laughing faces. She was still screaming Logan's name, and Piper realized she was headed outside to find him. Outside, where she could see headlights and taillights moving in the parking lot.

"Lily! Stop!"

She and Ethan gave each other one quick horrified glance, then both chased after Lily, calling her name. By the time Piper wrestled her way outside, Lily was halfway down the sidewalk in her white angel costume, still screaming Logan's name. She was thirty feet ahead of Piper when a green car came to a stop and the driver's door swung open.

Logan was across the roadway in two long strides, dropping to one knee in the slush and catching Lily in his open arms as she leaped. Piper stopped, panting from her panic and the run. Ethan was right beside her.

Lily was sobbing now, her face buried in Logan's neck.

"I'm sorry! I'm sorry, Logan! Please don't be mad at me anymore! Please don't go to Laska! I love you, Logan!"

His eyes were tightly closed. People were moving around them—some watching in curiosity, some just determined to get inside where it was warm and dry. Piper was sure Logan wasn't aware of any of them. Or of the snow gently falling. He was murmuring something to Lily in a low, rough voice to calm her. Piper stepped closer to hear.

"Oh, baby, I was never mad at you. Don't be sorry. It's okay. I'm not mad…"

Lily drew her head back and stared him right in the eye. "You're *not*? You promise?"

His mouth lifted into a shaking smile. His cheeks were wet, and it wasn't just from the snow.

"I promise, Lily. And you know what? I love you, too." He finally glanced up at Piper, his eyes full of emotion. And uncertainty. "But you need to get inside, sweetie. You have to go dance for everyone."

"Will you come watch me dance?" Lily asked, looking from Logan to Piper. "Please, Momma, can he?"

Piper's throat was too clogged with tears to speak at first. She nodded quickly before finally getting the words out.

"Of course he can." Then she remembered her son. And her in-laws. And all the complications. Logan stood, holding Lily in his arms. He looked straight at Ethan.

"Is that okay with you?"

"Whatever, man." Ethan shrugged. "But let's go. It's cold as sh…" He slid Piper an apologetic look. "It's cold out here."

"Let me go park the car." He handed Lily to Piper, and she waited there with Ethan, who didn't complain about the cold again. He just waited quietly for Logan to park the car, then return to take Lily from Piper.

As he took her, he gave Piper a warm smile. "I heard a story today about a very smart guy who once described love as elastic."

She gasped, feeling a stab of sweet sadness at the memory of Tom holding Ethan on his lap one afternoon over four years ago and rubbing her pregnant belly. Tom explained that Ethan's little sister was in there. Then he described how there would always be enough love to go around, no matter how many people joined their family. How did Logan know that story?

She nodded in agreement as they started walking toward the building. Ethan was playing it cool, but she could tell by the tilt of his head that he was hanging on every word.

"Yes, that was our Tom," she said. "Always so smart. He loved us all so much."

"And you loved him right back." Logan said in a low voice.

"Yes. We did."

"Can your love stretch to include someone new?"

"Are you asking if I can love you without loving Tom less?" They were just inside the doors now, where Roger and Susan were watching closely from near the gymnasium entrance. They waved, but stayed where they were. Ethan had pulled his phone out and was staring at it, but he hadn't left Piper's side. Lily was watching everything from her perch in Logan's arms. Piper smiled up at Logan. "I'd like to try."

He hesitated, and she realized "trying" wasn't

enough. Before she could clarify, he spoke, staring deep into her eyes.

"If you're not ready yet, it's okay. I won't push you. I love you and I'll never give up on you. I told you I'm stubborn. I mean, I'm plain old stubborn on my worst day. But for love? Hell, I'll be so stubborn the Taggart Inn will shake to the ground in a pile of dust before I change my mind. When you're ready. When the kids are ready. When your house is ready. When Christmas dinner is ready. When St. Patrick's Day rolls around. When *next* year's Christmas dinner is ready. I don't care. You're worth waiting for, Piper Montgomery."

It was hard to believe this man was hers. Truly hers. "You don't have to wait, Logan. I'm ready. I love you. Let's do this."

His free arm went around her waist and he pulled her close. Then he reached beyond her and tapped Ethan's shoulder.

"You in, kid?"

"Whatever." But Piper and Logan both saw the slant of a smile on his lips.

And right there, in the entrance of the St. Vincent's gymnasium, Logan kissed her. It was quick and chaste—they were in a church, after all—but also warm and full of love. For her. *And* her family.

It was…perfect.

EPILOGUE

IT DID NOT snow on Christmas Day. In fact, it was fifty degrees and everything was a muddy mess from three days of rain. It was still raining. Piper stood in her kitchen, staring out at the dreary weather. There would be no sledding today. No snowmen. And definitely no ice skating.

Logan walked up behind her, sliding his arms around her waist and kissing her head. She sighed, leaning back against him and soaking up his warmth.

"Good thing Gran ordered that ham the other day, huh?"

She nodded against him. "Yes. We'll have to use the turkey for sandwiches at the inn tomorrow."

"Think it'll be thawed by then?" He kissed her again, closer to the temple this time, and his lips lingered on her skin. She started to forget about the lousy weather. His kisses were like those lights in that alien comedy—one flash and your memory was wiped clean.

"Very funny. *You're* the reason I forgot to take it out of the freezer yesterday."

Roger and Susan had surprised them by inviting the kids to come wrap gifts at their place yesterday afternoon so Piper could finish getting ready for Christmas. Then they'd all meet at the Christmas Eve service at church and the kids would come home with Piper. It was a great plan. Until Logan came over to…um…help. And somehow he and she went from setting the dining table to being naked in her bed for three hours. She grinned to herself. They barely made it to church on time, but hey—they had to grab their moments when they could.

It wasn't until just before dawn that she'd woken with a start and remembered the still-frozen turkey that was supposed to be the centerpiece of her Norman Rockwell Christmas dinner today. By then it was way too late to thaw a thirty-pound bird. She'd texted Logan in a panic, and he'd gone to Iris, who announced she had a fully cooked honey ham in the fridge at the inn. She'd planned on using it for Christmas breakfast and luncheon sandwiches that week, but said she could improvise and do without it. Between the three of them, they were able to adjust the side dishes to make them compatible with ham. The Montgomerys would never know about the snafu when they all sat down for dinner in a little while. Logan's lips brushed her ear.

"Ethan seemed okay with his new game console not arriving on time."

"Ugh. Don't remind me." The website blamed the delivery company. The delivery company blamed the weather and the holidays and anything else they could think of. She'd spent what felt like hours on the phone trying to get it here before Christmas, but it just wasn't meant to be. Her oldest child didn't have the one thing he asked for under the tree. "But…yes. He's okay. I think that enormous rolling toolbox you got was enough to distract him."

"It was Roger's idea to put Tom's tools inside of it."

"Yeah, that really clinched it. Ethan came close to tears." She smiled. "I think we all did, to be honest. Roger saved us from a long day of endless, drawn-out *whatevers*."

He chuckled and leaned down far enough to kiss her lips. "And what did Susan save us from?"

She groaned. "A good night's sleep for the next year? A clean house? A life free of vet bills?"

As if to confirm her statement, they heard the clickety-click of tiny toenails on the hardwood floors, closely followed by Lily's pounding feet. "Rosie! Rosie! Come back! I haven't wiped your paws yet!"

A yellow bundle of curly fluff, ears flapping wildly, came skidding into the kitchen, leaving behind a trail of splotchy mud prints. And a laughing Lily.

Susan had given Lily a puppy for Christmas. A *puppy*. A goldendoodle, which Piper had never heard of. A quick search on her phone made it clear Rosie was going to be alarmingly large when she grew up. *Perfect*.

Logan released Piper to catch the pup, lifting her up in his arms and covering his denim shirt with mud in the process. He laughed, swinging the dog close enough to Piper to get her caught in the flying wet spray. She let out a squeal and jumped away, but it was too late. The puppy had enthusiastically licked her face, and left a smear of brown mud across the front of her white Christmas sweater, right above the red-and-green-plaid reindeer.

"Oops," Logan said, without looking the least bit sorry. She narrowed her eyes at him, but Lily interrupted before she could say what she was thinking.

"Thanks, Logan!" Lily reached up for the wiggling

dog, and he grabbed one of the new Christmas kitchen towels to wipe off the muddy paws before setting her down. Lily hugged the pup, who seemed to be trying to hug her right back. Piper's heart melted just a little. It was pretty darn cute. Lily laughed again, looking up with a wide grin. "Rosie and I are both flowers! The name was Miss Iris's idea. She's a flower, too!"

After a great deal of artificial grumbling that she would be fine on her own on Christmas Day—as if they'd ever let that happen—Iris had joined them for Christmas. She was in the front room with Roger and Susan now, enjoying a pre-dinner glass of wine.

Logan stooped down to Lily's height. "You know, I really love flowers. Especially Irises and Lilys and Rosies." He tapped Lily's nose with his finger. "But I don't know if your momma's going to like Rosie much longer if we don't keep her paws clean and keep her off the furniture."

"Oh, she's already *been* on the sofa!"

Logan's head dropped and his shoulders started to shake. At least he had the good grace to try to hide his laughter from her. Piper rolled her eyes in defeat.

"Lily, you can take Rosie back to the living room as long as she stays off the furniture." Then she brightened. "And while you're in there, remind Gigi and Poppa that Rosie is *your* dog, so when *you* go their house, so does Rosie."

Logan coughed, choking on his laughter as he stood. Lily and her puppy charged out of the kitchen, and he pulled Piper into his arms. "Remind me not to piss you off." He kissed her. "You're brutal. But I still love you."

It was probably her imagination, but it seemed the

heavy rain outside the window lightened a bit at those words. She'd never tire of hearing them. And she'd almost let him get away. A little shudder went through her, and he held her tight.

"Hey, come closer and warm yourself up on me, baby." She wiggled her eyebrows suggestively, making him laugh again before he shut her down. "There's no time for *that* kind of warming up. Maybe later, once the kids are asleep. I'll use that Christmas gift you gave me and sneak in."

He'd seemed baffled when he opened the small box that morning and took out a house key attached to a cheesy Rendezvous Falls key chain. Technically, he already had his own key, but she wanted to make a point, both to him and to the family. He was welcome here at any time. All the time, actually. Ethan got it right away, and had to explain it to Logan.

"She's sayin' just move in already, okay?"

Susan had stiffened a little, but Roger took her hand and shook his head. She was still working through her feelings about Piper and Logan, but she was trying. Logan had looked up at Piper in surprise, his eyes warm.

"Really?" He'd looked at Ethan. "It's cool with you?"

Ethan was busy going through the drawers on his shiny red toolbox. He'd just shrugged.

"Whatever. You're basically living here anyway."

Logan pulled the key out of his pocket now, dangling it in front of Piper. "Best gift ever. It's like you gave me a family for Christmas. The one thing I never thought I'd want, and now it's the *only* thing I care about. I don't want to move in tomorrow…well, I *do* want to do that, but you know what I mean. I don't want to overwhelm them. How do you want to handle it?"

She stared at the key, wondering what kind of future it was going to bring her. As long as Logan would be in her life, it was sure to be a good one. "Let's play it by ear. Maybe not tomorrow. But soon. Very soon."

Her hand rose to touch the tiny diamond-encrusted dolphin hanging from a delicate chain around her neck. She wasn't sure what she'd expected as a gift from Logan, but jewelry hadn't been anywhere near the top of the list. It reminded her of the dolphin tattooed on his arm, and he'd admitted he got it because it made him think of his two loves—her and the ocean. Thanks to the new consulting business he and Ted were creating, he'd still get to see his beloved ocean once in a while for business, but for shorter stretches. And he'd always come home to her.

He kissed the base of her ear, sending shivers across her skin. "Just so you know, that's not the last diamond you'll be getting from me."

"Oh, yeah? I never thought of you as the diamond type."

"Me, neither. But I can't stop thinking about how pretty a diamond would look on your finger." He held her hand up and grinned. "Don't you agree?"

She turned and wrapped her arms around his neck, burying her fingers in his hair. "Let's just say I wouldn't dream of refusing one if it came along."

He started to lower his head toward hers, then raised it again and sniffed. "Is there something burning?"

"Oh my god—the pies!" She ran for the oven. When she opened the oven door, sweet-smelling smoke billowed out. "Damn it, the cherry pie spilled over. And the crust on the apple is burnt." She grabbed for hot pads, and Logan helped bring the pies out and get them on the waiting racks. But they didn't move fast enough to keep the smoke from setting off the smoke detector, which started blaring. Voices rose from the living room and the puppy started howling. Logan closed the oven door and went to assure everyone the house wasn't on fire, while Piper waved the towels at the smoke detector until it stopped screeching.

He came back to the kitchen doorway, his shirt covered with paw prints, his hair askew from her fingers in it just a few minutes ago. She reached up and brushed her own hair out of her face, grimacing at the very crispy pies on the counter.

"No snow. No gift for Ethan. No sledding. No turkey. A puppy to train. Fire alarms going off. Burnt pies." She blew out a heavy sigh. "This Christmas has been…"

Logan walked over and cupped her face in his hands. There was so much heat in his golden gaze that she was a little surprised her clothes hadn't gone up in as much smoke as the pies did. He kissed her, tender and lingering, then raised his head and smiled as he wrapped his arms around her.

"This Christmas has been *perfect*."

She snuggled into his embrace as Lily called out from the other room.

"Momma! I think Rosie just pooped!"

Logan's chest vibrated with laughter, and Piper joined him.

"You're right. This is a perfect Christmas."

* * * * *

*Turn the page for a special preview of
the next book in Jo McNally's charming and witty
Rendezvous Falls series,*
Barefoot on a Starlit Night.
Coming soon from HQN Books.

BRIDGET MCKINNON WOKE the next morning desperately hoping the guy from the bar last night was just a figment of her imagination. She was in the midst of battling her father's family—*her* family—over turning the Purple Shamrock into a more modern "clean cuisine" American restaurant. So it made sense she'd have a nightmare about some Irish hottie with emerald eyes asking to move in downstairs. It would be just her grandmother's style to put a Celtic hex on Bridget's life.

Two mugs of scalding coffee and a bagel later, there still hadn't been a knock on the door. Maybe she really *had* dreamed him up. She propped her hip against the gold-and-white laminated countertop and watched the snow come down outside. Did he ever say his name? Did she ever give him the chance? Probably not. Bad enough some stranger walked into her kitchen on a busy night, but he'd walked in while she was having her near-nightly pity party.

She allowed herself only fifteen minutes or so each night, after food service was done and the kitchen was empty, to let her exhaustion and worry rise to the surface. Was she doing the right thing by staying in Rendezvous Falls? Would her grandmother be okay? Would the bar cover expenses this week? Was there ever going to be a day that didn't end with her back aching and her brain begging for sleep? Add in her worry over getting a tenant so she could cover her mortgage, and her brief pity session had stretched longer than a few minutes last night and a few tears had even managed to escape.

Her latest in a long line of cooks had quit, along with the busboy-slash-dishwasher, so she'd been alone over the sink. She figured it was safe to just let the tears flow. Until the tall, dark-haired stranger with the delicious Irish accent showed up, asking about the apartment. And somehow, as brief as their encounter had been, she knew that he knew she'd been crying. There'd been just a glimmer of something when his eyes had met hers. Oh, God...what if it had been pity? She shuddered.

Her temper had been on a hair trigger for months. Most folks approached her with fear, or at least a healthy dose of caution. But Irish was a stranger. Probably new in town, since he was looking for a place. Not knowing any better, he'd just barged into her kitchen, not even blinking when she unintentionally waved that knife around. He'd been sorta funny, with that *I'm from my mother* line. Polite, but just a little playful. Too polite to ask why she'd been crying. Not so playful that he'd tease her about it. But he'd known. It was only because he surprised her that he'd been able to get that close. She wouldn't let that happen again. She damn sure wouldn't let him move in.

She glanced at the clock. Eight thirty. Looked like he wasn't going to show anyway. Probably just some drunk guy who didn't even remember their conversation. Just as well. There was no way she was letting him rent her flat.

A knock at the door made her jump, sending her

coal-black coffee—her third—swirling in her mug. Fine. He was here. She'd show him the flat, then show him the door. He'd probably hate it anyway. It was furnished and decorated in soft pastels with overstuffed chintz furniture. Maybe it was just the accent, but he'd seemed like more of a hunting prints and leather kind of guy. She set her coffee down, then snatched it up again as she left the kitchen. She needed all the fortification she could get.

If he *didn't* hate the apartment, she'd come up with some reason why he couldn't have it that wasn't discriminatory. She headed down the center staircase to the foyer. It would be a pretty space if it wasn't so boxed in with walls and doors that didn't belong there. The furnished apartment on one side. An unfinished studio apartment on the right.

The previous owner had chopped this poor old house into apartments for college kids, but it was a little too far from campus for that. Most students wanted to be able to walk. Bridget never intended to be a landlord, but the price was right and she'd hoped to convert it back to a single family someday. In the meantime, the rent covered most of the mortgage. If she convinced the McKinnons to go with her plans for the Shamrock, and if they were successful, she'd have enough money to do it. It was a big "if" and an even bigger "hope," since she had no idea how to go about remodeling a house. She opened the door, crossing her fingers that maybe it was one of her cousins dropping by. But…no.

Irish stood there, bundled against the cold wind in a leather jacket that matched his black hair. That hair was short, but had a definite curl to it. Her first random thought was that he must have been an adorable child, with those black curls and intense green eyes. He was tall and lean and had a way of standing—legs apart, hands in pockets, head tipped to the side—that suggested he was confident and, judging from the slanted smile, perpetually amused. Just the kind of guy she didn't like, she told herself. Laid-back. An observer, with no ambition for himself. Some guy in touch with his *feelings*. No, thanks. A gust of wind blew snowflakes through the door, and Bridget realized she'd been staring at him while he got covered in snow. She stepped aside.

"Come on in, Mr....?"

The slant of his smile increased, causing his cheek to crinkle and a dimple to appear. *Yikes.* This guy was seriously good-looking. Women probably fell all over him. And *that* was a reason she could use to deny him the apartment. She didn't want it to be some playboy's bachelor pad, especially with the bedroom directly under hers. *Ew.*

He straightened and extended his hand. "Finn O'Hearn. My apologies for not introducing myself last night. I think that blade you were swinging around scared my manners outta me."

She'd been washing the cutlery and had her favorite chopping knife in her hand when he'd come in. Good. Let him be scared, like everyone else. She liked people best when they kept their distance.

"Bridget McKinnon. My apartment is upstairs." She shook his hand and nodded toward the mahogany staircase. "Your..." *Damn it.* "I mean...the available apartment is down here." She gave him her scariest glare. "If you take it, there will *never* be a reason for you to set foot on those stairs." She saw the spark of amusement in his eye. Ugh. If there's one thing she hated, it was being laughed at. She unlocked the door, then stepped back to let him in first. His brow rose in surprise.

"Ladies first."

"Not a chance. I have a cousin in real estate, and she told me to never turn my back on a stranger." Why was she babbling?

To his credit, he didn't laugh at her, or take offense. He simply considered her words, then nodded and walked by her. "Is that why you rent to women? You don't want some random scary man living downstairs?"

"Umm… I don't know how rentals work in Ireland, but here in New York, I can't admit to discriminating based on gender."

Finn's eyes shone even brighter. "Cleverly put, Miss McKinnon. You can't admit it, but you didn't deny it." He looked around the space that stretched the depth of the house and served as living room, dining room and kitchen. "More modern than I would have thought."

"And more frilly, I assume." But if she hoped the curtains and ruffled pillows would chase him off, she was mistaken.

"'Tis fine. Reminds me of my ma and da's house in Sallins."

They walked back toward the small kitchen tucked behind a laminated peninsula. She pointed to two doors on the left. "Bathroom. Bedroom. The bedroom has an additional small half bath attached. Nothing fancy."

Finn inspected the rooms. She thought maybe the peach-colored walls in the bedroom would put him off, but he didn't even blink.

"It's fine. I'll take it."

"Uh…excuse me, but I think that's *my* decision, not yours."

He turned and flashed her a full-on smile. Yeah, he was a player, alright. She'd bet he was good at it, too, between the looks and that accent. She cleared her throat and tried to sound as stern as possible.

"I don't allow *any* parties or nonsense down here. I don't want women—or men—coming in and out for random hookups, especially at night. No one gets a key other than the tenant. The walls aren't exactly paper-thin, but there's not a lot of soundproofing, either. I expect quiet after ten. If you're using the laundry room here instead of a laundromat, it's an extra twenty per month. And it's *my* laundry room, too, so you can't leave stuff around. There's absolutely no smoking. No pets. *I* get the driveway parking, since it's only one car wide. You'll park on the street or over in the bar lot and walk." She scrunched her eyes shut. Why did she keep using *you* like this was some kind of done deal? She *wasn't* going to rent to this guy. This guy who'd just walked back out to the living area, and was now opening and closing the refrigerator and stove. He looked over his shoulder at her.

"Like I said, I'll take it." Her mouth opened, and he held up his hand to stop her. "No parties. Quiet. Can't park here. No smoking. No pets. Don't leave my laundry in the dryer. No slutty behavior. I got it. I still want the place." He slid his hands into his jeans pockets. "I promise to lay low and stay out of your way. My credit…" He hesitated.

"There it is." She could hear the triumph in her own voice, and he could, too. "Your credit sucks, right? Let me guess—you need a little time to scrape together the security deposit, right? But I should trust you for it and let you move in anyway? Thank you—next." She waved her hands toward the door. "Bye."

"Easy there, Quick-Draw." He chuckled as he straightened. "I've *got* the money. I'll give you cash today if that'll do it. It's just that my…uh…divorce…" His voice trailed off as quickly as his smile did. "Stuff happened. My credit took a hit. But I've got enough cash to handle this. And steady income from the college."

She studied him through narrowed eyes. She wanted to boot him out the door, but she relied on the income from this place to cover most of her mortgage. Her previous tenant, Cyndi, had been a student. A junior, so Bridget had figured she was pretty stable when she'd moved in last August. But Cyndi had been transferring in from a school in Texas. After raving all through the fall months about how excited she was to see snow, she'd gone home to Houston for the holidays, then emailed that Bridget could keep the security deposit because she wouldn't be coming back. A couple early winter snowstorms were all she'd needed to see.

Bridget needed a tenant. Finn wanted to be one. It might be weird to have a guy living down here, but her door had a dead bolt. It's not like she'd ever seen much of her previous tenants—just the occasional pass in the foyer or bumping into them doing laundry. But if this guy had credit issues… She brushed past him and went to the front window, pushing the curtains aside.

"What do you drive?"

"What?" His footsteps came closer, but stopped a few feet away. She had to give him credit—he was careful not to invade her space. "A Range Rover. Why?"

She saw his SUV behind hers in the driveway. It looked new, but was so covered with salt from the roads that she couldn't tell if it was blue or black. The same was true of any other vehicle in upstate New York this time of year. The car was sturdy. Practical. Expensive. Not the type of vehicle some broke loser would be driving.

"Owned or leased?"

"Owned. And paid for."

She turned, surprised to find him closer than she'd thought. His hands were back in his pockets again. Did he do that on purpose, just to look supercool and unruffled? One hand slid out, and he ran it through his hair, leaving wavy curls standing up in its wake.

"Anything else you need to see? I can show you my passport. My work visa. My license. My bank statement. My library card. My campus parking permit…" She waved her hand at him to stop. He wasn't being defensive, just teasing because he could clearly see she was grabbing at straws, trying to find a way to deny him the apartment. And for some reason, that amused him.

"Okay, I get it." She bit back a smile. She wasn't usually one to be charmed by anyone, but Finn O'Hearn was definitely a charmer. Then his smile faded.

"Look, I *need* a place. I'm livin' at the Taggart Inn right now, and the college thinks I'm some kind of flight risk because of it. I can go to the bank and get two months' rent in cash, and be back here in half an hour."

She glanced at her smart watch. "Should have thought of that before you showed up so late. I told you I have to get to work at nine."

He huffed out a soft laugh. "The bank doesn't *open* 'til nine, Bridget." The way he said her first name made something funny happen in her chest. "I wasn't gonna stand at an ATM after midnight on a Friday night to get that kind of cash. You've got a tenant standing here ready to sign the line or whatever it is you call it. I'm basically a hermit with a bank account, which makes me a perfect tenant."

He was making good points, but instead of agreeing, she couldn't resist grabbing at the tiny red flag she'd just heard.

"A hermit? You mean the kind of guy everyone always describes as 'quiet and keeps to himself' after he goes on some murdering spree?"

The slanted smile returned, along with the spark of laughter in his eyes. "No. The kind of hermit who teaches history and finds an eight-hundred-page book on the subject of hygiene in the Middle Ages to be a fascinating evening read."

"You're not the type of professor who hoards piles of books and papers and stuff, are you? I expect this apartment to be kept clean…"

Finn's head tipped to the side in that way he had. She barely knew the man, but she could already tell this was a trait of his. "Do you ask your female tenants if they're hoarders?"

Oh, touché.

"It's a brand-new question on my tenant application."

He released a long sigh and stared up at the ceiling. "No, I'm not a hoarder. Of books or anything else. Feel free to schedule regular inspections of the flat if you'd like. Any more questions? Want to know my blood type? Need my fingerprints?" He waggled his fingers in the air.

Her mouth dropped open, and they stared at each other for a minute. And damn it, *she* was the one who cracked, bursting into surprised laughter at how he was mocking her. Most people didn't dare. Finn laughed, too, low and soft. He had a very nice laugh. She did her damnedest to come up with a reason not to lease to him, but couldn't. He knew it, and gave a quick nod and an even quicker smile.

"Right. I'll go to the bank and be back shortly. Will you be here or at the pub?" He started to turn, as if wanting to escape before she could ask any more questions. Then he caught himself and stopped. "Any chance I can get in before the first? Like…*now*? I'll pay a pro-rated amount, of course."

She had no reason to say no. Cyndi's security deposit covered the surprise loss of January's rent. But still, a little extra wouldn't hurt. She shook her head in defeat. "Fine. I'll give you the key when you come back with the cash. And I'll have a lease ready for you to sign. On the *dotted* line."

He thanked her and left with a mischievous wink, making the apartment feel suddenly lifeless. It was as if Finn O'Hearn had lit the place up, then extinguished the flame on his way out. So much for "no chance in hell," since it seemed she'd just agreed to let him live under her roof.

She headed upstairs to finish getting ready for the longest day of her week. Late night of Friday, followed by an endless Saturday on little sleep. Although in the wintertime, it should be a moderately slow lunch crowd, especially after everyone partied last night. Lately, it seemed a lot of days, unless there was a special event, were slow. It wasn't a good trend, and she couldn't figure out how to change it when she wasn't able to change anything at the bar.

Her mind slid back to Finn as she slipped on her down jacket. She thought of his face last night when he was in her kitchen at the Shamrock, grimacing at the mention of green beer. She agreed completely, of course—the stuff was gross. But it was a McKinnon tradition. At least for now. If she could ever convince her grandmother Maura to agree to her ideas, by next year the Purple Shamrock could be completely reinvented. Lots of locally sourced greens on the menu, but *no* green beer.

Bridget texted her cousin Sara to see how Maura was doing today. The response was slow in coming, and did nothing to reassure her.

Chemo's kicking her ass this week. No appetite. Super tired.

Bridget took a deep breath, blinking rapidly. It was way too early in the day for a pity party, and it was her *grandmother* dealing with chemo, not her. Priorities. She typed her reply.

Tell her I'll make a shepherd's pie for her with no spices.

It was one of several things Maura McKinnon couldn't handle since she'd started chemo after Thanksgiving. She used to love hot wings and Bridget's Irish tacos with jalapeño peppers. But now any spice at all set off her nausea. The woman was barely eating as it was, and couldn't afford to lose more weight. Bridget had put her phone in her pocket and slipped on her jacket, figuring Sara wasn't going to reply. She was on her way across the parking lot when the phone vibrated.

Bridget unlocked the back door to the pub kitchen, then locked it behind her. She shed her coat and started flipping light switches to get the place ready for whatever lunch crowd they might get in this snow. Once she had the lights on and the ovens, steamers and fryers warming up, she pulled her phone back out and stared at it.

She's losing more hair every day. She's bummed.

Her eyes fell shut. Maura was so proud of her thick curly auburn hair with just a touch of silver in it. They'd all known hair loss was likely, but Maura kept finding posts on the internet from people who *didn't* lose their hair, and she'd read every one of them out loud to Bridget and her four cousins. Repeatedly.

"See?" she'd say. "Not *everyone* goes bald! So I'm telling you right now, I am *not* losing my hair. I refuse."

Maura was petite—a little fireplug—and so full of energy before the cancer hit. If anyone could will themselves not to lose their hair during chemo, it was Maura. Bridget looked at the phone again. Her grandmother would take this loss almost harder than when she learned she had cancer. Her fingers moved on the screen.

Damn. Want me to bring her a new hat or something?

She could picture Sara, probably already sitting at her desk and working on her next novel. She was almost as driven as Bridget was, just in a much quieter and more private way. Determination must be a McKinnon trait. A few wavy lines appeared on the screen as Sara typed.

Can't hurt. Something bright and fun. And green.

A pause.

And DON'T talk about the Shamrock.

Bridget stared out the window for a minute, watching big soft snowflakes drift down from a gray sky. Across the lot she could see her house, a tall, narrow blue-gray shadow in the snow. When she rolled into town a year ago and bought the old house, she'd figured it was a brilliant move—right next door to the bar she'd soon own.

Daddy always said the Purple Shamrock would be hers someday, even in the days when she'd insisted she didn't want it. But it turned out Maura had held the deed on the Shamrock ever since her husband had passed on thirty years ago. Maura had loved Bridget's dad, but she'd never trusted him. Probably for good reason. Maura was thrilled to have Bridget run the bar. As long as Bridget didn't change a single thing. Ever. The rest of the family agreed, even though none of them were active in the bar. And now that Maura was sick, any negotiations—if there really had been any—were firmly on hold.

Understood. Talk later.

Finn's SUV pulled up to the side door and he hopped out, fixing a testy look at the sky, which wouldn't stop snowing. Letting him have the apartment was a colossally bad idea.

But she couldn't help thinking that her grandmother would love this guy.

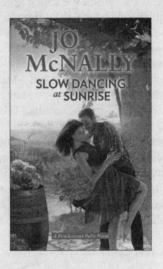